Isabel M. Howard

May 1959

A RING HAS NO END

This edition, issued in 1959, is for members of The
Companion Book Club, 8 Long Acre, London, W.C.99
from which address particulars of membership may b
obtained. The book is issued by arrangement wi
the original publishers, Cassell & Co. Ltd.

"*A blessed companion is a book*"—JERROLD

A RING
HAS NO END

*

THOMAS ARMSTRONG

THE COMPANION BOOK CLUB
LONDON

For my wife, in remembrance
of a few words written
on another St. George's Day

Made and printed in Great Britain for
The Companion Book Club (Odhams Press Ltd.)
by Odhams (Watford) Limited
Watford, Herts
S.559.V.UB.

PART ONE

1854 - 1894

*

CHAPTER I

A LAND of rape, lust, and feud to the death; where Khevsurs from remote valleys barter chain armour, double-handed swords and greaves of steel, still following the Crusading fashions passed down to them from the Middle Ages . . . a land where many men wear on the right thumb a cruelly-spiked ring, and of tribes who calculate the compensatory value of wounds by grains of barley and wheat alternately laid in length and breadth to the extent of the injury, reckoning two-thirds of the number of grains to be a fair settlement in cows. A mountainous countryside where the taking of an eye is punished by the loss of thirty good milkers, and where men, tilling the fields in the valleys, always keep warrior equipment close to hand.

This was the Caucasus, and those were the common people. In the main the nobility were different, preferring deceit and dalliance in Persian-like gardens, and the employment of treachery as a most amusing weapon—rulers much softer than those over whom they ruled.

It was to the Caucasus, ruled by a foreign, upstart Romanov Tsar, that swift horsemen of the Cossack Guard brought an Imperial Manifesto. It read, for those able to read:

By the Grace of God, We, Nikolai, Emperor and Autocrat of All the Russias, King of Poland, To all Our Faithful Subjects make known:

From the very beginning of Our Dispute with the Turkish Government, We solemnly announced to Our faithful subjects that a feeling of justice had alone induced Us to re-establish the injured Rights of Orthodox Christians, subjects of the Ottoman Porte.

At the outset We met with distrust, soon after with secret hostility on the part of the Governments of France and England, who strove to mislead the Porte by misinterpreting Our intentions. At last England and France now throw off the mask, consider Our differences with Turkey as but a secondary question, and no more dissemble that their common aim is to make Our Country fall from the powerful position to which the hand of the Almighty had elevated her.

Is Orthodox Russia to fear such threats? Shall she deviate from the sacred aim assigned to her by Divine Providence? No!

Let the whole Christian world know, then, that the opinion of the

5

Sovereign of Russia is the opinion which animates and inspires the whole family of the Russian People—that Orthodox nation, faithful to God, and to His only Son Jesus Christ, our Redeemer.

It is for the Faith and Christianity that We fight.

Nobiscum Deus—quis contra nos?

Given at St. Petersburg, the 11th day of the month of April of the year of Grace, 1854, and of Our reign the twenty-ninth.

NIKOLAI

This was the message which reached the Caucasus, where contrasts abounded: orange orchards and mountains eternally capped with snow; men swiftly fierce in their furies, and others whose passions were perverse and strange, the hallmark of decay.

To this wild country . . . where men in their cups computed the virgins they had ravished, or sniggered about even less decent things; where petty warring was constant and the *droit de seigneur* accepted as commonplace . . . to this wild country the Tsar's summons came.

When the Romanov's will reached his so-called loyal subjects south of the Don there was wild dissension in a council of the mighty. There were a few Georgians nostalgic-minded about the past, and many more Georgians caring only for their pleasures. Present also were Russians possessing estates both in Russia and the Caucasus, who at best hoped to keep all and for the worst plotted to maintain a grip on the more valuable. And there were Russians true to their Imperial Master.

Some among them pointed out that Russia was at war, challenging the united might of England, France, and Turkey. She would have little time and less means to crush rebellion within her borders. This was the moment to throw off Russia's yoke, to establish the sovereign state of Georgia in its former magnificence; here was the opportunity to uproot the black-and-yellow-striped posts, with the effigy of the double-headed eagle, which Russia, in her arrogance, had set up to delineate the limits of her far-flung possessions. In their wild enthusiasm holders of this belief quaffed fiery draughts of *aracq*, and splintered the vessels against pillars as a measure of their determination.

Others, more restrained, urged support of Russia in her hour of travail. In time, these far-seeing gentlemen declared, the war would be over and woe unto him who had attempted to stab the ponderous bear in the back. On the other hand active support of Russia would, in justice would . . .

"Justice from Russia?" screamed young Count Seshlyk, the apex of whose poppy infusion had passed. "As well expect the great Kubla to pass by a Circassian maiden reserved for a prince of Tartary and not deflower her in the passing."

6

The leader of the party of conciliation made another effort:

"Gentlemen," he urged, "we cannot continue indefinitely in this manner."

"Justice from Russia?" shrieked Count Seshlyk. "As well expect a Chikesska not to warm his bed with a pretty boy o'nights."

There was a roar of laughter; the Chikesskas' diversions were common knowledge between the Kuban and Mount Ararat. Just then their representative was snoring noisily, but his neighbour, Prince Gerasim Akashidze, gave him a dig.

"Did you hear that?" he shouted.

Surely Prince Akashidze was tempting fortune when he drew attention to himself. Had not his daughter married Prince Pavel Kaivanov and had not that young man, eight years before, died of excesses at the early age of twenty-five? And had not Prince Pavel's father, Prince Aleksiei Kaivanov, sworn bitter oaths that one of his blood should have been united with such rotten stock? Assuredly Prince Akashidze was tempting providence. For was not that grim man, Prince Aleksiei Kaivanov, presiding over the gathering?

Again Prince Akashidze poked Count Chikesska.

"Did you hear that?" he repeated. "Did you hear what was remarked, in passing, about you?"

Count Chikesska opened his eyes, and closed them again, tightly, as his lolling head moved into a patch of fierce sunlight which flashed through an unscreened gap in the jalousied window. "Wha's that?" he mumbled.

Prince Akashidze leaned over to him, and spoke softly.

Sitting at the end of the table, Prince Aleksiei Kaivanov stretched out to grasp the Imperial message with a beringed hand. Slowly he rose, an impressive figure in a Caucasian black cavalry cloak of shaggy felt, for the Prince Aleksiei, although a true son of Russia, believed in wearing, when in residence, the native dress and adopting the customs of the province in which he held territory. A stern presence, with belts buckled across his chest, each filled with dummy cartridges made of red gold. On his left breast hung the white enamel cross of Saint George. He rapped sharply for attention.

"Gentlemen," he said, "we have gathered together to make a decision of some considerable importance. So far, unhappily, much time has been frittered away in quite fruitless dissension, and I now insist that our counsels should be effectively and speedily brought . . ." He saw Count Chikesska fling back a chair and bare a dagger—saw the insane flash in the fellow's yellow-tinged eyes as he flung himself on Count Seshlyk.

"So I bed pretty boys, eh?" Count Chikesska screeched. "You son of a whore and spawn of darkness." His windmill downward thrust missed by a hairsbreadth. Overbalancing, he tumbled to the floor, bringing his opponent down with him in his fall.

"Separate them," called Prince Aleksiei.

"Let 'em fight, let's see good blood," Prince Gerasim yelled.

"Separate them," Prince Aleksiei repeated.

The panting antagonists were dragged apart.

"You'll die for this," Count Seshlyk gasped.

Prince Aleksiei invoked the traditional law of the Caucasian mountaineers. "*Adat!*" he bawled, and "*Azarpesh*", he demanded of a carpet-slippered attendant.

The horn of a mountain sheep, the Caucasian cup of friendship, was solemnly brought in. Scowlingly Count Chikesska drank down to the determined measure, and scowlingly Count Seshlyk drained to the dregs. Peace had been established between these two for ever, but a son, or a grandson, or a great-grandson, must in due course pay with his life.

"Gentlemen," began Prince Aleksiei, raising his hand for silence. "We must decide this matter."

Prince Akashidze threw back his head and tossed off a draught of burning *aracq*. "And what is Your Excellency's intention?" he asked suavely, as he set down his glass.

Prince Aleksiei turned to him. "I shall fight for my overlord, the Tsar of all the Russias," he said soberly.

Quizzically Prince Akashidze eyed his companions. His face slipped into a smile, and the smile travelled until it rested on the father-in-law of his daughter. "Of course, Excellency, you belong to a fighting breed," he remarked smoothly, adding insolently: "Or so it is said."

Prince Aleksiei's lips tightened. Watched in new-born silence, he slipped off the two cartridge belts on his breast. Dread purpose proclaimed by his deliberation, he took off his *burkah* and carefully spread it on the tiles. Taking position on one end of the cloak he unhurriedly loosened his dagger from its jewelled scabbard, and pointed with the gleaming steel to the other end of the cloak. "At your service, Your Excellency," he said grimly.

Prince Akashidze moistened dry lips, looked down at the tiny duelling ground from which a combatant may not, with honour, leave until death or mortal injury shall ensue. Then his face relaxed, the tension faded. "*Adat!*" he said, smiling.

"The tainted blood of the Akashidzes," said Prince Aleksiei bitterly. He shrugged, picked up and wrapped the *burkah* round himself, and buckled on the belts. "Gentlemen, I shall leave you," he said. "There is no advantage in continuing this farce. I shall

8

do my duty to Russia and the Tsar. You would well do likewise."

Prince Akashidze's sensual lips curved into a smile. "And we who are left behind, Your Excellency," he said softly, "will continue with our entrancing pleasures."

Prince Aleksiei Kaivanov did not deign to answer as he walked across the floor.

2

The Kaivanovs were a proud family, but it was the pride of achievement rather than of birth. Indeed, in Georgia they were declared to be *parvenus*, but as an Ataman, Kaivanov had held power of life and death over his followers for over five hundred years so that statement could hardly be accurate. In any event the gibe necessarily lost much of its sting when it emerged from the lips of those who had been surpassed by the forceful Kaivanovs in the race for lands and monopolies. Certainly the Ataman Guchkor Kaivanov, Prince Aleksiei's grandfather, had not been ennobled until the year of grace 1774, when his activities with the breaking wheel, gallows, and gibbet had done much to crush Pugachev's rebellion. An over-sanguine fellow, Pugachev, to dream that an ill-armed mob of Asiatic tribesmen and serfs from the mines of the Urals could hope to challenge the Imperial might. True, in the first few months of his rash effort he had ravaged the Don country, burnt great mansions and hanged hundreds of their owners. And true, the foolish fellow—an illiterate Cossack—had claimed to be Peter III, Tsar of all the Russias, thereby drawing to his banner some thousands of credulous peasants. This claim, for which there was no compromise, whose only outcome could be the insolent one's death, made for him an implacable enemy in Her who ruled.

All this the astute Ataman Guchkor Kaivanov foresaw. And in full season he caused the unlucky Pugachev to be thrust into a cramped iron cage, which had been placed on an artillery-wheeled cart drawn by four pairs of oxen. The miserable exhibit was dragged across the countryside, savagely cursed by those he had tried to elevate. In due course the tattered prisoner was brought before Her. Three days after that, with the pomp and ceremony proper to such occasions, that most puissant Sovereign, Catherine II, seated herself behind an open window which nicely overlooked a large square. From that position of vantage Her Majesty, a lady priding herself on her European culture, who earlier had gained the warm approval of Voltaire, witnessed the luckless Pugachev as he was rather carelessly quartered.

Her Majesty surely was in a good humour that day, for she did not reprove the hooded axe-man, and indeed sent the drunken ruffian an extra *pourboire* of ten gold roubles for his pains. Assuredly she was in a good mood, for she graciously received the Ataman Kaivanov with the significant words: "Welcome, Prince Guchkor," and equally graciously lifted him from his knees as he bent.

When Prince Guchkor left the Presence to ride back to his twenty-thousand-acre estate by the Sea of Azov, a paltry property as he now regarded it, parchments with many red seals entitled him to take possession of far-flung lands on both sides of mighty Don. With him he carried to his good lady, nestling in a purple-lined velvet box, a gem-laden ring, as a token of Her good will. And, as final proof of Her favour, he guarded, in a pigskin wallet deep in his vest pocket, a draft at three million for two million gold roubles on the Imperial Treasury, a commitment which that harassed body, unfortunately, never found itself able to meet. Still, the Ataman Guchkor had done well for himself, and from then on the Romanovs were the lights which guided his life. When, three years later, his son Dmitri was born, he felt that news of the advent of another Kaivanov, ever faithful to Her and Hers, should be conveyed to his ruler. Some seven weeks afterwards, to his intense gratification and in full disproof of the widely-held belief that the memory of Royalty is but a sorry thing, a sweat-stained horse and rider streaked up the lime-fringed approach to Yasni Dulba, the Kaivanovs' new palace close by rippling Don.

The Imperial message was short but agreeable.

It welcomed the budding of Our new subject and Our faithful Prince, Dmitri. It remarked on Our Royal Goodwill to the infant's father, and enclosed a Bauble for the Good Lady from whose loyal womb the little one had sprung. And in conclusion, sweet conclusion, it stated: "We have commanded that the child's name be written on the scroll of the Imperial Corps of Pages and that he shall, when proper, take up the station due to him at Our Court and at Our Pleasure."

The Kaivanovs had arrived.

Nor did Prince Dmitri, when he grew to manhood, do anything to retard the advancement of his family. A level-headed man, of sound character and purpose who, when his father died, grasped the reins of authority with effortless ease—a princeling intelligent enough to appreciate his sire's policies, and shrewd enough subsequently to remain aloof from the noble conspirators who slew the tyrant Tsar Pavel in his bedchamber in the first year of the nineteenth century.

Then he fell in love, irrevocably in love, with a bewitching girl of princely family, who wholeheartedly reciprocated his ardour. Fortunate it was that passionate desire and the material enhancement of a Kaivanov went so well in hand, for Princess Vara Daleologina brought him considerable hereditaments near St. Petersburg, a villa on the sunny shores of the Crimea, a town house in Moscow, and the fierce Daleologin temper.

Despite the latter they lived in great happiness, for the outbursts of *Madame la Princesse* were honest, of short duration, and left no scar behind.

Prince Dmitri Kaivanov and his beloved wife transferred their wholesome characteristics to their children, allying the vivid, witty ebullience of the Daleologins with the less polished but oak-like strength of the Kaivanovs. A sound combination, indeed.

They were blessed with three firm-limbed children. Olga, the eldest, was born when myriads of clear-cut stars carpeted the deep-blue heavens and a gentle zephyr sang its lullaby through the trees. A night of good omen, one might say, if one considered such trifles. Certainly Masha did, at least until an owl screeched and a yellow flame illuminating an ikon, a time-cracked painting of a haloed Saint, went out . . . Masha—devoted old servant of the Daleologins who had helped to usher Princess Vara into the world, and now was with her when *her* hour had come —found that double omen far too sinister.

As for Prince Dmitri, he saw neither the glory above nor the signs the trembling Masha had noticed. His world was the chamber in which he paced, and the room overhead where his beloved Vara was in cruel labour. He spun on his heel when the door opened, and stayed speechless; stared at the good doctor and tried to read in that kind face the news—too frightened to ask lest the hearing be ill.

"Calm yourself, Highness," said Doctor Bogolyubski.

"How is she?" Prince Dmitri snapped.

The good doctor remembered, not without qualms, that gentlemen of his profession were all things to all men. And, that being so, the quivering craven before him required comforting as other men.

"Calm yourself, Highness," he said with some boldness. "The confinement of *Madame la Princesse* is following the normal course which nature assigns to it. Nothing untoward has taken place and I see no indication of anything disquieting."

"Damn you, Bogolyubski," the head of the house of Kaivanov shouted. "How is she, I asked?"

The doctor swallowed uneasily, deferentially touched his patron's shoulder with a moist hand. "Naturally Her Highness is in some considerable discomfort," he said. "But no more so than the circumstances warrant. As Your Highness is aware, the first birth is always——"

"To hell with birth," Prince Dmitri growled, wiping his brow with a tuckered kerchief of Resht silk. "If I'd known previously. . . ."

But by morning he was near to forgetting his intended vow, when he saw his dear wife's shaky pride as her gaze lovingly caressed him and the nestling infant—her family. Filled with joy he bent down to kiss his beautiful little Vara, and, at her behest, tentatively pushed forward an uncertain finger until he touched the flesh and blood they had created.

For indeed Olga was a marvellous child. A fat cuddly creature, then a slim leggy elf who blossomed into glorious young womanhood, a transition so wonderful that even Masha forgot the birth portents, at least until after *it* happened, when she noisily insisted she had remembered all the time. Whenever a crowd of gallants gathered, it was reasonably safe to assume that the vivacious Princess Olga Kaivanova would be at their centre.

And yet for a challenge given in jest at the Cossack Horse Trials, she died. Older heads would have restrained her impetuosity, for the stone wall was high and the take-off difficult. She laughed provocatively at the young man who had dared to dare her, waved to her friends with the off-hand deviltry of youth, and smartly switched the flank of her pure Jevad. So she went, a taut little figure crouching low, to the drumming of hoofs which left a cloud of dust behind. It was a fine effort and had the wall been a single course lower all would have been well. But a series of sounds tells the tale: a click as a stone was struck, the intake of breath by those witnessing, the thud when flesh meets hard ground, and scampering by many to render assistance. Not a sound from her horse, for he, lucky fellow, had pitched on his neck and now, without harness and without saddle, with long mane and uneven tail, amid a horde of shoeless relations, was ranging the beloved steppes of the Kara Dagh of his dreams.

Fifty minutes later, Olga died in her stricken father's arms. As the earth's light was failing forever for her she whispered: "I wasn't frightened", a fitting epitaph for anyone, even for a girl of eighteen, even for a Kaivanov. That is the essence of the epitaph which yet may be faintly seen on the lichen-stained stone which covers her remains. Thus was the dire prophecy of the good woman Masha fulfilled.

But the hour-glass is running too speedily, for in relating the birth and death of Princess Olga Kaivanova a space of eighteen years has been bridged, and, as has been previously recorded,

Prince Dmitri and his Princess Vara were blessed with three children.

The second child, Aleksiei (we have already met him in a council chamber in Georgia) was born in 1802. A healthy brazen-lunged infant who . . . but more of him in a moment.

The last of the trinity, "little" Daly, came two years after her brother. Even when full-grown she was *petite*, a veritable Dresden doll of pink cheeks and pretty ringlets, over whom, in younger days, her mother's guests fussed and made such incomprehensible remarks as: "I could eat her", and other nonsenses; a miniature whom Prince Dmitri's friends loved to joggle on their knees. A happy little girl, a ray of sunshine in the princely house of Kaivanov and a joy for ever to the man she married. She gave Count Peter Yaroslav three stalwart sons, who joined with their father in worshipping their little mama.

Now we deal again with that lusty infant, Aleksiei, heir to vast estates on the Don, a villa on the sunny shores of the Crimea, town houses in Moscow and St. Petersburg, smaller properties bordering the sea of Azov and, possibly, his share of the scorching Daleologin temper. An important person indeed, Prince Aleksiei, to attract such a throng in the private chapel of the Kaivanovs while yet in his swaddling clothes. A marvellous place of worship it was, with mosaic floor, priceless paintings, wall decorations encrusted with sparkling gems, old ikons worth a king's ransom, and gold vessels by the score. In that chapel he received the water of Jordan from richly vested and mitred priests and the soft-footed satellites attending them. There, at Yasni Dulba on the Don, overseers and stewards, from St. Petersburg and Moscow, from Taganrog and palm-scented Yalta, saw the young master received into the arms of the Greek Church with all the colourful rites which that true body of Christ reserves for marked occasions.

As a boy, Prince Aleksiei Kaivanov was not oppressed by his august destiny. Perhaps that was due to the wisdom of his parents, for he played with the sons of his father's servants, stole pastries from the kitchens, and, mudstained, cut and bruised, sneaked back to his home after fighting short battles against small boys and long and dogged battles against bigger boys. Painfully he fell off his lively pony, and, biting his lip, climbed up again. His succession of tutors was driven frantic with his mischiefs, and two thousand Cossacks of the Don were mobilized when he played truant and disappeared for five days with a boundary-marking posse. The excuse he made—well, not excuse, for his family did not make excuses—the reason, he said, was that a Kaivanov should know the limits of his possessions. His father gave him a sound beating

13

and an encouraging slap on the back when the punishment was over.

Slowly the sapling grew into the young tree, and as surely the future of the Kaivanovs was rendered safe for another generation.

3

In the meantime Prince Dmitri did his duty by the Tsar and lost nothing in the doing of it. With his Cossacks he cut off stragglers and harried the lines of communication of Napoleon's army when that upstart, in his crazy insolence, invaded mighty Russia. Gallantly, amongst gallant men, he fought at Borodino, and when the day was lost employed that nimbleness of wit which is more valuable in a campaign than the gallantry of a thousand desperate men. For it was Prince Dmitri who insisted, against savage opposition, that every corn-bin in the ancient capital of Moscow should be emptied, and every ounce of foodstuff destroyed, so that Napoleon's starving men should find the embers of a city of desolation instead of the well of plenty for which they yearned.

So it was done, and the Emperor of the French, amidst stirring martial music, marched into Moscow, where valuable booty was collected: seventeen priceless pictures and two iron-banded boxes of gems. Of the sinews of war there were only bells, whose melting-down would have provided a sufficiency of bullets but not the strength his stumbling men needed to carry them. Victual-less, with winter at hand, there was only one thing a soldier could do. The order was given, bugles blared, tattered colours were unfurled to the icy wind, husky-voiced sergeant-majors painfully whispered words of command. The retreat was on. And throughout the long white wastes to Poland, Prince Dmitri and his lamb-skin-capped riders swooped down on shambling men. Their shaggy horses, by day and night, swept silently over the carpet of snow, cutting off companies, turning orderly retreat into disorderly rout. Of the six hundred thousand men who, with such overwhelming pride, had set out with the little Emperor, only one man in twelve saw his beloved France again. A fitting end, indeed, to those who trifle with our well-beloved Alexander I and Our Realms.

Certainly Alexander I was pleased with his faithful servant, Prince Dmitri Kaivanov. Did he not himself one morning pin the pale blue ribbon of the Order of Saint Andrew on to Prince Dmitri's *burkah*? That night the Tsar also received Prince Kaivanov in the privacy of his cabinet and there disclosed his plans for the final subjugation of the Caucasus.

As a result, Prince Dmitri lost no time in repairing to his estates on the Don. Aided by an order to all postmasters countersigned by the Minister of the Interior, he covered fifteen hundred versts in two hundred hours, and on the morning of the ninth day rested at Yasni Dulba in the bosom of his family. There, in preparation for his further absence, he was entirely occupied for a few days. Stewards had to be seen, altercations settled, and messengers sent across Russia bearing his commands. In the intervals he played with little Daly, teased Olga, or attempted to soothe that heated young man, Prince Aleksiei, who furiously contended that eleven years was a seasoned age for a Kaivanov to ride to war. Only for a short space in each day was he blessed with a few minutes alone with his beloved wife.

Gradually, over the years, the Imperial scheme took form. Levies from far and near, like ants moving up a fanwork of thread, concentrated at Rostov-on-the-Don. By 1816 the Army of the Caucasus was in being, and the advance began; over difficult country, with impenetrable forests, impassable mountains, and treacherous marsh.

Slowly the line, four hundred and fifty miles long, moved forward, forcing back Cherkesses and Abkhazians on the right, Kabards and Ossets in the centre, Checkens and Lesghians on the left. Forts were built behind to consolidate holdings, and every endeavour was made to avoid the guerilla warfare which offered little scope to time-honoured Cossack methods. In three years more the Russian frontier posts were far advanced, and His Highness Prince Kaivanov was so well pleased with progress that, by courteous arrangement with General Yermolev, Viceroy of the Caucasus, he took extended leave to visit his family: a relaxation from military activities marred by the accident which killed his daughter, Olga. Heartbroken, he returned to his duties, accompanied for the first time by his son, now a finely-built youth of seventeen.

Young Prince Aleksiei proved a shrewd student of military tactics, albeit a trifle reckless in the matter of raid and counter-raid. A sound fault, nevertheless, one which caused the projecting cheek-bones of the young gentleman's own Cossack *sotnia* to quiver with glee. The narrow black eyes of those Cossacks creased in laughter, and their wedge-shaped beards shook with homeric joy. For had not the Little Father sent young Aleksiei Dmitrio-vitch the deep crimson Order of Alexander? And had they not been with Aleksiei Dmitriovitch when he cleft a long-coated, slender-waisted Lesghian from shoulder to belly-button? And had not Aleksiei Dmitriovitch said that the Little Father's honour was for them as well as for him? And had not Aleksiei Dmitriovitch—may the Holy Trinity hold him in safe keeping—furnished them with two forty-gallon barrels of *quass*, four score of salted cucumbers, and sixteen roubles as the price of two mountain sheep for roasting? And had not Aleksiei Dmitriovitch in his graciousness joined their feast, and had not he played the balalaika to their stampings? And had not Aleksiei Dmitriovitch—may all the Saints in the Calendar guard him day and night—in his condescension given them a quarter of a *pood* of Chavka tea?

Like them, Aleksiei's father was well content. In the years of fighting ahead, before these obstinate people could be subdued, the boy would have passed through trials to supreme manhood. His only son would be able, both by character and birth, to take his rightful position in the councils of the Autocrat.

So Russia advanced, and by the spring of 1820 had neared the boundary of the Kabardan country; fair progress. Indeed General Yermolev, with the lack of foresight characteristic of many proconsuls, wrote bombastically to his master. An Armenian secretary brush-wrote the script, and relays of horsemen sped the red-sealed roll to the Imperial Presence. It ran:

"The conquest of Daghestan, begun last year, has now been carried to an end; and this land, proud, warlike, and hitherto unvanquished, has fallen before the sacred feet of Your Imperial Majesty."

A statement of attainment roughly forty-five years too previous.

And the Tsar of all the Russias made reward to those his faithful and well beloved. . . .

"To His Excellency the Prince Dmitri Kaivanov and the heirs of his body in perpetuity: A grant of that land in Our Provinces of Karthalinia and Imeretia bounded on the north by the River Dur and on the west and south by the range of mountains Linaki-Aghra-Kuram, together with all rights of concession, minerals and timber. And of Our Country of Trans-Caucasia the copper mines of the Chorokh Valley, the bitumen beds of the Omseti coast, the tobacco plantations of Mukhum, together with the vineyards at Kalazan, lithographic stone works at Emlivi, and the hot-mineral springs of Abas-Oman."

Truly a princely heritage alone.

Prince Dmitri Kaivanov, after inspecting his new properties in company with his son, and placing their charge in suitable hands, returned to his family and to the rounds of feasting and visiting his advent entailed.

A year later, at the time of the Semika feast, the young Prince Aleksiei met the Countess Zoe Eremeteva in the palace of Tsarskoe Selo. He, an upright figure, carrying himself with the unconscious pride of achievement, wearing the blue and silver dress uniform of his beloved Cossacks; she, hair in tiny curls on the top of her proud head, snowy-white shoulders rising from a low-cut bodice, and a dimple on her elbow showing between long white glove and short upper sleeve. He stared at her, and she demurely dropped her eyes before his bold regard.

Most certainly the young Prince Aleksiei stared, for the vision he saw, so befittingly backed by lapis lazuli decorating the wall, was one he knew he would never forget. Even her reflection in the ebony flooring, reaching to his feet over the inlay of mother-of-pearl, seemed to call him.

Six months later, amidst the odour of incense, surrounded by a brilliant throng, the gold crowns were placed on their heads. Assuredly it was a true love match, and a suitable match also for the heir of the Kaivanovs, for the princely name of Eremetev had been deeply rooted in Holy Russia's history for seven centuries, reasons which made the bridegroom's parents all the more content, for is it not said: "A ring has no end to it"? Certainly the new connections were comparatively poor, but that might be expected of a line of poets and lovers of the Arts, who by tradition lavished their surplus to the advancement of any *protégé* gifted with the trick of painting, music, or a pretty hand in the making of verse. Very different were they from the solid Kaivanovs or the quick Daleologins, but this latest admixture might well benefit the future strain. That was how the Prince Dmitri and his wife felt as, arm in arm, they watched the happy couple whirl away from Yasni Dulba in a French-built carriage drawn by six blood-horses yoked abreast, to wild shouting and the mad jingling of silver bells.

In due course, a lengthy Grand Tour over, the Princess Zoe Kaivanova, in a softly-sprung carriage drawn by decorous beasts, returned to the palace alongside the blue waters of Don. And the good Doctor Bogolyubski, now a fragile old man, once again became greater than even a Kaivanov in his own house. Below, as his father had done, Prince Aleksiei paced frantically. With heavy hearts and falsely bright faces, they tried to comfort him; while, above, the good doctor worked to save two souls, and yet knew that one must elude him.

"Why don't they tell me?" Prince Aleksiei shouted.

His father grasped his arm consolingly, and his sister Nathalie spoke to him . . . Daly, who at nineteen had become betrothed to Count Peter Yaroslav and had, in consequence, suddenly acquired the dignity of a *Grande Maîtresse* of the Household. "Don't worry so much, Aleksiei Dmitriovitch," she said, and then pursed her lips knowingly. "Quite often little complications set in. Possibly not very serious in themselves but——"

"Little complications," gasped her brother. "I tell you that's a damned lie."

"Aleksiei Dmitriovitch!" said his father warningly.

Prince Aleksiei turned. "I'm sorry I spoke to Daly as I did, but what she said is not the truth. How many hours have I been waiting here and how many times have I seen Mama's artificial smile? And where is Bogolyubski? Why doesn't he tell me what is happening?" He buried his face in his hands, and continued brokenly: "To think that my dainty Zoe Martinovna is being tortured. And that I am responsible."

"We men all feel that way, my son. I remember when poor Olga was born, and how I behaved, and the oaths I swore and the vows I made."

"As bad as I am?" Aleksiei asked.

Prince Dmitri nodded.

The young man raised his head and looked at his father curiously. Could that rather stout man have gone through these agonies?

In the entrance, grey-faced, stood Doctor Bogolyubski. Slowly he walked into the salon.

"Speak, man," said Prince Aleksiei.

Then, at last, the doctor painfully spoke: "Her Highness, the Princess Zoe Kaivanova, sends her respects to you. And wishes you long life."

"Dead!" sobbed Aleksiei. "My little darling dead. Never more to hold her living flesh in mine, and never more to see the light in her beautiful eyes."

"The infant——" began Doctor Bogolyubski.

"Never will she be able to do what she so longingly desired," Aleksiei moaned. "To sit with the new-born babe by her side and receive gifts, as Another received 'gold, frankincense, and myrrh'."

"The infant——" persisted the good doctor.

Through an arched opening came the chaplain, already attired in the gay colours, costly silks and velvets of his calling, for ill news travels fast and by then the bell tower trembled with its message of grim tidings.

"Peace be unto you," he intoned in a bass voice.

The company crossed themselves. "And to you, father," they murmured.

"In this hour of sorrow, Aleksiei the son of Dmitri," continued the deep voice, "I bring you comfort."

"The infant, Your Highness," said Doctor Bogolyubski desperately. "A fine, healthy boy, sound in wind and limb, a

18

consolation to him who is left to face life without his loved one at his side."

Prince Dmitri placed an arm round his son's bowed shoulders. "The next heir of the Kaivanovs," he murmured.

Prince Aleksiei looked about vaguely. "Yes, she is dead," he whispered. But his eyes opened wider, as if only then had he realized the meaning of what he said, only just understood what it meant to him.

The priest elevated the symbol of his office. "When He above," he began, "in His infinite wisdom and mercy, removes from our midst any one of His people, it is because He has Divine knowledge beyond the ken of humble sinners. God, I say, has reason——"

"God!" Aleksiei sneered. "There is no God."

"My son——"

"There is no good God, I tell you," shouted Aleksiei. "A God who takes my little Zoe Martinovna from me is evil, and a liar, and a foul cheat."

Those hearing, his father, sister, and the doctor, crossed themselves fearfully.

"Aleksiei, the son of Dmitri, you blaspheme," the priest said sternly. "I call upon you to repent. Nay, I demand that you repent and humbly withdraw words so rashly spoken."

"Why should He take my pure little wife?" Aleksiei demanded.

"But he who wickedly uses His name shall be cursed," continued the priest. "And his children shall be cursed, and his children's children. He shall be cast into Hell Fire, and shall suffer the terrors of the damned during his mortal life and in the life to come. Flames——"

"Father!" Daly implored.

"Flames shall lick round his limbs, and knotted cords press into his temple. He shall be big-tongued with thirst, but denied. . . ."

Sobered, Prince Aleksiei sank to his knees, bent his head penitently. "I have sinned, Father, but be my punishment what it will, it can be nothing to the loss which was the reason for my transgression."

The priest blessed him, and held down the crucifix for the kiss which washes away all stain. "Of that, my son, we will converse later," he said in benediction. "For the moment you must observe the ceremonies due to your station and to that of the blessed lady who has borne you a son to the glory of the noble house of Kaivanov."

Doctor Bogolyubski blinked back a tear. "Aleksiei Dmitriovitch," he quavered. "Your mother, *Madame la Princesse,* has supervised that which was necessary in the chamber of her who is no more. Perhaps you——"

And Aleksiei had done what was due to his station in this, the first great tragedy of his life. The second tragedy occurred when his son, the infant Prince Pavel, grew near to manhood. But that is another matter.

Yes, Prince Aleksiei did all that was due to his station. From that moment until the last, from the steps of the flower-heaped catafalque to the humid vault, he did his duty. He opened the door of the room in which she lay, in the finery of her wedding dress, on a bier placed beneath the sacred pictures. He tenderly kissed the closed eyelids and the cooling lips, and instructed the placing of a further score and one wax candles to her greater glory. For eight hours, and thereafter once each hour, he listened to the Psalms which were read without intermission until she left for the last resting place of all.

And on the day of sorrow he took his rightful place in the sad procession, walking behind Lukich, Metropolitan of Novgorod, and Ambrosius, Archbishop of Kazan, impressive figures chasubled in stiff gold cloth. Flanked by acolytes carrying pictures of the Saints, and a chorus of chanting Psalm-singers to the rear, he slowly walked. Amidst weeping and loud lamentation he walked, ever conscious of a loved head decorated with a crown of gold tissue and a pinched countenance exposed to view—his Zoe Martinovna. Without hearing he heard the pathetic burial service, and without seeing saw Kaivanovs, Eremetevs, and Daleologins embrace the corpse. Almost without knowing he slipped a Passport, obtained for a consideration from the Metropolitan's secretary, into his dead wife's tiny hand; the Passport she would hold in her coffin, that piece of writing which gave her Absolution for her trifling mundane sins.

Later, as was proper, Prince Aleksiei absented himself from the christening of the infant Pavel Aleksieivitch and from the long and complicated prayers and exorcisms which attend this ceremonious ordinance. At that office the "Receivers" handed over the babe to the austere Lukich, Metropolitan of Novgorod, and witnessed, as was their obligation, the triple immersion, first in the name of the Father, second in the name of the Son, and third in that of the Holy Ghost; and watched the sign of the Cross made on the child's mouth, ears, nostrils, eyes, breast, hands, and feet; and heard "The Seal of the Gift of the Holy Ghost" at every sign, when each of these parts of the infant was smeared with sacred ointment, an ointment prepared and consecrated with deep ceremony at Moscow once each year, on Thursday in Passion Week, and comprising of over twenty holy specifics—it was obtainable from the Private Chaplain to the Bishop of Moscow, for forty roubles each stone jar.

While all this was happening the child's father paced alone.

Thus, as was fitting, Prince Aleksiei Kaivanov absented himself while his son was received into the loving arms of the Church of Churches, and, as was likewise befitting, saw the child when the ordinance ended. And that was the only time he saw, or desired to see, his son for eleven years. He left the infant to the breasts of a suitable foster-mother and to the charge of his mother, the Princess Vara Kaivanova. For the Caucasus had broken into rebellion, and in campaigning was there not hope that he might forget?

So Prince Aleksiei fought for Russia against enemies who welcomed death because Paradise awaited them. As the young Mullah Shamyl raised the Moslem tribes of Daghestan against the oppressor he cried: "In Allah's name begin the Holy War. Paradise greets him that falls."

In consequence Prince Aleksiei had little time for introspection, and when he had . . . well, he was building a great house at Amsibu in the midst of the Caucasian possessions of the Kaivanovs, a palace of wide terraces and narrow-fluted columns appropriate to warm lands. Surely with these preoccupations and the mellowing influence of time he must have been nigh to forgetting his loved wife?

Perhaps, perhaps not; but certainly none other of her sex came into his life, though opportunity was not lacking, for Prince Aleksiei received many an inviting glance from dark, languorous eyes. But he, foolish man, whether shapely Georgian, blonde Kurd, or dark Tartar, ignored them all.

Thus, fighting or in consultation with skilled artisans, the years slipped by for Prince Aleksiei Kaivanov, their regular tenor being broken only by the miracle of Mount Ararat, which crowded the new military highroads of the Caucasus with a slow-moving army of non-combatants painfully trudging to the New Jerusalem. The war between Persia and Holy Russia had ended, and the biblical lands surrounding the sacred mountain were now part of Russia's Empire. Throughout Muscovy it was implicitly believed by many that Christ would return to inaugurate "the thousand years of glory" at the foot of the mountain, and so, from the Frozen Sea and the Siberian steppes, from Little Russia and from White Russia, pilgrims ecstatically flocked.

Once each year Prince Aleksiei saw his father and mother, for Prince Dmitri's lumbago was growing increasingly chronic, and the hot springs of Abas-Oman proved even more efficacious than those of his favourite Austrian spa. At such times Prince Aleksiei received from his mother, and received most impatiently

21

too, news of his son, the young Prince Pavel. And heard also, from that forthright, white-haired lady, her plain opinion of one who cherishes a grudge against a child. To which the Prince Aleksiei listened with courtesy and then changed the subject.

Prince Aleksiei busied himself greatly with his new palace at Amsibu, sending emissaries to purchase stone pillars from Greece, cedar wood from Lebanon, and glazed tiles from Persia. But in 1830 there was sterner work at hand. The wild tribes of Chechnia were again in revolt, and Imperial Russia, true to her God-given destiny, moved to crush these blind people.

Four years later, while His Highness the Prince Aleksiei Kaivanov fought in the remote country of Hamzad Beg, six wild riders swept between the limes of the Kaivanov palace by the Don, on a mission to summon him. It took them long to find him, and when Prince Aleksiei eventually reached Yasni Dulba, after a swift journey of relays of foundering horses, his dear father had been dead for ten days. His mother, bereft of the lover of her youth, died in her son's arms the same night.

Then, at last, Prince Aleksiei had to face alone the problem of his son and heir, the eleven-year-old Prince Pavel. In doing so, he created the second tragedy of his own life.

A nice-looking boy, Prince Pavel, happy to see an almost legendary father, and aching for love to replace the love the grim reaper had so recently taken away. Had his father clasped him in his arms all might have been well for the house of Kaivanov. If the father had seen the timid affection in his young son's eyes much might have been changed.

Prince Kaivanov consulted those who had charge of his heir. He was told the young master rode passably, and that in the matter of studies there was little cause for complaint.

This seemed satisfactory and so, leaving his son's training to tutors and senior family servants, Prince Aleksiei coolly bade farewell, and returned to that intermittent rebellion which was to exasperate Holy Russia for another thirty years, a sufficient distraction to make it difficult even for the most conscientious of men to attend to private affairs. Yet Prince Aleksiei was grimly conscientious about the stripling who bore his name. As the years rolled by he ensured that Prince Pavel enjoyed every advantage due to him.

When Pavel Aleksieivitch was twenty he decided to visit the palace his father had built in the Caucasus. Other Kaivanov possessions he knew well: the town houses in Moscow and St. Petersburg, the seaside villa in the Crimea, where he had spent many solitary summers, and, as contrast to the magnificence of Yasni Dulba, he was acquainted with the rather primitive mansion, on the shores of the Putrid Sea, where the Ataman Kaivanov had so surely laid the foundation of Kaivanov prestige. But now, a beauty-loving soul, he longed to see the sweet chestnuts, red and silver firs, and smilax and clematis of Georgia; the gold and silver work of Kaitago and the mother-of-pearl of Tabassaran.

At this time Russia's arms were faring ill, and the authority of the Mullah Shamyl extended from the walls of Grozni to Elisu, and from the Daryal to the Caspian. Thus, while Prince Aleksiei desperately led thin companies against men unafraid to die, Prince Pavel travelled south. In a sumptuous equipage with silver gear, the Kaivanov arms emblazoned on the sides, and an escort mounted on blood stallions, he made easy stages.

His critical eye found little fault in the new palace at Amsibu, fifty versts from Tiflis, where he settled contentedly, in due course receiving, and returning, the visits of Georgian nobility—a lonely young gentleman to whom was made known the boon fellowship the Georgian can so fulsomely give. And, in full season, Prince Pavel greeted Prince Gerasim Akashidze, and met that soft-spoken nobleman's daughter, Alia.

To the heir of the Kaivanovs the seventeen-year-old Princess Alia was an entrancing vision of all that is sublime, from her long-lashed eyes to the rich swell of her breasts, from the rounded turn of her arms to the perfection of white limbs in wide diaphanous trousers. Her touch set his pulses throbbing, her carriage sent the blood madly coursing through his veins.

For once the Kaivanov strain came out strong, and while his father, and two thousand other weary men, sought to relieve General Gurko, who at Temir-Khan-Shura had been surrounded by the forces of the Mullah Shamyl, the young Prince Pavel acted. In a Georgian church he took to wife the Princess Alia Akashidze; in a high, almost inaccessible church, surrounded by a lofty wall and closely-spaced watch-towers, he placed his destiny in the hands of an Akashidze.

As for the Princess Alia Kaivanova, she was glad. Prince Pavel was handsome, and courteous, and kind, and as pliable as a warmed wax taper in her hands. And was he not the heir of Kaivanov, the richest family in Holy Russia? As for the Prince Gerasim, he, too, was glad, for his daughter's husband was of a soft nature, who would be loving to his child, and maybe even a comfort to an Akashidze in financial stress.

Prince Pavel settled into his fleeting Heaven. As could be expected, he was duly flayed for this misalliance. "A thrice damned fool," Prince Aleksiei thundered, "to marry into a brood of whores and whoremongers. To contaminate the proud Kaivanov blood with such a stinking stew."

None of which the young man believed. After all, only thirty-eight weeks after he bedded her, his beautiful Alia presented him with a glorious child, an heir to the Kaivanovs who would, once again, enjoy a father's companionship. This was a delight which must, naturally, wait until the baby, Mikhail, grew a trifle older. Meanwhile, fortunately, other pastimes were at hand.

Perhaps Prince Pavel was becoming a little less sensitive, drinking a trifle too much, coming under the enervating influence of Prince Gerasim Akashidze too frequently. That might be the explanation. Or perhaps his decline began from the day he discovered his wife had lovers. Only one thing was positive: that when his only child was four years of age Prince Pavel Kaivanov, in the twenty-fifth year of his life, suddenly died. The cause of death was an overdose of Spanish Flies, an aphrodisiac much favoured by Georgian gentry.

4

For six hundred years, in a climate which promoted laziness, debauchery and licentiousness, the deliberately coarsened quatrains of *The Man in the Tiger Skin* had been bawled by thickened voices from the divans surrounding Georgian dining-tables. In the distant past, when the armies of mighty Empires fought for supremacy over their lands, the nobility of Georgia had retired into themselves, and in doing so took the first step towards soft living. Slowly, but very surely, they embraced the voluptuous standards of Persia, creating about them minor courts in which they aped the lecheries and seraglios of Isfahan.

A country in which the staple food of millet and pork fired the carnal senses, and wine was in abundance and fair women cheap; a race with a record of treachery and cruelty, of princes who wielded privileged sovereign power, and of vain, childish, callous men capable of assassination, abduction and rape. Where men, between orgies of love-making, sucked lollipops while toying with embroidery frames; where young women were trained to strike attitudes of inflammatory appeal; where the sauces at feasts were shrewdly mixed to stir the baser instincts.

It was the grandfather of Prince Gerasim Akashidze, himself long impotent, who caused drugged men to wake up in a "heaven" of musicians, sweet singers, and posturing, naked strumpets; who caused the same young men, when hidden eye-witnesses had been sufficiently amused, to be plied again with deadening wine. When stupefied, each victim was conveyed back to the place from which he had been brought. A rare jest it was when a young man swore through the countryside that he had acquired his pox in true Paradise.

The next Akashidze elegantly improved this play, as well he could, not being tainted with the dread rot. To the gardens chaste and simple maidens were now similarly conveyed, and there Prince Gerasim's father and his bosom friends, in the robes and guise of saints, joined them. And, with the months, fatherless babes came into a sorry world and bewildered girls were scourged for wicked sacrilege in naming their creators as being holy men of the world to come.

In such a vitiated atmosphere Prince Pavel Kaivanov lived and died. For the addict of Spanish Flies, or the taker of the bitter *ginseng* of Manchuria, must pluck the fruit for which he yearns, and trembling hands may easily dispense a fatal overdose.

For nine days after he received the news of his son's death, Prince Aleksiei Kaivanov sped south in an open *calash*. On the tenth day he removed his grandson, Prince Mikhail, from the custody of the child's mother, Princess Alia Kaivanova.

One grave error had Prince Aleksiei made. He vowed that he would not make another with his little grandson, the heir to all he possessed.

That resolution was ever in his mind. He was thinking of it as he prepared for departure to the seat of war, where the French and British were landing.

CHAPTER II

HALF-WAY up the bluff of the Maktuk, where the creeper-covered walnuts and planes of the lower slopes were replaced by beech and aspen, there was a rectangular clearing. Here, alongside a swift, alder-screened stream, was a woodman's hut, usually with a faint trace of smoke eddying from its crude chimney. From this position, with the smell from burning kindling and dried cow-dung in the climber's nostrils, there was a magnificent prospect of the palace, a noble pile of pinkish marble cunningly sited on a wide terrace. From this height the perfection of miniature landscape gardens and the gleam of artificial pools could be seen, even the calligraphic ornamentation which the architect—drafting the art of Persia on to his drawing-table—had so skilfully woven into this reincarnation at Amsibu of the princely home of a Khan.

Hidden on the far side, in the vast yard where five hundred

pampered blood-horses boasted marble-built homes, there was great activity. This was the day when His Highness the Prince Aleksiei—God guard him—left for the new war. Indeed he should have departed a full hour ago, but . . . his personal *sotnia* of a hundred picked riders, curbing their high-mettled steeds, sneered at an ornate equipage standing near. Some had dismounted to lead curveting beasts to and fro along a strip of tan, and they, too, curved their mouths at the sight of that alien vehicle with its quintet of bedizened attendants.

"A driver . . . and a second driver," scoffed a few, while endeavouring to restrain the iron-shod plungings of beloved animals.

"And two footmen to stand behind," jeered still more.

"And a black boy from Ethiopia," capped another. "He's for the lady's pleasure when——"

And all roared with deep-chested laughter. All of them: proud riders of the Cossack escort, domestics, flunkeys, strollers, itinerant traders—all roared. Yellow-faced Kalmucks abandoned their praying wheels as they doubled with glee; Tartar women cracked the paint on their cheeks, and grave Bashkir men stroked shaven heads in quiet mirth. Silver coins, corals and beads on the breastplates of the Tcheremiss women jangled with joy, and Mordva swan girls danced until their white puttees became flapping loose. Only the money-lenders in long stiff robes and round caps trimmed with fur, with busy beards and luxuriantly curled hair shining with oil, did not join in the demonstration. For the lady, if not rich, had great expectations and had already received accommodation on those expectations.

Nevertheless the carriage, revealing the hand of the master craftsman, M. Georges Shillibeer of Paris, was a thing of beauty. Of modernity, too, for it was fitted with the latest innovation, rubber tyres. And strikingly elegant, with crimson spokes picked out in gold, and shining panels decorated with Cupids in storms of flowers. Very different it was from Prince Aleksiei's severely practical *calash* which, loaded with valises, waited for the command of His Highness.

Both these equipages were emblazoned with the Kaivanov coat-of-arms, and yet those riders of the escort, in scarlet and gold livery, sneered at that pretty carriage. Indeed many of the stablemen present used the carriage's C-springs as scrapers for dungy boots.

The babel in the yard grew louder. Caucasian weapon-makers who so tempered steel that a full sword swing against stone would not mar the razor-like edge, clamoured for the favour of a few words with the Keeper of Weapons. Jews in caftans insinuated a

26

couple of roubles into the ready palm of the Assistant to the Assistant Steward, and kept back ten roubles gold for presentation to his superior, together with a bag of gold for the most important official of the household, the Steward himself.

Within the palace Prince Kaivanov glanced at a French clock and decided to terminate an interview.

The apartment was vast, its high ceiling supported across the centre by three malachite pillars. The walls were painted scarlet, lavishly ornamented in gold, and massive crystal candelabra hung from the ceiling, each suspended by four stout silver-linked chains.

Across the marble floor the quick steps of Prince Aleksiei suddenly stayed as his feet sank into a Daghestan rug. He turned slowly and inexorably. "Madam," he said coldly, "because you bear the name of Kaivanov I have listened to you with patience, and in doing so have delayed my departure in the service of the Tsar. That I do not propose to do any longer. Nor do I propose to reiterate the reasons for my actions."

The dark eyes of the woman shone with anger as she clenched her small fists. "I utterly refuse to accept your decision. I shall see Mikhail Pavlych when I wish and I shall take him away with me whenever I find it convenient to——"

"Whenever you find it agreeable to fit him in between your lovers, madam, I presume," said Prince Aleksiei.

White teeth bit into carmined lips. "That is an insult," she gasped, "for which my father or brothers, had they been here, would have killed you."

An ironic smile crept over Prince Kaivanov's firm mouth. "You may be right, madam," he observed. "Unfortunately you are not at the moment supported by the strong arm of an Akashidze. But painful as it is for me to speak in this manner to one of your sex, I am compelled to do so by your own persistence, persistence which only seeks to gain control of Mikhail Pavlych in his tender youth so that at my death you and your brood may dip your hands into the treasures garnered by the industry and integrity of his ancestors. That, God willing, I shall not permit. It is six years since my son died and six years since I removed my grandson from your charge. If I am spared a few years longer I shall have disciplined Mikhail Pavlych into true manliness, and then indeed, madam, will your hopes be destroyed."

He looked at his daughter-in-law, from modish hat to greasily-shadowed eyelids in the heavy, dead white face. Somewhat different, at twenty-eight, was the Princess Alia Kaivanova from the seventeen-year-old Princess Alia Akashidze who had almost provoked Prince Pavel to madness with her display of soft-fleshed charm. Her face was beginning to wreathe with fat and her hips to spread, the sad fate of women of the indolent East.

"That is my design for my grandson, madam," he continued. "On my return, if you wish it, I will renew my indulgence that you visit him once each quarter . . . a reunion with your son of which hitherto you have been extremely forgetful." Sardonically he watched her carefully dabble her eyes with a tiny handkerchief.

"I couldn't bear to see my little darling only to have to leave him," she sobbed. "But now, while you are at war, Mikhail Pavlych's place is with me. A boy of ten needs the care of a loving mother."

"I am in agreement with you," said Prince Aleksiei briskly. "Unfortunately Mikhail Pavlych . . ." he shrugged, rang a silver bell which lay on a Buhl table, and glanced at the slipper-shod footman who promptly appeared. "The carriage of *Madame la Princesse*."

The man bowed low. "Yes, Highness."

Princess Alia Kaivanova's eyes gleamed venomously. "So you think——" she began.

Her father-in-law checked her. "Say no more, madam. But remember one thing when you consider tampering with my wishes. Hitherto you have had revenue adequate to your dignities as the wife of my dead son. May I remind you that the assignments are not irrevocable."

"The carriage of *Madame la Princesse* awaits, Highness."

The Prince Aleksiei crooked his arm. "Allow me," he said courteously.

Preceded by the Major-domo, and leaving an overpowering trail of perfume in her passage, Princess Alia Kaivanova left the palace of Amsibu. Her elegant equipage now stood on the wide drive.

"Travel well," said Prince Aleksiei, handing her in.

Came a snapped word of command, the crack of a whip, footmen scrambling to jump behind, and a cloud of dust as corn-fed horses fought to get their heads.

Prince Aleksiei walked purposefully up the terraced steps, flinging peremptory commands to right and left: "Arkasha, my cap and *burkah*; Timofei Egorovitch, my *calash*; Porfiri, thou grinning scoundrel, inform the leader of the escort; Theodore, thou disappointed one, my compliments to the tutor of His Highness Prince Mikhail, I wish to see Prince Mikhail immediately; Peter Petrovitch the Steward to me at once."

In their various directions his servants doubled to carry out his bidding. After a last comprehensive glance which covered the portents of the weather and the bountiful products of his lands as far as eye could reach, Prince Aleksiei entered the room with malachite pillars.

"Ah!" he said, chuckling as he pinched his sister's cheek, "I thought you and I had already made our farewell. Or was it that you were a little inquisitive, eh?"

The widowed Countess Nathalie Yaroslava looked at him with serene eyes. She was a gracious old lady, with unlined face, snow-white hair, and still-youthful carriage. "Certainly not," she declared indignantly.

"Of course," said Prince Aleksiei, his eyes twinkling, finger and thumb snapping. "You wish to remind me of those messages. I can assure you, my dear, that your terrorizing has engraved them indelibly on my mind. As soon as I meet my nephews at Sevastopol they shall have their little mama's greetings."

Countess Nathalie stamped her foot. "You *are* irritating."

"I am sorry, my dear," said Prince Aleksiei gravely.

With overdone casualness his sister remarked: "I see she has gone."

Prince Aleksiei snapped his thigh, hugely delighted. Then, slowly, the creases of humour disappeared and his mouth grew bitter. "A woman who wept for the love she bore her only child," he said. "But a woman so intent on her policies that she forgot to ask for him."

"A horrible creature. Did——"

Prince Aleksiei took his sister's arm, and drew her into a small room to the side, where maps of Kaivanov properties hung on the walls. "Come, my dear," he said, "let us not talk of unpleasant things. In a few minutes I shall be leaving and there only remains for me to thank you again for taking charge of Mikhail Pavlych."

"Thou silly." She smiled reminiscently. "I vow I shall thoroughly enjoy mothering a small boy again, and I am sure it won't do any harm to Mikhail Pavlych either."

"You imply——" began Prince Aleksiei sharply.

"Tut tut, there you go again," Countess Nathalie interrupted smilingly. "No, I simply mean that a little joyous laughter about inconsequent things will not spoil the boy's character." She became deeply serious. "Since I came here a week ago I have been worrying about Mikhail Pavlych, my dear. He is far too . . . too apprehensive." She rested her hand on his sleeve. "Just think, Aleksiei Dmitriovitch, of us two and Olga, when we were children. The love which encompassed and . . ."

"But damn it, my dear Daly, I love Mikhail Pavlych and I

wouldn't harm a hair of his head. But I am ever cognizant of the Akashidze blood in him. I left my son to his own devices, and you know with what result. I am only ensuring that Mikhail Pavlych shall be a true Kaivanov, capable of carrying forward still further the glorious history of our house."

Countess Yaroslava sighed. "I understand, my dear. But do remember Mikhail Pavlych is still a child."

Prince Aleksiei nodded vaguely. "It has been wonderful to see you again, my dear," he resumed. "Although how I had the presumption to ask you to leave St. Petersburg I can't imagine." He placed his arm affectionately round her shoulders. "My dearest Daly, when Spring comes take Mikhail Pavlych up to the Don. You were always fond of Yasni Dulba."

He was smiling down at her when the Steward appeared in the doorway, prostrating humbly, and to him he beckoned imperatively.

A tall, well-built man, the Steward, dressed in a flowing robe of fine broadcloth tied by a silken girdle; with wide brow, broad nose, white teeth, brown eyes and mouse-coloured hair parted in the middle.

"You will take close heed of my commands, Anton Vasilevitch," said Prince Aleksiei curtly. "Henceforth Her Highness the Princess Alia Kaivanova is not permitted anywhere within my Caucasian estate. You will make my will known to whom it may concern. Dereliction of duty on the part of any one of my servants will entail fifty blows with the *nagaika* on the arched back, and thence dismissal from my service."

"Yes, Highness." The Steward bowed.

"Your punishment I should personally attend to on my return," Prince Aleksiei remarked. "And now, are there any other matters which merit my attention?"

Anton Vasilevitch straightened himself, waved his hands before his master. "There are many who crave for a glimpse of Your Highness's countenance. The merchant Rosencratz begs your commands for cloth for clothing your Highness's souls, and the brothers Samadze, weapon-makers——"

"Disburse them two hundred roubles, and my compliments on the excellence of their work. As for the others, you will make such contracts, month by month, as may be necessary."

Almost immediately after the Steward had backed out of the room, a young boy ran in. He was tall for his years, with slender limbs, dark eyes and hair, and a face not far removed from feminine beauty. In one hand he held a narrow-necked glass flask with a coloured bird blown inside it, a present from which he declined to be separated since his grand-aunt gave it him; in the other hand, first finger inserted to keep the place, a slim, leather-bound book.

"Grand-aunt Daly," he said excitedly, tugging her arm. "May I read this to you?" His face fell as he perceived his grandfather.

"What is it, my dear?" asked Countess Nathalie, stroking his head.

"It is . . . it is poetry," he stammered. "The poetry of Mr. Keats."

"Poetry!" barked Prince Aleksiei.

"You can read it to me tomorrow," interposed Countess Nathalie. "Your grandfather hasn't time to listen to it now." She frowned at her brother, who stared in stupefaction before belatedly realizing her meaning, when he hastened to make amends. "Well, my dear Misha," he said to his grandson, slapping him jovially; "what have you been doing today? Riding this morning on Cou-Cou, what?"

It was Mikhail Pavlych's turn to stare when he heard the affectionate diminutive. "No, sir," he replied. "I rode Ilya. Yesterday Cou-Cou threw me, so Nikanor Ivanovitch thought it would be better if I had Ilya for a few days."

"And so thou, a Kaivanov——" Prince Aleksiei began abruptly, but, under the warning gleam from his sister's eyes, his reproof tailed off. "Well, my boy," he went on, "I am leaving to fight for His Majesty the Tsar as you will also, should the necessity arise, when you are old enough."

The young Prince Mikhail licked his lips.

"Of course he will," said Countess Yaroslava.

"Surely he can answer for himself," said Prince Aleksiei. "Can't you, Mikhail Pavlych?"

"Yes, sir."

"For the Kaivanovs have always fought, and always will fight, for the House of Romanov," continued Prince Aleksiei. "You remember, Mikhail Pavlych, your great-great-grandfather . . . your great-great-grandfather——"

"My great-great-grandfather, the Ataman Guchkor Kaivanov," the boy began mechanically, "who with a handful of loyal men courageously fought against and conquered the rebellious Pugachev when, by wicked lies, that traitor persuaded masses of ignorant peasants to arms against the benevolent rule and authority of Her Gracious Majesty, Catherine II, Queen of all the Russias. And my great-grandfather, Prince Dmitri Kaivanov, who at Borodino turned proud Napoleon's forces into a host of broken men . . . who received at the hands of His Gracious Majesty the Order of Saint Andrew and a Commission which his Emperor,

31

the well-beloved Alexander I, feared not to trust to a Kaivanov."

He ended a little breathlessly, while his grandfather shot a glance of justifiable triumph at Countess Nathalie.

"Splendid, my boy," said Prince Aleksiei. "And remember this: if you, and I also, keep their illustrious examples before us, we never shall tarnish the bright lustre on the shield of their achievements. Never forget that, Mikhail Pavlych."

"No, sir." There he stood, the young Prince Mikhail, facing his grandfather. With his arms behind him, holding a volume of verse in the screen of his back, he stood.

"And remember also," continued the stern voice, "that in my absence you are the sole male bearer of our name in the Caucasus, and that men look to a Kaivanov. Comport yourself. . . ."

"I am afraid, my dear, that you will have great difficulty in reaching Count Bazkoff's dinner-table if you delay your departure much longer," remarked Countess Nathalie.

Again Prince Aleksiei eyed her. "True," he said, stooping to embrace the boy. "Good-bye, my dear Misha. May God cherish you in His safe keeping."

Mikhail Pavlych retreated half a pace. "And you also, grand-father."

"Run off now to your lessons," said Prince Aleksiei. "Monsieur Favel will be awaiting your return."

The youngster made a hurried inclination, a deeper bow to his grand-aunt, and scampered away.

"A good-looking boy." Prince Aleksiei sighed. "And I can detect no tendency to taking after his mother's side."

"Really, Aleksiei Dmitriovitch," Countess Nathalie observed reproachfully, "you frighten him out of his wits with your solemn talk. You *must* remember his age, my dear."

Prince Aleksiei chucked her under the chin. "I will endeavour to keep in mind my masterful little sister's behests. But come, my dear, I must be away." He led her into the apartment of malachite pillars. "Arkasha, thou scoundrel," he shouted, "my cap and *burkah*." Smoothing down his hair, he placed the cap on his head, and, assisted by two retainers, slipped into the folds of the garment.

"And you should not have sent him back to his lessons," scolded Countess Nathalie. "He would have loved to watch your escort start off. What does a few minutes' absence from his stuffy lessons matter?"

He smiled ruefully, stroking the side of his neck thoughtfully. "Now I know why your big sons go in fear and trembling of their mama. Theodore, my compliments and my apologies to Monsieur Favel. I wish His Highness Prince Mikhail to witness my departure," he called out as he buckled across his chest diagonal belts gleaming with red-gold cartridges, and round his waist another belt bearing a pair of pearl-handled daggers in jewel encrusted scabbards. With servitors clustering near he joked, and was chuckling at a jest against himself when he noticed amongst them the Groom of the Household, who hurried forward at his sharp command. "Nikanor Ivanovitch," he said, "you will ensure that His Highness Prince Mikhail takes his exercise on Cou-Cou and on no other beast. Even if he be thrown a dozen times each morning."

"Yes, Highness."

"Oh, Aleksiei Dmitriovitch," Countess Yaroslava murmured.

Her brother turned. "There are some things for which there may be no tenderness," he said sternly.

In due course he kissed her fondly on the forehead and on both cheeks, and, clasping his grandson firmly by the shoulders, looked searchingly into the boy's eyes before saluting him similarly.

Sinking to one knee, the company doing likewise, Prince Aleksiei received the blessing of the vestmented priest, and then walked firmly down the broad terrace. The side springs of the *calash* yielded as the step took his weight, and sprang up again as he sat down, when servants tucked bearskin rugs about his legs. Next he raised his hand, smiling at his sister and the boy. Two seconds later the hand fell, and Prince Aleksiei Kaivanov had begun his journey to the war.

Over the drive his *calash* lurched and sped, outriders on either side, eight fan-harnessed beasts ahead, a dozen tinkling silver bells swaying from the carriage's arched *dooga*; in front, the mad drumming of two score wrought-up horses; behind, two score of cursing riders choked by dust.

Thus the Prince Kaivanov travelled. For is it not said: "Pray to God, but service to the Tsar"?

2

At the top of the ridge the four horsemen paused to view the panorama, for it was indeed of interest to men who had been confined so many months in Sevastopol, the fortress known as "the second heart of Russia". Immediately before them, where slow-falling hills reached the sea, was the narrow bay and the naval harbour, access to which was denied by the sunken hulls of Russian line-of-battle ships, whose masts were always discernible above a tideless sea. Across the harbour ran an improvised bridge of boats, and beyond that, scarred by round-shot and burnt-out areas, was the town, guarded by a semi-circular line of forts, each supported by shrewdly conceived earthworks.

The bleak Khersonese peninsula, rising behind Sevastopol, was dotted with the tents and batteries of English and French besiegers and the lines of Sardinians and Turks, and these were dimmed by smoke curling from a multitude of camp fires. A scene almost of peace, that battleground, where men's bodies lay rotting. But mating birds were singing, and only a desultory shot or the distant sounds of a working-party broke into the cadences of their soft-throated pleas.

The oldest member of the party focused his glass. "The English are making rapid progress with their supply railway from Balaclava," he announced. "When that is completed many more men will be released for duty in the trenches, with consequent greater pressure on us."

One of the young men was patting the neck of his horse. "Surely, Uncle Aleksiei," he expostulated, "you do not doubt our ability to drive out these invaders?"

"I doubt any conception based on a confusion of thought, doubt it greatly," Prince Kaivanov replied sternly. "Already I have sent a courier to His Majesty with my appreciation of the situation, for it ought to be remembered that our opponents have insufficient men to invest our defences both north and south of the harbour, and that we are not cut off from support. Therefore reinforcements, instead of being poured into the town, should be diverted for the most part to the open country, and used in one smashing blow against their lines of communication."

"We essayed that at Balaclava, sir," said Count Adam Yaroslav.

Prince Aleksiei nodded. "Yes, my boy, and had that been successful you would have witnessed the English and the French fighting, not against our men, but to gain foothold on transports. The war would have been over between rise of sun and fall. Ah, well!"

He gave a last glance at the ruins of Inkerman on the left, at Fort Saint Pavel commanding the entrance to the dockyard below, and at a division of English ships, led by *Britannia*, which were tacking well outside the line of sunken hulls, a noble sight under gleaming canvas. "Yes," he remarked, reining round his horse, "I think we may take our day's pleasure without unease."

The animals carefully picked their way down the stony sides of the mound until a narrow track was reached. Winding along this, with occasional views of the Black Sea and the battleground, they slowly proceeded as far as a strip of flat pasture land, along which an invigorating gallop was possible for some distance.

"Excellent," Prince Aleksiei declared as the party reached a rough highway.

Count Adam Yaroslav pointed down the road, his whip following it for verst after verst as it twisted towards the horizon. "Plenty of sinews of war coming up for us," he said, acknowledging the humble greeting of a driver.

Indeed there were. Great wagons, drawn by rippling-muscled oxen, their heavy artillery wheels sinking into the ruts of the previous winter's traffic, axles frequently scraping the ground between, creaked and groaned along. Down this ribbon from Simferopol came foodstuffs, clothing and munitions of war. Crude greatcoats from Moscow, forage from the Ukraine, and small but inordinately heavy wooden chests from Tula—Tula, mighty workshop of the Empire where, in proof of the Orthodox nation's gigantic effort, eight thousand men laboured during the hours of light and turned out weapons at the unbelievable rate of one hundred and twenty thousand stand of arms per annum; Tula, in which no expense was spared, where a steam engine from England drove forty lathes on which musket barrels were turned, while wide-eyed spectators gaped.

Count Kirill Yaroslav jerked his thumb contemptuously towards the rudimentary vehicles. "We should have iron rails traversing the country in every direction by now," he said, "instead of having to rely on methods belonging to the days of Ivan IV. Modern war is decided by mobility, and the strong spear-thrust which is attained by secretly. . . ."

For a while the young men argued this out, until their senior, amused long enough by their good-natured wranglings, interrupted them: "May I now suggest to you gentlemen that we are bent on relaxation, and today we might forget the war."

The brothers grinned, and the party continued on its way. They left the road, passed through a beechwood so dense and oppressive that, apart from an odd jay or woodpecker, there were no birds, and then climbed again, alongside a fast-flowing, clear stream. Near a beautiful stalactite cave Count Adam gazed ostentatiously at the provender in his saddle-bags.

"How much further yet to these ancient ruins?" he inquired.

"You'll be feeding soon, just over the other side, and in comfort," Count Boris answered, hunching his shoulders in affected cold, for the day was balmy. "Here it is as chilly as St. Petersburg at the time of The Blessing of the Waters, but there. . . ."

The ridge was a sharp dividing line. On one side there was the stark Khersonese peninsula with stunted shrubs and sparse vegetable life. But before them were evergreens, magnolias, pomegranates and olives, with wild roses and vines stretching down the slopes.

"And the monastery?" remarked Count Adam.

Shading his eyes, Count Boris nodded towards a cluster of dark-green cypresses. "There, thou impatient one."

Count Adam put his beast down the slope, the rest following in single file. At the bottom, on a carpet of light green grass and dark green mosses, they trotted along, feasting war-weary eyes on the beauty unfolding about them.

In front still, Count Adam had passed the bend of the stream. Suddenly he reined his mount to its haunches. Signalling silence, he waited until the others drew level before pointing to figures sitting on the remnants of grey walls. "English officers," he whispered.

"Humph!" Prince Aleksiei muttered. "It appears we shall not have the solitude we expected. However. . . ." He cantered through the clearing, his nephews pressing behind.

In the precincts of the disused monastery the three enemy officers, aroused by the sound, put down food and drink and rose to receive the visitors with a grave salute.

"Good day to you, gentlemen," said Prince Aleksiei courteously. "It appears that you have anticipated us."

A tall, lean Englishman replied. "I'm sorry, sir," he said. "But I do assure you we had no idea this delightful spot was . . . was reserved. With your permission and our apologies we will betake ourselves elsewhere."

"Not at all," said Prince Aleksiei. "Indeed I should not permit it. As you see, gentlemen, there is ample room for all."

The Englishman cocked an eye of interrogation towards his companions before turning to Prince Aleksiei. "Perhaps you will join us here," he suggested. "My friends and I would be honoured with your company. We can offer you some decent hock, and quite respectable cheese and biscuits. As for the remainder . . ." he shook his head dubiously, "I am afraid we have nothing better than raw-ish salt pork and mouldy bread; rations I wouldn't give my dogs."

Prince Aleksiei smiled. "Perhaps we may be allowed to contribute to the advantage of your table, gentlemen. Fortunately, we are well provided."

And so it was, for in his nephews' saddle-bags were Crimean and Caucasian wines, caviare from the Kur, fresh round loaves of rye, and a salad of salted cucumber and cabbage.

Introductions were next made, before the newcomers' horses were tethered to the old cedars and their nosebags slung. After that the party settled down, the Russians crossing themselves devoutly before eating. For a few minutes there was almost complete silence, with nothing more than a chance remark, the pleasant chink of glassware, and the gurgle of liquid.

But later, conversation grew, and had become animated indeed by the end of the meal, when Prince Aleksiei opened a box of cigarettes made from "Turkish" tobacco grown on his plantations at Mukhum. The Englishmen had picked up the habit of smoking cigarettes from the French during the campaign, and the fragrant fumes of this fine tobacco circulated freely as various topics, from serious to gay, were discussed. There was, of course, a British roar of laughter when an officer of the 49th solemnly mentioned his Commander-in-Chief's habit of referring to the enemy as "the French," this much to the discomfiture of those gallant allies. Lord Raglan, he explained to the perplexed Russians, had last seen service in the Napoleonic wars, and custom was proving too much for him.

Then there was a lively discussion about horses, which ended with two members of the party heading towards magnificent beasts bred on the Yaroslav estate in the Ukraine. As the pair strolled along, differing good-temperedly, a Dragoon Guard's hand was resting on a shoulder ornament of the Pavel Regiment.

Those left behind were also arguing amicably, though there was complete unanimity about the charge of Balaclava, admiration and astonishment being evenly mixed.

"No," Prince Aleksiei remarked as he brushed a few crumbs from the folds of his blouse, "I had not the privilege of witnessing your Light Brigade's courageous ride. Unhappily at the last minute I was prevented from leaving the Caucasus by the traitorous activities of the old Mullah Shamyl, who began by plundering the Alazan valley. In the course of that he seized the castle of Tsinondal, from which he carried off, to be held for ransom, the sisters Chavchavadze. Of course"—his mouth curved sarcastically—"to be caught by surprise is quite characteristic of the Georgians."

"Don't know much about 'em," said the Scots Fusilier, smiling. "Except I've heard their women are deuced attractive."

Prince Aleksiei's mouth tightened. "That, sir, is a matter of opinion. And does not a delectable outer crust often hide the stinking abomination beneath?"

The awkward moment passed, and thereafter the conversation ranged over less inflammable matters: hunting, sport and the like. Even the course of the war was re-fought, but in the most amiable spirit by these men who might meet in battle on the morrow.

The pity of it all. But Her Majesty, Queen Victoria, had

declared that she felt bound "to afford active assistance to her Islamic ally the Sultan against unprovoked aggression", while Russia's Sovereign held that his vast country "fights for the Christian faith, for the defence of her co-religionists oppressed by implacable enemies."

Fine words both, to arise out of a petty quarrel between Greek and Latin monks in Palestine who sought preference in the Holy Places.

CHAPTER III

THE armed forces of Russia were fighting desperately to hold the forts Malakoff and the Redan, against which French and English had copiously and to little advantage expended themselves. Already the thrice storming of the Malakoff had left but four dead soldiers of France in its confines, and the English, in their costly attempts on the Redan, had fallen far short of that achievement.

During a lull, General Prince Kaivanov leaned over the sandbags reinforcing the parapet edge of the Redan, and looked towards the sheltered position to which the English had retired after their last failure.

"I am of the opinion that the enemy is massing for another attack," he remarked to his A.D.C. "Pass the warning."

"Very good, Excellency."

Prince Aleksiei continued to scan that quarter-mile strip of battle-scarred land, from a pile of English bodies heaped below at the foot of the steeply-inclined *glaçis* of the fort to enemy trenches revealed by the shining tips of moving bayonets. Attention caught, he brought up his spy-glass to scrutinize an English sap-head. "Colonel Keliani," he rapped out. "Your riflemen, half-right, a man crawling with a flag."

A sharp order was given, followed by barrels sighting over the parapet. There followed another order, the ear-splitting crack of simultaneous detonation, an acrid smell, and then more ragged reports as the rifles were reloaded and fired again. Eyes tingling, Prince Aleksiei strained to pierce the drifting fumes. "Aim straight, damn you," he shouted.

The figure in British naval uniform leapt to his feet again. Gripping a six-foot staff he ran towards the gap between the Malakoff and Redan forts, jumping over abandoned earthworks, slithering down hillocks; passing the glazed eyes of the sky-gazing dead and the imploring faces of the broken. Ever attended by tiny spits of dust which spoke of good marksmanship he raced along, finally scaling a mound. On the summit, lead buzzing by, he stuck the pole firmly into the ground and cleared the red bunting, which had fouled. Turning, he dived for his own lines, twisting and swerving as he tore back.

"A brave man," commented Prince Aleksiei, glancing towards the enemy batteries. He had not long to wait. Flames stabbed from the guns, a thunderous volume of sound arose, and rolling clouds of black smoke. Directed by that flaunting fragment of red, the guns corrected for line and, in steps, raised the range until their ninety-pound iron spheres smashed through green foliage masking the pit of the Russian battery.

"Good shooting, sir," said Colonel Keliani wryly.

Prince Aleksiei's brows beetled in anger. "If your damned men could have shot straight the destruction of that battery would not have taken place."

The rifleman shrugged thick shoulders. "Your pardon, General," he said. "But the fault lies not so much with my men as with their rotten weapons."

"A new issue?" snapped Prince Aleksiei.

Colonel Keliani's full lips curled, his heavy-lidded, dark eyes blazed. "Made from base metal supplied by contractors who place profit before human lives. That, sir, is the reason why our guns burst and our ammunition is faulty."

Prince Aleksiei gripped his companion's arm. "I know, my dear Colonel," he said. "There is much that needs investigation."

Colonel Keliani faced his superior officer. "Why should all our wants be supplied by a Moses, or an Aaron? Why do we trust these matters to a race who lack loyalty to any land of their adoption?"

"The Jews have the gift of commerce, my dear Keliani," observed Prince Aleksiei.

"And other attributes which make them a running sore in the side of the unfortunate nation upon which they batten. I tell you, General, it would be better for Russia if the pogroms drenched the Empire with Jewish blood down to the last of their accursed race."

Prince Aleksiei lowered his spy-glass, and thoughtfully considered his companion. "My dear Keliani, you take the menace of the Jews too much to heart. I can assure you——"

From the Allied batteries, beginning with the French on the left and sweeping along to the flank of the English, came a storm of cannonading. In the Redan red-hot balls of iron started to fall, while chains of bucket holders poured water to minimize the risk of fire.

On the left, charging against the Malakoff, the French swarmed from their earthworks. Well ahead of them was a debonair young captain of the *Chasseurs d'Afrique*, who for the moment had abandoned his regiment to join comrades on foot. With all the *élan* of their nation the infantry strove to catch up with the flying cavalryman. Thinned by devastating fire still they raced on, only to be brought up at the foot of the fort, where a pile of bodies began to grow.

Before the Redan, the English had not made another move, but their time was near. Through drifting powder fumes, smoke from smouldering fires, and steam from quenched cannon-balls, the watering eyes of Prince Aleksiei watched their earthworks, where the lighter colour of upturned soil was sharply delineated against the dark drab of the rocky plain.

"They come," he announced calmly.

Sword-beckoning officers in front directed and encouraged the bobbing bayonets behind. At a steady trot the British line moved menacingly forward.

"Rapid fire," shouted Colonel Keliani.

Men fell, the attack reeled, and yet the decimated ranks advanced. In the Redan defenders screamed, groaned, or died unknowingly. An English party reached the foot of the *glaçis*. The defending riflemen, that rich target so enticing, left the protection of the sandbags; bending over the parapet, they poured point-blank fire through the swirling eddies.

"I believe the English have brought with them . . ." Prince Aleksiei began saying to his A.D.C. but was compelled to wipe streaming eyes before peering down again. "Damn this smoke, it makes it impossible to see anything," he swore irritably. From below a wild cheer resounded as an English officer started to ascend and, just then, Prince Aleksiei obtained a glimpse which confirmed his suspicions.

"Scaling ladders," he shouted. "Pass the word to stand-to."

Up the sides of the fort, one hand for climbing and the other grasping a weapon, the British mounted; some of them, falling inert against the ladders, formed an additional obstacle for those following; or their fingers loosened and down the side of the *glaçis* they slithered, to be brought up with a thud against the warm heap of blood and sinews of the dead and dying below.

On the ladder nearest the Malakoff, a captain of the Coldstreams sprang on to the parapet but, foreshortened above the knees by a mighty sabre swing, toppled backwards, bringing to death in his fall three blaspheming men who clung to the lower rungs of the ladder.

Colonel Keliani was everywhere, fighting with demoniacal abandon, utterly regardless of self. Now he pointed.

"Wipe out those two," he bawled, his words lost in the din.

In the centre of the parapet, a faithful sergeant stepping off the ladder behind, stood an officer of the 49th. Thrice his keen blade hissed through the air, and thrice a son of Holy Russia passed from this life. But the odds were too uneven and, almost immediately, with bayonet wounds through his body and a ricochet Deptford bullet lodged in his side, this gentleman fell from the sandbag wall; dying already, a crimson flow gushing from his mouth, he staggered on the terrain.

In repulsing the assault, which faded out shortly afterwards, Colonel Keliani had been hurt.

"My dear fellow," Prince Aleksiei said, hastening to him, "it indeed grieves me to find you in such a plight."

With the crude but efficient surgery of the seasoned campaigner he swiftly bandaged the wound.

"Obtain a stretcher party," he said to his A.D.C. as he rose. "Have this officer conveyed at once to the hospital, where you will present my compliments to the physician in charge. Advise him that should he require anything beyond the hospital's ordinary resources, nourishing foods, broths and the like, my cook will furnish them."

"Assuredly, General."

Feebly Colonel Keliani turned his head, and looked up from the improvised palliasse of overcoats on which he lay.

"I'm done, General," he whispered.

Prince Aleksiei took stock of the grey face and the beaded forehead. "It may be so," he agreed, for it is not kind to buoy up a soldier with false hopes. "But that we shall see, my dear fellow."

That said he resumed his urgent duties.

The desperate throw of the Allies on that June day had failed, and throughout the battlefield friend and foe searched amongst the fallen, gripping inanimate shoulders and touching the eye-balls in still faces, when the outcome was usually either a shake of the head or a closer examination from a kneeling position. Around the Russian earthworks greasy-skinned priests were moving, pausing occasionally to give unction to men too weak to brush off the flies which pestered them, while from the town a string of old-clothes dealers arrived with a view to a ghoulish deal.

With eyes familiarized to the everyday happenings of war, Prince Aleksiei glanced over this scene from his command post, noting the tacit armistice during which the mutilated received rough aid and the stiffening were rolled into the cover of shallow holes. Then, replacing field-glass in leather case, he issued terse instructions—for repairs to emplacements, a new disposal of batteries, and the collection of scattered weapons left by dead and sorely-wounded men.

Prince Aleksiei did not retire to his austere quarters until the setting sun's blood-red afterglow had started to darken with the grey shades of approaching night.

2

The room was long and low, its arched roof supported by square, stone pillars. Weeks earlier the walls had been white-washed to the height of a man's head, on the instruction of a fanatically up-to-date doctor who had "ideas" on antisepsis. Above the limit of the flaking lime the wall continued in its old mantle of dirt, with webs and skeins of filth hanging from the ribs of the vaulted ceiling.

This was the Ekaterinskia Soldiers' Hospital in the fortress town of Sevastopol, where, cheek-by-jowl, lay one hundred and seventeen men on one hundred and seventeen pallets, and one man lay in a brass-knobbed double bed.

Sitting on an empty ammunition box, Prince Kaivanov stretched across to rest his hand gently on the wasted arm of the occupant of that outstanding bed.

"Let us consider the matter settled, my dear Colonel," he said, smiling. "As soon as you are fit enough I will have you moved by easy stages to Yasni Dulba, where you will be in the care of my dear sister. And perhaps later you may complete your convalescence on my estate in the Caucasus, possibly taking the waters there. They did my father immense good after a serious blood-letting."

A film of hope shone in a pair of sunken eyes. Indeed the patient tried to jest as, with a trifling movement of the hand, he attempted to draw attention to his surroundings . . . grimy windows cracked by the concussion of the guns; orderlies carrying buckets piled with reddened rags; priests with deep voices intoning the last offices; and a passing doctor whose forearms, revealed by rolled-up sleeves, showed sickly traces of a grim occupation.

"It would seem a trifle different, General," he remarked. "But as to your most handsome suggestion——"

"Another thing, my dear Colonel," Prince Kaivanov interposed. "It has been my great pleasure to report your valiant conduct to Prince Mentchikoff, about which I have no doubt His Majesty the Tsar will signify his pleasure most suitably. Deservedly so, for throughout the siege your courage has sparkled as a glorious example to every Russian soldier."

Deeply moved, Colonel Keliani for the moment was unable to speak. But his expression changed once again as, with an effort, he raised himself slightly from his pillows. Weakly he waved aside those near: two orderlies, a doctor and three priests. When he spoke he coloured faintly, as though confessing to some abominable sin.

"I could not do otherwise," he said painfully. "You see, General, the proud history of the Kelianis was besmirched by my grandfather. He . . . he took in marriage a Jewess. For that reason, an extra effort——"

Prince Kaivanov nodded. "I do not care myself for marriages between those of different religions," he said.

"But there is a paramount reason beyond that," Colonel Keliani replied. "I refer to the quality of Jewish blood, which is——"

Again Prince Kaivanov interrupted him. "The Jews, my dear sir, are a remarkably strong people or they would never have survived centuries of merciless persecution. Of a surety there are worse alliances than your grandfather may have made."

"My dear General . . ." Colonel Keliani protested.

"Much worse alliances, *damnably* worse," Prince Kaivanov went on, his tone sombre. "And if it were in my power to replace another strain in the stock of my descendants with Jewish blood, then gladly would I essay the operation. It would encourage me to have greater hope that in the future men bearing my name would acquit themselves as gallantly as you have done."

"*You* have fears on that score . . . doubts . . . doubts about Kaivanovs to succeed you?" the invalid stuttered.

Prince Kaivanov's reply was indirect. "We have a proverb, 'A ring has no end', and it can mean so much in certain instances," he replied grimly. "Can there be any doubt that the strength of unborn generations is affected, for good or ill, by the breed of the woman upon whose finger a man of proud family places a golden marriage ring?"

As if to indicate the subject could no longer be discussed, he drew on his white gloves.

"*Au revoir*, my dear Keliani," he said.

Squaring his shoulders he turned about and, escorted by the senior surgeon, walked the length of the ward to the outer door, a dignified figure watched surreptitiously by all.

The war was still in progress when Colonel Keliani, in a well-sprung carriage, travelled slowly along the rough roads to the

43

Don. The conflict also showed little sign of ending by the time he was able to take China tea and lemon with the Countess Nathalie, who throughout his stay at Yasni Dulba administered so efficiently to the needs of the invalid, her brother's guest.

Nor was the struggle over when the sick man, definitely much improved by then, journeyed down to the Caucasus, a drive of many stages during which nightly rest was taken in princely houses thrown open with warm hospitality to a friend of the house of Kaivanov.

Meantime Prince Aleksiei did his duty as might be expected of him, unyieldingly, right through to a golden September day when the French, towards the close of hours of carnage, placed their flag on the summit of the Malakoff. Elsewhere the defenders of the Redan beat off five British attacks, but with the French in flanking possession of the Malakoff the position of Prince Aleksiei's forces was untenable.

That night the Russians withdrew from the south side, crossing to the harbour's northern shore by the bridge of boats, marching in shambling fours, an endless column of weary men illuminated by the red glare over Sevastopol, fired by demolition parties. At the southern end of the bridge Prince Aleksiei stood, urging these numbed men with savage, penetrating orders. It was of vital importance that every able-bodied Russian soldier be safely evacuated. These, the men who could still hold a musket, were an asset to Holy Russia.

So the columns trudged by, and on the morrow, from the McKenzie Heights, the smartly-accoutred Russian staff looked down appreciatively on the devastated region the enemy had obtained for their pains, and hour by hour an impression strengthened. Over bottles of Crimean wine the rebuff glowed more rosily, until it swelled into a great tactical victory. That being so, there followed a spate of new plans for the final discomfiture of the invader. Fort Konstantin on the seaward flank at last received a supply of sound ammunition, while the Avlinka Bastion and the Gortschakoff Battery both added extra lines of grim muzzles to the front, though these would have been more significant if each had not lacked a breech-block at the rear.

Afterwards, from the north side of Sevastopol, with a narrow strip of water between, the Russian forces faced the Allies, and there both sides remained. The Allies had insufficient men to advance, while the Russians, their levies broken by long marches through the interior, were in no position to take up an offensive. In any event each of the combatants discovered a specious reason for satisfaction.

The Allies, by the employment of the electric telegraph, were able to announce to London and Paris: "The Fall of Sevastopol" and the Russians in St. Petersburg to counter with: "We still hold the fortress, impregnable against all attack" . . . neither party finding it convenient to mention that half of the defences held by the other.

A very satisfactory outcome, which caused Her Majesty Queen Victoria to order a gigantic bonfire to be lighted on the summit of Craigeowan, which subsequently held the attention of that lady when a plaided attendant pulled back a plaid curtain.

The Tsar, delighted by the glowing despatches he received, made progress down to Sevastopol—or rather as far as Bagtché Serai, north of Sevastopol, sufficiently distant from the battle area as to deny him any glimpse of the fortress.

At Bagtché Serai His Majesty talked with members of his glittering staff, presented medals, and inspected regiments of heroes carefully prepared for the ceremony. For three days he worked strenuously amongst his loyal soldiers, and on the fourth, having a little spare time, made his Imperial Will known. Horses were groomed afresh, gear cleaned and polished, for Alexander II proposed to inspect his fortress at Sevastopol. At the last minute a despatch for his Imperial Master arrived from the Minister of War, into which his on-the-spot advisers read a deeper significance than appeared on the surface. The outing was cancelled, for His Majesty, duly weighing representations respectfully but strongly submitted, deemed it wisdom forthwith to take the first stage of his return to the capital.

That night in Bagtché Serai a banquet was given, a banquet at which neither the Prince Kaivanov nor any of his plain-spoken friends were present. Fourteen exuberant field officers, all of whom had sworn fealty to the House of Romanov, celebrated a most amusing piece of chicanery before being carried to their soft beds.

3

The last of the English transports was hull-down, leaving astern a country which had been humbled but not crushed.

On that bright afternoon, prior to departure to the Caucasus, Prince Aleksiei Kaivanov ended a three-day tour of the battlefield, from the River Alma to Inkerman, and thence to the Redan, razed to the ground by the Allies. And now, on a bluff above the narrow harbour of Balaclava, he gazed on the terrain lately used by the Allies as a base. About him was the aftermath which an army leaves in its passing: stores, discarded tents, rusty weapons, even a heap of unused wooden crosses. Busily employed salvaging in the vicinity were many soldiers. Their clothes bulged with odd-ments.

Prince Aleksiei stared at the animated scene outside the double doors of a large hut, where men were levering off the tops of packing-cases or re-nailing those already inspected by a firm-chinned young officer standing near.

"My dear General," this gentleman cried out, moving forward. "It is indeed a pleasure to see you again."

The young man was a soldier of promise who had fought bravely in the war. Prince Aleksiei smiled genially.

"And what treasures have you found?" he inquired.

"Varied," Count Petrov laughed. "Quite remarkably varied." He counted off on his fingers. "Razors, pomade for the hair, English greatcoats, and six thousand boots—all left-footed . . ."

"You will have some difficulty, Volodia Leoniditch, in turning those to advantage," Prince Aleksiei remarked.

The young officer shook his head, and jerked his thumb over his shoulder. "I have already disposed of them to the merchant Rakenstein."

"Mmm," murmured Prince Aleksiei, bending to examine an English greatcoat hanging over the edge of a crate. "Well-made coats, these."

"Decidedly superior to the rubbish issued to our men. But as my windfall is large, General, will you allow me to present you with a case or so? They might serve for your stable-hands, game wardens and the like."

"No, my dear fellow," said Prince Aleksiei, "though I greatly appreciate the offer."

Pleasantly bidding farewell, he lightly spurred his horse, trot-ting her briskly as far as a steep slope leading down to the sea.

The young officer thoughtfully watched the disappearing figure. The next day, on his instructions, two wooden cases filled with British Army greatcoats were manhandled to a jetty built for the convenience of officers of the British Black Sea Fleet, where they were rolled into a Tartar fishing-boat, to depart on the first leg of their southward trip to Amsibu. For young Count Petrov was poor and ambitious, while General Prince Kaivanov was wealthy and powerful, and in the patronage of such men younger men may go far.

4

The brief scene between the two Kaivanovs, the dominating grandfather and his heir, a girlish frightened boy, had left upon one witness an impression he found difficult to shake off. And

way for this flying, snow-spattering equipage, for it was not deemed wise for members of that House to linger. Not in days of ever-rising anarchism.

Each with staff in hand, there were bearded hawkers of the Sacred Pictures who, as it would be sacrilege to accept money for such wares, traded only on a basis of barter; and on every corner pinched-faced beggars held out tin cups, humbly imploring charity.

On the other side of the broad thoroughfare was the blue-grey expanse of the frozen Neva, dazzling white where steel horse-shoes and tapered runners had laid a powdered track towards Finland; and, merely a short trip across the ice, grim-looking Saint Peter and Saint Paul dominated all with its silent menace, a fortress, a mausoleum and a prison.

All this might be seen through the windows of the Kaivanov residence on Palace Quay, a far-reaching building of shining Italian marble which was as magnificent as any along that street of splendour, where the abodes of the Grand Dukes, the _élite_ of the Holy Russian Empire and the embassies of foreign powers vied with each other in the front they presented to the capital.

The room was stifling as a hot-house, its atmosphere cloying. There were high banks of arum lilies and tuberoses in pots, and the earthy smell from masses of chrysanthemums warred with the odours of Paris perfumes.

Prince Mikhail Kaivanov, while his servant buttoned the shoulder fastening of his white silk shirt, toyed with a bracelet on his wrist, glanced indifferently at traffic passing silently along the lamp-lit Palace Quay, and less indifferently around his dressing-room. His scrutiny ranged over divans and brocaded screens, from ibises in Chinese porcelain to exotic hangings and piles of colourful cushions. As his dulled eyes moved, his long fingers fondled a white-and-yellow tom-cat whose claws were sinking into the padded fabric of the stool on which it stood, back arched.

"That is done, Highness."

His master did not reply for the moment. Prince Mikhail was preening before a mirror, gazing at the reflection of a man with sleek jet-black hair and dark eyes, fine features haughtily commanding, whose mouth would have been perfect had it not been a little slack. Though now thirty-six, he still possessed much of the feminine quality of his youth.

He moved nearer the mirror, stroked his eyebrows with a fingertip, and made his will known. "A little more powder, I think," he said softly, accepting the puff which the servant, with ready anticipation, had lifted out of a jewelled bowl. Then, without looking round, he held out his hand for a moistened glass stopper, with which he left a smear of costly fragrance behind each ear.

"And now, Leonid Borisovitch," he said, extending his arms to slip into a *cinquecento* costume of black-and-white stamped velvet.

He examined himself in the long pier-glass while Leonid Borisovitch manœuvred the devices which made possible a view from every angle.

"Quite attractive," he murmured, smiling quizzically at the waiting servant.

"Most excellent, Highness," said Leonid Borisovitch, standing farther away to obtain a better perspective. "If your Highness permits, I have seldom seen Highness look more effective."

"Effective!" Prince Mikhail frowned. "Hardly the word——"

A tap on the door of the outer chamber interrupted him, and —his man gone to answer the summons—he took a cigarette from a diamond-encrusted box, and thrust it into the bowl of a pipe-shaped cigarette holder. This done, he stood helplessly.

Soft-footed, the servant returned. "Your Highness," he began.

"A light, dolt. . . . Well?"

"*Madame la Princesse* presents her compliments, Highness. She would be honoured if you would join her."

Prince Mikhail's striking eyebrows were elevated. "So!" he remarked. "I quite forget when I last received such a message. It must be . . . h'mm. . . ."

"Highness, it was——" Receiving a savage cuff, Leonid Borisovitch abased himself. He had the uncertain expression of one who at times is allowed familiarities, though in his deep-set eyes there was something more. "Pardon, Highness," he said humbly.

But Prince Mikhail had forgotten. Slowly he pirouetted. "My cloak," he demanded.

When he had been carefully wrapped into this garment, he glanced finally at himself before mincing from the dressing-room.

Leonid Borisovitch sighed, expressively held his palms to Heaven, and departed on his duties to his master's oppressively scented bedroom, where he laid out a night-shirt of pink surah trimmed with Valenciennes lace.

"The largest ass will not make an elephant." The snarled murmur escaped his thin lips, and fearfully he looked about.

Prince Kaivanov traversed vast corridors, before knocking on a door which was opened by a French maid. The new decorative scheme of the boudoir beyond, in red and blue, caused him to hesitate on the threshold, and momentarily he closed his eyes.

The Princess Mikhail Kaivanova, a lady slightly plump but very attractive, broad of brow and wholesome-faced, abandoned her nails and glanced over the back of a silk-covered sofa.

"You will recover from it, Mikhail Pavlych," she said, her voice dry.

"But really, my dear, these colours," he said, shuddering.

Her mouth curved, indeed she looked regally scornful. Perhaps her *kokoshniki*, a high jewelled head-dress, and a *sarafan* and tight waistband as worn by ladies of the Court, served to add to the impression.

"I sent for you, Mikhail Pavlych——" she began.

"Ah!" Prince Mikhail's eyes gleamed. "Then you are making arrangements for Marienbad. Truly the vanity of woman is extraordinary. But remember, my dear Lizaveta Petrovna, that when the luncheon horn blows you must eschew such delicacies as paprika, *wiener-schnitzel,* sausage in butter, and stuffed pigeons if you would gain your purpose, and . . . er," he tittered, "lose flesh."

"You are intolerable," Princess Mikhail retorted.

"Then!" he shrugged. "Why do you command me to this . . . to this rather unaccustomed place?"

She laughed bitterly. "Is it my fault that you find my apartments strange?"

Prince Mikhail gesticulated. "Need we?" he inquired suavely.

The green ribbon of a *Dame du Palais* rose and fell sharply. She bit her lip, averted her head, and occupied herself intently with a velvet nail-polisher. When she spoke her voice had steadied. "I wished to talk to you about Ivan Mikhailovitch," she said. "He is our only child and——"

"My dear Liza," Prince Mikhail quivered. "Must you be so frightfully crude?"

"I should imagine that you find it so," said his wife icily. "The only thing which puzzles me is how you succeeded in begetting him. Perhaps the fear of your grandfather, and his demand to see the next heir before he died, provides the explanation. Let us trust that, wherever he is, he is still satisfied with his enterprise."

"He rots in Hell, I hope."

"That you will be able to ascertain in due course," said Princess Mikhail calmly, crossing shapely, lace-stockinged legs.

Prince Mikhail threw away a cigarette stub. "And Ivan Mikhailovitch?" he asked.

"I wish him to leave the Imperial Page School. His years there have done him endless damage, and already, at fourteen, he is a man of the world. Soon he will receive an appointment to the

53

Court and I neither want him to go there nor into the Guards as he would do subsequently."

"And why should a Kaivanov decline privileges which so many would give their souls to possess?"

Princess Mikhail stretched out, and laid her hand on his cloak. "Misha," she said earnestly, "Ivan Mikhailovitch has proclivities which the atmosphere of the Court would bring to fuller bloom. There are too many bored women there to whose petting I fear he would respond . . . women who would not scruple to use him for their own amusement."

Prince Mikhail nodded distastefully. "I understand that an Imperial Page has other duties beyond damping knee breeches to ensure their being skin-tight and creaseless," he remarked.

"A youth of Ivan Mikhailovitch's inclinations needs discipline. The adjustment of a lady's garter should not be done by such as he."

"And you suggest. . . .?"

"I called at the Admiralty yesterday."

Her husband's eyes narrowed, and he smiled ironically. "And what does my bluff, brother-in-law sailor, Admiral Sememski, have to say?"

Princess Mikhail glanced uncertainly. "Vasili Petrovitch says that Ivan Mikhailovitch could go into the Naval Academy, and thence into the Navy for a few years. The training would do him good. You . . . you are not angry with me, Mikhail Pavlych?"

His humourless smile still persisted. "Why should I be, my dear Liza? You must remember that Ivan one day will succeed to my rank and station, and naturally I desire that he should be fitted to the position we Kaivanovs hold in Russia."

"Then——?" Princess Mikhail's brown eyes were hopeful.

He airily circled a finger. "I will consider, my dear," he said. "And now——" he bent to kiss her hand.

Princess Mikhail, no doubt pleased by this outcome, spoke on a topic more congenial to him, pointing to the velvet costume showing through the half-open cape. "You are going to Princess Tchalmin's *Bal Costumé*?" she asked wistfully. "I suppose I shall have a thoroughly stuffy evening with the Grand Duchess."

Prince Mikhail nodded. "I propose doing so later, but first I shall indulge myself for a while at the Mariinsky."

"The Mariinsky!" Her mouth hardened.

Gazing at the ceiling, he lost himself in an enchanting reverie. "The *décors*, the miming of Zucchi," he murmured. "The consummate artistry of . . . But you do not seem to share my enthusiasm for the Italian Ballet, my dear."

Princess Mikhail's eyes flashed. "On the contrary."

"So . . ." He laughed softly. "My dear Liza, surely you are not jealous of the talented Zucchi?"

Slowly, very slowly, she shook her head.

A mirror was convenient—Prince Mikhail found it so. He was meticulously viewing himself as he spoke: "No," he said carelessly. "Then is it Marie Paretti who arouses your distrust?"

Infuriated by his indifference, she sprang up. "No," she shouted passionately, "neither Virginia Zucchi nor Marie Paretti; I only wish to God it were."

Prince Mikhail was pained. "Really, my dear Liza. . . ."

The Princess Mikhail Kaivanova sank on to a stool, buried her face in her hands. Her shoulders shook; the carefully-tended nails left marks on her palms.

"Leave me, you loathsome creature," she sobbed.

Quite unmoved, her lawful husband obeyed her command.

2

There was unease in many princely dwellings. It was incredible that the Nihilists had been able to touch off a compact charge of dynamite under a dining-room in the closely-guarded Winter Palace. Nevertheless it was an inescapable fact that the Autocrat and his family had escaped joining the half-hundred killed and wounded only through being a few minutes late for dinner. Here again was an example of the inefficiency of the police, here further proof of the widespread ramifications of the plotters.

Many frightened men and women eyed faithful old retainers suspiciously, for the outrage against the Tsar's person, it was asserted, could not have been attempted without inside co-operation.

This was the nightmare of those who woke bathed in sweat, and in the thoughts of others who in a paralysis of inaction sat up tautly in bed while conjuring infernal machines into the tick of a French clock. They remembered how Prince Krapotkine had been assassinated the previous year; how General de Masentzoff twelve months before that perished horribly. Damn the Government with its velvet hand, the paltry dozens it allowed to be executed, its ridiculous commutations on the eve of the scaffold, the inadequately few train-loads of rebellious dogs consigned in chains to Siberia.

"Inside co-operation." The phrase caught on.

True, General Malikoff, shortly after Empire furniture was blown to dust in the Winter Palace, had been given extensive powers. But was he sufficiently the man of action for a necessary but bloody task?

The cravens among them wondered, and worried about a noise which might be water-hammer in pipes or. . . . These anxious creatures huddled under silken bed-clothes and waited impotently, for that which has to be must be. Others, just as scared, nevertheless took their pleasures as they found them.

The massively-furnished banqueting hall of the Kaivanov mansion had undergone a striking change. The floor was deeply strewn with sand, stunted palms were everywhere, and in the background, seen through opened double doors, was the perfectly created illusion of a Pyramid. Most pleasing was this reincarnation of an Egyptian scene, but then so were all Prince Kaivanov's conceptions. The dinner party at which his guests were robed in monks' garments was still talked about in St. Petersburg.

On this evening the full three hours of the repast had gone, faces were becoming more flushed, and a priceless Napoleon brandy was on the board. The host, half-reclining on a neighbour's shoulder, listened courteously to an older man, General Count Petrov, who sat opposite.

"And so, Mikhail Pavlych, I sent your grandfather English greatcoats from Balaclava," this gentleman remarked.

Prince Mikhail sent his glass flying over the polished surface of the table. "I know, my dear Volodia Leoniditch," he said thickly. "As a small boy I was morbidly interested in them when they were unpacked at Amsibu."

Baron Ustinburg, a pock-marked gentleman, guffawed. "And as a grown man you wouldn't be much different, eh, what, Mikhail Pavlych?" he said, sniggering. "God!" he continued, almost falling off his chair as he appealed to the company, "wouldn't he shriek for his smelling salts if confronted with anything savouring of war?"

There was a roar of laughter, the drumming of heels, and Prince Chermoiev, whom humour took in an unusual way, was violently sick. Even Savinkof, the wild-eyed and highly-strung poet, and Nikolai Tsereteli, composer of stark music, tittered unrestrainedly at this slur upon their patron. But Antonio Rozzi, wearing the costume of the last act at the theatre and still painted, only permitted himself a faint smile.

Prince Mikhail, supporting himself on the young ballet dancer, rose unsteadily. "Sir," he began, catching Baron Ustinburg's eye, "I regard your observation as offensive."

"I should utterly ignore him, dear Mikhail Pavlych," said Savinkof, remembering the rent.

The empty glass had been filled by the attentive Leonid

Borisovitch. Prince Mikhail tossed down the vodka. "I, who as a boy fought at Gunib——" he resumed stormily.

"Egor Ignatevitch was but jesting," interposed Nikolai Tsereteli, not to be out-manoeuvred.

"Jesting!" Prince Mikhail bawled. "Jesting, you say. On such a subject, to one of my name."

The black rafters threw back bellows of glee. Prince Chermoiev, green as grass, staggered to his feet. "Let's have it, Mikhail Pavlych," he shouted.

Apart from General Petrov, who appeared somewhat weary of present company, the suggestion was acclaimed. Those near made ill-judged attempts to slap Prince Mikhail encouragingly, others loudly reiterated Prince Chermoiev's demand.

The fury in their host's face died. He smiled, bowed in acceptance, and signalled to the swarm of liveried servants.

"Gentlemen, we will drink a toast," he declared and, as soon as the glasses had been replenished, struck a more erect pose. "Gentlemen," he resumed solemnly. "To the Kaivanovs who have always fought, and who always will fight, for the House of Romanov. To my great-great-grandfather, the Ataman Guchkor Kaivanov, who with a handful of loyal men. . . ."

So he went on, word-perfect in the lengthy tribute to his forebears as taught him by his stern grandfather. At its conclusion pear-shaped spots of liquid marred the surface of the table as he flourished his glass.

"Gentlemen, to them," he cried shrilly.

Heads jerked back, bumpers were drained, and in a trice lovely glassware splintered into fragments when hurled enthusiastically against the wall.

"Bravo," screamed Baron Ustinburg. "Well said, indeed."

Prince Mikhail stiffly inclined his head. "You think so, Egor Ignatevitch," he said icily. "And now, gentlemen . . ." his glance of abhorrence passed over disordered dishes, soiled linen, and vomit, ". . . let us to the Islands."

"To the Islands," screeched the poet Savinkof, overbalancing.

General Count Petrov, murmuring about another appointment, made his excuses. Those gentlemen who needed it were assisted to their feet; and into voluminous furs, caps, and fur-lined carriage boots. Then, with his arm around Antonio Rozzi's shoulders, Prince Kaivanov stumbled to the door, outside which he handed the good-looking young Italian into the sledge, usurping a footman's function by tucking a bear-skin rug about his guest before taking his place alongside.

"You will be warm enough, my dear Toni?" he inquired.

Signor Rozzi, a member of the troupe at the Mariinsky Theatre, turned luminous eyes. "Quite, dear Misha," he said softly.

Still Prince Mikhail was not satisfied. He gave a curt command and an extra foot-wrap was speedily brought. Meanwhile the bulkily-clad coachman, busy with mettlesome beasts, jerked his head to the horseman who, at the great man's bidding, scrupulously inspected a blue-silk net which would protect their august master and his guest from fragments of snow kicked up by flying hoofs.

"The Villa Aydée," snapped Prince Mikhail.

The three impatient animals, responsive to the slightest touch, tore at the harness, and the equipage, silver bell alone giving notice of its approach, sped over the newly-fallen snow.

"Ah!" Prince Mikhail settled himself. "A most excellent evening so far. But now," he smiled on his companion, "I find it far more entrancing."

Rozzi was lost in contemplation of the towering spire of the Admiralty, outlined against the blue vault of the star-lit sky.

"My dear Toni," said Prince Mikhail anxiously. "You appear to be indifferent to my society. In what way have I offended?"

The vehicle, silently blaspheming coachman tugging at the reins in his efforts to obey his master's standing order, swept swiftly along the streets. On a sharp corner the *troika* side-slipped, straightening with a sharp jar to the shorter track taken by the high-spirited beasts in front. Prince Mikhail's gloved hand tightened on the side grip. Half pulling himself up he slashed out with the whip provided in his vehicles for this purpose. "You dog," he yelled. "Have I not given you instructions as to the pace you will drive?"

"Highness——" The coachman could say no more for the moment, but when his impetuous team's pace had been reduced he twisted on the lofty box. The peacock feather in his cap bobbing, he looked down with scared eyes. "Highness," he begged, only to receive a cut across the mouth. "The new feed——"

"Excuse yourself, would you?" Prince Mikhail snarled. "Report yourself to the Custodian of the Stables in the morning. I . . . I will give him his instructions." He smiled thinly as he sank into the comfortable seat. "These disobedient louts, my dear Toni, must needs receive tuition from the kiss of the knout."

Again Antonio Rozzi did not make any comment.

"Toni!" said Prince Mikhail. "I insist upon an explanation. Why are you behaving so?"

In the flickering light of the carriage lamps he noticed the young Italian's smile, a smile he thought suggestively secret. "Toni!" he said, "I trust none of my guests was distasteful to you?"

Rozzi came out of his reverie, almost, shaking his head

dreamily. "On the contrary," he sighed. "In particular I found Baron Ustinburg most charming."

Abruptly Prince Mikhail sat up. "Egor Ignatevitch!" he said harshly.

"So *simpatico*," the Italian murmured. "Yes, I like him."

"That ill-mannered lout." Prince Mikhail's voice was depressed to the deep tones expressive of the melancholia of his country. "No doubt you like me, too."

"Of course, Misha, of course I like you."

Prince Kaivanov pointedly moved deeper into the corner. "Like!" he jeered.

Wistfully the young Italian strove to make amends. "Let us not quarrel, dearest Misha," he cried.

"And yet you can tell me you . . . you like me," Prince Mikhail declared passionately. "The identical feeling you would have for a picture, or a vapour bath, or the iron with which you curl your hair. You like me, eh?"

Rozzi's jewelled ear-drops swung more rapidly, in scintillating arcs, when he started to weep.

"Toni!" Prince Mikhail begged.

"But you have hurt me," his companion explained. "And so soon the company leaves for Berlin."

"You shall not go," said Prince Mikhail vibrantly, removing a glove under cover of the thick rug. "Toni, my dear," he entreated, "I beg you to entrust your future to me. Here, in Petersburg, I have influence to ensure that your talents obtain the recognition they merit, and money sufficient——"

"So you think I am interested in money?" Rozzi inquired frigidly.

"My dear," Prince Mikhail was apologetic. "You must remember that it buys many of the things you enjoy."

Rozzi struggled to withdraw himself. "So you consider that I am to be compared to a certain mercenary Georgian creature? Oh, yes . . ." he added waspishly, as Prince Mikhail stirred in confusion, "I have heard about him."

"A youth of talent on one of my estates whose future I endeavoured to assist," Prince Mikhail said with indignation. "What lying tale is this?"

For a while they quarrelled like fishwives, but the atmosphere changed for the better when Rozzi began to pout rather attractively. In this manner the journey to the Islands was passed.

There were many establishments on the Islands, each possessing its respective appeal. Some were discreet places where one might dine with a brother officer's wife without being embarrassed by the sight of one's own wife sharing the rim of a glass with another gentleman of the regiment. And places where such diversions were openly flaunted, where wives, sullen in their own homes, waved gaily to straying husbands across the crowded napery.

And other roofs where choice entertainment provided some measure of satisfaction for jaded minds, beneath which much sweet champagne was drunk and satiated eyes had plenty to assess: gowns which left shoulders and bosom bare; *artistes* clad simply in gold paint and a live snake necklace; posturing women more decently habited in a triangle of transparent chiffon, and whitened bodies effectively delineated against a back-cloth of dull black velvet.

And here were yacht clubs and clay-pigeon shooting establishments; and gaming dens from which stricken gamblers declamatorily left either to die or with the intention of miserably exiling themselves to the provinces . . . unless they chanced to notice one of those innumerable signs promising revenge for the next night. Of these a shooting star was gilt-edged.

Then there was the Villa Aydée, membership of which was reserved exclusively to the stern sex, entrance by the naughtily curious being denied by the immense *dvorniks* guarding the door. Contrarily enough it was a place where high-voiced gentlemen acclaimed the "point" work of small-waisted youths, or quarrelled shrewishly for the next turn on the floor with young men of stilted gait and effeminate profile. A select private club where males blushed vividly under compliments, or, gossiping to their heart's content, daintily used a lace-edged handkerchief while scurrilously betraying one of their kind.

3

The Imperial Page School was housed in the handsome palace of the Emperor Paul, son of Catherine the Great, a fitting environment in which to teach noble youths the exactitudes of an exclusive craft.

These scions of aristocratic houses wore tight-waisted black coats covered with bars of gold embroidery, tassel-hilted swords, knee breeches and shiny top-boots. From a distance they could be mistaken for officials of the Court, but a nearer view disclosed their limited years.

Nevertheless the members of this privileged body considered themselves fully seasoned. Few were virgins, and indeed soon after an admission on this point had been extracted from a blushing new entrant it was usual for him to sneak off to Eranskia, where he mounted the stairs of a house reeking of cabbage water.

There, in a room containing little more than a tumbled bed, for a total outlay of twelve roubles, including two roubles for the building's porter, a broad-hipped dame repaired the omission in his social education.

Following upon this immense leap forward into manhood quite a number of these young gentlemen grew into the habit of keeping an open eye for more tender morsels. And many a Maid of Honour, becoming alarmed after allowing a little fun to go a little too far, deemed it good insurance forthwith to lure some witless cavalry buck into a proposal of marriage.

In the common-room three pages were reading, sceptically, a freshly pinned-up item which intimated when His Imperial Majesty would be visiting the School—in days of fanatical bomb-throwing the adventurings-out of the Tsar were not so obviously heralded.

Elsewhere other boys were writing letters, shrilly chatting, or taking a hand at Preference.

At a baize-covered table a card game was in progress. There was the jingle of coins, laughter, and the oaths of gamblers who were faring ill.

One of the players was a supercilious-looking youngster, Prince Anton Filosofin, a Camer page who, rumour reported, would shortly be appointed to the Empress. Leaning back in his chair he drawled: "I wish to God you wouldn't make such a fuss about a few copecks, Ivan Mikhailovitch."

Prince Ivan Kaivanov, whom the goddess of fortune had deserted, replied haughtily: "My dear Anton Martynych, let me point out. . . ."

Not quite so good-looking, Prince Ivan, as his father, but decidedly attractive, nevertheless. Slim, dark-eyed, black-haired, a boy who already liked the best things of life, and—Prince Mikhail having a horror of disciplining the young—with the money to obtain them.

A hare's foot in his right pocket, and a small ivory elephant on the gold bracelet round his wrist, Prince Ivan wagered. He inspected a card, murmured while making a pass over it with a jade figure attached to another gold chain, and, flicking the pasteboard with a touch thoroughly professional, leaned forward eagerly.

"Hell take it," he snarled, kicking back his chair.

Prince Filosofin's thin nose distended distastefully. "Throwing your hand in?" he said suavely. "As you wish, of course." His fingers drummed on the edge of the table. "That leaves you indebted to me for a hundred and eight roubles."

"I'll give you my note," Prince Ivan snapped.

61

The winner's eyebrows went up. "I am already carrying a great deal of your paper, my dear fellow. Of course," he went on, shrugging expressively, "if you find it inconvenient to settle——"

"Damn you, do you think I can't pay?" Prince Ivan bawled, gripping the arm of a neighbour. "Peter Petrovitch, loan me the money, so that I can satisfy this needy adventurer."

Count Kschesslaev, a quiet-natured round-faced boy, pointed to the pile near his right hand. "Take it out of that, Ivan Mikhailovitch," he said, grinning. "And remember that I can't count on the coffers of *my* dear father."

Prince Filosofin had lost a vast amount of his recent poise. "So I am a needy adventurer, am I?" he said angrily. "I shall now have the pleasure of teaching you a lesson, my talkative lad."

An excited ring formed. Advice and taunts were hurled at the parties to the quarrel, and Prince George Savosef, who in his veins had Romanov blood on the wrong side of the blanket, was so confident about the outcome of the struggle that he offered to lay fifty to ten in gold roubles and found no takers.

"After him, Anton Martynych," he shrieked. "Give the stinking little bastard something he'll remember."

"Bastard!" mused Count Kotya Yaroslav. "You know, George Filippovitch, I seem to recollect that your grandmother was accustomed to unlocking her chamber door for the advantage of——"

"——A gentleman who found nothing compelling in the cow-like faces of the women in your family," finished Prince Savosef hotly.

Count Yaroslav chuckled. "I'll let that pass for the moment," he said, before roaring: "Hey, Ivan Mikhailovitch, go in and wipe him across his thin nose. Why the devil are you hanging back?"

Although Prince Ivan was white with suppressed fury, he was certainly managing to contain himself.

"Listen, Anton Martynych," he said, wagging his finger. "Perhaps I was a shade hasty, but I solemnly warn you that if you so much as put a hand on me——"

If this sensible overture failed, he may have intended correcting Prince Filosofin with a back-handed slap to the mouth, a contemptuous gesture latterly well thought of by the School since a Guards Regiment's commanding officer, with most delicious effrontery, had cut short the admonitions of his mistress's husband in this manner. To the regret of the circle of youths, however, a servant intervened with a message which could not lightly be disregarded.

"His Highness the General-Commandant desires your immediate attendance, Highness," he said, bowing obsequiously to the heir of the house of Kaivanov. "Your noble father, His Highness the Prince Kaivanov, awaits you."

Prince Ivan stared, but only for a moment. A father means little, but the General-Commandant. . . . He quickly fastened his neckband which, for comfort, he had unhooked, and drew in his belt two holes, to regulation tightness.

"Am I all right?" he asked anxiously.

The General-Commandant had been known to consider the least departure from correctness in one page as being representative of slackness in the whole. Prince Ivan was critically inspected by his fellows.

Prince Savosef nodded. "You'll do, Ivan Mikhailovitch," he remarked at length, before sniggering: "Smart enough for that hot little devil, the Chamberlain's daughter, to think seriously of taking you as a lover."

Prince Filosofin's high pitched laughter secured the attention of his audience. "Let us hope that Ivan Mikhailovitch's father, when he sees him, doesn't take the same whim."

Prince Ivan, ears burning, did not dally.

His departure was the signal for an outburst of conversation on the subject of Prince Mikhail Kaivanov. The majority of the Junior Section were bade to make themselves scarce while their seniors retailed the latest scandal, but a few of the younger ones, who had formed attachments in themselves a source of local scandal, were permitted to remain.

It was a very short interview. Prince Mikhail, on his way there, had seen several most alarming sights, and had no desire to linger. He made his will known; his intentions for his son's future were accepted by the young gentleman, somewhat surprisingly, with enthusiastic approval. Within ten minutes he had taken his departure.

Once again in the *troika*, Prince Mikhail Kaivanov commanded his coachman to whip his team to full pace, and, crouching so low as to give the impression that the luxurious equipage was empty, he sped to Palace Quay.

In the old Palace of the Emperor Paul a young gentleman whose course had been so abruptly changed smartly saluted the General-Commandant, bowed so low to that martinet's wife as to bring a protesting creak from his breeches, and then returned to his quarters.

"Well?" said Count Kschesslaev, a curious soul.

Prince Ivan, smiling mysteriously, gave an order to a servant, and shortly afterwards a well-piled dish of a fairy-light *boubliki* was brought in.

"Help yourselves, you fellows," he cried, pointing hospitably.

Eager hands stretching out, the pastry fingers were quickly disposed of.

"Well?" persisted Count Kschesslaev.

Prince Ivan took his time. "Oh, I'm entering the Naval Academy, that's all," he announced.

There was an astonished roar, and much comment. "Not going into the Cavalry Guards? . . . Become a dingy *mitchman* when you could be a cornet in the *Preobrajensky*? . . . Be buried in a tin box when you could have the opportunity of displaying yourself in the Grand Parade of the massed Guards on the Field of Mars? . . . My dear Ivan Mikhailovitch! . . . Not ride at the Cavalry Festival? . . . Ivan Mikhailovitch, what are you thinking about? To go to *sea*?"

Ivan smiled scornfully. "You fools," he said. "While you schoolchildren have to creep out to assignments I shall be amongst the accommodating geishas of Japan. And when some of you deputize for a Grand Duchess with a sheet hanging from your shoulders, and others practise holding the blasted train, you must picture me with the Baltic Fleet amongst the women of France, Italy, Greece and Spain."

"Isn't our Ivan Mikhailovitch a devil for the ladies?" said Prince Savosef.

"He's forgotten the Black Sea Fleet," another remarked, grinning.

The future naval officer scowled. "I'll wager you're all envying my chance to escape from this," he snapped. "As for Court functions. . . . Bah! Who'd want to carry an eighteen-yard train with an old bitch snapping every time there's a turn in the corridor, when in place of that a chap can have his fling with the girls of Hawaii—and Creoles—and black women. They tell me that a black girl——"

Count Yaroslav seemed incredibly astonished, nevertheless he succeeded in slipping a wink to the Page Captain. "My dear Ivan Mikhailovitch," he drawled. "Do I really understand that you have never enjoyed a blackie?"

"Well, I'm damned," the Page Captain ejaculated. "Little snow-white, eh?"

"And he boasted he was a regular man of the world," scoffed Prince Savosef, the corners of his mouth wet as always.

Prince Ivan was scarlet with mortification. "Listen," he urged desperately. "I . . . I. . . ."

"Black women! Phew!" Count Kschesslaev whistled in homage

at the ceiling. "I remember on one of the occasions when I indulged myself. . . ."

That started the uproar, for the staid young Peter Petrovitch could not conceivably be imagined in the kind of erotic situation he was apparently about to describe.

In vain Prince Ivan tried to shout them down, but little heed was taken, even when he was reduced to frantic abuse.

"You dogs should be whipped until you can neither stand nor walk," he bellowed. "By-blows of tainted flesh, the lot of you."

His audience, of the proudest families in Holy Russia, did not take umbrage. Indeed, they stirred afresh in anticipation of new diversion.

"A pity Anton Martynych is not here to hear that," Count Yaroslav remarked, poker-faced.

"Filosofin!" said Prince Ivan. "*That* needy adventurer. By God, I'd have taught him something if he'd touched me."

The quiet youth, Count Kchesslaev, perhaps elated by a recent triumph, tried another shot.

"Well, I never," he marvelled.

This again was too much for his hearers, who laughed until they were exhausted. Before then, however, their butt, quivering with chagrin, had stamped out of the room.

4

On the day following the explosion in the Winter Palace, Prince Mikhail Kaivanov had seen too much for his comfort when driving to the Imperial Page School. Shopkeepers, with prudent anticipation, were fitting stout steel shutters; lancers swept along the streets; armed police zealously moved on loiterers, impartially shifting ordinary onlookers, plotters, and *agents-provocateurs* alike, so earning for themselves suppressed curses from the hundreds of His Majesty's Secret Police who, in rags or in the guise perhaps of a simple bee-keeper from the country with dirty bundle on shoulder, sought with keen eyes for rebellious fellows.

On the pavements sullen men gesticulated at luxury establishments and scowled at the few ornate vehicles which flew through the streets, while in the tops of high wooden towers police officers usurped the stations of fire-watchers and, signal flags in hand, scanned below for the first trace of unlawful assembly.

Not a pleasant place at such times, St. Petersburg, with *drosky* drivers openly insolent to passengers, and by no means content merely to tug at coat sleeves for a larger tip.

In these circumstances Prince Mikhail did not disdain to attend to a menial task. He drained a glass of champagne his servant had poured from a bottle in the silver cooler and then, kneeling on the floor, thrust clothing into a travelling valise with his own soft hands.

"You gave my message to *Madame la Princesse*?" he snapped.

It was against the conventions for Leonid Borisovitch to speak to his master while busily folding trousers. Suspending operations, he bowed and replied: "Yes, Highness."

"Hurry up, damn you," said Prince Mikhail, nodding irritably towards a steamer trunk. "And did I not tell you I am travelling light? God help me that I am attended by such an imbecile."

A moment later Her Highness the Princess Kaivanova arrived. "You seem somewhat disturbed," she remarked.

Suppressing an impatient oath, her husband rose to kiss her hand.

"I confess I am, my dear," he said, smiling wryly. "A sudden call to Amsibu which I find exceedingly inconvenient. Some trouble down there, I fear."

"Not the trouble here in Petersburg?" Princess Mikhail inquired, her tone quite neutral.

Prince Mikhail drew himself up to his full height. "My dear Lizaveta Petrovna," he said, his expression chilling.

"My friends might consider that an explanation; not that I believe their opinion would distress you," she said, adding wearily: "Oh! I must be out of my senses to attempt to restrain you. As if I cared what people say . . . now."

"They had better not let it come to my ears," said Prince Mikhail.

His wife did not comment on this. There was that far more important matter.

"And Ivan Mikhailovitch?" she asked anxiously.

Prince Mikhail glanced at the clock and made an imperative gesture to Leonid Borisovitch, who was methodically strapping the valise.

"Really, my dear Liza, I am in some haste. But I have seen Ivan Mikhailovitch and he raised no objection to my wishes."

"You called at the Admiralty afterwards?"

Prince Mikhail frowned. "It was a little out of my way. Perhaps I can leave the arrangements in the competent hands of yourself and Vasili Petrovitch."

"I shall go to the Admiralty in the morning," said Princess Mikhail firmly. "Whether or not there is rioting."

The upturned hands of her husband were expressive of his thoughts. "You will please yourself, of course, my dear," he said, shrugging. "But after that, if I were you, I should retire to our villa in Livadia. The weather there will be wonderful, and you would be far away from the annoyance of this insurrectionist scum."

Princess Mikhail nodded. "I might, but not until I have obtained His Majesty's permission to withdraw Ivan Mikhailovitch from the Page School." She hesitated. "Are you travelling alone, Misha?"

This time Prince Mikhail all but swore aloud. Really, if the woman were about to moralize it was full time to bid her farewell. He did so courteously but speedily.

But she had reminded him indirectly about a matter. He seized a pen, scrawled a short note, and added an enclosure of a thousand roubles. It was most disappointing that Toni could not travel with him, but he had no intention of crossing the city to the Mariinsky district.

His eyes narrowed reflectively as he sealed the envelope. The money was a matter of no account but—bearing in mind the need for loyalty to his own class, now suffering so much senseless calumny—the terms of the letter rendered it inadvisable for them to be seen by any of the lower orders.

"You will take this at once," he said. "And you will deliver it into Signor Rozzi's hand only . . . his alone."

"Assuredly, Highness," said Leonid Borisovitch.

One further matter remained, the abasement which every good man gives to Him before beginning a journey. Prince Kaivanov commanded the attendance of the Chaplain.

The private chapel of the Kaivanov mansion was dim, illuminated solely by flickering waxlights and delicately-chased metal lamps hanging by chains in front of sixteenth-century Moscow ikons, each forming a small yellow pool of light which, in scores of twinkling pinpoints, was reflected by ancient church utensils, jewelled crosses and gem-studded frescoes on the walls.

With the odour of incense in his nostrils, Prince Mikhail prostrated in sundry acts of humiliation before the sacred picture of his tutelary Saint. He made confession of his sins, received the Blessed Absolution, and, rising refreshed, made a donation of five thousand roubles for a most deserving object which the worthy father chanced to mention.

But then, from childhood upwards, Prince Mikhail had always been most devout. As his cosy, hay-filled travelling-sledge sped along the dead-straight roads of White Russia he uncovered, bowed and crossed himself whenever a river had to be ventured or was safely behind; and on every occasion of a sign from Heaven.

So the journey passed, through hundreds of villages in which snarling country dogs jumped to snap at the noses of sledge horses strange to them; with calls at post-houses at each of which the distinguished traveller magnificently threw vodka money, for there was always the possibility that the news from St. Petersburg had eddied wide.

In this wise, snow replaced by slush, steel runners by axled wheels, the gleaming palace of Amsibu was reached. There Prince Mikhail sank in thanks for a safe arrival, and donated four thousand roubles for a most deserving object to which the worthy priest casually alluded.

While awaiting Rozzi, Prince Mikhail occupied himself with painting and music, and there was one quite outstanding evening when he cleverly contrived to entertain a Chikesska and a Seshlyk, between whom lay a fierce blood-feud from the past. It was less amusing the next morning when he received one of his dead mother's clamorous relatives; to this gross fellow Akashidze he granted the loan requested but, with an all-too-vivid recollection of a similar function at which the most depraved women had been present, declined the invitation he was promptly given.

One sun-drenched day, when driving through Tiflis to the Governor-General's palace, he saw a youth bathing in a fountain. The boy was quite enchanting, his slender white limbs moving with infinite grace, and for the moment Prince Mikhail was so charmed with this spectacle that he seriously wondered about the desirability of allowing Rozzi the hospitality of his roof. But *the* solution came in a flash of inspired vision. This could be made into a situation of the most piquant possibilities. Dear Toni, wouldn't he be rent with jealousy?

Thereupon Prince Mikhail Kaivanov laughed softly, and spoke forthwith to his servants. Yes indeed, this would be highly diverting.

True, the youth's father, tramping out with ashen-faced determination to Amsibu, subsequently protested about the abduction and was severely beaten in consequence, this causing many eye-witnesses stealthily to scowl; and true, the lad's father must have been a weakling, for he died from the flogging. But was it the fault of the head of the house of Kaivanov that filthy clothing had infected flesh torn by the flailing stroke of the *nagaika*? How could it be?

Nevertheless, from then onwards, so much had local feeling been aroused, Prince Mikhail was compelled to journey around accompanied by well-armed guards. This was most tedious, but very necessary in view of the waves of disturbance surging through the Empire.

With the passing of a few months, however, some semblance of tranquillity gradually revealed itself in Holy Russia, though heavy rumblings of discontent quivered beneath the surface.

About then, surfeited with the pleasures he had managed to achieve at Amsibu, Prince Mikhail decided to travel wider. *En route* to Baden he visited his kinsfolk, the Yaroslavs, a family devoted slavishly to their horses, estates, and the nonsensical furtherance of a most dangerous heresy: a more liberal constitution for the country. While staying with them he drove into Odessa, and at the Opera House saw the so-called "divine Sarah"; and towards the end of the same week was in the Nobles' Club when anti-Jewish riots aroused by her name were reaching their height. This was the day after the world-renowned *artiste's* carriage had been stoned and, with one exception, the gentlemen standing in the lofty club windows were highly indignant about the outrage.

These observers had an excellent view from the first floor of what occurred below: a small party of Jews, men and women, hemmed into a corner of the square, were being relentlessly battered by the staves of a mob which went about its business ferociously.

"That single-mindedness is the greatest strength of us Russians," a youngish man exclaimed exultantly.

"What the devil do you mean, Keliani?" a fellow member asked.

Keliani's dark-eyed glance was withdrawn from the bloody scene as he turned to give an account, which seemed totally irrelevant, of celebrations the previous summer for his sister's name day, in which eleven hundred labourers on the family estate with their wives and children had joined. Briefly his point was that his father, General Keliani, decided as dusk approached that it would be discreet for the family to retire from an occasion promising soon to become an orgy of drunkenness and lust.

"That's what I mean," he explained. "We Russians give ourselves wholeheartedly to everything . . . pleasures, to *this*, or whatever it may be. And, by God, that is good."

Meantime the most distressing cries could be heard, even though muted by double-windows: screams, agonized pleas for mercy, dull thuds as viciously-wielded sticks broke human bones. Two incidents stood out clearly—the impalement of a venerable old gentleman on the spikes of railings, and the giant who, swinging a Jewish girl by her ankles, dashed out her brains against a wall.

"By Saint Stepan," an onlooker in the comfortable room said, gulping, "I think the police might put in an appearance now. These massacres may act as a safety valve, but. . . ."

"You're weak-stomached," Keliani declared with scorn. "Yes," he went on with obvious delight, "resentment is growing hourly, and all being well they'll be dragging these wretched Hebrews out tomorrow from every nook and cranny in the ghetto. Yes, tomorrow should be *the* day."

Nobody troubled to answer him, although the majority disliked what was taking place. But a few gentlemen certainly shrugged, and there were whispers and nudges. Why the Kelianis took such an immense pleasure in the pogroms was not definitely known, but many guessed quite accurately.

A lover of beauty and a hater of the crude, Prince Mikhail was relieved to leave this great marble-built city, but was not able to shake off the memory of these hideous sights until he had crossed the Austrian border.

In all, his trip abroad extended almost to a year, the final months being spent on the Riviera. By then, fortunately, conditions at home were reported to be definitely improving and he travelled back to St. Petersburg, where in due course he paid a courtesy call upon his wife, now in her own establishment, and also summoned his son, Prince Ivan, a naval cadet.

Precisely a month to the day after his return, the capital was shaken by a mighty Anarchist explosion. As a result of that explosion two men died: the assassin who lobbed the bomb and the target it hit—His Imperial Majesty Alexander II, Tsar of All the Russias.

Prince Mikhail left St. Petersburg the same evening, which caused a certain amount of ironical comment. For once, however, he was unfairly maligned; this hasty departure related to his peculiar pleasures, an incident for which even a Grand Duke, if similarly involved, would not have escaped banishment.

And so, when his monarch was laid to rest, Prince Mikhail was lazing in his villa at Livadia on the Black Sea. As he watched the sun-dappled waves on that day of mourning he idly reflected on the whims of fortune which had denied him, the head of the house of Kaivanov, participation in any of his country's greatest affairs of pageantry, both sorrowful and joyful. It was just a fleeting thought.

5

If Prince Mikhail Kaivanov missed his proper share in many majestic ceremonies, the same could not be said of his son, Prince Ivan, whose lot throughout life was to be present at great events forming the chronicles of the rulers of the earth.

He began quite young. When the torn body of Alexander II was laid to rest he walked slowly, head bowed, with his fellow-cadets; and on a lovely May day the year but one later, just a few weeks after a mass trial of Nihilists in St. Petersburg, he was in the ancient capital of Moscow, attending the picturesque crowning of the Emperor, Alexander III, and the Empress.

Ten years later still, in London, bunting-dressed and beflagged, the nuptials of the Duke of York and Princess May of Teck were celebrated. That ceremony, in St. James's Palace, was one at which the proudest royalties were present, among them the Tsare-vitch of Russia, in whose train was the younger Kaivanov, then a fully-matured man of twenty-seven.

Sixteen months afterwards, Prince Ivan was near-present when his own sovereign, assuming the greater crown offered by Almighty God and His Holy Son, renounced an earthly crown forever.

Alexander III, Autocrat of All the Russias, died in his beloved Livadia of a disease the nature of which was not known outside the Imperial Family. He was a strong and able man who, given a decent span, would gradually have done much for Russia. But quick ailment reduced him to pottering about his palace in the Crimea, in soft leather slippers and a little jacket striped red and white, each day shedding a little more flesh until his cheeks were skeleton-sunken. The dread course of events hastened Father John of Kronstadt to his side.

The bell in the Palace Church endlessly tolled the sad tidings. At this grievous summons a few great aristocrats of the Russian Empire and a half-score officers of the Army and Navy bearing illustrious names assembled in a cream-walled courtyard, together with, richly honoured, a handful of private soldiers and ratings. They formed a small circle round a vividly-vestmented priest; right hand uplifted, each swore the oath of allegiance to the new Emperor.

Prince Ivan Kaivanov, in royal attendance, was among that privileged company.

Within a few hours a simple procession was formed. The embalmed body of the dear departed was lifted into the coffin by his sons, with Nikolai II supporting the limp head. Borne by his relatives, as a poor charcoal burner might have been borne, he was taken on that November day to the cathedral of Livadia, a very modest place, too small for other than a few to join the Imperial Family. But Lieutenant Ivan Kaivanov, Imperial Russian Navy, was one of them.

With the next day came change; military and religious glory came into their own. The Remains, with appropriate pomp and ceremony, were reverently placed in the Imperial Yacht, for a slow but short sea passage amid two columns of grey ships of the Black Sea Fleet.

When the floating catafalque reached Sevastopol minute guns boomed sombre greeting, flags flew at half-mast and crêpe hangings swathed every balcony, although the latter, by order of the Chief of Police, were devoid of spectators. The Secret Police had been praiseworthily zealous, and the prison was packed with the politically suspect; an ingenious youth with a home-made camera was knocked senseless with the flat of a sabre, and a man suffering from tuberculosis committed suicide because, through excitement, he had forgotten the essential detonator for an infernal machine.

A dense crowd in Kiezt Square stood rigid and silent, but swayed uneasily when a septuagenarian gardener from the new Malakoff Park and Cemetery, fumbling for a rag handkerchief, caused four strangely-assorted men to swoop quickly; two marksmen with telescopically-sighted rifles crouched below the sill of an open window, and each blenched on hearing door panels splintering behind him; four very young men wrote tender letters to mothers—all perished, three beneath iron-shod hoofs, and the fourth, who had faltered, in a candle-lit cellar shortly after interrogation by the brethren of his underworld society.

Big throngs everywhere; professional men, merchants and their families in the small gardens on the Point; officials on the private stand in the Admiralty Dockyard; and uniformed officers, with black-weeded wives, were ranged against the marble side-walls of the Fleet Landing Place. Those in tatters congregated on the north side of the harbour and, more distant, country folk genuflected earlier at the Baider Gate, where the coast road bent to Balaclava.

There were regiments of foot soldiers, turned-about to face the spectators, and long gleaming rows of cavalry swords, outstretched and erect; ships' companies lined the sides of battleships, on whose lofty bridges senior officers stood stiffly at the salute.

Lieutenant Prince Ivan Kaivanov was among these thousands, black muslin wound about the hilt of his sword.

Thus Alexander III set out on a journey across Russia which would bring him to rest with his forefathers in the fortress mausoleum of Saint Peter and Saint Paul.

Accompanying him, in the naval escort, was Lieutenant Prince Ivan Kaivanov, of the Imperial Russian Navy.

PART TWO

1901 - 1914

★

CHAPTER I

ALL things are ordained, and, just as Prince Ivan Kaivanov of the Imperial Navy was destined from birth to see his sovereign's body carried upon a gently-heaving sea, so again was he, seven years later, destined to be present when the mortal remains of another mighty ruler passed between ships of war.

In His Imperial Majesty's ship *Plevsky* he was present when the husk of Her Britannic Majesty, Queen Victoria, lying in a white satin-palled coffin on the deck of her Royal Yacht *Alberta*, slowly travelled, behind a double file of black-painted torpedo-boat destroyers, from Cowes to the English naval base of Portsmouth, along a far extended line of her warships and those of other nations paying the final homage.

At the Royal funeral in London, Prince Kaivanov marched with the Navigator, two paces behind their Captain, a focal point marked on the tablets of each since birth, as inevitable as it was that Commander Prince Kaivanov should stub his toe so awkwardly on a sewer-cover as to derange his right epaulette when stumbling. Throughout his thirty-four years, irrevocably, the path of Prince Ivan Kaivanov had led to that circular piece of iron.

For several days longer, chilled by the raw-damp February air, Commander Prince Kaivanov languished in England's depressing capital. Then, very thankfully, he travelled down to Portsmouth, where his ship lay.

Meantime, in his homeland it had been found necessary to augment the five thousand two hundred and three censors who in times of peace and normality were sufficient to cover the suspect correspondence which passed in the Empire. Blue pencils and brushes dipped into black ticketing ink began to be worked harder.

The officers of the *Plevsky* had barely settled down to a round of gaieties in the French ports after leaving Spithead when the summons came. The Autocrat required all his faithful subjects close to hand; the coded telegram received by the Captain from St. Petersburg was imperative.

So the *Plevsky* weighed anchor at Toulon, signalled

courteously to the French flagship, vomited light-grey fumes of Welsh coal from her three tall funnels, hugged the coast of Spain, faced the rising sun in the English Channel, and stemmed the short steep seas of the German Ocean on her passage to the Baltic and the haven and anxieties of Kronstadt.

Barefooted seamen washed down, polished brasses, painted bulkheads, scoured decks, cleaned privies, shined scuttles, chamoised glass and burnished table silver. Below, stokers shovelled coal, scalded themselves with a badly-fitted joint, rubbed boiler mountings until they gleamed like mirrors, and were spurred to every effort to make stokehole deckplates fit to eat on.

And a few simple tactical exercises were carried out.

In the wardroom the conversation veered to the country to which they had just paid the most melancholy kind of official visit. A dull place and dull people, it was agreed, even under happier circumstances, and, after all, the name of "Perfidious Albion" had not been acquired for nothing.

"Why we allow their brutality to the Boers——"

"Those English hucksters are interested only in the diamond mines."

"We should be more open, and assist Kruger with active support——"

A voice came from the corner in which the members of the non-executive branches, engineering, medical and paymaster, usually kept to themselves. *Plevsky* was an unusual ship and, springing from small landowning families or those with mercantile or professional associations, these officers had found that this withdrawal saved many slights.

The Paymaster was a trifle pale, but determined. "Whatever the faults of the English, I think we could do well to copy some of their institutions," he said.

"Oh! On with that again," a princely, junior watch-keeper remarked contemptuously.

The Navigator followed that up. "We are a vastly different people from the English, Paymaster," he pointed out coldly. "They are law-abiding and lack the wild and far more virile blood of our countrymen. For that reason alone authority in Russia must be maintained by harsher methods."

Many angry faces were turned towards the Paymaster, who licked dry lips before continuing doggedly: "All the same," he insisted, "if the Emperor could be persuaded to initiate a more democratic constitution I am convinced there would be an end to these outrages and disorders."

This was too much for Number One, who flung his glass to the deck.

"By God, you," he bawled. "Haven't I warned you about your seditious talk?"

Tempers were rising, and the Fleet Surgeon and the Second Engineer broke off a low-voiced conversation about Count Tolstoi's letter of appeal to the Tsar, both aware that each revolution of the engines seemed to increase the general note of hysteria.

The Paymaster's troubled gaze wandered from fine napery on the table to the luxurious fittings of the broad compartment, and thence to the concentration of savage opposition confronting him.

"Listen a moment, Baron," he begged. "I'm as proud of my country as any of you, but I am no less a patriot because I think there is room for improvement."

"By God, we're in for a treasonable speech, are we?" the senior watch-keeper shouted.

"I'm no traitor," said the Paymaster desperately. "But any thinking man must realize there is something radically wrong."

"Go on, go on." The vicious chorus resounded.

The Paymaster hesitated, picking his words. "No one, even if he be the Tsar, should have the inherited power to control absolutely," he said huskily. "A great nation ought to take charge of its own destiny."

Number One, face contorted with rage, took an impulsive pace forward. "By all the Holy Ones of Kiev," he bellowed, spinning round as the wardroom ante-room curtain was pulled aside. "Ivan Mikhailovitch," he yelled to the slim, haughty-faced man who stepped over the coaming. "Come and listen to this upstart clerk."

But the Gunnery Officer, Commander Prince Ivan Kaivanov, had scant interest in polemics. Accepting the liqueur a well-trained servant handed to him on a brass tray and beaming broadly, he raised the glass.

"Well, Kronstadt in the morning, gentlemen, so here's to sweethearts and wives, bless 'em. And . . ." he tossed off the drink, "by John the Much-Suffering, let us hope that some of us may be lucky enough to be showing them the bright lights of old Petersburg tomorrow night."

A junior watch-keeper nearly fell off his chair, and the Navigator, hands on a table, shook with deep-bellied laughter.

That Guns, three years married, should be anxious to get home to his wife . . . fidelity and Ivan Mikhailovitch of all people. God, it was too excruciatingly funny for words.

"When a fellow has a wife and two children," Prince Kaivanov said, not without smugness.

Number One, reeling with mirth, jovially slapped a couple of shipmates, and finished with his arms round another officer's neck, by mishap the Paymaster's.

"And haven't you presented any charmer with a handsome turnout since you were married, Ivan Mikhailovitch?" he inquired over the Paymaster's shoulder.

This caused a fresh outburst. Guns's quaint habit of making a gift of priceless bloodstock and equipage to the ladies he favoured was well known.

"Not one," said the Gunnery Officer virtuously.

That set them off again.

The Navigator knuckled his eyes. "Do you remember the scarlet *troika* and the long-tailed stallions Ivan Mikhailovitch gave to that tit from Vienna?" he said weakly.

The junior watch-keeper grinned. "Or the widow with the four-in-hand, sir. When I first saw her driving down the Nevsky I nearly bust. There she was——"

On the threshold of the ante-room, at attention, stood a bare-footed seaman, bugle lanyard taut across his shoulders.

"Well?" snapped Number One.

"Five minutes to the hour, sir."

"Sound off, then. And report to the messenger of His Excellency the Captain."

As the bugle blared and the thudding of the engine lessened there was vigorous stirring in the wardroom. Swordbelts were buckled, white gloves taken from lockers, and revolvers examined; below, in cabins, officers changed into uniform frock-coats and adjusted their ceremonial cocked hats. The executive Commander, midshipman doggy behind him, hastened to the quarter-deck, followed by the Fleet Surgeon, whose face was lined with pain.

The crew were drawn up in divisions around a heavy triangular wood frame near which, between rifle-bearing guards, stood the petty officer who was to be the central figure of this impressive gathering.

Shortly after the officers and ship's company saluted the Captain, who arrived with retinue of chaplain, coxswain, and Number One, the proceedings for an offence as specified among the many articles of Admiralty Instructions started. A bearded warrant officer, head of the ship's police, tightly grasped a broad sheet of paper which rustled in the strong breeze.

"Whereas B. P. Borovansky," he began in a deep voice, "petty officer of the second class in His Imperial Majesty's Navy, did complain of the quality of the meat supplied to his mess . . . and whereas the said B. P. Borovansky, petty officer . . . did further aggravate his offence by causing such victuals to be consumed in the furnaces of His Imperial Majesty's ship *Plevsky* . . . thereby attempting to ridicule . . . sentence of . . . fifty strokes . . . before

76

his messmates and . . . as an example of what . . . God preserve the Tsar."

With the deftness of practice Borovansky was speedily stripped to the waist and tied to the triangle. A huge Lett spat on his hands and, with incredible speed, the knotted cords whizzed down. The delinquent bit back a groan, and white puffy lines stood out on quivering flesh which, with continued impacts, ran with red. The evolution was competently performed, for the strip of tortured pulp was narrow as a belt.

"Thirty! . . forty!" The Fleet Surgeon bent over the culprit. He turned back an eyelid, and then spoke imperatively to the Captain. "Sir——"

The Captain's face became sterner. "A couple more," he snapped.

From the ship's company, standing motionless with eyes dead front, a low and dreadful growl arose.

Without hesitation, the Captain reacted to the challenge of those who, however overtly, opposed one who holds the Emperor's commission.

"An additional five," he barked.

Then the men were dismissed, by sub-divisions, at intervals, and, in their own interests, sent below.

In the wardroom a rush was made for pre-luncheon *apéritifs*, revolvers and swords were discarded, cigarettes lighted, and blouses donned.

The junior watch-keeper was determined not to let the Gunnery Officer escape. "That four-in-hand, sir," he chuckled. "I remember——"

The curtain was flung back and the Fleet Surgeon, pallid, ran in. "He's dead," he screamed.

It was a lamentable breach of taste. Number One ignored the interrupter, ostentatiously turning away from him.

"I'll wager ten to one that St. Petersburg is diverted by a similar spectacle within twelve months," he said, laughing.

Prince Kaivanov slapped his palms together. "Done," he roared. "My dear fellow, the money is as good as in my pocket. In thousands, eh?"

"In thousands, Ivan Mikhailovitch." Number One grinned.

This bet provided the wardroom with a topic for the length of the Gulf of Finland, almost to the anchorage off Kronstadt. Then, of course, there were other things to think about: leave, sport, dining and dancing . . . and the lowering faces of the men.

There seemed change, some unfathomable spirit of unrest in the ship. Orders were carried out, but hardly with the same alacrity. Men worked, but whispered out of the corners of their mouths as they brushed away powdery snow piled on the decks by a short-lived squall.

On the bridge the Navigator pointed into the far distance, beyond broad-beamed ice-breakers which were opening the spring passage. Following the line of his gloved finger, the gilded dome of Saint Isaac Cathedral could be seen emerging from a low haze.

"Well, we're here, Guns," he said grimly.

Commander Prince Ivan Kaivanov nodded. "Yes," he agreed, not quite so boisterously as of late.

2

In the slush brought by thaw a vast crowd milled about outside the wide, railed-off space in front of the Imperial Opera House. Workmen, the early birds of the influx of carpenters, bricklayers and masons who arrived each spring from distant country villages to repair the damage winter had done to the capital, were there to gape, together with the poor from the holes and corners of the densely-populated Alexander Nevsky ward, who had nothing much in their bellies, and in that were not greatly different from the rest of the Empire at this time of famine. Many of these, with little in their pockets, kept easing their throats with a free drink of anti-cholera boiled water from one of the city's horse-drawn tanks.

The Imperial Opera House, flaming *flambeaux* high at the corners of the colonnaded portico, with mettlesome beasts tearing up to the canopy over its tiled entrance, was something to stare at on the evening of a gala performance. Small wonder that the crowd, straining on tip-toe, quickly forgot their resentment against a policeman who had poked a *drosky* driver with his sheathed sword; united as always against officialdom, their howl of execration went up, but soon faded. Even the students of the University, in the various garbs of Poland, Siberia, and Central Asia, carefully counting out three copecks for a hot glass of mixed ginger, pepper, potherbs and honey, a heartening substitute for prohibitively-priced tea, ceased to declaim about the wrongs of humanity; others, flat leather cases thrust under their arms, or linking hands with girl students, pushed and shoved to see as much as possible.

Crested vehicles, with bemedalled coachmen and footmen with cocked hats, sped into the square. There were Grand Dukes with their mistresses, nobles whose names were part of Russian history, and wealthy merchants escorting wives whose ample curves were supposed to confirm their husbands' commercial standing.

None tarried; the memory of how Bogoliepoff, the Minister of Public Instruction, had recently died, was too much in mind.

At the barrier end of the Square a traffic-jam had been abandoned in disgust by a traffic policeman, who, twirling white truncheon, stood on the pavement and let the mess sort itself out. Commander Prince Kaivanov's three-horsed *troika* was among the confusion of carriages.

Its owner frowned, moving his fingers irritably in fingerless fur gloves.

"Drive on, damn you," he commanded. "They'll shift all right."

Princess Kaivanova touched her husband's sleeve. The youngest of the four famed sisters Ghambashaidze, she was a supremely beautiful woman, with that compelling contrast of ash-blonde hair and sloe-coloured eyes.

"Ivan Mikhailovitch," she said softly. "I can't realize that you have been back nearly two months. Doesn't time fly, dearest?"

Her husband smiled; rather a sickly smile. "My dear Zeneide . . ." he began. Fortunately the *troika* then drew into an area of brilliant light. "Ah!" he said, sighting the silken calves of the major-domo. "We're here at last, my dear."

With the respect due to her station he handed her out. Within a fortnight of his return he realized his marriage—the second in his family to a Georgian—was a mistake, but no gentleman forgets the courtesies. Is it not said: "A wife is not a boot, to be pulled off and thrown aside"?

That evening Prince Ivan found a new interest, and on several occasions his opera-glasses were reluctantly lowered. Once, from the seat slightly behind his wife, he stretched for a programme resting on the plush-covered edge of the box, and in the gloom endeavoured to read its contents. Failing, he rose quietly, and opened the door into a lighted ante-room behind. After satisfying himself he came back, picked up the glasses again and, leaning his shoulder comfortably, followed every movement made by a graceful figure on the stage.

Ten minutes later a storm of applause greeted the end of the second act. The curtains met, the electric lights with which the Opera House had just been equipped flashed into crystal resplendence, and a scene as magnificent as any that might be seen in Europe revealed itself.

Prince Ivan's hand-clapping was sustained. His wife, already a little bored by their companions, smilingly glanced over her bare shoulder.

"You appear to be enjoying it, dearest," she said.

Count Kschesslaev chuckled. "Ivan Mikhailovitch always had a true sense of the artistic. I remember when we were embryo pages——"

Countess Kschesslaeva lightly slapped her husband's hand. "No tales out of school, my dear," she said.

Her husband sighed. "Brawling in public, what! Really, my dear, I wish you would bear in mind where we are." He nodded towards jewellery-bedecked and order-laden occupants of boxes and stalls who, as was the accepted thing during an interval, were continually looking about the house, craning to see whose wife was with whose husband, delighted when they discovered an unhappy allocation of seats which had placed a husband's mistress beside his wife's lover.

"Yes, my dearest," he said, shaking his head. "The spectacle of two husbands enjoying a box with their respective wives has caused sufficient comment as it is."

Prince Ivan scowled. "Ivan Mikhailovitch!" his wife exclaimed.

He pulled himself together, smiled, and touched his temple. "A deuced sharp touch of neuralgia, my dear. I think, if you will permit, a little cognac."

"I'd be off for some, old fellow," said Count Kschesslaev. "Nothing like it."

A stupid creature, Peter Petrovitch, with his nauseating idyll. Prince Ivan could have thrown the silly moon-face from the box for his puerile humour.

This ill-temper persisted. In the congested *parterre* Prince Ivan was decidedly short with a gold-brocaded Court servant, and somewhat sullenly acknowledged a group of friends who were pushing through the promenade towards the drawing-room behind the Imperial box.

Meanwhile the ladies and Count Kschesslaev scrutinized the ranks of the Diplomatic Corps, and commented upon anything anywhere which took their fancy.

"Oh, do look at Baroness Belsky," Countess Kschesslaeva tittered.

Opera glasses were simultaneously raised to inspect the Austrian-born wife of His Excellency Baron Belsky, who suffered the misfortune of a bright red saddle across her nose.

"It shows more than ever," Princess Kaivanova giggled.

"A surfeit of Viennese pastry, my dear Zeneide," said Count Kschesslaev. "Or her cigars."

His wife turned. "I've been told that——"

She half-jumped up, Princess Kaivanova's hand flew to her full bosom, Count Kschesslaev became deadly pale; there was the quite audible gasp of a multitude, and a woman screamed; one portion of the audience was rooted, and the other leapt to its feet. But it was soon over.

Count Kschesslaev wiped his forehead. "I think a piece of scenery must have fallen," he said.

In the promenade, all unconscious of an incident which had reduced so many to a jelly-like state, Prince Ivan obtained the information he required from an acquaintance of younger days with whom he had never got on.

Prince Filosofin wrinkled his thin nose. "Well, you know who she is, and what she is, and now you know where she lives," he drawled. "But believe me, Ivan Mikhailovitch, to you she is as remote as the top of the world's highest mountain. Ever heard of a gentleman named Robespierre? He was sometimes called 'The Incorruptible'."

"What of it?" Prince Kaivanov growled.

It could have been accidental, nevertheless Prince Filosofin blew a cloud of cigar-smoke into the inquirer's face.

"Which is exactly how you will find the adorable Kalutkina," he explained. "All the immense Kaivanov treasury . . ." He shrugged, pointed to his finger. "She will require a gold band there, my dear Ivan Mikhailovitch. And unfortunately you, my dear fellow . . ." he held up his palms expressively.

"I am simply interested in her art," Prince Ivan retorted.

Quivering with rage, he heard Prince Filosofin snigger as he walked away.

The next morning the showrooms of the Court Jeweller moved into smooth activity when a valued client was bowed in. A chair was provided for him, and valuable wares brought out for his inspection.

When dealing with an incorruptible the stakes are high; selection does not take long, price is the major criterion.

The staff bent to the ground. "At once, Highness."

A smart messenger, guarded by two of Messrs. Fabergé's commissionaires, was soon tapping on the door of an apartment, where he obtained a receipt for a flat silk-lined box.

In his personal suite in the Kaivanov mansion on Palace Quay Prince Ivan smiled in anticipation—until he saw the box again.

He swung the necklace from a finger while reading the note enclosed.

"So Vera Kalutkina regrets she cannot accept . . ." he muttered, half-disbelieving. Then he bit his lip and bawled.

"A hammer?" the servant stammered.

"A hammer, fool," Prince Ivan yelled. "And my *troika* to the door."

Within minutes the five-yard whip of the coachman cracked;

81

within minutes his master was once again in the cathedral-like establishment of a world-famed jeweller.

A plate-glass case exhibiting Easter eggs made from precious materials was reverently opened, and superb specimens of the craftsman's art were placed on appropriately-coloured squares of velvet.

Within an hour the *prima ballerina* Vera Kalutkina received a small oblong package containing a yellow enamel egg within which, faithful to the last detail, was a tiny gold coach, with wheels which spun, and exquisite doors that opened. The tiny vehicle was upholstered too, but the miniature seats and scarlet-lined interior were crudely marred by soft-gleaming fragments and pearl-white dust. The wanton destruction of the necklace would have cost a Frenchman a hundred thousand francs, an Englishman four thousand pounds, a German eighty thousand marks, or an American twenty thousand dollars.

An impressive gesture, indeed.

3

For many years the head of the house of Kaivanov had spent much of his time in the warmth of the Caucasus, although, of course, there were occasions when he went up to Yasni Dulba on the Don or to other family properties. Another advantage was that unrest had not percolated to any extent to the southern part of the Empire, which permitted a completely detached viewpoint towards the Government's methods—meaning that, without being disturbed by ear-piercing screams or suffering the dislocation which a thoroughly efficient mass pogrom entails, it was possible to discuss academically the Minister's guile in switching on to the Jews the blame for current conditions, and what a very satisfactory red herring that was proving to be.

Amsibu, so isolated, was also a most suitable place to entertain old friends, and on the same afternoon Vera Kalutkina returned a second costly package to his son, Prince Mikhail was there with his guests.

To be candid, one exception outstanding, none of them were enjoying themselves, for the situation was unprecedented, agonizingly embarrassing.

Prince Chermoiev, who even with the passage of the years had not vanquished a youthful weakness which tinged his cheeks green through a combination of much liquor and much laughter, was in a dreadful plight, but his *malaise* had nothing to do either with drink or mirth. Hoping to be unobserved, he edged further from the *person* who shared with him a cushion-filled divan, and with a palpably shaking hand leafed over the pages of *Mir Isskustva*, a magazine bitterly condemned by the capital's press.

"Anything interesting there?" Prince Mikhail inquired, attempting to ease an unendurable strain. "My dear, that young fellow Sergei Diaghileff! But have you read what the reviewers think of his ideas?"

Still so strikingly handsome that women often turned to look at him, Prince Mikhail shot an exceedingly nervous glance at Prince Chermoiev's near neighbour as he made this half-hearted inquiry. For over a year there had been the strangest reports about a change of sex in Savinkof, the wild-eyed and highly-strung poet, who had always been a member of their intimate gatherings. It had been an appalling shock when, the latest to join the house-party, *Mademoiselle* Savinkova arrived unexpectedly, less than an hour before, a poet*ess* who was daringly gowned.

This lady made a dead set at Prince Chermoiev from the moment of seeing him.

"Oh, *horribly*," she gushed in a bass voice, gazing meltingly at the object of her affections. "So, so unfair. Don't you agree with me, dearest?"

Expression hunted, Prince Chermoiev stared with numb entreaty at Nikolai Tsereteli, the composer of stark music.

This took place in the vast apartment with malachite pillars, a room noticeably less austere than it had been in the era of Prince Mikhail's stern soldier-grandfather. Massive candelabra still hung from silver-link chains, but the light's direct rays were pinkly shaded, and harmonizing draperies allowed only an occasional glimpse of scarlet walls lavishly ornamented with gold.

Prince Mikhail's inquiry about the *World of Art* led to luke-warm references to editorials which wrote off the publication as "corrupting", "morbid", or "likely to promote depraved tastes". It was a relief when, on the stroke of the hour, footmen came in carrying trays on which were thin-stemmed glasses and bottles of fine Echmaidzin wine.

One of the servants, in his teens, was a very graceful Khevsur youth, an outcast from a pious tribe which kept on the best of terms with Allah, Jehovah and the Lord by resting on each of the holy days of Friday, Saturday and Sunday.

Prince Chermoiev, glad to clutch at any straw, stretched a white hand towards this youth and, feigning deep interest, forced a semblance of tenderness into his voice as he stared up at dark, liquid eyes.

"And how is it I haven't seen you before, my dear boy?" he inquired.

Dipping frequently into a dish of sugared confections, the poetess had been lolling in an attitude decidedly abandoned for any lady.

"Oh really, darling," she said, shrieking with laughter. "You can't do that now *I'm* here, you naughty perverted man."

"I shall do whatever pleases me," Prince Chermoiev yelled.

Mademoiselle Savinkova sighed deeply before appealing to the company, a group of gentlemen each of whom was petrified with fear lest he should be singled out. Their host was selected for attention.

"What can a girl do about him, Misha sweet?" she asked, rolling her eyes tragically.

Prince Mikhail funked the issue. "Surely that . . . that is a matter you must decide for yourself."

Prince Chermoiev glowered at him. "A fine friend you are, Mikhail Pavlych," he stuttered.

In a startling, deep tone the poetess giggled as she rose and smoothed out creases in her dress.

"We shall have to see then," she said, patting her hair with her finger-tips. "And now I think I must retire to my room. I find that a rest before changing for dinner does quite wonderful things for one."

Before Prince Chermoiev could take action to avoid it, she bent to whisper to him, placing a muscular arm firmly round his shoulders.

"I shan't," he cried out.

The poetess simpered as she squeezed him more tightly. "Darling, you must," she said. "Do consider me, a lonely female amongst so many men. How could I ask any of them to maid me when you are here?"

After an unseemly struggle Prince Chermoiev broke free.

"You can fasten your own damned hooks," he bawled. "And if you touch me again I shall slap you the hell of a sight harder than you have ever been slapped before."

Not at all disconcerted, wagging her fingers flirtatiously, Mademoiselle Savinkova withdrew after that, silken underskirts swishing, fat hams swaying in a sheath-tight gown. From the doorway, before finally disappearing, she favoured Prince Chermoiev with a lingering glance which was as encouraging as wild-looking eyes would permit.

"She's mad," one of Prince Mikhail's oldest friends groaned. "And she has absolutely ruined this party," he added pettishly. "The nasty creature."

Prince Mikhail held up his hands for attention. "Gentlemen," he said, voice vibrating with feeling. "Innocent though I am, I owe you all my profound apology for the dreadful position we are in owing to this unwelcome intrusion. Why he, *she*, she ever decided to come here is more than——"

The picture of despair, Prince Chermoiev was pacing rapidly to and fro, mouthing incoherently. But he paused to beat a table with his fists.

"But why, in God's name, does she pick on me?" he shouted. "Why, why, why?"

Frowning with concentration, Nikolai Tsereteli gave considerable thought to this question.

"You and he were always bosom companions," he said gravely. "Obviously the feeling on his part has assumed a new significance."

A St. Petersburg painter, renowned for the startling quality of his canvases and of immense renown in an extremely limited circle, went even further.

"Marriage, of course," he said simply.

"God! I cannot bear this," Prince Chermoiev gasped. Mouth puckered, he seemed about to burst into tears.

At this stage, Prince Mikhail, who had an odd sense of humour, unexpectedly howled with laughter. This led to an hysterical scene with Prince Chermoiev. It was quite a time before peace was established, and thereafter Prince Mikhail was at pains to be exceedingly circumspect in dealing with his friend.

Afterwards, however, when revitalizing himself before dinner in a vapour bath, and during the subsequent light beating with leafy birch branches given him by his servants, he smiled again and again. And later still, sitting on a dressing stool while his valet attended to him, he often chuckled.

His good humour persisted but, when the gong sounded, the gay little snatch he was humming diminished and, a social engagement of importance ahead, he leaned towards a mirror illuminated by a score of candles.

The tune ended discordantly, "My hair!" he bawled. "A thread of grey! Have I not told you. . . ."

Leonid Borisovitch's jaw dropped when he saw the frenzy on his master's face, and he cringed on glimpsing the flash of a gold hand-mirror, whose edge cut into his forehead.

"Highness," he moaned, trembling.

Prince Mikhail made an effort to control himself, took a yellow cigarette from a jewelled box, but tossed it aside in favour of a scented cachou. "You will telegraph at once to St. Petersburg instructing my barber to present himself," he said more calmly.

"Yes, Highness."

Prince Mikhail viewed himself again, lightly touching his jet-black side pieces, which were entirely satisfactory. In improved mood he turned to watch Leonid Borisovitch stemming a stream of blood. "That will teach you to keep your eyes open, thou rascal," he commented.

"Yes, Highness."

In the mood for fun that evening, Prince Mikhail's expression grew menacing. "But you will report yourself to the Steward. Tell him to give you . . . now what shall it be?"

"Highness!" Leonid Borisovitch wailed.

Prince Mikhail, with cold intent, looked at him for fully fifteen seconds. "Yes, tell him to give you . . ." he paused again, "to give you a hundred roubles."

This said, he doubled with glee, amused by the sudden expression of surprise in the deep-set eyes of the man who had been in his service for so many years.

When the barber arrived, he discovered in his august client traces of a skin blemish. Two doctors were at once summoned from Tiflis and Russia's most renowned physician from the capital. Unhappily the small eruption did not respond to their treatment and, exactly ten days after the disfigurement had been pointed out, the horrified patient took further steps. Of a pious disposition always, Prince Mikhail poste-haste abandoned his friends—now settling down after Mademoiselle Savinkova's enforced departure—and journeyed to the holy city of Kiev, the Empire's font of Christianity.

On arrival he proceeded immediately underground to the Pestcheri of Saint Theodosia where, involuntarily screwing up his nose, he kissed the saint's skull, which sweated an odiferous ointment of immense repute, whose quality was that, if applied to the true believer, any disease would be cured.

That was the beginning of a Spartan régime, during which he fasted absolutely for thirty-six hours and with great severity for another fortnight. Throughout the period, in the Pestcheris both of Saint Theodosia and Saint Antonio, he crawled along the interminable passages of the sacred catacombs, face smeared with a costly salve, taper in hand to light the intense darkness. There were many niches hewn out along the route, each of them the resting place of a holy man, whose preserved body was dressed in silks; at every little chapel he stayed to pray and to pay the recognized devotions, kissing the shod feet of those dead for generations and with veneration holding stiff, gloved hands.

It was a trying ordeal. But, praise be, it proved efficacious—the blemish had gone.

On the morrow, before the relieved sinner Mikhail Pavlych left the city, the Metropolitan of Kiev and Galitz gave him three lovely presents: a copy of the Kiev edition of the Slavonic Testament, bound in two volumes and encased in red Morocco; a small book, covered with shagreen, relating to the history and antiquity of Kiev; and a plan of the Lavre Monastery and Pestcheri, printed on a square of thick, yellow silk. At the same hour the same relieved sinner thankfully donated a hundred thousand roubles to a most worthy cause.

After confessing, the penitent rose from his knees refreshed, when the Metropolitan was pleased to escort him to the Lavre Palace, where His Eminence was most gracious. Dispensing with the attendance even of the private chaplain, he and Prince Mikhail sat down to an appetizing collation of a variety of fish superbly prepared. These were laid with bread and fine wines, and the meal was topped off with a wonderful old brandy.

The next morning Prince Mikhail started out for Odessa, from where he proposed sailing to Batoum in the Caucasus. He was quite peaceful in mind and nearly fifteen pounds lighter in weight. On careful reflection, he thought the change became him.

4

For what little remained of that winter of famine, strike, and riot, Prince Ivan Kaivanov lunched daily at Kontants, an establishment where smart men delighted to squire smart women. Night after night, while university students wordily demonstrated in the streets, he dined at the Kuba't, an after-performance supper room patronized by the stage and ballet, where he picked solitarily at a few dishes, smoked a never-ending chain of cigarettes, moodily drank *zakuska*, and scowled at the asinine jests of passing friends who should have known better than to irritate a man in his deplorable condition.

Tongues wagged freely; every step in his pursuit of Vera Kalutkina was delightedly watched. And at an early stage well-meaning friends made certain that the obsessed fellow's wife should know.

Princess Ivan Kaivanova twice attempted to talk the matter over with him.

"My dear Zeneide," he said touchily to her on the second occasion, "why do you listen to this senseless gossip? Am I living with this woman? Or have I spoken to her more than half a dozen times?"

His chagrin did not escape her. "For a man of your reputation, Ivan Mikhailovitch," she said with some dryness, "you seem to have been singularly unsuccessful. But, of course, if you don't care about making a fool of yourself——"

87

Prince Ivan's dark eyes flashed. "Me, making a fool of myself?" he shouted. "Me?" He slammed the door.

For a moment his wife's beautiful sloe-coloured eyes became a little beady. That she, who had been one of the toasts of fair Georgia, should trouble her head about any man, husband or no! Anyhow, she had been rather a romantic young fool, and her married sisters had had reason to taunt her about married bliss, but after this. . . . Princess Kaivanova began to smile. It had been dull of late, and Count Resskov had been attentive. Yes, two could play at this game.

Her bosom, massaged every day to ward off the overlusciousness feared by the ladies of her race, began to rise and fall as her easily-aroused blood took charge. Excitedly, she summoned her maid with a silver bell and, considering an array of face-lotions, selected a preparation of cucumber juice and sour cream.

"Yes," she told herself, "now *I'll* amuse myself."

It was a decision she kept henceforth.

Meantime her husband pursued his lovely objective in every interval of leave, and shortly after the Court moved out to the fresh breezes of Peterhof he advanced a step. By good fortune the docking of his ship through workmen's deliberately scamped work coincided with a command performance in the Court Theatre at Peterhof. Luckily, also, the regiment of his quartercousin, Count Kotya Yaroslav, had taken up summer quarters in Krasnoe Selo, one of the few of the Imperial Guards regiments to be spared from the repression of disorders. Prince Ivan proposed himself as a guest, and then lost no time in taking a train.

That night, facing an embarrassing profusion of silverware—each retiring commander presented a piece—and flanked by a portrait of His Imperial Majesty in the particular uniform of their regiment each Guards regiment possessed, he impatiently dined with his kinsman and ninety other lively fellows. The next morning, hiding his impatience, he stood near a tent on a carefully-constructed hillock while his Emperor, a small figure surrounded by overtowering relatives and officers of the General Staff, followed the progress of the manoeuvres.

The performance that evening in the Court Theatre was brilliant, but even when *she* was on the stage holding the audience spellbound with her art he was impatient.

Next morning, however, when action was possible, before the *artistes* left to resume their relaxations by the sea, Prince Ivan found matters more bearable. Far remote from the state of siege which had been delared in the Province of Moscow, in a flower-fringed bower on one of the terraces, accompanied by the sweet sound of the fountains in the Palace gardens, he declared himself, passionately kissing her hand.

"I adore you," he said hoarsely.

A lovely young woman, Vera Kalutkina, with shining raven-black hair parted in the middle, drawn back to a low *chignon*. Her face was a perfect oval, and her complexion smooth-alabaster white, against which carmined lips stood out in entrancing relief.

Sunk on one knee, he implored her. "My darling," he said, at fever-heat.

Even in a capital boasting many beautiful women she was outstanding; dark eyes veiled beneath unbelievably long lashes, slim of ankle and slender of feet, with graceful, supple limbs, not over-muscular yet.

"Really, Prince Kaivanov," she said, withdrawing her hand. "Though I may be willing to accept that your intention is not to insult me, yet——"

"Insult you!" Facile tears welled down Prince Ivan's cheeks. "Insult you!" he repeated.

"How else can it be?" she said in a charmingly husky voice. "You have a wife and children."

Truly Commander Prince Kaivanov had broken down. Strickenly, he beseeched. "But at least I may have the privilege of your friendship?"

She looked at him gravely. "Is that all you want, Prince Kaivanov?"

By all the Saints in the Calendar he swore his oath. Give him her friendship and he would prove it to her.

Vera Kalutkina smiled a little. "You may call on me, then Prince Ivan."

"Prince Ivan!" he cried miserably. "Surely, my dear, Ivan Mikhailovitch is more fitting between friends?"

She conceded this later, slipping her hand under his arm as they were descending the steep slope from a flying bridge, though further along, on an ilex-bordered path, she warned him again. "But remember, Ivan Mikhailovitch."

"By the Holy Father and the Blessed Virgin," he began virtuously.

Laughingly she craved pity; and laughingly, two days later, showed her maid the contents of a velvet-lined box brought by an emissary from Fabergé's.

A gift worth a full ninety thousand roubles, one she expressed herself as pleased to accept. It was well understood that the little token of esteem changed hands in that spirit of give and take, "as between friends".

On that basis their association continued throughout the summer and autumn, but by winter one of the parties to the compact was chafing about the conditions prescribed by the other.

Matters between them reached a critical stage one November day, when on the Neva workmen with long-handled, spear-shaped saws started the seasonal cutting-out of blocks of ice for storage in the ice-cellars of the citizens of St. Petersburg.

It was a gloriously crisp morning, but level-headed folk hurrying along the avenues, between trees delicately outlined with a tracery of glistening snow, hardly seemed to notice it. Few dared stop to speak to acquaintances—nowadays, in this land of fear, any gathering of three or more constituted unlawful assembly.

In the fine residential street in which his mistress resided, the coachman of Vera Kalutkina, heavily swaddled in the *armvak* of his calling, kept himself and beasts warm by marching them backwards and forwards, every now and then exchanging a word with the driver and footman of an outstandingly appointed vehicle similarly engaged on the other side.

Prince Ivan was in the apartment, cosily warmed by a porcelain-enamelled stove. Fur coat had been thrown on to a chair, and his fur cap, which many of the nobility considered more sensible than too-revealing officer's headgear, was on the floor.

It was a handsomely-furnished room; or so most people would have said on glancing at off-white walls, pleated-silk ceiling, salmon pink chairs, and couches upholstered with ermine; there were bearskin rugs, a white grand piano with golden cashmere shawl overlaying it, and beautiful screens.

Commander Prince Kaivanov was an exception. "My dear, this place," he remarked disparagingly. "If you would only allow me to provide you with a more suitable establishment. Really my——"

"Ivan Mikhailovitch," a husky voice called, mock-sternly.

He uncrossed his legs restlessly, glanced at the open door of the bedroom and the half-open door of the bathroom beyond that, seemed about to rise and then thought better of it.

Stretched luxuriously in warm scented water, white teeth biting through one of Eliesieff's delicious bonbons, Vera Kalutkina trilled with laughter.

"My dear Ivan Mikhailovitch, haven't I told you time after time that I am perfectly happy here?"

"I know," he grumbled.

Unseen, apart from her maid, Vera Kalutkina frowned slightly. "Besides, my dear, what construction would St. Petersburg put on it if I suddenly went into a residence far beyond my means?" she asked.

Prince Ivan irritably lighted a cigarette. "Well, it wouldn't be true, would it? No, my dear," he added hastily, anticipating her reproof, "I am not complaining, but all the same I do hope you will permit me to do as I wish."

He continued to importune as she dressed and completed her *toilette*, and was still offering sound argument when she came in to show him the effect of cherry-sized black pearls on her slender neck. This was a gift which, having completed the round of white pearls, emerald bracelet, diamond diadem, ruby ring, and sapphire brooch, he had just presented to her as another mark of his homage.

"You really are a dear, Ivan Mikhailovitch," she said.

Winter was here and she had eluded him for five months. He was slightly sullen as he slipped a sable pelisse about her shoulders, and was a little sulky to begin with when, at the outer door, she spoke of another gift, the three blood horses straining before her sledge.

"I haven't got used to them yet," she confessed. "People stare so, as if they had never seen such a turn-out in their lives."

He thawed considerably, and beckoned to his footman. "I'll wager they haven't, save Persian. And I've brought you something else to surprise them, too. There, my dear," he wound up triumphantly, pointing to a pure yellow Semmelpinch terrier, a creature not usually seen outside the Imperial Household of Austria.

Vera Kalutkina, fondling the ears of the bright young fellow, was overwhelmed. "My dear," she gasped.

Prince Ivan, complacently eyeing the terrier and the pink-dyed manes and tails of the milk-white horses, nodded with satisfaction. "Thought you'd like the little chap. I sent a courier to Lippiza for him. But . . ." he glanced carefully along the street, to right and to left, "but I think we will be on our way, my dear." Speedily he tucked her in, and then spoke sharply to her coachman. "You know where to go. Drive fast."

"Yes, Highness." The man made haste to gather up the many blue reins of his spirited span.

The owner of the sledge, which lacked any betraying crest, looked her astonishment. "Oh! Ivan Mikhailovitch, why mine?" she asked.

"Just wanted to try out these three stallions," he explained, his speech clipped. "Told your man as I came in."

There was little conversation between them until the menace of the city was far behind. The scene was so peaceful, then: a white landscape extending into the distance, and every few versts the frozen swimming ponds of *dacha* resorts whose wooden restaurants and holiday cottages were boarded up for the winter. Never a soul in sight; no possibility of a madman with a bomb.

"My dearest," he said tenderly, seeking her gloved hand under the fur rug, "I am taking you to a villa the English firm of Maple is building for one of the Grand Dukes. If it pleases you and if you will permit me——"

"For his mistress," said Vera Kalutkina icily.

"Yes, for his mistress," agreed Prince Ivan. "But," he almost screamed, "is she anything less to be honoured for that? Would he be allowed to marry her even if he could obtain a divorce? Why shouldn't he have his years of happiness?" The melancholia deepened in his eyes. "Even if His Majesty refused me a dispensation I would be willing, nay eager, to defy the convention which forbids an officer to marry one of your profession. God knows, and you know, that I would. But can I, can I?"

Vera Kalutkina was trembling. "Then your wife, Ivan Mikhailovitch?"

"Refuses to consider my suggestion." Tragedy was in every line of his face as he stared at an orchard where, under snow-covered mounds of straw, fruit trees, roots at one side never allowed to grow, were hinged down for the winter. "I cannot wait any longer," he said. "I shall kill myself."

Her breath, coming more quickly, mingled steamily with his and was whisked away.

"Perhaps she might change her mind?"

"And if not?" he asked drearily.

She was quivering like an aspen leaf when the first moan sounds from the Steppes. "Perhaps then. . . ." He leaned to catch her words, "perhaps then I will," she whispered, scarlet mantling her pale cheeks.

Sparkle came back into his fine eyes. He slipped the glove from her hand and, protected from the keen air by the rug, bent to press burning lips against her soft wrist.

"My little one," he said rapturously.

"But," she faltered, "only if and when we know that there is no possible hope of her changing her mind."

He crossed himself with all the fervour of a newly-fledged acolyte in full view of a priest. "It shall be when, and only when, you say the word, my darling."

"I know," she said softly.

Commander Prince Ivan Kaivanov was well satisfied. A gentleman experienced with women, he had seen sufficient in her dark eyes. It would not be long.

At the Feast of the Epiphany, with its wearisome, long-drawn-out rites, Prince Ivan felt little discomfort when, snow falling thickly on regimental colours and the shoulders of those present, he watched His Imperial Majesty, Nikolai II, walking down a short flight of steps lined by white-habited priests to perform the annual Blessing of the Waters. While the bald shivered and envied those who had had the foresight to wear wigs, Prince Ivan dreamed dreams of consummation as the Emperor, to the Metropolitan's deep intoned prayer, dipped the Cross in the slightly surging water at the bottom of a hole cut through the ice on the Neva.

Blood pulsating, Vera Kalutkina was never out of his mind as he danced, drank and supped at the first of the season's state balls, a dull and crowded affair, spreading over half a dozen halls of the Winter Palace, at which two thousand guests were present, many of whom were light-fingered enough to smuggle out small ornaments as souvenirs, proofs of prestige.

Mania for her still seared his brain when, at the last state ball of the season, he was numbered amongst a small company of two hundred who left untouched the knick-knacks in a comparatively small ballroom.

Not long after that, Prince Ivan decided that the time was ripe. He was escorting her from the theatre, through streets buzzing with the news of the banishment of ninety-five students to Siberia and the immediate closing of the University of St. Petersburg. Quite resolved, he hurried her across a brightly-lighted strip of pavement into the security of the restaurant.

In a private room he helped her off with her furs, brushed aside the *maitre d'hôtel's* attempt to seat her, and anticipated her every wish.

The service was of the highest standard of the Medved. Dishes came heralded by a discreet tap, and a whispered: "Is it permitted, Highness?" Covers were whipped off, sparkling wines made their cobwebby *début*.

Borsch, hors-d'oeuvres of twenty-eight varieties, royal sturgeon, mushrooms in oil, meat-balls mixed with cream, small sausages grilled in butter; red wines, white wines, and the sweetest champagne.

"My dear Ivan Mikhailovitch!" she exclaimed.

He pushed a finger-bowl aside with one hand and with the other flicked outwardly a corner of his table-napkin, a sign acted upon immediately by those to whom it was addressed.

This was the moment. As the door closed he dropped to the floor and rested his sleek head in her lap.

"My darling," he muttered. "Zeneide still refuses."

Vera Kalutkina stroked the nape of his neck. "But, my dear," she consoled him, "you could hardly expect her to change her mind yet. We must give her time."

Eyes burning, Prince Ivan found his feet and drew her to him, seeking her soft, moist lips. "Time!" he said passionately. "Do you know what even a day means to me? God, how I count the minutes."

"But what can we do, Ivan Mikhailovitch?"

His hands, as if strength had gone, slipped from her shoulders. "We can do as others do, my darling," he said. "Only that."

She was twisting an embroidered handkerchief. "But I couldn't, Ivan Mikhailovitch," she said faintly. "We should be an outrage before His eyes."

Prince Ivan tossed off a glass of old vodka without the fiery spirit touching his palate. "But you love me, little one?"

Vision dimming, she touched his sleeve. "That is why I want us to be together only when there is no reason for regret, Ivan Mikhailovitch," she entreated. "Darling, we must have patience."

He was breathing hard. "But you said you would, Vera Nikolaevna."

Her face worked pitiably. "Not until it was certain nothing would move your wife."

Sneeringly, the correction was accepted. "And what about your God and your devotions, then?" he asked. "Come, my dear, do remember you are a woman of the world and not an ignorant peasant."

As he walked away she began to cry. "I can't," she said, following him. "Don't you see I can't, not until you have given your wife every possible chance. I have prayed and——" Suddenly she looked directly at him. "And then I promise you I will, Ivan Mikhailovitch."

He was swinging a tassel at the curtained window. "And how long, if Zeneide continues immovable, will that be, if I may inquire?"

Her long, damp lashes screened her eyes. "I promise," she said, her voice so low that he had difficulty in hearing, ". . . not longer than the end of the year."

Thwarted and infuriated, Prince Ivan jeered. "And it is only March now," he shouted, laughing half-insanely. Deep sobs racked him next, and tears rolled down his cheeks as, on his knees again, he tugged the hem of her gown. "My own darling couldn't do this to me. Sweetheart, I can't endure this torment. I . . .I can't wait the best part of a year, my little one."

"You must, Ivan Mikhailovitch," she said softly.

Appraisingly almost, he looked up at her, this beautiful woman who had for so long, as he was aware, serenely resisted the bloods of the Guards.

"Oh, please, Ivan Mikhailovitch," she said.

Lesser men than Prince Kaivanov might have pointed out that a lady who had accepted four hundred thousand roubles in valuable presents must be prepared to pay when, and how, the donor wishes. But he was a gentleman and, scrambling to his feet, bowed stiffly, icily asking her wishes.

In the *troika* she glanced at the proud profile, and tentatively touched his hand. At the apartment door she almost called him back after the most aloof of farewells.

But that little gesture Prince Ivan did not see; it was hardly to be expected that he would glance back. He flung himself into the vehicle, mad with disappointment.

"To the Islands," he bawled.

5

Prince Ivan's debauch continued for five weeks, during which his naval duties suffered severely. He gave many parties, one of them lasting four days, for which the ladies, *cocottes* exclusively, arrived in their latest silks and satins, heavily scented and powdered, their *coiffures* works of art. This began with a pleasant and well-mannered get-together over a buffet snack of crayfish and wine, went on until eyes were bloodshot with drink and excitement and women's hair tumbled to their waists. How it ended nobody could remember.

There was the orgy to which only gipsy girls had been invited, and a rough and quarrelsome affair it became before dawn; and another at which a nude young woman thumped her pink feet on the pedals of a piano.

Music, song, tinkling glasses, shrill laughter, uproar, fighting, screaming, ill-temper—parties, parties, and more parties.

In those five weeks Prince Ivan Kaivanov amply demonstrated that he had inherited some part of the perverse genius of his ancestors, the Akashidzes of Georgia.

"Very nice an' all that, Ivan Mikhailovitch, but . . ." Prince Savosef wagged an uncertain finger, "but paid women after all, you know."

This remark was made one day about noon in the Nobles' Club, where both gentlemen, heads feeling as large as balloons, were disposing of nauseous concoctions prepared by the chief barman. A potent pick-me-up was a necessity for Prince Ivan, who was already overdue at Kronstadt.

Audibly groaning, Prince Ivan carefully turned. "Paid women," he said vaguely. "What are you getting at, George Filippovitch, ol' man?"

"My fancy is always a virgin," Prince Savosef explained ripely. "There's something about a virgin . . . mind you, Ivan Mikhailovitch," he conceded, "I'm not blaming you for not providing the untarnished stuff. You couldn't any more than I could have done, now could you?"

Prince Ivan hiccupped. "No, I couldn't, could I?" Then he stared, a trifle pie-eyed. "Couldn't what?" he demanded.

"Virgins." Prince Savosef leered.

"Most certainly I could." Prince Ivan differed stridently. "S'matter of fact I have a pair of charmers in view already. Upper-class *burzhuis*, by the way, which makes for better sport. Want to bet?"

A couple of days after that, on the evening of Bacchanalia, when the light of street lamps was beginning to shine more strongly against the gathering dusk, the attractive twin daughters of the wealthy city merchant, A. P. Paroshinsky, slipped out of their home on a little outing. The jaunt was at the suggestion of the family butler who, though not long in their father's service, was already on excellent terms with the young ladies. More than once he had connived with them—not without monetary advantage to himself—in various small matters which, innocent notwithstanding, would have failed to win the approval of strict parents.

Unhappily, however, less than three lamp-posts from their home, the girls were bundled with breathless speed into a closed carriage, the curtains of which were tightly drawn. Two gentlemen were inside, one on each seat, and the better-looking of these endeavoured to silence their protests with what he obviously considered a reasonable explanation.

"My dears," he said as the vehicle raced along, "surely you know tonight is the Feast all lovely young women will join in celebrating? Don't tell me you haven't heard of Tora, the god of lasc . . . the god of having a nice bit of fun. Well, my friend and I——"

"Nothing to be afraid of," Prince Savosef intervened to hearten them. "Of course you must enter into the spirit of . . . er——"

Prince Ivan interrupted also: "Naturally there isn't anything to worry about, my dears," he said hurriedly. "A drive, a little refreshment, and so on. Could anything be more desirable, I ask you?"

For once Kaivanov urbanity failed completely, both then and later at the Villa Corné, a secluded property at the Islands catering specially for abduction and rape. In any event, when a man is out of condition it is not easy for him to cope with a she-devil.

Violently struck on the nose, eyes watering, and conscious of many pains, Prince Ivan released the girl.

"Of course if you feel at all reluctant about it," he muttered, gingerly exploring damage done to his cheeks by finger-nails, "then my carriage is at your disposal."

Devoid of colour, breast heaving and clothing torn, she was leaning against the wall, clutching a window curtain for support.

"I won't leave . . . without my sister," she gasped.

Wincing, Prince Ivan touched his right ear lobe. "As you please," he said haughtily. "Still, rather awkward, don't you think?"

The sheer hatred in her grey eyes silenced him so effectually that, without further demur, he limped into the corridor, where he cautiously opened and then as cautiously closed the door of the room adjoining on seeing the turmoil of white limbs within. Indeed, on returning to his partner he momentarily forgot those many aches.

"I rather imagine you will have to wait a little longer, my dear," he told her, squaring accounts between them with a slight but very significant smile. "But would you care for a glass of something until they are . . . er . . .ready to join us?"

He was quite disconcerted by her reply. And *really,* who the devil cared about her father?

Nevertheless, within a matter of hours, both he and his fellow rake were compelled to consider that city gentleman, A. P. Paroshinsky, and had St. Petersburg not been in an uproar the outcome might have been even more serious. The assassination of Sipiaguine, the Minister of the Interior, kept the little incident in its true perspective, however, though it was to be regretted that Prince Savosef, on the following afternoon, showed the white feather.

"I'm off to Vienna until it blows over, Ivan Mikhailovitch," he said frankly. "And you'll be wise to make yourself scarce."

"My *dear* George Filippovitch." Prince Ivan's lip curled.

Prince Savosef dabbed at the dampness seldom absent from the corners of his mouth. "Please yourself," he replied abruptly. "But if you read this morning's paper you'll find they're plundering in Poltava and Kharkoff, and that 'incendiarism' is a much used word. And soon . . ." he tapped his friend's shoulder, "they'll be after the persons of those who aren't connected with the political scene. Just lately my name has been a little too much in the public eye, and now this fellow Paroshinsky is on the warpath. . . . Yes, I'm making tracks elsewhere."

"Really, my dear chap." Prince Ivan eyed him coldly.

This self-confessed gutlessness upset him so much that he gulped down a glass of *slivovits* instead of deliberately savouring its full plum flavour.

There were other repercussions. Despite anxieties arising from major disturbances everywhere—the murders of high-placed officials, explosions in luxury hotels, the arrest of thousands, and the unpatriotic response of the masses to the growing threat of war with Japan—there were a few who took heed of Commander Prince Kaivanov's recent behaviour. In particular Admiral Sememski, now retired from the Service, heard at the Yacht Club much more than he cared about his nephew. As soon as possible he visited his sister.

"My dear," he said, "I was responsible for nominating Ivan Mikhailovitch to the Navy, and candidly, Liza, going off the rails as he is simply won't do in these troubled days. It is just putting weapons into the hands of the fanatics who are against us. Of course I'm perfectly willing to deal with the young fool, but. . . ."

Princess Mikhail Kaivanova's hair had silvered, and she was a trifle more plump. She smiled faintly. "You'd better not, Vasili Petrovitch. You'd develop your harshest quarter-deck voice, and . . . no, better not. You know it's that woman Kalutkina who is at the bottom of all this."

Worriedly tugging his torpedo beard, Admiral Sememski stared out of the window at the fine river panorama.

"Would it be of any use to speak to his wife?" he inquired. "Disagreeable, I know, but this can't go on."

She joined him and stood incuriously watching the scene: drivers abusing one another in the traffic, two beggars resting on staffs, and a Polish Jew stumbling along in a voluminous black *lapserdak*. Thoughts dwelling upon a husband who was neither comfort nor help, her glance followed a party of axe-carrying peasants, strangers to the city, who walked in file, the leading pair addressing the third over their shoulders as they strode along, all three devoutly making the sign of the cross on encountering a sallow-faced priest.

"I'll do something, Vasili Petrovitch," she sighed. "Yes, I'll have a talk with Zeneide."

As soon as the Admiral left, Princess Mikhail rang for her maid. Within forty minutes she was calling upon her daughter-in-law.

Princess Ivan laughed openly. "My dear Lizaveta Petrovna," she gurgled, "it is simply that Ivan Mikhailovitch and myself prefer to go our own ways."

A good churchwoman, Princess Mikhail had for months been

anxiously pondering about her son's relationship with his wife. Gradually she had drawn closer to a conclusion most distasteful to her.

"But one has to consider the children, my dear," she said, shaking her head in spite of herself. "Of course, Sergei and Anastasia need a father as well as a mother, but perhaps the harder way might be wiser for them in the long run. After all, my dear, you and Ivan Mikhailovitch have drifted apart, and lately I have often wondered why you haven't given him a divorce."

Princess Ivan shrugged. "Because it never occurred to me, and certainly Ivan Mikhailovitch has never asked me. In fact I rather think the freedom, *and* the safeguards, of our present situation are pleasing to both of us."

After that what else could be said, save a few inconsequential courtesies? Then, heavy-hearted as ever, Princess Mikhail went up to the nursery to see her grandchildren, in both of whom she discerned tendencies which troubled her enormously.

Just about that moment her son, possibly influenced by Prince Savosef's forebodings, arrived at a decision about Vera Kalutkina. What sort of a man is he who desists because of a rebuff? he asked himself indignantly. The Imperial Ballet's season had ended, and Vera was spending part of her summer vacation in Capri. He would follow her, if arrangements could be made.

They were, for his Captain subsequently heard him with sympathy when he bared his soul. The following morning, pasty-faced, black under the eyes, and somewhat scarred, Prince Ivan arrived at the station in the best of spirits. In the stationary Pullman he split a bottle with a friend of Page School days.

On the wall opposite the carriage a red-lettered poster stood out, a warning against drinking unboiled water. Raising his glass, Prince Ivan toasted this intimation as the train bell rang for the third time.

"But why drink water?" he demanded.

This observation, arising from sheer relief, was not remarkable for wit, as he knew, but any small piece of pleasantry is to be appreciated in a land overhung by a pall of gloom ever more lowering.

Prince Ivan's stay in Capri extended to five hours, after which he left in a furious temper without bidding farewell. Another venture two months later was hardly more prolonged and on that occasion, when shaking off the clinging dust of Florence, he resolved henceforth to dismiss from his mind a woman who could be so infernally stubborn and stupid. But in the autumn, when the Imperial Ballet opened their season in the capital, he resumed the assault upon Vera Kalutkina. Despite the fervency of his pleas, however, it was not until the turn of the year that she, fulfilling her earlier promise, gladly, shyly and fearfully gave herself to him.

On a mellow late summer's afternoon ten months later, in the superb ground floor *salon* of the magnificent villa he had given her, Prince Ivan was talking to a distinguished professional man from St. Petersburg. Their conversation in the main had been about a series of incidents in which troops had been compelled to shoot down a few hundred foolish creatures. But why, oh! why had these misguided people allowed themselves to be incited to revolt against a ruler set over them by Divine Providence?

Prince Ivan snorted. "And the tortuous-minded press of the West describe the action of our authorities as 'atrocities'."

"Over-harsh perhaps, Highness, but——"

"Atrocities! What next indeed?" Prince Ivan was fuming when an elderly woman, enveloped in a white apron, came in to speak to his frock-coated companion. "Let these leader-writers, who apparently support the assassins," he went on, "explain the inconsistency of underworld murderers who rant about the brotherhood of man and at the same time set timing-wheels for the destruction of their fellow-beings."

"Quite so, Highness, I do agree with you on that abhorrent aspect, for the Nihilists do slaughter indiscriminately. But if your Highness will have the goodness to excuse me?"

The debate was renewed shortly after the doctor returned with the news that the *prima ballerina* had been delivered of a fine girl. Differences between them were considerable, Prince Ivan asserting that any concession would subsequently involve a demand for impossible concessions, his opponent believing that wise concessions would achieve more than repression.

"Yes, it is all damned difficult, I agree," Prince Ivan said, so weary now of the subject as to take a middle course. "General strikes, train-wrecking, fanatical agitation ever increasing." Reflectively he stared across the villa's extensive park. "And now Japan is adding to our problems with her ridiculous interference about Manchuria. Not that the Mikado's threats should worry us."

The gynæcologist was not of the same opinion. "I am not so sure, Highness. Japan is a fighting nation——"

"Pff!" Prince Ivan snapped slender fingers. "We should crush them like that, my dear sir. You will see that Kurino has instructions not to press us too far."

Maybe so, maybe not. But the Japanese Minister was certainly in the news during the next four months. Before Christmas, face inscrutable, he drove to the Foreign Office, where he informed the Foreign Secretary that his Government, in the polite parlance of the diplomatic service, "viewed with grave concern the Russian delay in replying to Japan's most recent note". Just a month later, a few days after the annual Blessing of the Waters, when society was engaged in the mad whirl of the season's second half, Kurino made the same short journey three times in five days, and twice on the sixth.

There were adroit men among those who advised the Autocrat. Now if war should come, they pointed out . . . for it is well known that internal disorder fades when a country faces armed challenge from outside.

Russia procrastinated; her shrewd statesmen took the long view. Within a week Japan withdrew her Minister; two days after that newsboys in the capitals of every land displayed a few flaming words:

Japanese under Admiral Togo attack Port Arthur.

The great soldiers of the Empire smiled at the notion that the little yellow men could seize a fortress which would have remained impregnable against an attack by the world.

The fatuity of even contemplating that Holy Russia, with her millions of fighting-men, could fail. There was an ally, too.

As the Tsar declared in his Manifesto: "In God we trust. He is ever at our side."

CHAPTER II

WHEN the heir of a family with vast possessions is on the active list in wartime, it is prudent to make certain arrangements. This was why Prince Mikhail Kaivanov, who throughout the spring and summer since hostilities began had found Amsibu most disturbing, was travelling to the capital to see his only son, tied there by duties.

As the train neared the small agricultural town of Kletkoff, upon which a fierce August sun had been beating for ten hours, a wave of movement passed through a weary crowd on the baked-mud platform. Men stretched themselves; women, bowed under bundles of bedding, shouted at whimpering children; and reservists, driven there by fear of the consequences of neglecting the instructions on mobilization orders nailed to telegraph poles throughout the land, sullenly eyed the funnel-shaped stack of the approaching locomotive.

Slowing but still jolting, logs falling off the timber-piled tender, the engine passed between a grain elevator and a cattle loading ramp. Then the long train jarred to a standstill, steam hissing deafeningly.

Prince Mikhail, extraordinarily youthful-looking for his years, threw on to the floor of his private *coupé* a newspaper featuring a clamorous demand by Our Naval Correspondent, "Fore and Aft" —a pseudonym which, incidentally, concealed the identity of a colonel in the Operations Branch of the Army Staff—for a sally round the world by the Baltic Fleet to the Far East. This, it was confidently proclaimed, would result in the total annihilation of the Japanese Navy.

"If it pleases, Highness," Leonid Borisovitch asked, after forcing a passage from the rear of the train. "There is little to be bought from the vendors worthy of your Highness's attention, but I might obtain fresh fruit and tea."

Prince Mikhail nodded. "Do so."

"Assuredly, Highness." The valet squeezed past a pair of weeping drunkards, and scratched his head at the sight of a throng elbowing to reach the public samovar. "Maybe the station-master's clerk would let me have a brew if I slipped him a few copecks," he muttered.

To a gentleman used to a soft mode of life this kind of travel was most exasperating: no restaurant car, many stoppages, dawdling along. There were other annoyances. Stonily Prince Mikhail eyed a peasant who, displaying a magnificent set of teeth, gaped into the gilt and pearwood *coupé*. Would the lout have had the nerve at one time to flatten his nose against the window-pane? Prince Mikhail's brow beetled. His scowl next switched to a railway employee carrying an expensive-looking bag belonging to a pock-marked individual whose intention obviously was to intrude.

"The next compartment, if your Excellency will be so kind," the porter was saying.

"Stupid oaf," the owner of the valise roared, momentarily forgetting that peasants nowadays often turned mutinous. "No, this one, as I have already told you," he added more temperately.

Phlegm rising, Prince Kaivanov intervened. "Take that damned bag out."

"Your Excellencies," the railwayman wailed from between them.

Prince Mikhail thrust him aside and, advancing to the doorway, addressed the unwelcome traveller from the brass threshold. But he had not proceeded far when sarcastically interrupted.

"No doubt I speak to General Kouropatkin *en route* to assume command of our troops against the enemy," the other said. "But allow me to inform you, sir, that I am Baron——" He stopped short, stared unbelievingly, and before Prince Mikhail had time to resist he found himself warmly embraced.

"My dear sir," he cried, outraged.

"Surely you remember me, Mikhail Pavlych?" the unknown murmured, poking ticklish fingers into Kaivanov's ribs. "I'll freely concede that it is an agonizingly long time since we were last together, but *I* at least haven't forgotten either your Egyptian banquet or the monkish-habited dinner-party. Nor," he smirked, "dear Toni Rozzi."

Delightedly Prince Mikhail held up his hand. "I know who you are, but don't tell me. Yes, that's it . . . Egor Ignatevitch. My *dear* fellow."

As proof, he immediately started to fuss over this old friend, whom he had dropped years before because of an offensive remark. Would Egor Ignatevitch sit here or there? Was Egor Ignatevitch quite comfortable?

Surprisingly, Baron Ustinburg did not respond to this cosseting too freely, and the explanation was delayed until the train was rattling along again. It seemed that he was hurt at not being recognized more quickly.

"Have I changed so utterly?" he asked wistfully. "Please be quite candid; honestly, I should prefer it."

Prince Mikhail scrutinized him. "You look your age, I fear, Egor Ignatevitch," he replied. "And surely you could obtain a more satisfactory skin preparation, one which would do better in concealing those rather horrid pock-marks. They're not pretty; a trifle revolting, in fact."

For the next fifteen minutes Baron Ustinburg devoted himself entirely to the passing landscape, but just as he was paying quite exaggerated attention to a small village whose hovels were dominated by a handsome white church with a green cupola, there was an incident which brought about a more congenial atmosphere.

When the coach lurched violently to the sound of clanging metal both gentlemen grabbed the padded arm-loops, fearing an attempt at derailment. Four or five seconds later they were smiling feebly at each other.

"The points at Gorkashka Junction," Baron Ustinburg muttered, fumbling for a handkerchief.

Prince Mikhail also dabbed his forehead. "We live a life of nightmare, Egor Ignatevitch. Of course," he went on witheringly, "the weakness stems from the Government's fear of the effect of extreme measures upon a certain section of our own people . . . and its nervousness about public opinion abroad. Scandalous!"

Despite censorship, enough had filtered through to show that

London newspapers in particular were virulent about the Russian Government's method of dealing with unrest. This was referred to, which led to bitter denunciation of the English, a nation which, though not at war, supported the presumption of the little people by open financial assistance.

But nothing could for long divert the two travellers from their own problems. Each contributed his budget of woe.

"And in addition to ruining the equipment of one of my copper mines," Prince Mikhail continued viciously, "the dogs have fired three of my oil wells. There isn't a damned bit of regard for the sanctity of private property."

In Baron Ustinburg a touch of cattiness was always near the surface, and he still cherished a grudge.

"Let us hope the same brutal disregard is not extended to private persons. I must confess to being quite appalled when I heard about the attack on Prince Galitzin's friends. Things have indeed reached a dreadful pass when honoured guests of the Governor-General of the Caucasus cannot be adequately protected. Yes, conditions must be deplorable down there. I suppose, my dear Mikhail Pavlych," he rounded off with tantalizing delicacy, "that is why you are leaving your southern estates?"

Prince Mikhail reacted icily: "I am visiting St. Petersburg at the express request of my son."

Baron Ustinburg's eyes widened. "How *very* interesting!" he exclaimed.

This caused another silence, but eventually Baron Ustinburg tried to make amends. "That reminds me, Mikhail Pavlych," he said, nibbling a crystallized fruit. "Buy a parcel of Siberian Railway Bonds. Trains crammed with troops are running to the East, literally almost in an unbroken line. I have had a confidential view of the traffic returns, and they are astonishingly encouraging."

While this generous tip was being given, another train was approaching the train in which they were sitting; within seconds its engine passed the engine and front "hard" coach of their own train.

"I had a letter from a very knowing fellow on the Bourse," he continued, but was completely put out of countenance by a negligent wave. "Oh *really*, you Kaivanovs and your money-bags."

With a deafening *whoosh* and a full-bellied roar the passing train thundered by.

Both gentlemen, ducking and abandoning their seats, found themselves huddling together on the carpeted floor, their primary fear a home-made explosive mixture in a crudely-fashioned case.

"It is tragic that we are reduced to this nerve-wracked state," Prince Mikhail said tersely as he dusted off his knees. "Criminal!"

Ten minutes later there was another shock, when the wheels howled under heavy braking and the carriage swayed alarmingly. Rapidly losing speed the train crawled forward as far as twin water-towers, one of which had been flung from its tall iron pillars. Debris was strewn everywhere, but gangers had restored the rails of the tracks.

From the official in charge Prince Mikhail learnt that the explosion had taken place three hours before, a few seconds after the crack south-bound express had pulled out.

"There were no casualties?" he said.

"Not in the train, Excellency," the man replied. "But seven youngsters were blown to pieces. You see, Excellency, a train is a bit of excitement for the children in these lonely parts, and they come to watch the engine watering."

"Deplorable!" Prince Mikhail muttered. From his wallet he extracted a sheaf of hundred-rouble notes. "Here, my good fellow, he went on, "divide these between the parents of the bereaved."

When he closed the window and resumed his seat it was hardly remarkable that he and his travelling companion should speak anxiously of what might be expected in the capital.

Glumly Baron Ustinburg pointed out that St. Petersburg was the core from which the evil poison spread. "Things are declining so swiftly," he mourned. "I shouldn't be surprised if the gutters are running red."

In this he was wide of the mark, so wide that when, filled with foreboding, they reached the capital the following day each had difficulty in crediting his eyes: good-natured crowds and a sea of smiling faces.

Less than twenty-four hours before, St. Petersburg had been quite different, with soldiers and sailors shouldering off the pavements anyone well-dressed. The streets were in a state of wild confusion, packed with peasant-artisans, men of the forces, and thousands of students who had never returned to distant homes since the University was closed.

Orators were everywhere, but even they were forgotten when the news spread like wildfire of a defeat sustained by the Army in the Far East. A storm of cheering resulted, horrifying to the well-tried veterans of the Palace Grenadiers, who in a bent posture, hands clasped over muzzles of rifles, stood guard against the railings of the Imperial Monuments.

Mounted police, trying to disperse the masses, longed for the support of the Guards; support which the authorities held back lest ugly incidents should mar a day it was hoped would be one of national rejoicing. For everyone in the city knew that the doctors were with the Empress, and every soul in the Empire had heard of the hypnotic passes which were to bring an heir after a dreary procession of four Imperial Grand Duchesses. That was why people listened to speakers with one ear, and kept the other alert for the signal cannon.

Near a statue, a sailor stretched out a condemning finger.

"My comrades died when we had a shot at destroying the Arsenal at Kronstadt, and my brothers-in-arms in the Black Sea Fleet have mutinied at Sevastopol. But you lot here in Petersburg are shirking your duty. When *are* you going to march against the nobles and the *burzhuis*? What are you waiting for? For news of the German woman brought to bed with child? So that you can shout your bloody empty heads off with delight. . . ."

There was a vibrating growl of mob fury, lost as a column of demonstrators surged along the Nevsky Prospekt. Forcing the police before them as thistledown flies before the wind, they marched behind a double-pole banner on which their message, "Down with the Autocracy! Stop the War!" was beautifully sign-written.

Across the way a student wearing pince-nez drained off a glass of tea given him by a considerate stall-keeper.

"Now where were we, comrades?" he resumed huskily from his rickety box. "Oh, yes. . . ."

A fresh diversion as a few hundred Poles swept along, each singing or shouting. Some were yelling: "Poland for the Poles", and others, in unison, competed with: "We will revive . . . the ancient glories . . . of our kingdom." A contingent at the rear, challenging eyes seeking hopefully for any Russian who might differ, repeatedly chanted:

"Poland, our dear land, our home land, our own land,
Crushed under the usurper's iron-shod heel . . ."

A few paces up a narrow side street, a gaunt-faced old man, attended by a sparse audience exclusively female, raised his right arm tremulously skywards. Judging by the manner of his delivery and his flowing hair, general opinion put him down as a defrocked priest.

"My friends," he quavered, tears streaming. "They set the Saints' pictures in gold and rob Saints to do it. Yes, corruption, brothers and sisters. But is it not a saying of our unfortunate country?—'The cause is decided when the judge accepts a present'. . ."

There was tumult everywhere. Boys and girls added to the noise their fathers made, and women in bright kerchiefs contributed their own shrill note. Police agents prowled about, and porters serving blocks of flats kept ears and eyes open for tit-bits which might earn a few roubles from the Secret Police, two of whom were listening to a soldier frenziedly shouting from a stone balustrade.

A street vendor of salt herrings was so engrossed by the self-confessed deserter that she was unaware of darting hands emptying her basket.

"Dirty bastards," she screamed piercingly on discovering the loss. "Some thieving swine have . . ." she went on to explain, but no one took any notice.

At the other side a brazen-lunged man in mechanic's greasy clothing bellowed on: "Are we going to be shamed by our comrades in Kiev and Kharkoff? What have we done so far to boast about here? Oh, no I haven't forgotten Mister—we can afford to allow him a bit of a handle to his name now, eh?—yes, *Mister* de Plehve. Well, I'll not hide that it was St. Petersburg chaps who made sure that all that was left of His most mighty Excellency—*another* Minister of the Interior—was what could be scraped off the junk that was left of his fine carriage. . . ."

BOOM!

The first cannon. In street after street thousands of people stiffened to attention, counting. Inflammatory words died. It was not, of course, that anyone cared about the sex of still another Romanov, but money was at stake, wagers to be settled, and the market had shortened astonishingly of late.

"Ninety!" Another thunderous, rolling crack. Tension grew. "One hundred . . . one hundred and one." Then absolute silence until . . . the next echoing report, greeted by a storm of cheering and darkening of the air as hats and caps were joyously thrown upwards.

Long before the full three hundred rounds had been fired the brassy-voiced speaker summed up his shamefaced audience:

"Jelly-minded bunch of skunks you are," he said bitingly. "Bawling your blocks off because the German woman has at last whelped a mortal with something between its legs."

He was by no means appeased when his hearers, ignoring censure of themselves, roared with delight.

Thus the day went, to be succeeded by that of Prince Mikhail Kaivanov's arrival, on which the Tsar's Manifesto to celebrate his son's birth was published. His Majesty, in his condescension, made it known that every soldier and sailor fighting against Japan was to be a godfather of his heir. A political amnesty was also announced containing concessions which were at once bitterly criticized at the Nobles' Club. In full session, leading members deliberated in the Council Chamber, each occupying a chair on which his family's arms were carved.

By the next morning the pleasure which had shone on the faces of the Tsar's people had vanished. Lawless assemblies began to terrorize sundry quarters of the city.

Shortly after that, business completed in record time, Prince Mikhail left St. Petersburg for Yasni Dulba. Several friends accompanied him, each with a load off his mind at the blessed thought of a protracted respite from anxiety among the Cossacks of the Don, loyalest of the loyal.

Prince Mikhail's departure meant that he was unable to join with others two months later in bidding a moving farewell to his only son, whose ship was among the squadrons sailing from Libau on a long-range, perilous mission, an expedition arising out of journalists' ceaseless agitation rather than from any conviction the Board of Admiralty might have.

2

For the second occasion within a comparatively brief period a member of the house of Kaivanov spent some hours in the family lawyer's dignified room. A line of silk-bound documents was spread along the polished top of a massive table and, in readiness to wind up current matters, Isvoltoff stretched towards an ebony-and-bronze inkstand. When his distinguished client's bout of coughing subsided, he dipped a pen and, bowing, handed it over. Then, blotting-paper hovering, he attended Prince Ivan who, moving along the side of the table, scrawled his signature eighteen times.

"You must take care, Highness," the lawyer murmured. "Colds and chills——"

A faint smile showed fleetingly on Commander Prince Kaivanov's handsome but strained face. "Will not concern me much longer, my dear fellow," he said.

Horrified, Isvoltoff took a step backwards. "Your Highness," he gasped. "You don't mean that the doctors . . . oh, I see, Highness. I must own I misunderstood your allusion. And so that, Highness, is the opinion of the senior officers of the Fleet?"

Prince Ivan nodded. "Absolutely," he replied resentfully. "We sail east because the pariahs of the newspapers have forced it on us, for no sounder reason than that. As a crazy gesture, my dear Isvoltoff, we throw our antiquated fleet against the English-built ships of the Mikado."

"Highness!"

"I must bid you good-bye, my dear fellow," said Prince Ivan, striving to keep emotion from his voice as he held out a hand. "Carry out the provisions of my will, and telegraph His Highness my dear father as soon as you receive news of my death."

Isvoltoff, that able product of the School of Jurisprudence, was equally moved.

"Highness," he said, blinking.

It seemed fitting that a funeral procession should pass at that moment. Prince Ivan watched the leading men carrying the top-board, and stared at the humble bearers who grasped wooden staves supporting the coffin. His melancholy glance went to the white face of the much-shaken corpse.

"For the proud name of Russia we go. And for her dear sake we must accept what fate bestows," he said sombrely.

Through the falling snow he drove to his residence on Palace Quay. Prudently entering by way of the straw-strewn exercise yard, where every horse had its name on a brass plate over the stall door, he made his final commands known.

"And make certain I have the three swiftest," he ended.

In the upper hall of the mansion the Major-domo hovered nervously. "Your Highness, the merchant Paroshinsky has called again. He implores you to favour him with a few minutes' conversation."

"Tell him——" Prince Ivan snapped ... but what was the use when death was in the air? He would receive the fellow.

Paroshinsky, a portly figure dressed in the finest of English cloth, put up a very determined resistance.

"But, Highness," he persisted, "there can be no argument that there is a child toddling in my house, that it is my daughter's, and that my daughter was forcibly abducted by Prince Savosef."

"Does he dispute it? That is more germane," Prince Ivan inquired cynically.

The merchant's brown eyes flamed. "He refuses to discuss the subject."

"Then so do I."

Paroshinsky held himself in check. "But, Highness," he expostulated. "My daughter was a pure girl, not a woman picked off the streets."

Commander Prince Kaivanov was really amused. "I hardly think you are entirely accurate there, Monsieur."

"Her life is ruined unless I can obtain redress from Prince Savosef. If you, Highness, would be graciously willing to testify——"

"Against Prince Savosef? Don't be absurd, my dear fellow."

"But, Highness. . . ."

Irritably Prince Ivan made a sign. "Show this gentleman out," he told a knee-breeched, silk-stockinged footman who hurried to him. "At once."

Without another glance at the caller he went into another lofty hall and then turned towards a black-and-white marble staircase, which he slowly ascended. On the half-landing he paused briefly, grasping a sculptured figure for support, before wearily dragging himself up the remainder of the shallow flight of steps, head drooping a trifle.

Surprised at the top by his wife, who was standing there wearing a fur coat and pull-over carriage boots, he breathlessly apologized.

"A thousand pardons, my dear," he said. "I hadn't realized you were coming down. I'm just off for a last few minutes with the children, so suppose you join me. That is," he added teasingly, "if I shan't be detaining you. The dear Count, eh?"

Princess Kaivanova. who had been staring at him somewhat curiously, nodded. "Yes, we are taking tea at the German Embassy. But, Ivan Mikhailovitch, that perfectly dreadful cough."

He laughed. "Oh, it's nothing, Zeneide, my dear. A few days at sea will clear up this little trouble of mine. Nothing to worry about."

"Then the fleet definitely sails? One of the naval secretaries told me at lunch he was quite certain it would."

"Yes, my dear, the train for Libau is due out on the stroke of midnight," he said gravely. "But you mustn't allow me to keep you any longer, or you will be late for your appointment."

Her fine eyes flashed indignantly. "I shall have plenty of time for Hans when you have gone. In any case I haven't seen the children myself for quite a while. Much more important, however, I simply wouldn't dream of not accompanying you to them on the day their father leaves in the service of his country."

Greatly moved, Prince Ivan peeled back a gauntleted glove, and turning her arm, tenderly kissed the inside of her wrist.

"It will be a charming memory for me to take with me, my dear," he said.

Arm-in-arm they walked slowly along two lengthy corridors, between pictures and porcelain any of which the world's greatest art galleries and museums would have been proud to own.

The day nursery was a fine apartment, fitted with everything to please a child: a slide, a swing, an immense and beautifully-appointed doll's house, and a wonderful model railway; there were whole regiments of colourful lead soldiers, guns, forts, and ships of war. Surprisingly, not a single doll was to be noticed.

A minor disturbance was in progress. The four-year-old Anastasia, heart-shaped face a mask of resolution, was compelling her brother, a year senior, to relinquish his luxuriantly-maned rocking-horse.

"Get off, Sergei Ivanovitch," she screamed, the red silk ribbon on her dark pigtail flying. "Get off, I want to ride."

Prince Sergei whimpered as she slashed him with a toy whip across his ear, but before the commotion grew worse their English governess, Miss Brown, hurried from an adjoining room. "Anastasia," she called sharply.

Princess Anastasia's naughtiness was forgotten in the excitement of the rare visit. Prince Ivan swung his daughter as high over his head as he could, and his son just so high as that young gentleman could bear without flinching.

It is one of the tragedies of life that all good things must come to an end, even life itself.

Tears welling, Prince Ivan Kaivanov kissed his dear little ones, and with tears streaming down their cheeks he and his wife fondly embraced.

It was a poignant spectacle. Miss Brown, confusedly aware that her vision was misting, averted her glance from the disturbing sight.

This was not the end of grief for that day. There was still another who mourned Commander Prince Kaivanov's departure, a separation perhaps for eternity from the man to whom, with many a prayer to Him for forgiveness, she had given herself.

Vera Kalutkina would not for some weeks be taking up residence in the town house her lover had recently bought her, and their parting took place at her villa, after nightfall.

She managed to stifle her emotion until, bending, he brushed his lips against the raven-black hair of little Mimi, softly sleeping. But then she began to tremble and when, leaving nurse and child, they were alone again, she broke down utterly.

"I can't let you go, Ivan Mikhailovitch," she cried.

Consolingly he patted her hand. "My dear, duty calls and I must answer. And I know my little cabbage would not try to deter me from it."

She raised swimming eyes. "*Yes*, I would. What do I care about the Japanese? I don't hate them and they don't hate me."

"You seem to forget they are our enemies, Vera Nikolaevna," he said a trifle stiffly, but, relenting, went on more gently: "Come, come, dearest." To distract her attention, he spoke of more material matters. "I should like you to know that I have made further provision for you and dear Mimi, my darling, as shortly you will hear. And my lawyer also has instructions to communicate with you—should it be necessary."

Sinking into a chair, she covered her face with her hands. "Oh, don't, Ivan Mikhailovitch," she begged.

"But dearest, this is war, and I am on the active list, and we must consider the future," he said, reasonably enough. "And I was merely trying to assure you——" Eyes closed, he exhaled wheezily, and laid wide-spread hands against his chest.

She sprang up. "Darling, however you pretend otherwise I know you are ill, and I am certain the Admiralty would never allow you to sail if they knew. For my sake you must go to the medical department and——"

Commander Prince Kaivanov, Imperial Russian Navy, drew himself up, his small but pregnant gesture drawing attention to the sword and belt which earlier he had thrown on to a sofa.

"The Kaivanovs, Vera Nikolaevna," he said austerely, immutability in every line, "do not make excuses."

She sobbed in his arms, and they both sobbed as they clung together near the outer door, the servants mingling their tears with them. So Prince Ivan, leaving sorrow behind him and with what God alone knew before him, left for the capital again, speeding, to begin with, across a white waste, the night heavens a dark blue canopy glorified by a prodigal array of clear-cut stars.

Early next morning, with other officers, he was a passenger in a long, double-engined train, every window of which was securely curtained and every pane painted on both sides with opaque black paint. The signalman in the box at the end of the platform booked it out of St. Petersburg at 1.43 a.m.

In winter, when the Gulf of Finland was frozen, the Fleet moved south from Kronstadt to open-water ports in the Baltic. The round-the-world foray against the Japanese started from Libau.

This great naval base was a scene of intense activity. Working parties, cursing under their breath, trundled hand-carts piled with victualling stores along the wharves, closely watched from every guard point by doubled numbers of specially picked sentries. In the harbour, winches whining, two ships were still coaling; another, a battleship, feverishly discharged down her port side ammunition belonging to an armoured cruiser which she had accepted earlier through a faulty signal, while on her starboard hand a lighter containing her own ammunition drifted further away from a head-rope furtively severed with an axe.

The rusty sheaves of cranes squeaked, chattering donkey engines filled the cold air with clouds of steam, and fussy tank locos, stopping too suddenly, caused the clank of buffers to reverberate into the distance, and once brought about splendid havoc when couplings broke. On five ships gangs of resentful civilian employees of the establishment, brought aboard at pistol-point, completed essential jobs their passionate-eyed foreman had signed for as "satisfactorily completed" the previous day.

His Imperial Majesty's ship *Ekaterin Bazneva*, in which efficiency was subordinated to the advantages of a congenial mess, lay in one of the larger basins.

As her Gunnery Officer, Commander Prince Kaivanov, stepped from the gangway he perfunctorily acknowledged the salute of the distinguished sub-lieutenant who was keeping harbour watch, being more conscious of the scowling faces of members of the ship's company. When changed into sea-going rig he reported to his commanding officer, but as soon as courtesy permitted withdrew from an intimate family gathering, kissing the hands of four icily-composed ladies, the Captain's wife and daughters, before bowing himself out.

He next sought the wardroom, now a dismal sight—the grand piano gone, bulkheads stripped of beautifully-grained wood, and draperies and furnishings, anything inflammable, torn out.

A party of officers was grouped round the brightly-burning stove, keeping servants busy with their demands. They were all talking volubly, with the exception of the Captain's secretary who, crouching in a chair and staring into the depths of a glass cupped in his hands, steadily mumbled to himself.

The conversation covered an extensive field: the walk-out at the Putiloff Neva Shipbuilding Company, a foul stab in the back when ships were on the eve of sailing on a hazardous wartime assignment; the reason for the disaster to the submarine *Delfin* which, when on trials after a refit at the Baltic Works, submerged but never resurfaced; that morning's discovery of tampering with the thermometers in the flagship's magazines. There was also speculation on an hour-old rumour which confidently claimed that the little yellow men's destroyers were lurking outside, waiting for the Fleet to emerge.

"Christ!" the Torpedo Lieutenant muttered as he swept a lank strand of hair from his forehead and focused hazily on the newcomer. "Oh, hello sir, would you care for a drink, a lovely, lovely drink? Another down the hatch wouldn't harm any of us."

Commander Prince Kaivanov shivered, teeth chattering slightly. "It would be most welcome, my dear fellow. Don't know what the devil is the matter with me lately. A hot day bathed me in sweat if I lifted my hand, and now a touch of cold chills me to the marrow. Damned funny."

"Why not let the P.M.O. run you over, sir?" the Torpedo Lieutenant said.

This suggestion was dismissed much more abruptly than its kindly intention warranted.

"Nonsense," Commander Prince Kaivanov started off again, with such emphasis that he choked on his next words, breath whistling and shoulders beginning to shake. As though to ease himself he bent over a table, supporting himself on his palms. When the lengthy paroxysm ended he turned away from his shipmates, but two of them saw him surreptitiously examine in the shelter of his body a handkerchief he had placed to his lips.

"I say, sir," a junior watch keeper said with tipsy concern. The Torpedo Lieutenant also repeated his advice.

Quite recovered, Prince Ivan laughed heartily and clapped the younger men's shoulders. "My dear fellows, all I am suffering from is a chill of sorts which has been hanging on—well, rather too long. So pipe down, the pair of you."

Commander Zelouky, from the most favoured seat in front of the stove, glanced around. "Never mind, Guns, if you're not in Davy Jones's locker within the next few days you'll be all right," he said thickly.

Prince Ivan laughed again. "Of course, Number One," he scoffed. "To listen to these two Jonahs you'd think I wasn't fit to sail. What do they expect me to do? Run along to the Skipper and say 'Please, sir, may I be excused?'"

The junior watch-keeper, appreciably fuddled, found a knotty problem in this remark. "What a dilemma for a chap to be in," he said, awed by his own imagination. "I mean, a chap who starts feeling ill at the last moment before his ship pushes off on a dangerous job. What should the poor devil do?"

Commander Prince Kaivanov's voice throbbed with passion. "His duty, at *whatever* cost to himself. When a nation calls for her sons, a nation as sorely hurt by traitors as ours——"

Gulping down the remaining inch in his glass, Commander Zelouky raised blood-shot eyes.

"Discipline, that's what is needed everywhere, and less pandering," he growled. "Negotiations . . . ugh! I'd show 'em. Take Poland—can you conceive the Poles being allowed to raise the cry of 'liberty' in Warsaw when the Empire is at war? I'd give 'em liberty, the rebellious scoundrels."

A thin-faced young lieutenant, lolling in a chair at the port-side end of the half-circle, managed to find his feet. He steadied himself against a steel pillar, now denuded of its peacetime coat of glossy white enamel.

"Sir," he said with drunken gravity, "I have the honour to request formally that this subject be dropped."

"And who the hell are you to dictate to a superior officer?" Commander Zelouky demanded.

Count Wiazovsky swayed dangerously as he brought himself

to attention. "A nobleman of Poland, my good sir . . . a country in which my ancestors ate as gentlemen . . . when their neighbours in Russia fed out of troughs," he announced proudly between bouts of hiccuping.

With admirable swiftness Commander Prince Kaivanov took charge of a situation which, if not controlled, might have ugly repercussions. Speaking from the heart, he reminded them of the perilous undertaking upon which they would be engaged soon. He did not spare himself, but the effort, plainly for all to see, drained him of strength.

"No, gentlemen, I beg of you, this is not the time for dissension," he ended in a weak voice. "We are comrades-in-arms, and must be ever faithful to each other."

This, and what he had said previously, was stuff of a nobility so much out of keeping with his character that his audience resembled nothing less than an episode of historical importance depicted by *tableau-vivant*. No one spoke or moved.

An alien note was provided by the Captain's secretary. Leaping to his feet, glassy-eyed glance on the deck overhead and arm pointing in the same direction, he struck an impressive though wavering attitude.

"A fleet of doomed men," he declaimed sonorously. "I'm doomed and you're doomed, and soon we'll all be food for the little fishes. Dead, dead, dead."

Having relieved himself of this forecast, he fell flat on his face. That was funny enough, to be sure, but the laughter greeting his tumble had little genuineness in it.

A strange night, a night on which the shutters of signal lamps winked at novices' rate, and all too often winked inaccurately. A night of ships colliding, of engines racing astern when telegraphs, so those on bridges swore, tinkled for quarter speed ahead, a night during which ships' wheels or steering engines seemed to have difficulty in differentiating port from starboard.

Happily, the spirit of the Baltic Fleet improved before many days elapsed, after a successful night encounter with the enemy's torpedo-boats in the North Sea.

Morale became better all round, in wardrooms and on messdecks. Toasts were enthusiastically drunk, coupled with a note of regret, for no seaman cares to abandon enemies in the water. But where torpedo-boats are concerned it is essential to be wary about heaving-to.

The Fleet's new-born pride in itself, alas, lasted only to the first port of call, where a series of imperatively-worded telegrams were brought out post-haste by the Russian consul.

His Imperial Majesty, compelled to take notice of the British

Government's sharp note, directed that those officers responsible should answer to him for sinking trawlers of the English Dogger Bank fishing fleet. He further directed that the culprits be landed at Vigo.

With them, but not of them, was Commander Prince Ivan Kaivanov. *His* misfortune was a suspect pulmonary condition of a nature too obscure to be adequately investigated aboard ship.

From the nursing home to which he was taken Prince Ivan telegraphed to a Parisian doctor of international connections with whom he had a slight acquaintance. On arrival this gentleman examined him and decided that a period of observation was necessary. After discussion it was agreed that this might best be spent on the dazzlingly-bright shores of North Africa, where the climate was most suitable.

The doctor at once wired his secretary cancelling all engagements until further notice; and, exactly a week after the Baltic Fleet sailed from Vigo, left with his distinguished patient for Algiers. The journey was made most comfortably, in a steam yacht chartered for the purpose.

3

Russians have a gift for laughter envied by most. A perfect hurricane of laughter swept through the Empire when, in the New Year, it was officially announced that a saluting cannon used at the annual Blessing of the Waters had been inadvertently loaded with shrapnel, a piece of which had gone through a window of the Winter Palace.

Inadvertently!

This misuse of a word quite put out of mind the news of a week or so before about the inexplicable fall of Port Arthur.

Inadvertently!

It was so funny that one could forget the stupidity of the Putiloff Neva workers, who had again downed tools; and one could nearly forget the impudence of Father Gapon in leading a deputation of strikers to the Minister of War.

But Father Gapon's next indiscretion was less easy to overlook. The colossal impertinence of this priest, a man disowned by the Orthodox Church, to propose that the Tsar should leave his country retreat at Tsarskoe Selo to meet his people on the steps of the Winter Palace!

The day after this audacious suggestion became known, Baron "Decimate", at the Nobles' Club, was particularly wroth.

"By gad, that fellow Gapon," he fumed. "And now I am told

that this renegade father is egging them on to deliver a petition today."

"Judging from what we have seen already I should say something of the sort was extremely likely," remarked Menshek-Pelikoff, a gentleman with intelligent green eyes.

In the late eighties the Baron had quashed minor disturbances in the Urals by shooting one man in ten. This feat had earned him his nickname.

"But what the devil *is* the Government doing?" he exclaimed testily. "Why don't they bring out the Cossacks?"

Outside the club a never-ending procession of working-class men and their families moved towards Palace Square. Some talked quietly, others chattered; many craned upwards at the fine buildings along the route, children perched on their shoulders; and a few, while trudging on, painstakingly tried to read that morning's edition of a new newspaper, *The Copeck.*

The majority held themselves with patent dignity, for it was expected that Father Gapon would explain their position to the Little Father who, as soon as he heard about their poor wages and daily troubles—when he heard for himself and not through the mouths of lying statesmen—would soon right their wrongs.

"Cossacks!" Menshek-Pelikoff growled. "These people haven't a weapon amongst their thousands. They're nothing more than puzzled sheep, not murderers, nihilists or agitators."

There was a general laugh; Menshek-Pelikoff on his hobby-horse again.

"Have you ever seen these simple sheep running amok, butchering Armenians or Jews?" someone asked slyly.

"Yes, I regret to say I have," Menshek-Pelikoff admitted hotly. "But Russians by nature are credulous, high and low alike. They'll believe anything, and they're quickly incited. It is the extremists on both sides who are the most dangerous of all."

The sly individual got in another shrewd blow. "And on which side are the extremists worst?" he demanded. "Isn't it true that the extremism of those against the Government is more savage and beastly than the Government's reprisals, for after all the Government doesn't kill without discrimination or convict without fair trial. No one is either executed or sent to Siberia without legal investigation."

Menshek-Pelikoff sighed. "Yes, I agree with that. But," he fired again, "we're digging too deep. All that these people want is a wage sufficient to buy enough food, and if a little was left over for modest pleasures they'd be delirious with happiness . . . a few roubles in hand for Palm Week, to enjoy themselves with and to give a few presents—a singing sausage for the youngest boy, sugar wool for the old woman, a green weather frog with its little ladder for the kitchen. . . ."

In Palace Square matters were reaching their climax, the police helpless against the mass influx of still more thousands of people, themselves inexorably shoved from behind by further thousands, each of whom was excitedly hoping for a glimpse of the handing-over of a simple document.

A senior police official, shrugging off responsibility, spoke to a field officer, who nodded quite casually to a subordinate, a trifling sign which speedily set in train an ominous series of actions. As the word went round, *sotnia* leaders freed swords a finger's length out of scabbards; company officers issued sharp orders; the front ranks of infantry sank on to one knee, and second ranks, with a spit for luck, took aim over their comrades' shoulders.

Many of the immense crowd were without a notion of what was afoot, but, suddenly aware of the possibility of bloody violence, a sad change came over others. Confined by dense barriers of their own fellows, and so unable to obey the final warning to disperse, they pallidly waited, paralysed.

A fur-capped colonel of Siberian Cossacks rose in his saddle, arm outstretched. When he waved his sword forward and spurred his beast, hoofs began to drum as fiery-eyed men on fiery-eyed animals raced behind him, a spearhead which left a swathe of agony and death behind. Before then, however, many already had paid the penalty—a volley from the flanks had taken its toll.

In the Nobles' Club the North Sea indemnity claim was being discussed when the first thin screams of despair were heard.

"I suppose the English, being English, naturally expect compensation," a wealthy Bessarabian landowner was commenting. "But damn it, six hundred and twenty-five thousand roubles for a few fishermen and their wretched boats. . . ."

After that nothing was said for a time. In the billiard room cues thrust with blind haste at clips clattered to the floor; and in the gaming-room, playing cards fresh from new packs became soiled and crumpled with the nervous movement of clammy fingers.

Sounds heightened and fell; a distant droning was heard. The noise swelled, rising thunderously with the nearing presence of a multitude of flying feet. Along the street panic-stricken creatures came running; grey-faced or apoplectic, mouths wide open, slobbering, or snapped tight; silent, shrieking, laughing; eyes roving or fixed, darting or insane; filthy-tongued or calling upon the Saviour.

In the club, a strange quietness ensuing when the steaming herd had passed, there was a sudden release of breath.

"Damnable!" a gentleman said, one of half a dozen clustered around Menshek-Pelikoff. "We don't know precisely what has happened, but I am certain it will be another blot on our country's good name. It *must* end."

Baron "Decimate" put away his handkerchief. "I rather think it is ending already," he boomed. "Yes, gentlemen, such evidence as we have does suggest that the authorities are now really waking up."

He, who had brought sharp order into a small town in the Urals, was able to see for himself, when he drove across Palace Square later on, how these things look when done on an impressive scale.

Carts of every description were there: carts from the War Department and from the City Council; and log wagons, hay wains and mobile cesspit tanks—vehicles on skids and on wheels, hooded and open.

Into these conveyances squads of troops were lifting bodies, and fire-brigade men and sweepers were shovelling rust-coloured snow.

There was plenty of work to be done, for four thousand six hundred people had died.

Most nations possess a few weak vessels in the ranks of their administrators, and, quite frankly, Holy Russia was no better served than were many great countries. A case in point—the official who, six days after the incident in front of the Winter Palace, drafted an announcement to the effect that the situation was "now normal".

Normal!

With St. Petersburg momentarily stunned, but already showing signs of fanatically rising again; with Moscow weltering in blood, a battlefield in which many houses were packed with tenacious garrisons, the streets with field-guns; where youths occasionally streamed out of tottering buildings, hands above their heads— Moscow, where all that could be found of the remains of the Governor, the Grand Duke Sergei, could be pushed stickily into a small urn.

Normal!

With railway telegraphists working fitfully or on strike, the workmen of the Baltic Naval Dockyard out again, with a sugar refinery belonging to the Grand Duke Mikhail in the Province of Kiev destroyed, and His Imperial Highness, mind you, own brother to the Autocrat himself. With peasant revolts in the provinces, landlords murdered, country seats sacked and inmates brutally treated; with the estate of the dead Grand Duke Sergei in the government of Orel pillaged, and he another of the mighty House of Romanov.

But normal! What next?

With horrible murders at Baku; and the shooting of Vice-Admiral Nazimoff by his filthy-nailed orderly; with the shocking news of the naval battle of Tsu Shima and the annihilation of the Baltic Fleet causing, not sorrow, but demands for peace by swine who did not appear to understand that Holy Russia's honour was at stake.

Normal, by all the Saints!

With mutiny in the Black Sea by the crew of the *Kniaz Potemkin*, who killed all their officers save five because an odd rating had been shot in his tracks for rank insubordination; with Odessa *en gala* to receive the committee of twenty seamen who directed the passage of the *Kniaz Potemkin* from Sevastopol; with the scum of Odessa lamenting on their granite and marble front as dead sailors were ceremoniously brought ashore; with Odessa in renewed turmoil when the naval mutineers joined forces with their comrades ashore in a fight against the Cossacks; with shipping smouldering in the harbour, granaries burning, warehouses on the quays roofless and smoking, and with ever the report of rifles, day and night.

By Notre Dame d'Iberia . . . normal!

CHAPTER III

THE future does not always fall out as imagined. Not that Prince Ivan Kaivanov exactly chafed during that hot summer after his return from convalescence on the shores of the Mediterranean; it was rather that a vague sense of disappointment invaded him. A fellow working at the Admiralty needed relaxation, not staid dinners and bridge, or the company of simpletons whose idea of pleasure was to sit and chat while idly watching fireflies in the warm dusk. Now to have a few girls from the music halls, and bright fellows tearing over from summer quarters at Krasnoe Selo . . . that would be something. Liveliness, change; cars pulling up in clouds of dust.

"To tell you the truth, Vera Nikolaevna," he said, "I'm fed up with chaperoned misses from the Imperial Ballet School, girlish ecstasies about the Swan Dance, and with drinking infernal tea at English 'five o'clocks'."

Coaxingly she slipped her arm into his. "You're not, Ivan Mikhailovitch," she said.

"I am," he replied mulishly.

Vera Kalutkina proudly shook her dark, beautifully poised head. "I know what is the matter with you, darling," she whispered. "You're still brooding because you weren't with the fleet at Tsu Shima. But you couldn't help it, and it wouldn't have made a scrap of difference if you had lost your life as well. And you must remember also how much you have to be thankful for, how a slight tendency to weakness in your chest might have been so much worse—so terribly different, dearest."

They were standing on the terrace of Vera Kalutkina's red-and-cream country villa. From the shady lawns below, where chairs and tables were arranged, laughter and the talk of many people arose.

Prince Ivan, staring down an avenue of trees at swans on the shimmering blue lake, pulled himself out of his abyss of repining.

"I know, darling. And that is why I need something more stimulating than this . . . than these very good people. Look at 'em, my dear."

Vera Kalutkina was beginning to be most proprietorially cross.

"I think you are quite outrageous, Ivan Mikhailovitch. I am sure . . . His Imperial Highness," she gasped, gathering up her skirts. "Darling, I must run to receive him."

From his vantage point Prince Ivan sourly watched a member of the House of Romanov hand his *bonne amie* from an automobile before relieving her of a dust coat covering an attractive afternoon gown. Then the Grand Duke kissed his hostess's hand and acknowledged deeply-curtseying ladies and tight-waisted military dandies standing rigidly at the salute.

Prince Ivan's good-looking face was disfigured by even a worse scowl when he saw a nurse in a lilac-coloured linen dress wheeling a perambulator.

"My God!" he muttered.

As he made his way resentfully towards the steps at the end of the terrace he noticed a group of ladies fussing over his daughter. One of them, a *prima ballerina*, lifted out the child to cuddle her, and no doubt, he told himself savagely, baby-talk would be strictly in order.

When eventually he paid his respects to the guest of honour it was impossible to overlook the fact that the Grand Duke shared in this kind of nauseating nonsense. Both he and Mimi, who was deliriously enjoying "ride-a-cock-horse" on his knee, seemed equally pleased with each other.

"Ah, my dear Ivan Mikhailovitch," His Imperial Highness said, laughing fatuously, "you see they've found a job for me." But shortly after that his voice lowered: "Bad news from the south, I understand."

"Really, sir," said Prince Kaivanov. "My day off, you know, sir."

His Imperial Highness's corsets creaked as he leaned nearer. "The despatches were garbled and not too definite, but. . . ." For a spell he continued extremely grave, though not for too long. After all, for the ladies' sake one must not spoil a pleasant occasion.

"Quite, sir," his host agreed.

The Imperial nursemaid gently pinched Mimi's soft cheek. "And now, my dear," he said, "we mustn't make Papa jealous, must we? Up-si-ups, sweetheart."

So Commander Prince Ivan Kaivanov, his smile a shade bilious, found himself holding a lively and talkative little girl before a pack of grinning women, as he considered them.

The white-clad messenger, in the uniform of a chief petty officer, was a Godsend. Prince Ivan tore open a heavily-sealed envelope, read it through hastily, and thankfully handed the child to her day nurse.

His Imperial Highness waved apologies aside. "Not at all, my dear fellow. In these days we are lucky to have a little pleasant enjoyment at all."

Prince Ivan was still glowering when his Benz brought him within sight of the gold-gleaming steeple of the Admiralty. That he, who had embarked on this *affaire* with a light and joyous heart, should now be enmeshed in domestic tyranny. It was repugnant. Why, even Zeneide, and he *was* married to her. . . .

With his first view of the steeple Prince Ivan's brow furrowed anew; he began to wonder.

Admiral Count Tseragin's note had been strikingly peremptory.

A vase of long-stemmed pink roses and a heavy silver-framed portrait of Countess Tseragina were the only objects relieving the severity of official furnishings. Along one side of the table three chairs had been placed; at the other side, boring through his callers with keen eyes, sat a rat-trap-mouthed officer, Admiral Count Tseragin, called in by the Government at this late hour.

"Be seated, gentlemen," he said curtly.

The senior of the three officers, Captain Prince Shulovsky, high-cheeked, tight-lipped, with strikingly bushy red eyebrows, took the centre chair; on his right was Commander Tianov, to the left Commander Prince Ivan Kaivanov.

Count Tseragin lost no time. "Gentlemen," he began. "Our

seamen at Libau have destroyed the barracks, looted the victual-ling yard, and are now attacking the officers' quarters. The Baltic Fleet no longer exists. And in the south the Black Sea Squadron under Admiral Krieger has failed so far to compel the *Kniaz Potemkin* to surrender, and to involve the situation further the crew of the *Georgei Pobiedonosets* is in revolt. These and other influences, gentlemen, are the basic reasons for Russia suing for peace."

Commander Tianov gasped. "Are we confessing ourselves beaten by Japan, sir?"

Admiral Tseragin smiled grimly. "We are beaten by reason of the internal state of our country, towards which the ratings of our own profession have done no little to contribute. And that, gentlemen, is why I have cancelled your present appointments." His voice deepened. "This disease in our Service must be stamped out without mercy, and it shall be. You will proceed to Sevastopol, and there constitute yourselves into a permanent naval court-martial."

"But, sir," Commander Prince Kaivanov rose impetuously, "with respect I should prefer to be granted another opportunity of facing the enemy. I . . . I . . ." he laughed ruefully, "I have been denied once, as you know, sir, and death, with a deck under one's feet——"

"You'll probably die a good deal sooner this way," said Admiral Count Tseragin gruffly. "Sevastopol is ablaze, and the lives of members of the court-martial will not be a very sound insurable proposition." He lifted a paper-weight, picked up a telegraph form, and frowningly re-read a message long delayed. "Admiral Krieger hopes to restore order, or at least gain the upper hand, perhaps by now. It will then be your duty, gentlemen, to pass such sentences as will serve as a warning for all time."

For a few moments the Admiral was lost in contemplation of particles of dust eddying in a shaft of sunlight. Then he turned slowly.

"Gentlemen," he said gravely, "at heart I believe our people are sound, but our great Empire is almost *in extremis*, brought low by pernicious doctrines. Yours will be the task of cutting out some of the tainted flesh. I trust I have been clear, gentlemen. But if any of you have subsequent queries I shall be at my desk here until the small hours."

Captain Prince Shulovsky glanced at his colleagues, and then, red eyebrows quivering, shook his head decisively. "No, sir, your instructions are perfectly plain. They will be carried out to the letter."

"And gladly, sir," said Commander Tianov. "These dogs have

defiled the Cross of Saint Andrew flying over our ships, and for that—yes, gladly, sir."

Admiral Count Tseragin rose briskly. "Exactly, my dear fellow. Gentlemen, your train leaves at three o'clock in the morning and, inasmuch as it can be ensured these days, you will have priority on the line. And now all that remains is for me to wish you God-speed . . . and a safe return."

"Thank you, sir."

"Good-bye, Tianov, my dear fellow, my felicitations to your wife. And good-bye, Kaivanov . . . I trust your father emerged safely from the bloodshed in the Caucasus of a week ago. I understand he spends most of his time on your southern estates."

Commander Prince Kaivanov started out of a reverie. "Yes, he does, sir, although within the past year he's stayed quite frequently at our place on the Don. But the climate at Amsibu suits him much better than Yasni Dulba, and he went down again. Oh, I imagine he'll be all right, or I should have heard. Besides . . ." he shrugged. "The disturbances in the Caucasus, I gather, have been this time more in the nature of massacres, not seditious opposition to the régime."

That old man of iron, Admiral Count Tseragin, nodded understandingly. "Several hundred thousand more Jews and Armenians spread throughout the Empire would have saved us infinite trouble," he remarked dryly.

In an instant the air of tension was dispersed; two of his hearers bellowed joyously, each aware how easy it was to switch their own people to a new target.

Commander Prince Kaivanov was more restrained. His thoughts might have been different, however, had he known that these were the closing hours of a six days' race between a telegram addressed to his mansion on Palace Quay and the hour fixed for departure from St. Petersburg of a very special train.

2

Since the passing of the fanatical days of armed religious risings against Russia's suzerainty, the Caucasus had suffered spasmodic outbreaks of a minor character only: the usual local excitements arising from feuds, abductions, rapes and betrayals; holy wars proclaimed by fierce Tartars upon timorous Armenians; and pogroms, holiday events for the remainder, in which luckless Jews were butchered.

These disturbances were a nuisance to the authorities, to be sure, but nevertheless they were regarded as convenient distractions by the Governor-General and his troops in the pink-

and-white barracks at Tiflis, who usually kept to their quarters rather than march out to interfere.

This remained, broadly speaking, the position even when the nation was disrupted by rebellion and anarchy from Revel to Vladivostock. Little more than an occasional backwash rippled down from the fearful maelstrom in the north.

The shock to the landed proprietors was therefore all the greater when, within a night's space, towering waves of insurrection, like a heavy sea backed by wind and tide funnelling into a narrow estuary, swept through the province.

The revolution of 1905 had reached Georgia.

It brought madness to the lovely palace of Amsibu. Domestics were fleeing across the park, cursing flunkeys tugged off scarlet-and-gold liveries, the Assistant Steward crawled through the Persian garden dragging a sack bulging with pillage collected since that universally hated man, the Steward, less laden perhaps but with greater intrinsic value in a smaller compass, had slipped away earlier.

The air was thick with the suffocating stench of burning crops; pinpoints of yellow-red light, Armenian villages ablaze, dotted the mountainous countryside. When the wind favoured, screams could be thinly heard, those of wives and daughters of foremen and managers outraged before husbands, sons and sweethearts.

Two torchlit columns moved against Amsibu, the smaller, from the south-east, more or less purposeful and silent; the other, from the west, vociferous with exploits, noisy with the delight of cattle carried off and fine bloodstock maimed, churches and schools sacked, holy images torn down, Jews castrated and weak-kneed Armenians forced to accept Islam at the behest of the scythe.

From an upper window of the palace the youth Nubar Gashginkian, tear-streaks dried by sheer horror, mouth everlastingly working, trembled as he perceived a clangorous throng nearing.

He wore a faithful replica of the Steward's garb. That, and the power bestowed with it, had been a whim of his master's, and right mercilessly, for three months, had he used his authority. Now he thought of nothing but the possible reckoning.

As though bereft of strength he leaned against the window frame, staring out with dark liquid eyes, praying desperately for an intimation of the approach of the five *sotnias* of Cossacks who, on their master's order, should have reached Amsibu by now after a seven hundred miles' ride from Yasni Dulba on the Don. His ears were ever attentive for the silvery jingle of horse gear, for the mad hoof-drummings of excited little horses.

In the vast apartment with malachite pillars Prince Mikhail

Kaivanov turned from an arched opening, glanced at his servant and shivered. On a tall glass ornament, however, the image strangely reduced, he could still perceive the bobbing, yellow flames of the torches.

"Pardon me, Leonid Borisovitch," he said jerkily. "I am a little overwrought. Pour me a glass of cognac, if you please."

"Yes, Highness." The servant busied himself.

Face taut, Prince Mikhail was listening intently. "My Cossacks," he screeched suddenly. "Can't you hear them? Dammit, can't you . . . isn't it . . . ?"

Leonid Borisovitch, nostrils imperceptibly quivering, shaded his eyes to the night.

"No, Highness, I fear not," he said, sighing gustily. "And the other torches—merely a second party seeking Your Highness's hospitality, I suspect."

The noise outside was growing louder. Cat-calls could be distinguished; and vulgar jests, drunken wit, the shrill voices of women.

"Why, in God's name, I didn't get away . . ." panted Prince Mikhail.

The valet comforted him. "They but come for the Armenian youth, Highness. He exceeded all reasonable bounds."

It might have been better for the Armenian youth just then had he entered less alarmingly than he did, blunderingly, hissing and choking, an animal knowing the jaws will soon close.

"What the hell do you mean by rushing in here?" Prince Mikhail bawled. "Get out . . . hide yourself somewhere."

Clawing at his patron's silk wrap, blinded by tears and almost beyond speech, Nubar Gashginkian was gazing up imploringly when, from the lower terrace, they heard the quick patter of many feet. That sound grew progressively louder when the mob, pushing among themselves for precedence, raced towards the stairs at each end which climbed in stages to the outer portico.

Prince Mikhail tore off the restraining hands. "You have brought this on yourself, you thrice-damned fool," he gasped.

Eyes rolling, the Armenian found words. "They'll tear me limb from limb," he shrieked. Floundering forward on his knees he made a frenzied grab and clung desperately to his dear Misha's hand. "Save me, Highness, oh save me. You promised me your protection, Highness. You said——"

The head of the house of Kaivanov kicked out with merciless violence. "You have shown yourself as not worthy of my protection," he bellowed. "Even a half-wit would have recognized that I merely jested. Why should I be involved because of your crass folly, as I may well be?"

That restored the old fear, and colour drained from his cheeks. Ignoring the abjectly grovelling youth, Prince Mikhail huskily addressed his servant:

"Are you sure, Leonid Borisovitch, that they come only for this craven creature? Are you really sure?"

The valet met his master's glance boldly, with absolute assurance. "That is so, Highness," he said. "Nothing more than that, Highness."

Prince Mikhail's shuddering breath became easier, relief spreading like a soothing unguent across his face.

"Highness," Nubar Gashginkian moaned.

He was regarded quite dispassionately. "You would do well to take to your heels without delay, and if you can provide yourself with other apparel your escape may be facilitated," Prince Mikhail remarked. "You will find money somewhere or other in my——"

"Highness!"

"Though I imagine you will have purloined gold before now, and will be fully aware of where it is," Prince Mikhail resumed conversationally. "But I would advise you to make haste, my dear boy, extreme haste or otherwise. . . ."

But it was too late already, as perhaps the youth's strangled cry proclaimed. Springing to his feet he stared dementedly at the sea of faces confronting him; cruel faces everywhere, first jammed in the windows, and then pouring through the two doorways.

A pace or so inside, the intruders momentarily hesitated, such was the force of tradition; after that, foot by foot, they advanced further, fanning wider into the room.

Their spokesman was a dark-complexioned fellow wearing a heavy sheepskin cap, a long, moth-eaten coat, and blood-stained trousers tucked into high felt boots.

"The Armenian there, Highness," he snarled. "We want him."

Prince Mikhail's eyebrows went up, but he did not otherwise reprove them. "His behaviour, I now regretfully understand, has been somewhat overbearing," he said coldly. "I am not fully informed but I believe he has lent himself to practices I would not permit in my lawfully-appointed Steward. Is that so?"

A confusion of tongues informed him of the accuracy of this statement, with chapter and verse concerning many an offence. When the babel died down Prince Mikhail sternly judged the matter.

"It is not conduct I can condone," he said. "I shall see to his suitable punishment."

The leader growled. "We'll see to his punishment. And here and now, while we can lay hands on him."

Prince Mikhail had sized up his visitors, a mixed party of Christians and Moslems. These were simple peasants who could be overawed, not dangerous city demagogues.

"Indeed," he retorted, his fine eyes flashing. "And pray since when, my good fellow, has a Kaivanov allowed others to usurp the——"

"All the same, Highness, we're handling this ourselves," the spokesman interrupted doggedly. "We'll deal with this defiler of our virgins."

"A defiler of *virgins*?" Prince Mikhail ejaculated.

"Yes, Highness . . . many of them."

It was the most severe shock of Prince Mikhail's life. "He has taken *women*?" he asked, still incredulous.

"He has, Highness, our young daughters. And we have proof."

As soon as he realized beyond question what had been afoot, Prince Kaivanov reddened dully. Outraged, shaking with fury, he glanced briefly over his shoulder towards the youth. The Armenian, gibbering, shrank against the colourful hangings on the far wall, his hands constantly making tiny ineffectual movements.

"In that case," he said, in a voice quivering with loathing, "I must stand aside. There are offences *and* offences. This one is covered by laws centuries old, the unwritten laws of our Caucasus."

As if to dissociate himself from what must follow, he reached for a decanter and poured himself a stiff measure.

"Highness!" Nubar Gashginkian shrieked.

Apart from a high-pitched scream, cut off short, this was the last sound the youth made on earth.

When the evil-smelling throng shuffled out not long afterwards Prince Mikhail sniffed delicately, wafted a handkerchief and petulantly eyed crumpled Persian rugs and marks made by dungy feet. Once, considering the impertinence of the intrusion, he clasped his fists in rage and bit his lip in anger, but his mood changed when he noticed the bloody horror in a corner.

"Leonid Borisovitch," he said, close to vomiting. "That horrible thing, as ghastly in death as, unknown to me, he must have been in life . . . have his carcass removed . . . and fetch perfume . . . and a spray. This place is simply dreadful."

A steadily increasing noise, the tramp of feet, drove from Prince Mikhail's mind any further thoughts about the young Armenian, or his remains. He darted to a window and, peering down, watched a column of men winding along the curving avenue. At the last bend, leaving the lines of tapering poplars behind, the leading files swung to the left on a tiled walk in the landscaped garden, their torches reflected in the dark water of the artificial pool.

"Who are these?" Prince Mikhail whispered, handkerchief fluttering to the floor from limp fingers. "What do they want?"

Most carefully Leonid Borisovitch scrutinized the newcomers. "A mere desire for wordiness, I would say, Highness," he remarked, shrugging away any possibility of danger. "But is it your Highness's wish that I ascertain the exact reason for their call?"

"Do so." Prince Mikhail's nod carried further than his reply.

Leonid Borisovitch expressively held out upturned hands when he returned. "They but crave speech with your Highness and await your pleasure," he repeated as if fully justified. "And, Highness, if I may be so bold as to suggest——"

"Yes, yes?"

The valet leered. "A little refreshment for them afterwards, Highness. It is wisdom, if your Highness will pardon me, to pander to such as these in this unfortunate time."

Fear was ebbing from his master's face. "You will arrange it while I attend to them," Prince Mikhail said eagerly. "Wine in abundance, vodka by the tub——"

Firmly Leonid Borisovitch intervened: "No spirits, Highness," he said.

Servant looked knowingly at master, master looked understandingly at servant.

"I . . . I shall not forget this, Leonid Borisovitch, thou *very* faithful one," Prince Mikhail said, immensely moved.

Left by himself, Leonid Borisovitch wandered down the room, drawn despite himself by a fearsome sight, the body of Nubar Gashginkian. Then turning away, he reached towards a jewelled box for a cigarette. A divan was nearby; he sank on to it, crossed his legs comfortably, and struck a match on the chasing of a silver lamp. From an array on a low table he selected a slender flagon and tossed the stopper away in a high arc; the small piece of cut-glass rolled scintillatingly and, as liquid gurgled, he watched its movements with deep-set eyes. Impassively he drank, impassively he took a second drag at the newly-lighted cigarette before flicking it behind him with thumb and finger.

After that he rose, and, stifling a yawn, decided to seek his master. He followed a different route, however: through an arched opening, past low gates, beautifully wrought in silver, which he savagely slammed, thence into a long corridor. At the extreme end, outlined against the night by the flickering light from below, he perceived a long-familiar figure.

From the extreme end of the upper terrace the head of the house of Kaivanov stared down three flights of steps, towards the crowd at the bottom.

"My good people," he said, smiling and persuasively, "if one of you at a time will address me we shall proceed much quicker."

After vague rumblings, a young man stepped forward, the yellow flame from the torches shadowing the contours of his thin face.

"Mikhail Pavlych Kaivanov," he began, with a pompousness oddly at variance with a gangling appearance. "In pursuance of orders issued by the Tiflis Committee of the People's Government of the Caucasus which has been established for the solemn purpose of casting off the shackles whereby the common——"

"Get to what counts," a gruff voice advised him.

Obviously the student contemplated an objection, but a glance at the grim faces of those about him was a sufficient deterrent. Nervously he started off again but, though he adhered to a memorized oration, he discarded entirely an accent of spurious gentility, the result of two years at the University of Rostov imposed upon a peasant upbringing.

"We, an accredited detachment of the People's Army of Tiflis, being instructed to bring to summary justice the persons of those who have offended against the will of the people. . . ."

"Christ, how much longer," someone shouted.

For an accredited military body they were a motley crew; some in ankle-length *caftans*, others in the stiff black *cherkesskas* of the mountain folk; shaggy felt cavalry cloaks were there, and shoddy suits of the western world.

"Up the steps!" The brazen-lunged cry reverberated, its echoes thrown back by palace buildings. "Up the steps!" The demand grew.

Through slowly drifting smoke Prince Mikhail Kaivanov's frightened eyes glimpsed a strange assortment of weapons, and fearsome devices to mutilate and hurt. There were men with a spiked, flesh-tearing ring on their right thumbs, and others who, despite a surfeit of cartridges carried in belts criss-crossing their chests, could flourish nothing more soldierly than a butcher's long knife or the cruel *nagaika* for whipping.

"Hold!" he screamed to them. "We must discuss sensibly any complaints you may have. But perhaps, to begin with, you would care for something sustaining, say a glass or two of. . . ."

The torches swirled and swayed in spirals as their bearers were convulsed with belly-deep laughter. Within a matter of seconds, however, the dance of those flaring points of light became erratic, red sparks flying when a bitter struggle began between the exponents of revenge on the spot, without further parley, and the supporters of quasi-judicial procedure. The academic-minded, quickly thrust aside, were replaced by men with blood-lust in their eyes.

"Hold!" Prince Mikhail screamed again.

Had he stood his ground valiantly from the onset he might have dominated them, as Prince Aleksiei Dolumsky had done at Vladkhaz, ninety versts away; or possibly, with an exquisitely subtle jest, he could even have turned this audience into a flock of hilarious sheep—two days before, in that fashion, Prince Andrew Ramankinov had saved himself and his family.

But nothing of this nature occurred—Leonid Borisovitch shoved him much too hard for that.

For eleven steps and a landing, three flights repeated, Prince Mikhail somersaulted and slithered, every moment of his headlong descent heralded by an ear-piercing cry.

But at the bottom he was quite silent when, bleeding and bruised by his fall, he confronted his enemies. Strangely enough, an attempt at escape did not appear to be in his mind. It may be that, under the acute stress of his hopeless situation, he had been able to draw upon the power and strength of his redoubtable grandfather. Whatever it was, in those dying minutes of his life —and for the first time in his life—Prince Mikhail Kaivanov fleetingly showed himself as a formidable personage.

"You unpleasant carrion," he remarked, very distinctly.

About then he chanced to glimpse his valet. Leonid Borisovitch was standing a couple of paces behind, smiling openly, unholy satisfaction in deep-set eyes.

His expression quite unchanged, Prince Mikhail went on: "The dregs of humanity, every one of you," he said with devastating scorn. "The scum of the earth would be a flattering description of you."

A growl of anger was rising when with the swiftness of a panther he spun about. Leaping forward, he seized Leonid Borisovitch and, using his now-shrieking servant as a shield, jumped into the thickest part of the press, an onslaught so violent and unexpected that torches were knocked out of hands, and men, excited and often off-balance, struck with gleaming steel not always as accurately as was desirable.

A period of confusion followed. At its conclusion two men were dead: Prince Mikhail Kaivanov and Leonid Borisovitch, the servitor who had betrayed him.

Although forever oblivious to earthly pain and physical blemishes, Prince Mikhail received further attention. His body was hacked, stabbed and clubbed again and again, and when each and all of his assailants had contributed an honourable share, what remained of his handsome face was kicked in. As final embroidery, they bent his legs backward and folded them around his neck.

After inspecting this human spider, one of them remarked with a broad grin: "He ran from the wolf and fell in with the bear."

The following morning Prince Mikhail's Cossacks found his stiffened, gruesome remains. Four of them tugged to replace the main members in a more life-like position, and others rough-stitched him together. Then he was washed carefully.

A *sotnia* leader wrote out a message. Thirty of his men guarded him on a furious ride to the railway and the telegraph line.

That telegram was destined to see many sunrises as it flashed along the wires, and many sunsets as it languished uncared for on some untidy desk.

It went first to Tiflis, over which, wherever the capital of the People's Government of the Caucasus might be, the Russian eagle still flew, though only at the expense of martial law. From there a soldier telegraphist who had taken over a revolutionary's post re-despatched the message, consigning it the long way, for the line to Batoum was down in a hundred places, broken faster than repairs could be made. He tapped the letters out grinningly—and so speedily as to provoke indecent language from the civilian operator at Baku.

Across the fierce Khevsur lands, where coats-of-mail, iron-bound shields, hour-glasses, chain armour and two-handed swords were in commonplace use, the news of death travelled, winding along high mountain passes from whose summits the angry glow of natural beacons could be seen, a blaze of combustible gases issuing through surface fissures from the incalculable oil-bearing shales below.

So to Baku, where Parsee fire-worshippers witnessed more than they bargained for when disgruntled workmen from the "black" part of the city, after firing refineries and naphtha stores, surged to the "white" part of mosques and fine buildings and converted them also into crackling pyres. Here, nearly choked by thick smoke, the civilian operator, who was out of humour with his buffoon of a military opposite number at Tiflis, relayed the ill-tidings to the other side of the Caspian, a journey of a hundred and sixty-five miles.

Thus to Krasnodorsk, beginning of the Trans-Caspian Railway, where a ragged telegraphist ate hard-boiled eggs with spring onions; and, to fill up, shovelled caviare into his mouth with a crust of chaff-adulterated black bread.

Next, after some delay, into the telegraph office at Merv, where blinds were tightly drawn against a blistering sun. There the staff were squat in figure, with dark yellow complexions and slits of eyes; here they smoked and played cards day and night, mortgaging pay for years ahead to settle gambling losses. At Merv a branch line swerved off to the borders of Afghanistan, a well-kept track which, carrying little merchandise, was viewed with no small concern by military and political officers in India.

Now Kara Kum and the silent Oxus river, a sizzling stage.

To Bokhara, a Venice in the desert, where looms shuttled lazily and power to drive them would be considered a grievous sin against Allah above.

Into oven-hot Samarkand, in which Russian flags were being trampled underfoot and eight men, for a start, swung by their necks in a line. And so on to Tashkent in Turkestan, and what a revel of Jew-baiting it was there. That afternoon a noble gentleman won fanatical applause by jumping his horse over a Hebrew hearse; the next day, freakish fate, he was himself spiritedly hunted out of the town.

But by then the sad intelligence was beyond the northern tip of Lake Aral, where the singing wires glimpsed a barren shore off which seals played in blue waters stretching for two or three hundred miles.

Three days after a *sotnia* leader had been pencil-chewing while in the throes of composition, the telegram arrived in Orenburg, where it might easily have ended its journey. In the telegraph office, illuminated by flames from a clothier's warehouse, a hook-nosed clerk was unquestionably neglecting his duty. Round and round he walked, mouthing incoherently; again and again he tried a lock, wedged still another piece of wood behind the door, peered once more with blood-streaked eye through a knot-hole, stopped his ears to harrowing screams, or rubbed sweaty palms together while desperately wondering what to do.

His glance fell upon a pile of forms. Perhaps in work there might be forgetfulness; he seated himself, picked up the top sheet, meantime his right hand, which in normal conditions went about its business automatically, vacillated for an appreciable period above the ebony knob of the transmitting key before Samara's call-sign began to be tapped out. In due course he became more absorbed although once, after glancing at the clock for timing purposes, a thought struck him and, hurriedly rising, he examined himself side face and front in a mirror, paying the closest attention to a nose whose boldness bespoke its origins. Whimpering, he shook his head and was returning disconsolately to his stool when brought up starkly by a thunderous assault on the door.

That was how a flimsy addressed to the new head of the house of Kaivanov, which chanced to be in the upper layer of the batch, passed forward in the nick of time, long before the Chief of Police learnt that the sole remaining telegraphist had lost his life during the course of a deplorable affray.

At Samara, whose buildings were always coated with grey dust from the big flour mills, conditions were very different, jolly and sociable, with poker players indistinct through the eddying smoke of particularly choice tobacco. Wines and spirits were stacked everywhere, fruits also of a fortunate raid.

Then onwards, across mighty Volga, flying past villages—distinguished by a signpost stating name and number of souls—completely surrounded by wattle fencing to contain the community's live-stock, where country clergy peacefully tended their land and used their axes as skilfully as any other man, whether for felling a tree or fashioning a neat overlapping joint.

Now into the extensive junction at Penza where, owing to the more direct line to Ryask being "dead" for fifty-five hours, all telegraphic traffic was switched north.

To Nizhni Novgorod and the stink of tanning, where business men laboured, such is optimism, to set out wares attractively in the stone buildings of the Fair Town. In this ancient mart the telegraph department was functioning quite admirably, but in an earth-closet adjoining the office two nervously-sweating clerks had just opened a massive square box. It was labelled "Perishable"; sent by comrade miners in the Urals it had reached them safely, thanks to co-operation by railway workers. Swiftly the pair did their respective jobs, one with dynamite and the other in the fine setting of cog wheels, both with ears alert for a sudden visitation from those remorseless devils of the Okhrana.

They were interrupted by a colleague, a thoughtful-looking, youngish man with a lantern jaw, who very deliberately put a cigarette in his mouth and prepared to light it.

"So this is what you're up to, is it?" he said.

Panicking, one of the clerks leapt forward to snatch the match. "You'll kill all of us if you're not careful," he hissed.

"And that would be a real miscarriage of justice, wouldn't it?" the newcomer mused. "And, by the way, there's a question I'd like to ask you—have either of you had a close view of a bomb explosion just after it's taken place?"

His behaviour was so strange that the others looked at each other quickly, and then, eyes narrowing, at him.

"What's wrong with you?" one inquired, thinly.

"Only this, that it's all right trying to kill the high-ups, *so long* as you can be sure of hurting them only."

All three were blood-brothers in the same secret society, but two by now were convinced of danger in their midst.

"So you're not with us?" the elder said, half under his breath.

Slowly the lantern-jawed man shook his head. "Not in this, comrades," he admitted, paler than ever. "Because it means more often than not the maiming and killing of innocent people. I've seen it for myself, and I shall do what I can to stop such an inhumane business."

The younger clerk appealed to him. "Mitya, we're aware that others frequently suffer, and we grieve about it, but that's part of the price we have to pay."

The objector again shook his head. "No, the paying is often done by men and women and children who are guiltless in every sense." He turned, adding as he grasped the door-handle. "Just think it over, you two."

It did not need thinking over and, before the catch of the door clicked, each of the clerks had made up his mind. That night a man would be denounced as a traitor to the society whose oath he had taken, which would mean his death within days.

Meanwhile the advice of a nobleman's hideous departure raced through the rye country, where servant girls with long shining hair, plaited and ribboned, still sang in chorus at night or danced to the bagpipes and the balalaika. Twenty feet above the shimmering track of the Siberian Railway the humming Morse now ran, passing eastward-bound trains crammed with glowering troops munching away at their daily ration: three pounds of rye bread and an ounce of salt to dust over it; passing other trains, too, trains stuck in sidings for hours and days, waiting for a lull in the stream of more essential freight. These trains, made up of sorry-looking rolling stock, windowless and unsprung, were packed with one-way warrant passengers, male and female, consigned to the penal settlements of Siberia.

But a movement even more secret and important than that of military reinforcements was expected, and through the evening and in the succeeding darkness of night the pot insulators at the tops of creosoted poles looked down, every dozen versts or so, at small camps whose fires, within the zone of light they cast, gleamed upon the bared bayonets of closely-spaced soldiers standing on both sides of the track, a gapless steel-guarded corridor extending for many hundreds of miles through which, this day or maybe another, an all-blue train would rush, drawn by an engine displaying on its boiler the Emperor's eagles in shining brass. Or, rather, there would be two identical trains, and at the first sign of the leading one, in which the Autocrat might or might not be travelling, these soldiers would take up the Third Position: about turn, bringing their backs to the metals, count one-two, then quick-march away at right-angles to the railroad line, with eyes rigidly to the fore, advancing into cornfields or waste until the rumble of iron wheels faded in the distance, when a return could be made.

A breathtaking leap to Moscow, where "patriots" and revolutionaries alike overturned horse-trams to form street barriers.

On its final section to St. Petersburg the telegram to Commander Prince Ivan Kaivanov lingered in both Tver and Bologoe.

At Tver the station-master's room and the telegraph office were a sad spectacle, filled with the survivors of a train which had crashed over a nearby bridge, from whose middle span wreckers had removed a section of rail.

Gravely injured men, women and children, bleeding, moaning or unconscious, were still being carried in. A shabbily-clad doctor attended to them—he gave of his utmost, meantime swearing unmeaningly about a convention, honoured by his own kind, which insisted that it was against professional etiquette for a medical man either to send in a bill to a patient or even state his charge if he were asked.

The Governor of Novgorod was the target at which the sabotage had been aimed. He was quite unhurt, though pale and shaken.

"I shall recompense you for your services, Doctor," he said wearily. "It will be in thanksgiving to the Almighty for sparing me."

"Who the devil is bothering about money?" the doctor snarled. His expression changed. "God!" he went on, wiping perspiration off his brow with the back of his hand. "No, your Excellency, I am not really concerned about payment. What I am concerned about is that these things should be . . . that in this year of grace the mentality of so many Russians has not progressed beyond that of Genghis Khan's cruel followers. What else can explain these blind excesses, this lust to destroy the few at any cost?"

Next on to Bologoe, where a highly-intellectual eye-shaded telegraph operator, deliberately breaking contact both ways, settled down to read Pushkin in the soft rays of a kerosene lamp. That is, until he heard the errand on which his be-shawled, full-bosomed wife was bound—that of acting wet-nurse to the Provincial Councillor's child. Yes, a few roubles always come in handy, but in a flash he became a red-hot revolutionary and in his rage hurled a metal Coronation goblet at her, splitting open her forehead.

In St. Petersburg the telegraph staff was working slowly, very slowly, reasoning quite soundly that absence of information and messages hopelessly delayed add their quota to the general confusion. An important priority communication from the Commander-in-Chief, Sevastopol, had been held up for three days, by unspoken agreement between the telegraph boys along its route, before it reached the Admiralty. That was good.

But a telegram handed in by a *sotnia* leader at a remote sub-station in the Caucasus was six days before it arrived in the capital. That was bad.

The clerk who received it snorted, and swivelled in his chair. "Some of these country bumpkins haven't as much wit as a Romanov," he announced, waving the offending message. "This should have come through faster than the wind. News of this sort—another big pot *unexpectedly* gone to glory—demoralizes the noble scoundrels."

Newspapers, cigarettes, cards, books, all were abandoned. His colleagues had to laugh.

"Here, you," he went on, trying not to laugh himself as he spoke to a youthful messenger. "Get this delivered, sharp. And never mind telling me it's after the official time. I know that myself."

So it was that at twelve minutes after midnight, two hours and fifty minutes before the scheduled departure of a special train to Sevastopol, Commander Prince Ivan Kaivanov learnt of Prince Mikhail's murder.

That evening, for once, he and his wife were together, host and hostess at an impromptu party in their home. As soon as he read the fatal lines Prince Ivan quietly rose and, the gravity and sorrow in his expression evident to all, apologized to their guests before gently drawing Princess Zeneide into the next room, where he showed her the telegram.

"My poor dear father," he said, a catch in his voice.

Princess Ivan, a full-blooded woman, had never been enamoured of her pervert father-in-law. But it was now certain that conditions in the Caucasus were extremely critical, and she was a Ghambashaidze, after all.

"How horrible," she gasped. "Oh, I do hope Papa and Mama are safe. I haven't heard from them for ages."

Though she was a Georgian, and he had married her, Prince Ivan's respect for the nobility of those parts was not outstanding.

He shrugged. "They'll wriggle out, one way or another."

That was hardly pleasant, and his wife, eyes flashing storm warnings, would have been justified in taking umbrage. However, he immediately captured her interest with a worried comment.

"This places me in an awkward position," he muttered.

She stared. "Whatever do you mean?"

"I have this urgent appointment in Sevastopol, haven't I?"

"But I still don't understand," she persisted.

Patiently trying to explain, he began to pace to and fro, brow furrowed with perplexity, hands clasped behind his back. To begin with he spoke with great warmth about Isvoltoff, the sole person with the knowledge and capacity to deal with affairs in his absence.

"But you see, my dear, even a lawyer has his limits," he continued. "He may be quite sound with deeds and settlements and what-not, but practical details to do with vast estates are out of his line of country. It really is a ghastly dilemma."

Princess Ivan did not appear to be any more enlightened. "But why?" she asked.

He turned towards her. "My dear," he said, "you seem to forget that my unfortunate father had enormous properties, which I inherit."

Touchy already, this remark was taken by his wife as a reflection upon her own family whose lands, such as remained to them, were mortgaged to the hilt.

"Of course," she snapped, "the many realms of the Kaivanovs, each a small kingdom in itself, with their mines, oil wells, granaries, private railways, timber mills——"

Pained, he restrained her. "I own much, I know," he said. "And with it I now have great responsibilities."

At that they parted, she to return to their friends, to whom she would present his excuses; he to his study, where he could think matters over.

Shortly before one o'clock Prince Ivan hit upon a partial solution to his problem. Before the first quarter after the hour struck he reached a room in the Admiralty, where once again he sat within arm's length of Countess Tseragina's portrait.

Sixteen minutes later he made still another desperate appeal. "But, sir, in a week or perhaps a little longer——"

Admiral Count Tseragin was tired; a bluff old salt-horse, a strict sense of duty only had made him accept a post confining him to a desk. He appreciated keenness in his officers, but he was weary of being badgered.

"My dear Kaivanov," he interposed as calmly as he could. "You know perfectly well, gloss it over as you will, that you could not be ready in two weeks, let alone one. The difficulties you have mentioned arising out of your father's lamented death and the imperative need to resolve without delay the complexities in his French investments make any trifling period ridiculous. It can't be done without reasonable time."

Crestfallen, Prince Ivan nodded miserably. "I suppose not, sir. But . . ." he was shaken with quick anger, "I'll take damned good care in future that not a copeck of our money is ever invested abroad."

Admiral Tseragin was not interested in high finance. "You will be given immediate leave, and you will report for duty again in two months' time," he said abruptly.

Prince Ivan gazed unseeingly into the dark night. "I missed Tsu Shima, sir," he murmured. "And now I am robbed of serving those Sevastopol dogs with their deserts."

"My dear Kaivanov, there will be plenty for you to do when you come back." Admiral Tseragin's smile was grim until he noticed the wall-clock, when he swore irritably as he thumbed a bell-push. "I'm sending Commander Zelouky in your place. That is," he growled, "if I can find the fellow."

"An old shipmate of mine, sir." Prince Ivan quite failed to disguise his envy. "Wasn't it he who cleaned up the revolutionaries in Reval?"

"Mopped 'em up and dumped them into fire buckets," Admiral Count Tseragin grunted. "But where the hell I shall find him at this hour is more than I know."

His caller ventured a request, faltering a little boyishly. "I've an idea of old Dmitri Semenovitch's favourite haunts, and if, sir, you will permit me to have a shot at rooting him out I . . . I shall feel that in some degree I am contributing to your plans."

This explains why, at a quarter to four in the morning, Prince Ivan was assisting a nearly-sobered ex-shipmate into a special train whose despatch, on Admiral Tseragin's orders, had been held back until the arrival of the most recently-appointed member of the court martial. Present also were Captain Prince Shulovsky and Commander Tianov, with whom, as the signal for departure was given, Commander Prince Kaivanov tearfully shook hands. Prince Ivan was indeed woefully affected and, as the train pulled out of the screened-off and guarded platform, he stood a lonely figure, head sunk into chest, unaware of comrades who, waving farewells, sought to hearten a man so much in the grip of despair.

In the absence of Miss Brown, nursing a cold in bed, and of their apple-cheeked old nannie, who was visiting a nephew wounded in street fighting, the Kaivanov children were having a wonderful day.

It began on a high note, when their father came to the nursery to break the news of their grandfather's death. The occasion was solemn, naturally, but it was thrilling also, especially when Mlle Sachot, their French mistress, rushed off in an hysterical outburst.

In effect that "wonderful day" belonged exclusively to the daughter of the house. Thanks to Mademoiselle's nervousness, and her inability to enforce discipline, both of which involved frequent disappearances, Princess Anastasia had suffered few checks, and to date her brother had been bayoneted as a Japanese, executed as a revolutionary, manacled as a prisoner, shot as a traitor, tortured as an Armenian, and very nearly burnt as a Jew.

A box of matches, and his sister's demoniacal expression, finished Prince Sergei entirely. "You're not, Stana," he sobbed. "You've hurt me already, and——"

"Oh well, big baby," Princess Anastasia jeered and amused herself by striking matches quickly until none were left. "And..." she thrust gleaming, unwinking black eyes forward until their faces were only an inch apart, "and if you tell tales to Brownie I'll... I'll peel the skin off your nose."

A piece of quicksilver always, and desiring refreshment, Anastasia abandoned her brother. This release provided Sergei, who had taken a back seat all day, with a spell during which he might show off. Belatedly bent on making an impression he hurriedly dragged out a stool and, clambering on to it, stretched beyond a shelf containing among other books, *David Copperfield,* which their governess was now reading to them at bedtime. Arm at full length he triumphantly grasped a Danish clay-pig money-box, which he rattled noisily to draw attention.

"I know how to get money out of this," he boasted. "Bet you don't know how to get——" His sister was making a hideous row sucking an orange, and he was compelled to repeat himself in a much louder voice. "And nobody," he finished up slyly, "can tell anything has been taken out, not even Brownie."

Young Princess Anastasia dashed the back of her hand across a juice-glistening mouth. Eyebrows elevated, faint smile derisive, she glanced at him with supreme boredom.

"*Really,* my dear," she drawled, imitating an aunt.

Tongue out, Prince Sergei fumbled away with a purloined table-knife and, although failing several times when near achievement, he might subsequently have captured one of the coins if his watchful sister had not, at the critical moment, undermined a mammoth tower. The avalanche of wooden bricks startled him, and the elusive piece of silver, jerked from the blade, slipped inside again.

"That isn't fair," he stormed. "You made me jump."

Considering his temper, which hardly assisted delicate manipulation, it must have been more good luck than good management which caused his very next attempt to be successful.

"Look, Stana," he screeched. "Here, in my hand."

Anastasia promptly kicked over a neatly-arranged company of the Empress's Own Crimean Regiment.

"That's only one," she scoffed. "It would take you years and years and years to get four out."

Tears not far distant, her brother at once relinquished the clay-pig and ran to his beloved playthings. "It wouldn't," he wailed, "and leave my soldiers alone. And . . . and . . ."—his lips quivered when he found a broken leg—"and I'll bet you can't get them out any quicker."

In a furious medley of English, French, German and a little Russian, Anastasia expressed a contrary opinion.

" 'Course I can, dolt," she wound up contemptuously.

Beside himself with anxiety, Sergei was still kneeling. "You've broken three of my . . . bet you can't," he said shrilly.

That was sufficient. Princess Anastasia snatched up the money-box which a moment later was shattered into pieces against the playroom wall, its silver contents falling to the floor, where the coins rolled in diminishing curves.

"Now can't I?" she crowed with wicked glee.

The only daughter of the house of Kaivanov, dismissing without a second thought a partially-completed pen-wiper which Brownie had set her to do for a Christmas present, sought fresh diversion. To her intense gratification, as if she had waved a magic wand, she decided privately, this immediately arrived in the person of Mlle Sachot, who entered as rifle reports in the streets, heard for many days and nights, fortunately rose to a larger volume than of late.

"Oh, mademoiselle," she cried, running to the wan-faced French mistress and clinging to her arm. "Those awful revolutionaries are much, much closer now. Do you think they will dare to try to burst our doors in?"

In endeavouring, without Miss Brown's support to fall back on, to cope with this wilful young creature, Mlle Sachot had had a dreadful day. For weeks, too, she had been quaking, firmly convinced that barbaric Russia, so uncivilized compared with *La France*, was on the eve of an epoch whose horrors would be far more fearful than those that stained her own country's annals a little over a century before.

"But certainly not," she replied not at all convincingly. "And, my dear, you must be quieter than you have been. I have a terrible headache."

Her charge's expression revealed sweet concern only. "Poor, poor mademoiselle," Princess Anastasia said, lowering her voice to a tender whisper. "Of course, I will be as quiet as a little mouse. But please, dear mademoiselle, do tell me what those nasty men would do if they came in. Would they kill Papa and Mama, and Sergei Ivanovitch and me, as they did poor Grandpapa?"

"Anastasia!" Mlle Sachot gasped.

"How was Grandpapa killed?" the inquisitor asked wheedlingly, in the same considerately hushed tone. "Did they slit his wind-pipe?"

"Anastasia!" Mademoiselle said faintly.

To that young lady's carefully-concealed delight another fusillade started in the neighbourhood, and she at once racked her agile brain for a means to take further advantage of this background of strife. Her efforts were not unsuccessful, for within three minutes Mlle Sachot was again tottering off tearfully to her room.

In actual fact, except in the opinion of luckless individuals surviving hits by stray bullets, or sorrowing relatives, the firing was insignificant, and as such was quite ignored by Princess Anastasia's father, whose dressing-room windows were on the same side.

At the identical moment of Mlle Sachot's withdrawal from the playroom, Prince Ivan's sailor servant was speaking to him.

"Highness," he said, "there is the luggage to be put aboard the train. When I have finished packing is it permitted I cast off for the station, Highness?"

Prince Ivan nodded. "By all means, Pavel Pavlych. You reserved a *coupé* for me, eh? In the name of Amsibu, as I directed?"

"Yes, Highness."

Cogitating, Commander Prince Kaivanov's glance passed from gold-mounted walking-stick to an elegant Homburg hat, thence to a mirror in which he saw himself in a well-cut dark grey worsted suit from whose breast-pocket a tasteful handkerchief peeped out. But he frowned on perceiving a pair of lemon-coloured gloves, and had them exchanged for others more nearly in keeping with mourning.

"Mmm . . ." he murmured after that, eyeing the Homburg again. "You might as well take that hat to the station, and bring me an old cap in its place. Also . . . yes . . . find me a light overcoat, one somewhat . . . er . . . dingy in hue, for me to wear now while crossing the town. In these days, Pavel Pavlych, isn't it folly to run unnecessary risks?"

The servant grasped his meaning. "Assuredly, Highness," he agreed. "And, anyhow, Highness, is not the coat as warm without the lace as with it?"

"An old saying, and a very true one," Prince Ivan commented gravely.

There were still two outstanding private matters to attend to: he must again speak to his widowed mother, this time to make his excuses for not calling upon her before departure; and he must bid his wife *au revoir* in person.

Towards disposing of the first of these, Commander Prince Kaivanov vigorously turned the handle at the side of the wall telephone.

Princess Ivan Kaivanova's boudoir was a scene of domestic bliss. A yellow-backed French novel lay open on a rug and, although the afternoon was mild and the intricately-scrolled main stove not lighted, flickering rays from a wood fire in an open grate were reflected brightly in shining silverware on a low Turkish table.

To the left of the fireplace a good-looking young man, one of the Secretaries of the Embassy at Tokio until the outbreak of war, reclined in a graceful attitude, balancing a plate on his knee with consummate ease. Close to a small, bubbling samovar, his hostess sat at the other side of the table, charming in a lacy *négligée* into which she had changed after returning with her escort from a *matinée* at the Dvorianskoe Sobranie in aid of wounded soldiers, at which Kyasht had danced to a capacity audience.

Earlier they had decided that Prince Mikhail's death need not interfere with their plans, but now Princess Ivan was pouting.

"But really, my dear, a fortnight," she protested. "Honestly, I simply can't stand this place even a week longer. But the country is in too frightful a condition to risk going to the Crimea, and as for opening the villa at Peterhof . . ." she shuddered. "No, not with those fiends of sailors so near at Kronstadt. So, darling, you must please realize I shall do exactly as I have said, which means I shan't be in Russia much longer."

"But, Zeneide, my own, surely you can wait. After all, His Excellency has promised me leave before the month's end, so why not be sensible?"

Princess Kaivanova's dark eyes flashed. "You could get away sooner if you really made an effort."

"My dearest, I shall travel by the earliest possible train."

Having made this emphatic promise Baron Kovolin rose lissomly, walked round the table and, bending over her shoulder, passionately kissed her in an intriguing hollow which allowed him a sight of swelling white breasts.

"All the same, darling, I shall definitely start out for Budapest on Tuesday," she told him, quite mollified. "You know I have telegraphed Papa insisting he and Mama should meet me there. Of course, if they were unable to join me," she murmured, veiled amusement in her eyes, "you would be there to console me, and what a blessing that would be, dearest."

"I would try, my darling," Baron Kovolin promised, his voice deepening.

They looked at each other with mutual satisfaction and understanding. Moved by thoughts of pleasures in store she stretched across to squeeze his hand, while he undoubtedly would have given further proof of his ardour had not her husband arrived.

"Ah, my dear Baron," Prince Ivan said heartily, rising superior to the sorrow and cares so plainly besetting him. "And felicitations to you, my dear . . . as lovely as ever, I see."

"Thank you, Ivan Mikhailovitch." His wife smiled.

"My condolences, Prince." Baron Kovolin spoke with suitable feeling. "A shocking business, my heart bleeds for you in the loss of your dear father."

"Yes." Commander Prince Kaivanov stared into space.

A few moments later he again endeavoured to put aside personal tribulation, and referred to the children.

"I've said good-bye to 'em," he remarked with a chuckle. "And, by Jove, isn't Stana becoming a little devil? She'll be a handful to some fellow one of these days . . . or to quite a few, more likely."

His wife's exquisite face was transformed by a scowl. "You know I am utterly weary of Miss Brown or that silly Frenchwoman asking for a talk with me about her . . . or positively demanding it," she said fretfully, gesticulating with annoyance. "After all, one employs people for these things, and. . . ." The topic was shrugged aside when she pointed to the samovar. "Of course you will join us, Ivan Mikhailovitch?"

Prince Kaivanov held out his hands regretfully. "I'm afraid I haven't time, my dear. My train, y'know."

"Paris the divine, isn't it?" Baron Kovolin said. "I am truly sorry about the circumstances clouding your trip, but surely it will do you good—a wonderful change from this rabble-filled hole."

Ruefully Prince Ivan shook his head. "It won't be easy for me to forget that while I am absent I shall be contributing nothing practical towards crushing these vermin. That, as I needn't remind you, is a duty incumbent on every true patriot."

Baron Kovolin stiffened. "It is an aspect which has not eluded me," he said.

Despite the conciliatory phrasing there was a touch of malice in Prince Ivan's reply. "My dear Baron," he expostulated, "I intended no reference to yourself. You people in the Diplomatic are in quite a different street from officers in the fighting services —your battlefield is the conference room, ours in combat . . . each, I daresay, as deadly as the other, though possibly a little more comfortable in one case."

Inwardly elated by the nasty dig he had given his wife's lover, Prince Ivan subsequently told the inside story of what hitherto had been regarded as a strange suicide. Confidentially related to him the previous night by Commander Tianov, it concerned the late Austro-Hungarian naval attaché, Count von Schmalandorf. This gentleman, recently married to Princess Irma Anovachevskova had shot himself before breakfast time of the day following the nuptial night.

"You've heard of the Austrian custom in which the bridegroom makes a gift to his bride for the loss of her virginity," Prince Ivan went on, hard pressed to keep his face straight. "Well, apparently von Schmalandorf was the perfect gentleman to the bitter end. Next morning he duly presented his Countess with the *morgengabe* and then walked off to his dressing-room, where the damned fool put a bullet through his head."

"But everyone knows what Irma Adolfovna is," Princess Ivan exclaimed delightedly.

Baron Kovolin was taking alternate bites from a candied peach and a preserved strawberry. "With the exception of the simpleton who made her his wife," he remarked.

A volley from the direction of Vasili Island, rattling the windows, recalled to Prince Ivan the Paris train and flying minutes.

"Well, my dear Zeneide," he said, prelude to farewell.

The Princess, avid to pass on this tit-bit to her sister, was reaching towards a telephone hidden beneath the wide skirts of a beautifully-dressed doll.

"I must tell Linaida," she giggled.

"But you must excuse me, my dear," Prince Ivan said. "And do start out for Budapest as soon as you can. St. Petersburg is hardly the place for you, or any other woman. Don't you agree, Baron?"

"Emphatically, my dear fellow."

Prince Ivan's eyes sparkled and had he been of a more volatile nationality, and less under restraint from grief, he would unquestionably have kissed his finger-tips in adulation.

"Wonderful place, Budapest," he said. "The Erzsebet Park, the marvellous shops in the Karoly Korut and no hooligans to disturb you if you loiter to look in 'em; Franz Josef's Quai, enchanting to stroll along at the right hour; the shining waters of the Danube . . . superb!"

Still smiling, Prince Ivan bent to kiss his wife's hand and exchanged final compliments with them both.

When he went down, swarms of servants scurried out of his path as he passed through the second hall and the lower hall to his *troika* which, crests carefully painted out and its coachman attired in dun-coloured clothing, waited for him at the western door.

The drive to the station was not pleasant—along streets in which laying of tramlines for the new electric tramcars had ceased, where tools remained where they were when dropped by labourers rushing off to join the popular movement. Sometimes there would be a clear run ahead; at others neither master nor coachman dared to proceed at more than walking-pace when hemmed in by growling throngs who snarled abuse at the *burzhuis* occupying the carriage. Shrill agitators abounded and, a whim which had caught on, lines of hysterically-laughing citizens, competing in forcing jets of urine highest, relieved themselves against the Imperial monuments where, quite unmolested, distressed-looking white-bearded Palace Grenadiers in high shakoes and gold-embroidered uniforms stood on guard. There were quieter zones also, in lengthy streets through which cavalry might charge. In these, with scouts posted, sweating men rubbed soap on the cobblestones, while others slid about until the surface was sufficiently slippery to endanger even the surest-footed little Cossack horse.

A most disconcerting crossing.

No less disconcerting was the long railway journey through Russia, during which every water-tank out of order implied the probability of some hellish plant. The train ran hours behind schedule; every stop was an anxiety, and every town along the route a matter of apprehension until the state of the local revolution could be ascertained.

When, at last, freedom from care was attained, which meant that the gauge had changed and the frontier was now behind, Commander Prince Kaivanov belatedly remembered that in the haste of his departure he had quite forgotten Vera Nikolaevna. That must be remedied—perhaps at Vienna, or preferably in Paris, where he would have more time.

Unhappily he did not recall this firm resolution until the evening of his first full day in the French capital, just as he was paying off a *fiacre* in the Boulevard des Italiens, a few paces from the brilliantly-illuminated entrance of the Opera Comique. It was too late then, of course.

Even more unfortunately, he was guilty in this connection the next day also. Still, when one is lunching and supping a remarkably pretty young actress, and strolling with her in the late morning along the Avenue du Bois de Boulogne, a lapse of memory is excusable.

Nevertheless four days after his arrival Prince Ivan managed to put his conscience to rights.

To Vera Kalutkina he telegraphed undying love and his fervent hope that her heart, strained by too-severe rehearsal, would soon recover, so that, when the season began, she would once again enchant her audience at the Mariinsky. To little Mimi he sent a thousand kisses, and also telegraphed five hundred roubles' worth of flowers to each.

To his wife, the Princess Zeneide Kaivanova, he telegraphed his love and good wishes, and by another telegram instructed that the same value in blooms should be placed in her suite to greet her at Budapest.

Social observances fulfilled, he dashed off a short-tempered letter to his lawyer Isvoltoff, and another, highly blasphemous in the Navy manner but respectful—to Admiral Count Tseragin. In each he mentioned an infuriating difficulty he was experiencing, that of bringing French financiers to the point.

3

In September of the year of Prince Mikhail Kaivanov's foul murder Holy Russia was compelled to sign an ignominious treaty of peace with the Empire of the Mikado.

Yet, even with the war ended, even with that cause for unrest removed, a strike on the Trans-Siberian Railway was engineered, the blind fools responsible not realizing that this action penned in the Far East tens of thousands of their so-called soldier-comrades, every man of whom lusted to return home.

To bring an end to lawlessness in one swoop the Autocrat, in his condescension, countenanced a new constitution permitting greater civic freedom, a widely-extended suffrage, a legislative Duma, and real municipal responsibility—a measure which should have caused the malcontents to fall on their knees in homage and gladness. True, wild enthusiasm followed for a day or two, but after that, for month upon month, the old reign of terrorism was renewed by animals nigh incapable of being taught.

But taught they must be. That was imperative owing to the drift of the international situation. Was not Germany taking on airs? Well, if her insolence went too far she would receive a salutory lesson when Russia's vast armies marched through her trim lands, with France crossing the Rhine to strike deep into her vitals at the other side.

However, the matter of internal order was of major priority, and funds were needed to deal with that. In consequence a Loan was broached, to be issued at 88 and to bear interest of five per cent; the total amount was sixty million pounds, of which, it was proposed, Paris should take four-fifths and the London Market make itself responsible for twelve millions.

The success of the Loan was a full vindication of the repressive measures adopted by the Government within Russia's borders, and a hard-cash proof that the investors of France and England were aware there could be one conclusion only to the struggle between the Tsar and a minority section of his people.

It was a little strange to find England participating in this financial accommodation, but then the English always had an eye to a good bargain, perhaps too keen an eye. Nevertheless fair's fair, and the English were certainly not as bad as the Prussians made them out to be.

The truth was that England and Muscovy had always been supremely ignorant of each other, which breeds ill-conceived ideas. In particular, the English had a most peculiar sense of humour. For instance, there was the cartoon in the periodical *Punch* which appeared long before the Gold War was forced upon the simple, God-fearing Dutch people of South Africa, undoubtedly for the immense riches beneath their farm-lands. The Gold War! Well, perhaps now it would be more politic to call it the Boer War—the English, if humorous in their own quite extraordinary fashion, could be extremely touchy if their moral standards were in the least questioned. This cartoon was supposed to symbolize the Franco-Russian *entente* by showing a Russian bear dancing to the tune of a French loan. Damned idiotic, it was, puerile, stupid, ill-mannered. Still, as the *Journal de St. Petersburg*, the semi-official organ of the Foreign Office, pointed out, one must try to understand these strange people.

The new attitude prevailing, the launching of the *Dreadnought* by King Edward of England was given much prominence; she was a marvellous ship, too, worthy of the world's most powerful sea power and, candidly, somewhat superior to anything the Russian Navy possessed.

Ah well, Russia's friend England could have the sea with pleasure, for she herself, rapidly reorganizing, would soon be supreme on land whatever that sabre-rattling actor the Kaiser thought!

Little by little as the seasons passed, incidents which might have deferred this much desired outcome became less frequent, though regrettably there were still bomb-outrages, strikes, lockouts, and at least one attempt to blow up the train conveying His Imperial Highness the Grand Duke Nikolai Nikolaich from Tsarskoe Selo to St. Petersburg. Famine, too, was always near at hand, and hosts of ever-loquacious agitators never ceased to shoot up with their parrot cry of "Freedom, Equality and Amnesty".

Yes, despite these annoyances conditions steadily improved internally until a man could be tickled by simple things, say the juicy disclosure that the Assistant Minister of the Interior had been named as implicated in a grain scandal. Once again it was possible to drive out in reasonable safety to William Island for a lazy afternoon at the Krestoffsky Club, to wager against friends fancying their skill at clay-pigeon shooting.

Abroad, Russia's prestige grew. More than ever she and France were in the closest accord, and as to England, it is sufficient to state that the Russian squadron which visited there received a reception so remarkably warm that the authoritative press in both countries pronounced it as still another stabilizing factor in the preservation of world peace.

In this manner Holy Russia, the stigma of defeat by the little yellow men receding, came into her rightful place. Under the guidance of the Emperor and his chosen ministers she pursued her God-directed course, smiled upon by her friends of the great democracies, who rejoiced that her parliament was now a living entity. Unfortunately it was true that the Duma was opened and then dissolved with the rapidity of a Jack-in-the-Box, but this could be attributed entirely to the preposterous demands of a section of its members. They alone were to blame.

Thus it came about, two years after Witte and Komura, on behalf of their respective governments, affixed their signatures to a treaty of peace, that Holy Russia, her desperate travail ended, attained normality, *real* normality.

Praise be to God on high! Praise be! Our thanks, O Lord!

How different it was: soldiers dancing gaily to wildly-swinging concertinas; good cheap food for the poor; freely wandering pilgrims selling a light from a sacred flame kindled in the Holy City; freshly-painted sentry boxes and guards smartly presenting arms; shrieks of *joy* from skaters weaving along canals illuminated with coloured lanterns.

Once more friends gossiped merrily into the small hours around a whistling samovar, and drank delicious, honeyed tea without fear of their innocent meeting being interrupted by a police raid.

Jolly crowds attracted by startling flashes—from the horseless wonders, the new electric tramcars—which turned snowy roofs, lintels and trees into a glittering fairyland, would not move on, so enthralled were they. Highly delighted tram-drivers contributed their own quota of excitement—smoke, and frequently flames, would rise when, attempting to start with sensational speed, motors were burnt out; as for stopping, brakes were crashed on a few paces only from the picking up places, throwing hilarious passengers higgledy-piggledy as the contraption, wheels locked, howled to a standstill in an excruciating slide.

With these crowds the police did what they could, but many picked members of the force, sent to France or to England to learn the niceties of traffic control, had not yet returned; those left did their best with shouting, gesticulating, and at times cursing—seldom anything worse than that.

At last, whatever a small percentage of mealy-mouthed creatures might say, dear Russia had come into her own.

Since Mlle Sachot had voluntarily relinquished her engagement with the Kaivanovs, the children of the house had driven away a batch of French mistresses. Miss Brown, firmer than any of these ladies, was more of a permanent fixture, but on the morning young Prince Sergei left home to join the ranks of the Page School she was as near as she had ever been to hysterics.

Twenty minutes after her brother was driven off, Princess Anastasia, dark eyes smouldering, reached her climax, an uncontrollable little termagant flushed an angry scarlet from throat to temples.

"*Look*, another tramcar," Miss Brown said quickly, seizing any opportunity to distract a thoroughly naughty girl, as she most inadequately described her pupil to herself. "If you watch carefully between those buildings——"

"Tramcars!" the young madam shouted. "I don't want to watch the silly things. I won't either."

Before the governess could intervene an army of costly toys had been viciously jumped upon, or kicked against the wall.

"If you don't behave, Anastasia," Miss Brown said sternly.

"Why should I stay at home?" Princess Anastasia screeched. "Why should Sergei Ivanovitch go to the Page School without me? Why can't I go?"

"Because, dear, you're a girl."

"That wouldn't have mattered," Prince Ivan's daughter said contemptuously. "Besides, I'm not frightened like Sergei Ivanovitch is. . . ." On and on she raved, betraying possession of the Daleologin temper of her great-great-great-grandmother. "And," she ended, "*I* wouldn't have been scared of the boys who are there. I'd soon have frightened *them*."

The old nannie now appeared, waggling her hands above her head in dismay. But the clamour made by a fire-brigade caused a brief respite. Anastasia, diverted by the noise of bells and iron-shod wheels, rushed to the window and gazed down at a dog streaking through the street alongside a furiously-riding mounted policeman. Not far behind, racing in excited pursuit of the lurcher as they were taught to do, came four fleet-footed horses pulling the fire-engine, whose elated crew hung on by the skin of their teeth.

This interval of peace was merely the prelude to a fresh storm.

"I could still catch up to Sergei Ivanovitch," Anastasia started off again. "If . . ." she tugged Miss Brown's arm. "If I ordered Papa's own special beasts I could."

Her governess summoned up the ghost of a smile. "Come, dear," she coaxed her. "You know those boys would tease Sergei Ivanovitch *dreadfully* if a little girl went with him to his new school."

It is problematic whether even Prince Sergei would have appreciated his sister's attendance when he was introduced to the Page School, but the possibility certainly existed that her company would have been welcome on one stage of his drive there.

This was in Mikhailovsky Oulitsa, close to the vestibule of the Europeiskaya Gostinitlza, through whose double doors three gentlemen were emerging.

The first of these pulled up sharply on the sanded pavement to eye three vehicles. A broad grin quickly spread over his face.

"My God," he roared. "Look at that, and Ivan Mikhailovitch's boy is in one of 'em. Rich, isn't it?"

A swift glance was sufficient for his companions, who promptly doubled with laughter.

"If only the ladies were in the others," the hindmost remarked.

"But their pets are taking an airing, and should be well trained," the third added with a chuckle. "What are the odds on the clever little creatures turning up their noses and cutting each other?— their mistresses would."

It was hardly feasible that Prince Sergei, at his years, could have connected their glee with the juxtaposition on the broad street of his own magnificent *troika* and the two bizarre conveyances at which he was gazing incuriously. Until then he had been miserably preoccupied in wondering what might await him before nightfall at the preparatory establishment attached to the Imperial Page School—his cousin had made his blood curdle with tales of the awful things done by the bigger boys to newcomers.

Another burst of merriment aroused him and, looking round, he saw a number of gentlemen staring his way.

"They're making fun of me, damn them," he said between clenched teeth. "They know it's my first day."

By now, the amusing news spreading, the efflux from the hotel had quickened. Hastily turning up Astrakhan collars and throwing fur coats over low-cut gowns, smart men-about-town and their feminine counterparts tumbled outdoors to cheer a spectacle already the subject of considerable comment in the capital.

Convinced he was the subject of unwelcome and cruel attention, Sergei crouched lower.

"I'd like to spit in their faces," he hissed. Pushing aside lap rugs and carriage-furs, he leapt up to beat his fists into the coachman's many layers of clothing. "Drive faster, dolt," he screamed. "Use the whip, I tell you."

The genuine cause of the fun, two sledges each so unusual in colour as to attract everyone within range, had passed the corner of the Philharmonic Hall from Mikhailovsky Square. That nearer the kerb, drawn by three prancing stallions with floating manes, was occupied by a Pekinese clad in a padded yellow jacket, which sat on a cushion goggling at all and sundry. In the second, which had a trio of high-stepping milk-white Bohemian horses, a quaintly-clipped French poodle, protected by a thick, vermilion-hued tailored wrapper, peered gravely over the side.

These equipages had first astonished St. Petersburg four days before, but were not seen on the following day. After that, reins in the hands of embarrassed old drivers, both flaunted themselves again.

The vehicles were upholstered in soft leather, dyed respectively apricot and *Rose du Barry*. That painted bright green picked out in gold, together with the Pekinese, was the property of Natasha Brakaieva, a young and pretty ballerina of the Mariinsky Theatre; the other in sky-blue embellished in silver, together with the French poodle, was owned by Tamara Tolinskova, also a young and pretty ballerina of the same theatre. Both outfits, and their four-legged passengers, were gifts to these charming ladies from Captain Prince Kaivanov, Imperial Russian Navy.

Nine-tenths of St. Petersburg giggled, retailed the quarrels of the two ladies with infinite pleasure, and applauded the donor as the hell of a fellow.

Outside the Europeiskaya Gostinitlza, whose bars and discreetly-shaded lounges were now empty, a brisk business was being done by a dapper young officer balanced precariously on the iron bar of the boot-scraper.

"Come along, ladies and gentlemen," he bawled. "I'll still take a slight shade of odds against the poodle snubbing the Peke. Yes, sir. . . ."

Within a little over a minute wagers in thousands of roubles were offered and accepted; men exhorted lightheartedly and *soignées* women trilled joyously. And what a rollicking roar went up when Tamara Tolinskova's Suzi yawned—disdainfully, her gratified backers swore—at Natasha Brakaieva's pop-eyed Fifi.

Then the crowd scampered into the warmth of the hotel, bent on following their pleasant diversions. Within an hour the scene so recently witnessed had taken second place to an item of gossip about the apartment in which Matviei Artemevitch—the Guards one, not the courier fellow—had installed a young woman; or, more noteworthy, the toilet seat in the apartment, which Matviei Artemevitch had arranged to be covered with ermine. The long bar rocked with laughter and Matviei Artemevitch, fondling his moustache, could not stave off a flush of satisfaction.

Elsewhere big gatherings continued to watch the electric street-cars, sharing in the scorn of the *drosky* men whenever they went wrong and smiling sympathetically as a *drosky* driver, after giving full vent to his feelings, turned to kiss his beloved horse.

Yes, the old pattern of life had returned.

The silver-embellished card-saloon of the St. Petersburg—Cannes express was invariably crowded; poor children on outsize skates, without more dangerous mischiefs to lure them, skimmed over the roughish ice of the Neva; and the Principal of the Board of Control of the Imperial Ballet School, stuffy-headed with long rehearsals, thought nothing of taking an extensive drive in the invigorating air.

Indeed, things were normal.

The pity was that Holy Russia had weltered in blood unnecessarily, and that a few misguided creatures had lighted a fire they could not control. They were as the careless housewife, of whom it is said: "She fried a pancake and it ran out of the door."

Praise to the Almighty. Once more Russia had found her dear soul.

CHAPTER IV

DURING the ensuing years uneasy undercurrents were at work in the Western world.

In England trade progressively became worse, with Germany a bitter and—many Britishers maintained—a shoddily-sharp business competitor. Taxes increased, but when the Government, against Von Tirpitz's Naval Appropriations, proposed limiting the building of Dreadnoughts to four, a universal outcry went up: "We Want Eight and We Won't Wait." It was an expensive gesture in times of strikes and still more strikes, many carried to the point of violence. There was political deadlock, too, between Lords and Commons, and a country divided into two camps on the question of Irish Home Rule.

No, matters were not encouraging in England, whose Captain Scott, for all his heroism, had been forestalled by Amundsen; where maritime engineering pride was lacerated, and the nation stunned, by the loss of the *Titanic*, "The Unsinkable Ship". Circles not outstandingly connected with commerce were feeling the pinch also: art treasures sold to wealthy people abroad rose from a trickle to a stream and, unpalatable though it was, Americans were able to afford better polo ponies.

France, although less dependent on export, *entrepôtage* and the returns from foreign investments, was not without her own problems, but her people drew together at the time of the Casablanca affair, which could have brought her into armed conflict with Germany. She, too, suffered many paralysing strikes, with riots so grave that infantrymen were compelled to open fire. Even more serious, there were occasions when troops mutinied and naval reservists refused to do their duty, a calamitous state from the security point of view.

In Germany trade was booming. The military party, constantly enraged about the monies filched from the Treasury by the Admiralty, longed to try out a magnificent war machine perfectly capable of deciding any issue without help from a minor Service. The toast was *Der Tag*: England the thinly-veiled objective against which the bumpers were pledged.

In Austria the Foreign Secretary's fascinated glance kept stealing towards Servia, though he should have been curbed by the knowledge that Russia always afforded protection to the Slavonic peoples. Despite this known factor Count von Berchtold continued to look towards the south-east, the man destined to be the most blood-guilty of all.

But in Russia there was profound tranquillity, the tranquillity of a mighty nation which, her old strength regained, shuns no challenge, a giant unafraid. The Empire was prepared for any eventuality, and her friends, France and England, were heartened by the quietly forceful words of General Soukhomlinoff, "We are ready", and he was in a position to know.

In this manner the years slipped by, until 1914 came, with its glorious summer. There was improvement in other matters also: in England an uncanny lull in the demands of the workers was noticeable; in Germany the Junkers relaxed on the sun-drenched Baltic coast, and the organizers of the German Navy League, suspending their all-out programme for once, ceased to barnstorm vociferously from town to town. In Russia the submerged opponents of the Government, of whom a few still existed, allowed their secret presses to stand idle, and took a holiday themselves.

The barometer of the international situation climbed to "fair", higher than it had been for an age. Sir George Warrender and his squadron visited Kiel, and were impressively honoured by the Kaiser. Further north Sir David Beatty led the First Battle-Cruiser Squadron to Kronstadt, and two of his light cruisers steamed up the Neva as far as the Nicholas Bridge to show the White Ensign: all were entertained hectically for a week, the privileged guests of the Tsar.

A little later an Archduke named Franz something-or-other was assassinated at Sarajevo, wherever that was, but the Austrian authorities did not seem to be in any hurry to make a move and, except locally, the death of this gentleman caused little stir.

The peoples of Europe continued to bask in wonderful weather.

2

The July sun beat down cruelly, and the burning lands of the Don shimmered with haze. On the broad river the pilots of rafts hung limply over rough-handled steering sweeps; and on their farms and holdings baggy-trousered Cossacks, sweat streaking, allowed lolling-tongued horses to amble along as they pleased.

It was certainly not the season Captain Prince Kaivanov would have chosen to visit his estate at Yasni Dulba. But an anthracite concession proposed by an American syndicate, with revenue figures equivalent to those of a minor kingdom, had been argued by his agents and attorneys to its penultimate stage and his personal attendance was needed for completion. Reluctantly he left the cool breezes which made his villa in Finland so delightful in summer.

On the second day after arriving at Yasni Dulba an express "preference over all traffic" telegram reached him from the Admiralty, its message a single code word whose meaning he fully understood: to present himself at St. Petersburg without delay.

Many of Russia's senior officers received a similar order, but for him especially it meant setting out immediately on a long and tedious journey, scorching by day and sultry at night.

Fortunately nothing else was needed from him except his signature, twice. When he had dashed these off, bidden farewell to guests and advisers and retired to his suite to prepare for the return trip, his agents and attorneys, to celebrate the end of the strain of intense negotiation, settled down to what, if they knew each other, would degenerate into a heavy carousal. But the three

Americans, despite expostulation, started out on a tour of the palace accompanied by the Assistant Steward.

From vast chamber to vast chamber the foreigners passed, scrutinizing massive silver coffers and drinking cups so broad as to require both arms to lift; or pausing to finger heavy gold plate and to stare at breathtaking jewels in ikons.

The New York lawyer lingered before a wall faced entirely with amber in different designs. "What a place," he murmured.

Next they went down a pink marble corridor off which, striking change, a passage led into the long-dead Prince Aleksiei's austere, soldier-like quarters. Further along, obviously a show-piece from the Assistant Steward's expression, were the apartments of Prince Aleksiei's grandson, a gentleman of very different character who, instead of passing away in honoured age, perished horribly in an immense Khan-like residence belonging to his family.

An extremely dignified banker whistled as his bemazed glance roved over the exotic scene. "Say," he muttered.

Prince Mikhail had always had his own ideas about interior decoration. The varied hues of divans, brocaded screens, oriental rugs, deep cushions and silken Chinese coverlets instantly caught the eye; there was a long pier-glass with an extraordinary range of swivelling side extensions, and a glittering array of cut-glass bottles of perfume; the legs of the furniture were covered with pearl inlay, while the atmosphere, even after the lapse of nearly ten years, was redolent of myrrh. The bedroom was panelled with mirrors and the bathroom in brilliantly-burnished silver on which were ceramic figures of nude boys.

The visitors halted, but none of them spoke until the mining man picked up a pair of gold-handled curling-tongs.

"Reckon this guy must have been a queer bird," he commented.

"Queer!" the lawyer ejaculated. "Take a look at this."

He pointed to a beautifully-bound but well-used Testament lying between a swansdown puff with carved ivory head and a silver bowl partly filled with pinkish face powder.

"I'll be shot, durned if I won't. Yes, it *is* a man's," marvelled the banker, who had examined the fly-leaf. "Well, I suppose queer is the suitable word."

After an exhaustive round of sightseeing they were ushered into a room with a bottle-laden sideboard and a circular table laid for a meal. There was also a buffet with a startling number of dishes, all based upon fish and vegetables. So appetizing were these that, to their dismay, the Americans tucked away a meal in itself before the main service began. Subsequently, however, their guilty sense of repletion was magically smoothed out by generous portions of solid soup. This renowned delicacy, made in winter from mutton, beef, hare and fragrant herbs, was preserved until needed in a subterranean chamber freshly re-lined during the dark days of each year with blocks of ice as high as a Kirghi man. Chilly to the tongue, with a wonderful flavour, it was most acceptable in hot weather.

"My, that was good," the lawyer sighed.

The sound of a large automobile accelerating reverberated from outside. Smacking his lips, and nodding agreement to his colleague, the mining engineer left the table and wandered to one of the windows, taking his wine with him. A chauffeur-driven open touring car, with four tyre-covers strapped on the back, was now standing at the main door. A large and lively crowd was there already, several hundred in all, composed of the palace's staff and estate workers who chanced to be near enough, grooms, woodmen, gamekeepers, carpenters and gardeners.

"Seems like the Prince is leaving shortly," he remarked. "And lordy, what a send-off."

Interested, his associates joined him. "I wonder what all the rush is about?" the banker said, frowning slightly. "Dammit, he sounded plumb mysterious to me. Anyhow, let's see him off."

They had not long to wait, for their host was about to leave his own room. Standing with heels close to slashing teeth in a snarling mouth at the end of a white bearskin rug, Captain Prince Kaivanov made sure the Steward had not forgotten an order given earlier.

"You telegraphed to His Excellency the Governor of Rostov requesting him to hold the St. Petersburg express for me?"

The Steward bowed. "Assuredly, Highness. A swift horseman set out within a few minutes of my receiving Highness's command."

In consequence of his profession Prince Ivan was seldom at Yasni Dulba, an estate wholly agricultural and correspondingly uninteresting to him. This was probably responsible for his initial surprise as his glance fell upon a once-prized possession, bought when he had been a midshipman in the Eastern Fleet. The ingenious trick-picture vividly portrayed a naked young woman tempting a black-robed young priest—a barely-perceptible mesh studded with brilliants was superimposed, so contrived that a light tug on a tassel at one corner transferred a singularly obscene motion to the cleric's frame.

Smilingly recognizing the device, Prince Ivan went across to test it, bursting into hearty laughter when he caught out the dignified Steward, who was broadly grinning.

"So thou also consider it comical, Georgei Andrievitch," he

chuckled. "Thou, a good-living man stern to all others, a shining example on high to his fellows."

Brown eyes twinkled and magnificent white teeth still showed. "But not too high, Highness," was the delighted reply.

"Ho! ho!" Prince Ivan chortled. "So thou hast thy secret little pleasures, eh? When next we meet thou must acquaint me with them, without fail thou must. But time presses, Georgei Felixovitch. . . ."

From one of the smallest banqueting halls the three American gentlemen witnessed his departure, their eyes opening wider when they perceived servant after servant kissing their lord's hand. The crowd was bigger by then, augmented by six or seven hundred Cossacks, with countless more racing in.

As the Benz moved off, a stentorian cry of Godspeed rose from the throats of bareheaded men, the women sinking effortlessly in a prolonged curtsey, full skirts spread out about them.

"Medieval . . . the old boyars," the mining engineer muttered. "And only a few years ago the country seemed in the mood to wipe out the whole bunch. Folk who'll change at the throw of a hat, the Russians, I guess."

Leaving clouds of dust behind, the car sped along the avenue between fountains whose jets sent up lofty plumes which glittered in the bright light.

Beyond the park the dirt road ran straight and level for three versts before climbing a slight gradient between the charred timbers and grey embers of a village burnt down entirely a few days earlier, through the dreaminess of a young woman when frying beans. At the top of the slope the flying car missed a few squawking hens and, a rear wheel simultaneously encountering a vicious pothole, its owner was thrown so far round in his seat that he faced, seen across the flat countryside, the great residence built and maintained by the courage and resourcefulness of his ancestors.

Close to Yasni Dulba on the east were the shining waters of the Don, a broad ribbon reflecting the darkening blue of the near-evening sky. On the other side of the house there was a never-changing vista, stretching to the distant horizon, of the golden ears of the second harvest. The copper-hued rays of the westering sun illuminated the palace, shading one edge of the slender white bell-tower, deepening the richness of red-painted walls, and toning even more beautifully blue enamel and gold leaf on the church dome.

As night fell the Benz was far away from this magnificent residence, racing through the cool glades of a silent forest. Progress was swift and, as outcome, the crack Vladikavkhaz-

St. Petersburg express was detained by no more than a mere seventy-eight minutes at Rostov-on-the-Don.

It was as well that Captain Prince Kaivanov had not been dilatory. The next morning, from his elegant *coupé*, he saw a satchel-carrying rider nail, without dismounting, a buff-coloured piece of paper to a telegraph post on lonely crossroads: the summons for general mobilization.

There were delays due to troop movements along the line after that, and many hours before he reached the capital Holy Russia and Germany were at war.

In St. Petersburg, soon to become the old Slavonic Petrograd, processions swarmed through the streets bearing immense portraits of the Tsar. Flags flew from every building, grand pianos were flung out of the upper-storey windows of premises occupied by Germans, and the pavements opposite shops of Germanic signs and lettering were littered with broken violins, crushed concertinas, trampled trumpets and the befouled sheets of Bach and Wagner.

At the Imperial Opera House Chaliapin sang *God Save the Tsar* on his knees, close to the footlights, to an audience unashamedly weeping.

There was no fear. "Saint Nikolai the Miracle Maker" would take care of them. And had they not the glorious Russian Army? And was there not France with her gallant soldiers? Then there was the unvanquishable English Navy. Yes, there *should* be England, with her unvanquishable Navy, but. . . .

The largest crowd in St. Petersburg, extending far on to Trinity Bridge, demonstrated noisily in front of a wing of the red Soltikoff mansion, which housed the British Embassy. Time after time His Britannic Majesty's Ambassador waved from a window above the house porter's winter box; or, more occasionally, stepped out to deliver a few noncommittal phrases while gripping—tightly, some observers declared—the wrought-iron balcony rail. But he never said what they wanted to hear.

Much more enjoyable were visits to the embassies of the Dual Alliance, when savage booing was the least harmful of many different ways in which hatred was expressed. Enthusiastic calls, of course, were paid to the dove-grey French Embassy on the Quay for a renewal of frantic cheering, tribute to a dear and loyal friend who had proved *her* good faith by declaring war.

The throngs, as always when the Orthodox Nation was threatened, stimulated themselves by singing the 104th Psalm, their voices rising in wonderful unison. And, shortly after the last word died away, a bright soul referred loudly to two statues of naked Teutonic figures, hitherto undamaged, which called attention to the German Embassy. Roaring with approval, thousands at once decided to right matters; panting with excitement, eyes bloodshot and mouths open, they rushed off.

When the offending emblems had been destroyed, those thousands galloped back again to the British Embassy, their haste so extreme that many among them, tripping, were trampled on by those madly following.

What would England do? Would she honour her bond to Holy Russia?

These were the inquiries which were bawled, screeched, yelled and screamed.

PART THREE

1916 - 1918

*

CHAPTER I

THE third winter of war in Petrograd, where drawn-faced officers returning from the front showed none of the joy of the British subaltern reaching London, or that of the erect young German fighting-man arriving at Berlin or Munich for a precious few days' leave.

The third winter of war in Petrograd, a hard winter of ice, snow, sleet and mud, with winds so often whistling viciously along the quays.

Apathetic wounded, trundled out of ambulance trains at the filthy Nikolai Station, were driven past the statue, queerly shaped in frost-protecting wrappings, of Alexander III bestriding a full-feathered shire horse; beyond that, a multitude of temporary wooden buildings housed many lost babies and refugees whose homelands had been overrun by the enemy. And here and there evidence of graft was to be seen—perhaps a private courtyard piled with logs.

From patchwork ambulances these wounded soldiers glimpsed many doleful sights: tramcars, a few in service and more broken down; bakeries with queues of shivering creatures hoping to obtain a loaf of black bread, made from mouldy cereals and straw at that; and ragged humanity shifting feet outside the windows of every grocery shop.

Without a *pood* of coal to burn in them the central heating appliances of the hospitals were useless, and chilly wards—once so admirably equipped from the private fortune of twenty million pounds entirely withdrawn from England for this generous purpose by His Imperial Majesty—were now short of every essential from clips to peroxide. Even the small British Colony hospital on Vasili Ostroff was hard put to raise a few rolls of gauze or a sound pair of rubber gloves, and the bottom of the barrel had been scraped for lint, chloroform and linen.

Petrograd in the third winter, where the Tsar's Delaunay-Belleville car was never seen on the streets; where the once-arrogant staff of the War Office were not too proud to be seen twice weekly trudging along, gladly carrying home a paper bag containing sugar, rice, flour and soap; Petrograd, in which the higher officials of the Civil Service were still using reams of expensive paper to communicate rambling instructions to bewildered governors of provinces and police chiefs.

Subversive pamphlets smuggled in from Switzerland competed with a thousand secret presses; ambitious politicians "viewed with alarm" any success of Russia's armies, and said as much in the Duma. Popular Socialist argued vehemently with Constitutional Democrat, Social Revolutionary and Social Democrat jumped wordily into the dog-fight. Grigori Rasputin had been murdered, but although his cold body had rested in an Imperial Chapel, the dissolute Bishop Teofan abruptly ceased any further championship of the dead miracle-worker. Other great ecclesiastics wetted their fingers to the wind and, following the lead of Bishop Hermogene, attempted to gain the people's favour by noisily reviling their former friend.

Wheat rotted in sidings of the Siberian Railway while starvation stalked the capital; munitions of war never got a smell of war. Soup kitchens doled out warmish coloured water, and mirrors on the high-ceilinged walls of the Winter Palace blurred to the breath of man. Richly varnished carriages of princes of the Orthodox Church waited near, but not too near, the white colonnaded Stock Exchange; the Kolchugin Copper Works made a profit of twelve million roubles on a capital of ten million, and the Tver Company returned a nett hundred and eleven per cent, thereby causing the shareholders of the Moscow Textile Company Riabushinsky, receiving only seventy-five per cent, to have a legitimate reason for complaint.

Erotic humbug or no, Grigori "The Saint" had said that his end would mean the end of the ruling house of Romanov. The British Ambassador, more practical, telegraphed his Government: "If the Emperor continues to uphold his present reactionary advisers a revolution is, I fear, inevitable." Six weeks before Christmas he took up his code-book again: "If there is trouble the troops, I am told, will refuse to fire" was the message he sent.

These words were not generally known, but the Tsarevitch's were: "Dear Mama weeps when the Germans are beaten, and dear Papa weeps when the Russians are beaten. So when," rumour reported the perplexed little boy as asking, "ought I to cry?"

Petrograd in the third winter of war.

*   *   *   *   *

Depression resolutely banished, as it should be within a fortnight of Christmas, there was almost the usual seasonal air of gaiety on Nevski Prospekt and the smart Moskaia that mid-week morning. Handsome *troikas* carrying pretty women and attentive escorts drew up at the imposing doorway of the Ural Stone Shop, and scores of coachmen, chauffeurs and footmen waited nearby the severely-simple, velvet-draped windows of Fabergé's. Business premises were beautifully decorated with tinsel and greenery, gifts on display ranging from costly jewels to brilliant coloured peasant-craft embroideries and quaintly carved wooden toys. A laughing, well-dressed throng passed to and fro, the more devout crossing themselves on sighting the ikons above shop doors.

Two youths of perhaps sixteen, with the unmistakable stamp of the *Corps de Pages*, were leisurely placing their orders in Eliesieff's. Followed by a long-suffering attendant they sampled many rare crystallized dainties, each garrulously advancing the merits of the sweetmeat he fancied.

With time to kill, they hesitated on emerging into the rigorous cold.

"What about popping round to reserve seats at the Michel, Feodor Antonych?" the taller suggested. "A damned good leg show, I'm told."

This proposal seemed out of keeping with the speaker's appearance. Count Boleslas Wiazovsky was slender, with an artist's long hair and a definitely poetish look about him.

"Oh, I don't know, Bolo," his companion remarked with a shrug. "Nothing much better than usual, I fancy."

A Pole, and as touchy as his father, a captain in the Imperial Navy, Count Wiazovsky preferred his ideas to be treated less casually.

"No doubt you have a better notion," he retorted coldly.

Skid chains crunching on frozen snow, a Packard flying a corps flag on the radiator cap pulled into the kerb. A well-groomed young officer, wearing the silver aiglets of an A.D.C., descended and handed down two exceptionally attractive young ladies bundled in chinchilla and mink. They were followed by a white Borzoi.

Count Wiazovsky nudged his friend. "Damned funny how Anastasia Ivanovna carts Mimi Ivanovna about so much when they're so different, isn't it? You'd have thought——" He broke off to stare intently at one of the girls in the little group gossiping on the pavement. "God!" he muttered, "I'd like to bed Anastasia Ivanovna."

Eghbokoff grinned. "From what I gather, it wouldn't be impossible," he drawled. "Though I believe that shapely tit her half-sister would prove a little more difficult."

Despite the vivid make-up which made the two young ladies, in common with all society women, of the same pattern as the most expensive *cocottes* in the capital, the fact that Princess Anastasia Kaivanova and Mimi Kalutkina were closely related could be seen at a glance. It was true that Anastasia Ivanovna's slumbrous eyes were nearly black and Mimi Ivanovna's a soft sapphire blue, but each had shining raven-black hair and a heart-shaped face. Both were slim, Mimi Kalutkina's lines particularly being those of her famous ballerina mother, and although Princess Anastasia's Cupid's-bow mouth was rather fuller, there was nothing about her to indicate that eventually she might develop the creases of fat which had resigned her mother, Princess Zeneide, to a life of sloth at Amsibu.

"You are too kind, darling," Mimi Kalutkina was saying.

She was glancing mischievously through long lashes at Count Petrov. Of middle height, he was a dapper young soldier whose pleasantness of expression did not disguise that he was a man who knew his own mind. His family, a military one, had known the Kaivanovs since Crimean War days.

"Ridiculous," my dear," he retorted. "Keep the bus as long as you want and when you and Stana have finished with it send it back to the Ministry."

In this manner Princess Anastasia Kaivanova and her half-sister shopped that morning, a staff car in attendance.

"So worthy, Cyrus Konstantinych," Anastasia remarked subsequently. "You know, my dear, I believe he cherishes ideas about you."

At this reference to Count Petrov, Mimi flushed vividly.

"Don't, be absurd, Stana," she said.

"My God, but you're blushing." Anastasia was delighted, and avidly continued with a mocking account of what married life would be like with an old man of Cyrus Konstantinych's years. "My dear, he's thirty if he's a day, and you're fifteen . . . or is it six——"

Roused, Mimi intervened spiritedly: "And you're by no means out of your teens yet, Grandmama."

Anastasia giggled. "That's just evading the issue, my dear. All I am really trying to say is that any girl tying herself up too soon is just a damned fool. My God, the very word husband is boring."

"It would be to *you*." Mimi laughed outright.

When young Eghbokoff and his companion met the two young ladies they persuaded them into Conradi's. Over sugar cakes, cream cakes and rich, steaming chocolate the quartet discussed various titillating topics: the masked fête on the Chermoievs' skating-rink; a delicious scandal involving a mutual acquaintance and what she did, drunk as usual, on her name day; and the latest marrieds and the latest divorced. Feodor Antonych Eghbokoff added a screamingly funny tale about an unlucky couple caught in a state of nature by a husband returning from the Carpathian front, and his Polish friend made a suggestion about a wonderful *café-chantant* he had recently discovered.

"Why not, Anastasia Ivanovna?" Count Wiazovsky went on eagerly. "I thought we'd sup at this spot . . . I'd book a private box and——"

Princess Anastasia bubbled with laughter. "Evil thoughts fill your head, my dear Boleslas. But I'll wait, darling."

"Wait?"

"Until you're old enough, my dear." She was glancing at her tiny watch when her would-be entertainer rose angrily.

"By Grigori the late Saint," he snapped, "I'll show you whether I am old enough if ever I get you alone."

Mimi, who had been feeding titbits to her dog, clicked her tongue reproachfully. "Boleslas, dear," she said as though speaking to a child. "You mustn't be crude."

Icily composed by now, Count Wiazovsky bowed stiffly. "I must apologize for my outrageous proposal. I regret exceedingly that it was so repugnant."

"Silly boy." Anastasia laughed. "Perhaps I might, sometime."

He seized quickly on that. "You promise?"

"I never promise," she replied impatiently.

The two young gentlemen saw them into the waiting car. As it accelerated Count Wiazovsky drew out a gold cigarette case on which, as was the rage, the monograms of a number of his friends were traced in jewels.

"One way of putting a fellow off," he said, still white with fury.

Feodor Antonych was more philosophic. "It all depends on her mood, and next time she'll either agree or wipe you across the snout."

"She shall have her chance," his term-mate growled.

They turned into Moskaia and, a little beyond a small group of people who were reading a war telegram posted in a window, encountered a couple coming from the perfumed premises of a *Coiffeur de Dames*. Both youths saluted punctiliously, and both forgot themselves so much as to crane their necks around for another look at the pair: a handsome young man elegantly trapped out in the distinctive uniform of one of the smartest regiments, who was attentively squiring a lady decidedly longer in the tooth than himself.

"Some lad," Eghbokoff remarked with genuine appreciation.

These would-be men-about-town again glanced at Prince Sergei Kaivanov and Princess Merzelena who, while laughingly being helped into a *troika* with the Kaivanov crest, lightly slapped her companion's cheek, a flirtatious gesture which completely ignored the presence of many witnesses.

"I wonder how far he's got with her?" Count Wiazovsky speculated. "Of course," he continued with a knowing air, "she has the reputation of promising more than performing."

Young Eghbokoff grinned. "Still, Sergei Ivanovitch needn't rush his fences. General Merzelen is another of those husbands who's at the front."

Count Wiazovsky shrugged. "But even before that they lived tolerably, like the dog and the cat," he said.

After exchanging a few jests on Prince Sergei's opportunism, and chatting a little longer about his apparent distaste for young women more suitable to his own age, the two boys argued as to their next diversion.

In due course they settled upon a rouble's worth each at a well-known place of entertainment, a small gold-mine to three generations of owners, into which country clodhoppers were lured, little knowing that their feverish pursuit of nimble-footed naked girls would give immense pleasure to a line of spectators occupying stools at peep-holes behind the wall.

It proved a particularly diverting session and the Imperial Pages had plenty to discuss afterwards. Indeed, when walking alongside expensive but ageing cars parked outside the Europeiskaya Gostinitlza they were still so engrossed that they missed the two young ladies with whom they had been earlier.

Princess Anastasia Kaivanova and Mimi Kalutkina, who were entering the hotel, passed through double doors held open by the heavily-wrapped doorman and a liveried inside porter. In the welcoming warmth they were assisted out of furs and then headed towards the bar, waving *en route* to dashing officers of the Technical Department, who were permanently quartered in the hotel.

"You're not seriously thinking of spending an evening with that child Boleslas, are you, Stana?" Mimi asked. "No, no, Chuffka," she added fondly, crooking her finger through the collar of her dog, who was showing a tendency to stray.

"Of course not, stupid," Anastasia began but, her eyes lighting up, smiled almost immediately. "Although boys do get so frightfully worked up and it could be quite fun. And," she went on laughingly, "it might be interesting to know what Valya Androvna's reaction would be to my dallying with her son's friend. And my God, here she is."

Feodor Antonych's mother, Princess Eghbokova, a somewhat brassy-looking woman, pushed through the press towards them, cup of champagne in one hand and cigarette in the other. Married much too young to a hidebound gentleman, she was now in the early thirties and had been going the pace ever since General Eghbokoff's death on the Galician front.

"Stana, darling," she cried excitedly. "Whatever engagement you have you must cancel it. I've discovered two most divine Cossacks of the Savage Division . . . *unbelievable* Moslem he-men, women tamers and that sort of thing. They're taking us to lunch at Kontant's and afterwards—guess what?"

"They're taming us," Princess Anastasia suggested gleefully.

Princess Eghbokova's titter in response was completely lost. The uproar was deafening and, at the other side of the smoke-filled long bar, striving to keep pace with demands, the coloured barman and his white-coated assistants continued to pour cease-lessly from large coffee-pots containing liquids of potent alcoholic content.

"I tell you the Empress is at the bottom of our troubles," a captain in the Volhynsky Regiment declared thickly, leaning on the chest of a naval commander to force home his point. "I tell you. . . ." He belched and laughed inanely about it.

A group of hilarious young men and young women were roar-ing with amusement about an incident at the ice-hills the previous night. This party claimed Mimi Kalutkina immediately she was seen.

As not a square inch of table space was available in the vicinity, Princess Eghbokova thrust her lipstick-soiled cup into the hand of an astonished stranger, smiling at him bewitchingly and adding a word of thanks which hardly enlightened him.

"Isn't Mimi Ivanovna quite extraordinary?" she remarked. "Those wretched ice-hills—sliding down and trudging up again. I should be bored to death."

Mimi Ivanovna's half-sister shrugged. "She enjoys it," she said. "And if one enjoys something why not?"

"One lives but once, eh, Stana?" Princess Eghbokova said with a giggle as she borrowed a saying peculiar to her companion.

But Anastasia was weary of the topic. "And now, Valya And-rovna," she inquired, "where are these alarming men?"

"They're over there." Princess Eghbokova nodded.

The two ladies started to move along the room, but paused to have a few words with an auburn-haired young woman who had so often shared with them adventures scandalizing even to many in their own circle. She was, of course, at once acquainted with the nature of her friends' present rendezvous.

"My dears," she gasped most effectively, flashing slightly pro-tuberant blue eyes. "You really tempt me to join you."

Princess Savoseva was a partner in another ill-assorted union and, though so recently married, did very much as she pleased, contemptuous about a husband prematurely aged by excesses, of which one example was the abduction, many years before, of the daughters of a wealthy merchant. In that venture Prince Savosef had been associated with Princess Anastasia's father, Prince Ivan.

"Really, you do, my dears," Princess Savoseva went on, glancing provocatively at her companion, a colonel in the Pavel Regiment. "But truly I can't desert Filipp Egorovitch. Really, after the undying protestations he has been making I should feel simply horrid if I did. You do understand, darlings?"

"Of *course*," said Princess Eghbokova.

Anastasia laughed. "Meanwhile a thrilling experience awaits us timid creatures. I gather from Valya Androvna that if we don't reach two most impetuous gentlemen very soon they are quite capable of taking decisive action."

"How *wonderful* for you," Princess Savoseva said, thrilled.

Princess Eghbokova giggled. "Wait until you've met them, Stana."

Princess Anastasia's dark eyes were challenging. "It might be more interesting to stay here until they form themselves into a hot-blooded raiding party of two to fetch us," she said.

In the lounge the orchestra struck up the bunny-hug, and in the bar a semi-tight woman began to wriggle her shoulders and to snap finger and thumb. Low down in a tiny cleared space, a Don Cossack officer was demonstrating a dance while holding the blades of a pair of dirks in his mouth; blood streamed down his chin as, with knees doubled, his legs shot in and out. Frantic applause greeted his efforts.

It was all great fun. Here one could, for the moment, cease to worry about Germany's supposed intention to create anarchy behind the Army; one could forget the taunting leaders in German-subsidized newspapers which declared the British Ambassador to be the Pro-Consul of Russia.

But there were others who never relaxed, brave and level-headed men and women engaged in an uphill fight against bribery, corruption, chicanery, pusillanimity and jealousy. In Prince Obolensky's mansion on Mokhovaiya Oulitsa a handful of loyal people talked and planned. The Empress Dowager was no longer in residence at the red Anitchkoff Palace on the Nevski, but many true men, despite Her Imperial Majesty's well-known desire to avoid any step likely to embarrass her beloved son, risked her disapproval and sent couriers to her retreat at Kiev with advices about the growing perils of the situation.

Night and day rumour filled the air. And the latest catch-phrase, "All unhappiness comes from Germany", referred to the Emperor's consort, not to the enemy country in which she was born.

The English "five o'clocks" were prolific fountains of information. Many important matters were debated, often heatedly when the late Rasputin was under review. Scores of distinguished ladies had attended the dead Saint Grigori's séances, and still believed implicitly in him. Others stoutly asserted that his miracles were faked—the sickly little Tsarevitch, they suggested as an instance, was given noxious drugs by an accomplice in the Household, and when Her Majesty anxiously sent for the so-called healer he simply administered the appropriate antidote to the child.

Perhaps the most outstanding titbit was announced in a red, velvet-hung drawing-room during that period of talked-out quietness when the majority of the guests were contemplating descending to the lower hall for fur-lined boots and mantles. It was made by a former Mistress of the Robes who had patiently waited for the right moment. Very nonchalantly she remarked that the Palace of Tsarskoe Selo was connected by private wire with the German High Command Headquarters, which explained why the moves of Russia's armies were always anticipated.

"Oh, yes," the centre of attention continued, "I have it on the most *impeccable* authority that the Empress speaks to General Hindenburg from her boudoir *every* morning, a little after His Imperial Majesty has received the . . ." she allowed an effective oratorical pause ". . . the Minister of War."

That tale swept through the capital; within twelve hours it was being repeated in every mansion and in every slum.

On the whole the gentlemen were more practical, but nevertheless human enough to prattle about the Mongolian specific which the Tsar was reputed to be taking for medicinal purposes, at the risk, be it understood, of burning out his brain. Problems about the war engaged them more absolutely, however, blunt old veterans and corseted swash-bucklers alike, whether at the Nobles' Club or behind the putty-sealed double window-frames of the exclusive Yacht Club.

Certain facts were known: that nowadays six or seven Russian infantrymen were compelled to share a rifle—many of the obsolete 1878 pattern—and the artillery was unable to fire more than two rounds to the enemy's three hundred. What was not known was why—after Russia's prodigal expenditure of life and material in the Masurian Lakes which saved Paris and the Allies' cause in the early days of the war, when the Ambassadors of both France and England were informed that reserves of ammunition had been used up—the English failed to fulfil their promise of adequate supplies of munitions.

On this, a few gentlemen ventured to point out that Russia had, before the war began, openly bragged about being once more a great military power; her present allies had then been informed she was fully prepared, even for a struggle of considerable duration.

These critics were as bitterly assailed as others who, supporting the secret feelers for peace in Stockholm of a month or so before, had the impertinence to declare that Russia was no longer in a condition to wage war.

Issues were not always so clear-cut, and often there was an inordinately funny element in them. What man alive could help grinning when a former Governor of the Province of Orel, who had amassed a substantial fortune during his employment there, viciously denounced grafters and profiteers? And take old Admiral "Back-Stairs", whose sea-going career had been highlighted by ridiculous blunders. Quite oblivious that his leg was being pulled, he could be relied on always for a ripsnorting analysis of British tactics at Jutland. Throwing his arms about like a marionette when censuring Sir John Jellicoe and Sir David Beatty, he had to be seen to be believed. Laugh?—you nearly died.

2

The Mariinsky Theatre was warm with the indefinable mixed smells from perfumes, steam heating, fine tobacco, and Russian leather. Lights in glittering chandeliers blazed on a Grand Duke in the central box and upon jewelled women and well-groomed men in the stalls and the tiers.

The national anthems of the Allies were played to a stiffly-erect audience, *God Save The Tsar* in a silence so intense that a dropped programme made a quite disproportionate noise.

As the house stirred into movement again, Prince Sergei Kaivanov bent over a woman whose neck, though attractive, was not as firm as once it had been.

"My dear," he said softly. "Shall we?"

She smiled up at him, warm-eyed. "If you wish, Sergei Ivanovitch," she said, pouting a little. "I'm on the Committee so I suppose I ought to put in an appearance."

A gallant figure wearing the insignia of a staff appointment, Prince Sergei escorted her along the crowded parterre, where many people whispered on seeing them, then beyond doors deftly opened by gold-braided Court servants, past the saluting Chief of Police, and down a broad flight of shallow steps whose sides were filled with tubs of hot-house flowers.

"And later?" Princess Merzelena asked quizzically in the *troika*. "To the Islands, darling?"

"I rather thought that when we'd shown ourselves at this 'Comforts for Airmen' reception or whatever it is," his fingers tightened on her knee, "you might care to offer me the hospitality of the Merzelen mansion."

A woman who knew her world and how to handle the men in it, she laughed quite openly and was still smiling about his naïvety when they reached the Yaroslav residence.

"Well?" he demanded, dark eyes excited.

"Of course, silly darling," she said, highly diverted with him.

The Yaroslavs' white-and-gold ballroom, divided down the centre by a line of marble pillars, was a picture of rich colour from the Cupids painted on the high ceiling to the lovely dresses of ladies and the order-splashed uniforms of men moving beneath.

People seemed to be thoroughly enjoying themselves at this affair got up for charitable purposes. But to a few the evening had small possibilities, and so when Princess Anastasia Kaivanova, who had arrived before her brother, chanced to see a young girl of about Mimi Ivanovna's age she speedily removed herself from a group consisting of her fresh-air-loving, goody-goody kinswomen, the Yaroslav girls, and a few British submarine officers up from Reval.

Xenia Menshek-Pelikova was delighted to be singled out by Anastasia Ivanovna, upon whom she secretly modelled herself without interference from anyone whatsoever. Granddaughter of a renowned poet and daughter of a liberal-minded aristocrat who, for all his breadth of political vision, had perished with his wife in a Nihilist outrage, she lived with an ailing grandmother and, wealthy in her own right, did exactly as she pleased.

"Oh, hello, Stana," she said. "My God, you're superb tonight. Suppose you've something rather special on?"

Smilingly Anastasia looked her up and down. Xenia Menshek-Pelikova was very tiny, though exquisitely proportioned, a perfect miniature with flaxen hair and green, almond-shaped eyes.

"You're a pretty nice packet yourself," she commented handsomely, adding teasingly: "And I'll swear on any old bone you name that I'd guess you to be at least three years older than you are, which should fill your infantile heart with rapture. But I'll have to leave you now . . . with Valya Androvna I am renewing acquaintance with two Mohammedan gentlemen in the Savage Division. I don't know how many wives mine has already, but I'm inclined to think he intends this night to put me on the strength in an ex-marital classification."

"It's not true, Stana," Xenia Menshek-Pelikova gasped.

Anastasia laughed, "Which, what?" she said. "Well, the general outline is, honest."

Xenia drew a deep breath. "You are a devil, Stana," she said admiringly.

"On the contrary, I am a perfect lady," Anastasia retorted. "And as a well-brought-up young woman I am now leaving you to bid a courteous farewell, with suitable but not precisely accurate excuses, to our host and hostess. So good-bye, darling, and good hunting in due course."

Bracelets tinkling as she waved adieu, she went off to pay the courtesies mentioned. This social observance completed, and now freed for livelier diversions elsewhere, she crossed the ballroom again but was held up by the two youngest Yaroslavs, who had in tow two fresh-faced British naval officers. The girls' business was borrowing—sledges and a few extra horses from the Kaivanov stables, for an excursion later in the week.

"Of course, my dears," she said, nodding, but her smile changed into a scowl when, through an arched opening, she saw her brother dancing attendance upon Princess Merzelena in the vestibule beyond. Her annoyance was noticed, and in consequence, to clear up misconceptions, she had to explain: "Why in the good God's name should I mind, so please do grab absolutely everything you're short of from our place. As a matter of fact I *am* in the hell of a temper—but it's because I've just spotted Sergei Ivanovitch making a fool of himself."

Her air of disapproval, a term of understatement, was plainly in evidence when she met the couple a minute or so afterwards. Prince Sergei, who feared his sister as much as he had as a child, greeted her with the breeziness often assumed by weaker vessels.

"Ah, Stana, my dear," he said. "Surely you don't allow the English Navy to displease you, or is my eyesight at fault? Or perhaps, for all your adaptability, my dear, you're not cut out for the kind of parlour games I'm certain they'd suggest."

With the respect due from a young lady, Anastasia curtseyed demurely to his companion, which at once placed Princess Merzelena in the category of older women, indeed elderly women.

Seething, Princess Merzelena partially controlled herself. "It is apparent that Anastasia Ivanovna considers seasoned men only," she said tartly to Prince Sergei. "Overgrown schoolboys are obviously not in her line."

Princess Anastasia's appraising glance roved slowly over her.

"My dear Princess, a Kaivanov trait is to prefer maturity," she remarked with smiling insolence. "At times even the *passée*."

An English officer eyed the trio curiously, noticing the fury of

a most skilfully made-up woman, the indecision in the face of the
exquisite young soldier with her, and the undisguised contempt of
the third, a dazzlingly beautiful girl. The eternal Russian triangle
again, he decided as he headed towards a boisterous group who
were arranging a skating party for the following evening on the
lake in the ornamental gardens of the Taurida Palace.

Not very much later, after champagne, chicken cream, and a
few pastries at the buffet, Prince Sergei and his companion
decided to leave. The outside porter was instructed to call up the
Kaivanov *troika* whose coachman, along with many others, had
been warming himself at a red-glowing charcoal brazier.

"There, my dearest." Prince Sergei, somewhat unwieldy in his
many wrappings, tucked the bearskin rug about her.

Princess Merzelena was still in a nasty temper. "How dare you
permit your sister to insult me?" she demanded.

"Stana will have sound reason for regretting her foolhardiness,"
he countered sternly. "But I am afraid she has always been . . .
how shall I put it? . . . rather possessive about me. Now she sees
me with the most attractive woman in Petrograd, and she sees
how I feel about that woman. And so, naturally. . . ."

She was quite sparkling by the time they reached the Merzelen
mansion. In the lower hall a footman deftly eased off his mistress's
fur-lined carriage boots; of two other footmen, both with the
deftness of a lady's maid, one untied an Orenburger shawl which
covered her close-fitting fur cap, the other gently relieved her of
the weight of a high-collared *shuba*.

Chatting vivaciously, Princess Merzelena and her attentive
escort, who had also discarded heavy clothing, ascended the broad
marble stairs and crossed a vast room with gilded mouldings,
white satin upholstery, gilded furniture, and crystal chandeliers.

The boudoir beyond, hung with rose brocade, was pleasantly
warmed by a beautifully-chased porcelain stove, but the bedroom
leading out, where an odiferous pine-log fire hissed agreeably in
an open grate, seemed even more inviting.

"Ah, my dearest," Sergei said, his manner teasing as he pointed
to bottles and decanters set out in orderly readiness. "So you did
think we might come here?"

She laughed. "One does well to prepare, Sergei Ivanovitch."

For a little while they occupied themselves in their own ways,
Princess Merzelena sinking on to a curved stool from which, face
and bare shoulders bathed in the flattering glow of discreetly-
shaded lights to either side of the dressing-table, she closely inspected herself before using powder and perfume. For his part
Prince Sergei audibly and most amusingly discussed with himself
the need for care in selecting the wine she should have, but was

genuinely careful to ensure he was not observed when dropping a pink tablet into her glass.

"Darling," she said, smilingly interrupting his nonsense. "Do please ring for Celeste."

With the air of an authority he scrutinized gold-capped jars and phials before shrugging negligently.

"My dear," he protested with engaging gravity, "there is really no necessity. You will find I can maid you most adequately in every sense . . . cosmetics, your hair, and the rest. But before I present my testimonials here's your cup of cheer, and no heel-taps, darling."

While she drank he remained curiously watchful, but afterwards played the fool outrageously, posturing with an antique silver hand-mirror before turning his attention to a small, jewelled casket.

Princess Merzelena laughed with girlish extravagance. "And whatever do you think is in that?" she asked. "One of those *rather* special cards we have heard about?"

Well-versed, he knew to what she alluded: a Private Home, with a high-walled garden and a door on a quiet, lampless street, in which unwanted children, outcome of the love affairs of ladies of rank, married and unmarried, were secretly placed. The transaction was usually carried out under cover of darkness; swiftly, without prearrangement, and with no questions asked. A hired carriage would drive up, and the knocker would be hammered. Immediately the door opened a swaddled bundle of humanity, with a generous donation pinned to the clothing, would be handed over into waiting arms. In return a numbered ticket was received, valid for ten years, after which the holder could not claim the child even if she desired.

"Be that as it may, my dearest," he said with a chuckle when the good name of five or six ladies of their acquaintance had been torn to shreds. "I'm not at all sure that old Prince Nitchkoff doesn't bluff these matters out better than your revered sex, for I'll swear he's fathered several of his own footmen. I know I've the devil of a job to keep from cackling when a cluster of flattened Nitchkoff noses swarm round to remove my outer garments."

She gurgled about that, subsequently wafting a handkerchief against her cheeks, so hot had they become. That was when Prince Sergei, confessing himself a little warm also, retreated for another drink. Strangely enough, however, he chose a spirit whose qualities were fiery rather than cooling, tossing off a glass of vodka which took down with it an oval, white pill furtively placed beforehand on his tongue.

"And how, Madam, may I now assist you?" he inquired gaily

on coming back. "If you are retiring I suppose I should turn down the bed . . . or whatever the operation is damned well called."

She revelled in his drollery and tried to contribute on an equal footing. Giggling, she watched him as, in feigned professional style, he exposed the satin sheets on the Empire bed and plumped-up a pile of pillows.

"Bravo, darling," she exclaimed, clapping her hands. "Really, I shall have to engage you in Celeste's place."

Prince Sergei solemnly bowed. "And would Madam now wish to disrobe for the night?"

Princess Merzelena tittered. "Madam doesn't intend retiring yet. But . . ." her breathing had become quicker, ". . . but you can help me into something looser than this gown."

"May I?" he said.

"Yes . . . yes, darling," she replied.

Shakily, white arms over her shoulders, she was reaching for the catch of a pearl necklace when he drew her tightly to him. Passionately he kissed her, bruising her lips in a sustained caress.

"My darling," he whispered.

"Dearest," she said, trembling.

"My own," he said longingly.

Her eyes were closed. "Oh, Sergei Ivanovitch," she said faintly. "I . . . I have never felt quite like this before."

Tiny beads of moisture appeared on Prince Sergei's brow, but he was shivering.

"Perhaps until now you have never met a man to stir you as you were meant to be stirred," he murmured. "And, God help me, never before has a woman moved me as you do."

Breasts rising and falling deeply, she had difficulty in replying.

"Do I?" she said tremulously. "Oh, and you do me, so so terribly."

"*Then*, my own darling," he said.

Prince Sergei picked her up with such brutal disregard that the string of her necklace broke. Cradled in his arms he carried her a few paces across the room, leaving a trail of matched pearls behind, spheres softly gleaming on the carpet.

About half past eleven that night, after quickly finding another social gathering dreadfully slow, Princess Anastasia Kaivanova and her friend Princess Eghbokova, together with two officers wearing the Islamic green star and crescent in their furry hats, left the Nitchkoff's house by way of the conservatory, which had been transformed into a capital replica of an Italian garden, with white statuary, singing fountains and, peering through the tops of olives, a shining moon.

At midnight the quartet enjoyed soup, cold sturgeon, champagne and non-stop cabaret; and at one o'clock a call was paid on Vera Kalutkina.

The *prima ballerina's* big *salon* had an aspect of cosiness from the red wallpaper patterned with gold scroll to a gay Turcoman rug crumpled on a divan. The atmosphere was lively, homely and yet elegant; the samovar bubbled, and glasses of amber-coloured tea were in constant demand, taken with lemon, honey, jam or cognac. Rich sugar-coated cakes were in abundance, and there were plenty of laughing and chattering people to eat them.

Their hostess was flirting tantalizingly with two gentlemen, open rivals for her favours who so far had barely addressed a civil word to each other. Vera Kalutkina, a lovely woman who had lost little of her beauty, was deliciously convinced that an explosion might occur at any moment. She was roguishly deciding how, without committing herself to either, she would deal graciously but a trifle reproachfully with any conflict when, glancing round, she saw that some of her visitors were contemplating leaving.

"Going so soon, my dears?" she asked.

"We must, darling." Anastasia replied, winking slyly. "By the way, Mimi, would you and Cyrus Konstantinych care to come along with us? Neither of us, thank God, is on duty at the hospital tomorrow, so you could stay in bed with an easy mind in the morning."

Slender ankles crossed, Vera Kalutkina's daughter was sitting on a footstool close to her *fiancé*, her face radiantly happy.

Count Petrov answered for her: "I don't think we'll join you, Stana," he said, bending and brushing his smoothly groomed head against gleaming black hair. "Eh, darling?"

Mimi looked at him, adoration in the limpid depths of her blue eyes. "If you'd rather not, Cyrus Konstantinych," she whispered.

Indifferent to the kindly smiles of a number of onlookers, Count Petrov immersed himself in those bewitching eyes.

"I'd rather not, sweetheart," he said huskily.

A blush, stealing up Mimi's slender throat, gradually displaced the magnolia-white of her complexion, until her cheeks matched the vivid carmine of her lips and the full richness of the Zirman carpet. She gave one quick glance at her lover, snuggled nearer, and slipped her hand into his.

It was very touching, that intimate little group: the alert-looking young man so humble and proud, a bonny girl so much in love with him, and Chuffka part of the piece, lying with his nose on his mistress's instep. Small wonder that Vera Kalutkina fumbled for a handkerchief.

At three o'clock in the morning Princess Anastasia and her party were out at the Islands, listening to gipsy music against a background of overloud laughter and the pop of corks. Twenty-five minutes later she and Princess Eghbokova, together with Princess Savoseva, whom they had run into there, gave an exhibition dance in the middle of the floor, to applause enthusiastic enough to lift off the roof.

Probably aroused by his partner's *houri*-like performance, the shorter of the two Moslems became a little too pressing.

"By the Prophet, I know what you are," he bellowed when his undisguised references to the advantages of a private cabin were disdainfully checked. "A 'ticer, that's what——"

Anastasia's dark eyes darkened further. "I give to whom I choose, and when I choose," she said icily.

Hawk-eyes flaming, rage bubbled in his throat. "You do, do you?" he growled, stumbling forward. "And now, my beauty, I'll show you how a Lesghian gentleman takes what he wants when he wants."

With every ounce of her strength she smashed a heavy cut-glass decanter across his even teeth. Bleeding profusely he swayed and, spurs entangled, toppled over, striking his head as he fell against a bronze bust of Pharaoh, part of the ornamental leg of a massive table.

The room buzzed with delight, men standing up to watch and women climbing on to chairs. And when, groaning, the warrior from Shan-tau sat up dizzily for a few seconds, before passing-out utterly, a stream of dinner rolls assailed him from all angles. Crisp outside and unbelievably white inside, they bounced and rolled everywhere, many of them destined, soiled or otherwise, to be smuggled out by the waiters into humble homes which had forgotten that bread could be other than leaden and strange.

A swarthy Guards officer of perhaps thirty approached Princess Anastasia and pointedly clapped his hands as though leading the applause for a star turn.

"Bravo!" he cried, staring hard at her. "Splendid, my dear."

"Thank you," she replied, staring back as unwaveringly.

He bowed. "It *is* Anastasia Ivanovna, isn't it?"

Holding out her skirts, she bobbed peasant-fashion to him.

"And it *is* Matviei Jacobych, isn't it?" she retorted. "But I don't seem to remember you as a tiny tot at my first dancing class."

Baron Matviei Tchalmin's smile in response almost reached his pale eyes. Wounded in the early months of the war he had, since then, been attached to the reserve battalions of his regiment. His reputation was of that species of notoriety which compelled even the most innocent of women to eye him surreptitiously.

"Alas, my dear lady," he deplored. "In those days I was an outstanding veteran of the Page School, and so our ways were far apart. But may I inquire if you think the time is ripe for us to extend our knowledge of one another?"

Anastasia dimpled. "It could be entertaining."

A feeble winter sun was struggling through a yellow-grey sky as many of these roisterers put on their carriage clothing. To those sufficiently awake to notice when they reached it, the city looked different. Only a handful of vehicles waited outside the big hotels and restaurants, whereas normally there would have been lines of them even at that hour. There was also an unusual stirring of soldiers, second-class troops composed of aged reservists and young untrained men.

A sleepy observer remarked that the authorities were criminally at fault in these trying days not to ensure the availability of a sufficient number of the crack regiments, whose loyalty was unquestionable.

After all, he added between yawns, Petrograd was the hub of the Empire.

CHAPTER II

THE Cossacks were praiseworthily good-humoured with the crowds, even laughing at those who sang the *Marseillaise*. A few hundred feet overhead an immense six-seater Sikorsky roared by, but did not return; the sun was obscured. Only whispers broke the uncanny quiet which hung over the capital, and there were neither tramcars nor cabs. On Millionayskia there was scoffing at the notion that G.H.Q. would, at the Duma's bidding, countermand the order to certain Imperial Guards regiments to hasten to the capital from the front, but there was also anxiety about it. The occupants of many other comfortably warm houses did not undress at night, officers were apprehensive, the police openly fawned on the public, and the well-manicured white hands of departmental bureaucrats began to shake.

The spark which fired the powder trail may have been caused by women weavers who suddenly went on strike in the Vyborg quarter, by a crowd whose pressure cracked the plate-glass windows of a provision shop, or by the consumptive woman who threw a brick at a baker's window in the populous Rozjdestvensky ward.

Endless throngs of excited people began to invest the streets. The better-dressed were unceremoniously jostled, more bricks were produced for other shop windows, dirty snow was thrown at the police.

The few detachments of Cossacks, strained with play-acting, started with relish to whip men, women, and children alike. Spade-shaped beards quivering with joy, they loosened swords in scabbards—now, in the age-old parlance, they could "take measures".

Military patrols were doubled, but a red-flagged army motor lorry ventured out and found it need not retreat. Reserve units of the Pavlovsk Guards, intended to feed the front-line battalions, fired first on the crowd and then on their officers after returning to barracks.

As the day waned the Palace Grenadier guarding an Imperial monument not far from the Kaivanov mansion, stern self-disciplinarian though he was, stamped his feet and relaxed his sharp-set pose to glance askance at red material tied over the face of a Romanov. Many bodies were around him, predominantly those of mutineers belonging to the Keksgolm Life Guards; corpses of loyal sailors of the second Baltic Fleet lay there also, men who might still have been living had they waited until their shipmates put *the* burning issue to a show of hands, when a transference of allegiance was unanimously voted.

Lugubriously the Palace Grenadier shook his grizzled head.

From her window Princess Anastasia Kaivanova saw the next fight, a pitched battle further along when a frantically-running mob, pursued until then by infantry in extended order, received welcome aid from a drink-mad horde of comrade soldiers and sailors.

A countrified-looking young woman in a severe black silk dress, whose hair was plaited and bound with a green ribbon, tremblingly picked up a powder-bowl swept to the floor by her mistress.

"Highness," she faltered, "don't you think it would be wiser if I——"

"Shut up, damn you," Anastasia snapped at her maid.

Stolen limousines flaunting improvised red flags sped along Palace Quay, the muzzles of rifles peeping out on each side, usually with at least one passenger drinking from an upturned bottle.

Valya Igorovna gulped. "If Highness would only permit me to turn off the lights. Any of those drunken things might take a fancy to shoot in here."

"If you're frightened," the daughter of the house of Kaivanov replied disdainfully, "you may go below to the other servants. They've darkened behind there, I gather." A rapid volley, dangerously close, caused her to reconsider. "Oh, very well," she called over her shoulder. "Switch them off if it makes you feel safer."

She looked out again. Several hundred soldiers, red cockades on sheepskin caps, were now doubling from the right, bawling as they came along, to join forces with a few score sailors who were leading a thousand or so workmen-comrades armed with axes, officers' swords, knives and broken bottles.

Muddled by propaganda, the outnumbered loyal troops retaliated half-heartedly; slowly and then more quickly they gave ground, yielding altogether when the example was set by a party of their own fellows switching over to the opposition. This triumph was greeted by a bestial roar, and the watcher's lips momentarily became compressed.

"Draw the curtains, Valya Igorovna," she said sharply, turning. "Put one light on again and then get Her Highness Princess Eghbokova on the telephone."

As the maid drew thick coverings over the tall windows she noticed a large automobile cruising by, with a soldier stretched out on each running-board—rifles wavering and shoulders jammed between mudguards and bonnet-sides, they were firing ahead, quite haphazardly, it seemed. In the light of lamps further down the quay she saw a black flood of civilians converging upon a residence which had an Imperial right to the name of Palace—in all probability they were strikers, of whom it was announced that morning there were a quarter of a million.

"Highness, please!" she gasped. "Awful things are happening, Highness, and you must escape."

Her mistress pointed impatiently to the telephone. "Nonsense, you stupid fool," she said.

There was no response from the Eghbokoffs and the telephone exchange, collapsing under the strain, reported variously about Vera Kalutkina's number—either "engaged", "no reply", or "out-of-order".

But Valya Igorovna succeeded eventually in obtaining a connection with the Savosefs, and for the next three or four minutes, until the line went dead, Princess Savoseva caused the receiver to crackle with her hysteria. But Princess Savoseva always lacked balance, and was in a great house whose few remaining domestics, aged servitors, huddled in misery. In addition her elderly husband, he with Romanov blood on the wrong side of the blanket, had left hurriedly at midday for the Crimea. The Spaniards have a saying, "fear runs down the reins", and some of Prince Savosef's fear, though she had scoffed about it only at lunchtime, must have been communicated to his young wife.

". . . my dear, I shouldn't worry," Anastasia comforted her. "This annoying rabble will speedily be repressed. As soon as they hear a whiff about the Imperial Guard's return, which can't be long now, they'll melt away before you can say——"

Mimi Kalutkina rang up shortly afterwards, with ominous news of bloody assaults on persons and the sack of restaurants and residences.

"You must leave there quickly, Stana," she told her half-sister imperatively. "These beasts are only thinking of the large mansions and the palaces, and they won't bother people like Mama sent me. So put on some of your maid's clothes, and come over to us at once."

"Oh really, Mimi darling," Anastasia expostulated. "It will all end as swiftly as it began."

She was not alone in thinking that. Many men and women, who should have known better, were trapped that way.

The officer class had been picked on for the earliest humiliations, when in the first hours the soldiers said to them civilly enough: "Surrender your weapons, your Honours"; and an element among the sailors, though more severe, merely delivered painful but not bone-smashing blows with rifle-butts against the faces of those who remonstrated. The tempo changed in due course, however, and crowds surging from working-class districts into the fashionable quarters became much harsher in their methods of disarming. By nightfall, streets in those parts were littered with swords thrown away by prudent owners, and with the mutilated bodies of officers who had proudly but unwisely refused to throw them away.

That evening in Angliskaya Neberézhnaya, approaching the Yaroslav mansion, whose studded doors had been prised off their hinges by a determined band a few minutes before, a young man walked hurriedly, his lips twitching. He was clad in an exceptionally well-cut officer's uniform, but lacked weapons, shoulder ornaments and sword belt. On his badgeless cap scarlet ribbon was fashioned into a crude rosette, and on his right arm he wore a woman's red garter.

The Yaroslavs' unwelcome visitors were entertaining themselves hugely, as febrile laughter proved. In the tiled outer porch, the hall candelabra illuminating the ugly spectacle, an old gentleman was being relentlessly pummelled to death.

On the pavement, four excited hooligans were stripping down to her soft white skin a daughter of the house. Surrounded by implacable hatred, held so that she could not escape, the fourteen-year-old Princess Yaroslava stood almost naked in the icy cold, tatters of underclothing about her feet. Eyes piteous, her distraught glance darted about.

In the circle of light from a lamp she saw fleetingly a passing figure, and although the man's head was averted the expensively-tailored lines of his garments conveyed a message to her bemused brain. There, she knew instinctively, was one of her own kind. Desperately she cried out, unaware of beseeching aid from a distant kinsman.

"Help, please help me," she screamed, frenzied with fright and shame. "These horrible beasts——"

The young man swerved away, so abruptly and so blindly that he collided with an individual attired somewhat unusually in a lady's fur coat and patent-leather shoes over which bell-bottomed trousers billowed.

"You're surely not disturbed by a bit of fun are you, comrade ex-officer?" the naval rating jeered. "Those lads are only after satisfying themselves with the pampered little bitch."

The young man stammered. "I . . . I . . ."

"You don't look over-enthusiastic, ex-officer comrade," the sailor remarked with mock concern. "In that case . . . mm . . . you see, we Kronstadt boys have the trick of being able to make the most unlikely folk gush with real bloody enthusiasm; one way or the other, that is. Aye, them we suspect either pledge themselves damned quick to the new order, in a right gush as you might say, or a red stream gushes out of their throats even faster, it's as simple as that."

While Leading Seaman Georgei Kuznets laboriously started to explain this macabre jest to comrade-sailors, soldiers and workmen attracted by his bellow, the young officer sidled off, taking to his heels as soon as he dared.

On Liteynyi Prospekt he had another series of shocks. A dozen workmen, squatting on sacks bulging with the night's spoils, were wolfing down caviare, digging it out of hotel-sized tubs with silver spoons which, when finished with, they amused themselves by bending into fantastic shapes before throwing away. They held him up for a while.

Panting, his shuddering breath steam-like in the keen air, the young man hurried along, but was brought to a stark halt when gruffly hailed by a soldier near the Udyellanaya Church.

"Comrade ex-officer, is it seemly to pass the House of God without rendering tribute to God?"

"No . . . no, of course not."

The man laughed delightedly. "Then, comrade ex-officer, you

shall take part of my burden, so enabling me to pay respect to Him above. And if you try any tricks . . ." his smile evaporated as he snarled: "I'll shove a bayonet into you one way and a sword down your gullet the other until they're having a fighting match in your guts. Understand, comrade ex-officer?"

The young officer did. Most carefully he carried an ivory miniature framed in gold embellished with precious stones, a pair of glossy leather riding-boots, three many-branched silver candlesticks, four silk shirts, a pearl-and-silver crucifix, a green fringed tablecloth, and a woman's toque hat.

The private of the Lithuanian Regiment, who had been able to doff his flat cap at the church door, thanked him genially and even tried to explain:

"You see, comrade ex-officer, everything belongs to the people now. If you behave yourself you'll get your share. If you don't——" Bowed down as he again was under his load he made a single expressive gesture.

In the next street a mob clustered round a wine merchant's door. The choicest products of Crimean vineyards, red and white, poor stuff for men doing deeds, were hurled away scornfully, while over the heads of the crowd, passed from hand to hand, came bottle after bottle of cognac and vodka. The senseless were everywhere, and the loquacious and the ugly. Bottlenecks had been struck off, and many greedy drinkers' mouths were bleeding.

Close by an officer lay moaning in the gutter, his feet bare and hideously lacerated by broken glass upon which, compelled by bayonets, he had danced.

The young man's horrified gesture was noticed by two swarthy dockyard fitters. Hairy arms were slipped about his neck and, hanging on to him with maudlin affection, they deliberated with each other across his chest.

"Our comrade's belly is a mite particular," hiccupped one.

"Sh'understandable," his companion pronounced. "All the same, it's our duty to remind him of the glory of the revolution."

Fortunately both were in the mellow stage and their victim was allowed to escape after he had memorized and loudly repeated four lines of filthy doggerel about the Tsarina.

Thereafter the young man's passage was easier, particularly when he fell in with a stern-demeanoured battalion of the Knights of Saint George, with whom he was able to keep company until the houses of the district, thinning out, became immensely larger.

On Palace Quay he was checked by the shouting of mischief-seeking crowds who, brandishing loaded sticks and other improvised weapons, were advancing towards him, outlined sharply against the snow by the lights at the tops of ornate standards. Half-sobbing he dived through a gateway, tumbling headlong on a patch of unsanded ice. Picking himself up painfully he started off again, frantically climbing walls and spiked railings before pausing breathlessly to take bearings.

To his relief, though the rear quarters were not very familiar, he recognized the Kaivanov mansion, a dark mass silhouetted by a red glow in the sky from burning buildings beyond. He ran again.

Frenziedly assaulting the lower windows he found a protective bar loose at the fifth, and, using cap as shield, broke the outer and inner panes. Crawling inside, he found himself in a warren of passages as unknown to him as the laundry and drying rooms, through which he eventually fumbled in darkness.

For a few minutes he was hopelessly lost in his own home, but at last reached the echoing reception hall at the front. Then he raced up a curving shallow-stepped staircase, and along marble and polished parquet floors.

The noise he made brought his sister to the door of her boudoir, but by then he had passed. Beautiful evening-gown rustling, Princess Anastasia followed more leisurely to his suite.

As she entered his dressing-room, where the contents of four or five drawers were spilled on the floor, Prince Sergei was tearing at his neck-fastening.

Nerves unsteady, he spun about. "What the devil are you doing here, Stana, and rigged out like that?" he gasped. "Looking for trouble?"

A shade impatiently, Anastasia took a cigarette from a box and tapped it on the back of her hand. "Why shouldn't I be here?" she asked. "My dear Sergei Ivanovitch, the doors have all been strengthened recently and Papa had the ground-floor windows stoutly barred after the other revolution, when Grandpapa was murdered at Amsibu. Don't you remember what a hell of a life we led the masons who fixed the bars?"

"Bars!" Sergei retorted. "If they're any good why do you think all the servants have done a bunk?"

Quite astonished, she stared at him. It was true that the more senior members of the staff had refused to allow conditions to interfere with their attendance at a ball for upper servants at the Yaroshanovs; and though it was possible that others, like excited children lured by anything novel, might have taken French leave to watch the fun outside, surely some remained.

"No servants!" she was exclaiming when a most amusing notion struck her. "Sergei Ivanovitch," she went on, laughing, "how on earth did you get in?"

"What the devil does that matter?" Sergei shouted. "And don't tell me about the damned bars again, because they won't keep out those butchers."

Anastasia looked above her head, either at a neat smoke-ring or in resigned exasperation.

"They'll hold long enough," she remarked. "And don't be so infernally tiresome, Sergei Ivanovitch. You know perfectly well that the Guards will be let loose at any moment now, and they'll quickly scatter the riff-raff. I told Mimi Ivanovna so when she telephoned begging me to rush there."

Sergei had opened the stove and, crouching, was rubbing grime into a suit of Scotch tweed.

"The Guards left here are mostly replacement units, not of the old calibre," he said, lips curling strangely. "And they've gone over to the mutineers with the remainder of the garrison."

Eyebrows raised, his sister inquired: "Have they indeed? And which regiments, pray? And for God's sake don't set the place on fire."

He jumped up furiously. "All of them, you damned fool," he yelled. "The Moscow, Preobrajensky, Siemionov, Volkynian, Ismajloff—every damned one, and they're killing off their officers to begin with. And we'll be killed if we don't hurry out of this death-trap. We've seconds left, not minutes."

Emphasis to this warning was given when, before she could reply, a charge of dynamite placed efficiently by a sapper sergeant blew in the doors of the adjoining mansion northwards, along the quay.

The Kaivanovs' town house was not molested immediately. But when a thunderous attack began upon the front it was heard only faintly at the rear, where Prince Sergei, dirty and disreputable-looking, was climbing out of the window he had broken not long before. His sister was behind him, wearing ill-fitting boots, the soiled cloak of a wash-place woman, and a black skirt of shoddy material which hid the delicate hand-made underclothing of one of the most fashionable young ladies of the capital.

Having done their share by killing all officials from chief engineers to Grade Two foremen, it seemed as if comrade-workers at the power stations, determined to furnish comrade-liquidators elsewhere with all possible technical assistance, stepped up the voltage. In fine residential streets lamps shone with unparalleled brilliance upon broken bodies, rust-coloured snow, trampled oil paintings, and the litter from priceless manuscripts and illuminated missals destroyed for destruction's sake.

The sky was aflame also: mansions burned, the police buildings at the corner of Gorokhovaia and Zagorodnyi Prospekt smouldered, the Law Courts flamed yellowly, and the town house of Captain Count Wiazovsky, Imperial Russian Navy, whose invalid wife had been tossed outside in her bed, was a leaping pyre of fire.

Machine-guns barked, often inadvertently mowing down the comrades of the comrades manning them; and manacled gaol-birds released from prison—though not from handcuffs, whose keys could not be found—went on pillaging until weary of the intense cold, when they tramped back to detention-houses where the warders who had once guarded them swung limply from ropes.

On their journey to Vera Kalutkina's, of which one dominant impression was the tinkle of glass as windows were broken, Prince Sergei and his sister saw many ghastly sights: a family horribly butchered because a pair of silver-plated spurs, a Horse Trials prize, was displayed on their dining-room wall; the fiendish torture given to two Cossacks; the delicate-faced girl who had hanged herself with her own silk garters. And more personally, the drunken soldier, festooned with machine-gun belts, who thrust his hand into Anastasia's bosom.

A sailor wearing good conduct badges, who was idling further along under the red lamp of a brothel, evidently also considered her sweeter meat than the bare-breasted, cheaply-scented strumpets inside. He was alert and stone sober.

"No use struggling, my spitfire comrade," he said with a thin chuckle. "When pretty young comrades show themselves without the people's emblem they must expect what they get."

Anastasia ceased to resist. "As you will, comrade," she said coolly. "There's no police to lock me up now, praise be."

"Police?" The petty officer stared suspiciously.

She began to cough painfully and, bending lower to ease herself, gingerly felt her crutch. With hand still in that place she spoke hoarsely to the man.

"It's got me, comrade," she told him frankly. "Aye, it must be three months now since the accursed doctors refused to renew my permit, though I was only in the second stage then. But still," she leered, "if you're game, comrade."

"Hey!" he growled.

Her expression changed. "If I had that chap here now," she snarled. "In the Orel Rifles he was, the dirty bastard, and he must have been as rotten as a Mongol egg."

The sailor swore viciously. "On your way, you bloody whore," he said.

In this wise the Princess Anastasia Kaivanova escaped, but

neither she nor her brother spoke about it until well out of earshot.

"Self-preservation every time, my dear Sergei Ivanovitch," she murmured then. "Nothing like it."

Prince Sergei was shaking with fright and rage. "What did I tell you? I warned you, didn't I? Here you are."

This time she did not refuse, and tied round her arm the scarlet bandana he thrust on her.

Cautiously they slipped along dangerous streets, pushed forward on busier streets, and raced for alleys and doorways with hundreds of others when unexpected bursts of firing reduced crowded thoroughfares to unpeopled voids.

In the Hotel Astoria, where a massacre of Russians had been averted by the uncompromising attitude of Allied officers billeted there, only a few pilot lights were burning, in the hope of avoiding further attention.

Anastasia nodded towards the hotel. "I know heaps of men there. Perhaps——"

The crunch of many footsteps on the frozen snow prevented further discussion, and the mob pouring into the square was too menacing for them to think of remaining in that neighbourhood.

"No, *walk*," Anastasia hissed. "Loiter, Sergei Ivanovitch; anything except run."

A few hundred palpitating yards were covered before they reached the comparative safety of a narrow back-street in which, from rough wooden slabs, Chinese were selling human flesh. It was labelled "For animals only", and there were elbowing throngs of hungry-looking cat and dog lovers.

The crowds grew more dense and more vicious as brother and sister neared their destination. It soon became apparent that their half-sister had been too optimistic. Very select Sergeivsky Oulitsa, in which Mimi Kalutkina lived with her mother, was packed with people and looted property; three houses were on fire, and occasionally terrible screams could be heard.

"It could be suicide going to Mimi Ivanovna's," Sergei groaned. "I hope she'll be all right."

"God, so do I," Anastasia muttered, her cheeks whiter than they had been that night. "But we couldn't help and it might be better for them if we weren't there. A couple of scarecrows like us would quickly be suspected for what we were, if found with them."

Prince Sergei, before turning away, glanced towards the far end, which seemed reasonably quiet.

"I don't think either of them will be touched," he said. "After all, Vera Nikolaevna was one of our greatest ballerinas, and

Russians of every degree, which includes the degraded specimens around us, have always venerated such an *artiste*."

They had been speaking in English and, perceiving several inquiring glances, Anastasia roughly tugged his arm and went off into the Malorusskij dialect she had picked up in Cossack lands.

"Come on then," she snarled. "But you'd better know this, you miserable milksop, you'll either pinch a posh dressing-table set for me, with a nice china ring-holder *and* some rings to hang on it, or I shan't be so damned long before I'll give the glad-eye to a chap who will."

She continued to upbraid him, until they had left behind a circle of people who, from being curious, were now grinning broadly at these Little Russian country folk, enjoying the scared young fellow's discomfiture and as much as could be gathered from the virago's attack on him.

That effort tired Anastasia. "Oh, where can we go, Sergei Ivanovitch?" she murmured.

An hour and a quarter later they found refuge in Zacchariev-skaya Oulitsa with an elderly gentleman who had coached Prince Sergei in the all-important period of the final terms at the Page School. Mr. Collins welcomed the sorry-looking pair with open arms.

"Come in, my dears," he said, locking and bolting the door before bustling them into a book-lined room. "Now don't worry, you'll be as right as rain here, because if any of these scoundrels come trying their games on, well, they'll get the rough edge of my tongue. And you needn't laugh at me, Anastasia Ivanovna, for when Patrick Arthur Collins gets his rag out, as your nuisance of a brother is fully aware . . . there, there, my dear."

Princess Anastasia had, at last, yielded to strain. "You haven't seen what they've done, Patrick Arturovitch," she said, quietly sobbing.

For four days, during which the capital was given to foul horror, Sergei and his sister remained in that house. When they emerged it was to hear of the Tsar's abdication:

> "We have deemed it good to abdicate . . . not
> wishing to part from Our beloved son . . .
> We transfer Our inheritance to Our brother,
> the Grand Duke Mikhail Alexandrovitch. . . ."

From a newspaper they learnt also that the ex-Tsar's train had been shunted into a siding when returning from Army Head-quarters at Mogilev, to be left there until it had been decided what was to be done with the once-august traveller. Now, readers were told, he was to be known as Colonel Nikolai Romanov, a humiliating fall in military rank, one might say. But, contrary to the custom of the majority of kings and princes, this little man, tender father and mystic ruler, had never accepted any higher military title in the whole course of his simple life.

Prince Sergei and Princess Anastasia heard about other matters also: the Grand Duke Mikhail Alexandrovitch's refusal of the throne, and (received dazedly) an account of the Grand Duke Kirill parading with his sailors in support of the revolution. They also saw soldiers, sailors and workmen taking all roads to the Taurida Palace, to proclaim their recognition of the authority of the Duma.

In common with others of the nobility, the Kaivanovs suffered immense material loss, and mourned many acquaintances and friends. Vera Kalutkina was among these. She was dead, from natural causes; natural causes in her case presumably being the effect of shock on a heart weakened by dancing too long after the doctors forbade it.

But a nearer tragedy affected Anastasia and her brother far more, the disappearance of their half-sister. Mimi had vanished completely.

2

The worst disorders of Moscow and the capital did not extend to the South; in point of fact, apart from the abdication, the gravity of the situation was incompletely realized on the shores of the Black Sea.

Admiral Prince Kaivanov, returning from Sevastopol in response to an urgent telegram, put the position admirably to Admiral Prince Shulovsky, who likewise had been called from his duties at Nikolaiev by his family. The two gentlemen had met at Yekaterinoslav, where the less important Nikolaiev coaches were coupled on to the sleeping, library, smoke-room and restaurant cars which formed the well-appointed Sevastopol-Petrograd express.

"My dear fellow," Prince Kaivanov said emphatically, "every member of the Imperial Family warned the Tsar. We all have known that unless changes were made utter disaster might follow."

In the warm and comfortable *coupé* he continued to expound. Prince Shulovsky grunted occasionally, apparently more interested in glowing embers of wood from the engine or in powdery snow thrown up by the plough, which sometimes blanketed the window.

"That's all very fine, Ivan Mikhailovitch," he broke in as they were nearing Kharkoff, and attendants were smoothing well-laundered linen on to sleeping berths. "Severity was my line when I presided over the Sevastopol court-martial which cleaned up the *Kniaz Potemkin* disorders in '05—you didn't go, you remember—but I don't think the same attitude would be sound policy now, when we are in the midst of a much greater war. There are also too many unknown factors. For my part, I agree entirely with Admiral Kolchak."

It appeared that Admiral Kolchak, Prince Ivan Kaivanov's superior at Sevastopol, advocated, and insisted upon, a velvet-handed course of action.

"Namby-pamby measures, in my view," Admiral Kaivanov said arrogantly. "And I may say I had no hesitation in so informing the Commander-in-Chief. Moreover many of the officers present at the conference supported me. Actually, I later summoned an informal meeting to discuss the matter further."

Prince Shulovsky impatiently threw away a cigar, and with hardly-suppressed irritation poured out a glass of cognac.

"Which is exactly what I fear, Ivan Mikhailovitch," he said curtly. "The greatest failing of us Russians is to hold innumerable meetings and to fall out at 'em. If the officers divide, well . . . God help 'em in the end. He'll be the only ally."

At the tone of censure Admiral Prince Kaivanov reverted to the formality appropriate to the difference in seniority.

"Nevertheless, Sir, I think we shall find that in Petrograd the majority of senior officers incline to my attitude," he said stiffly.

Distinctly aggrieved, he excused himself and, a night's gambling in mind, set off along the corridor towards the superbly-equipped card room.

In Petrograd the Provisional Government's *Prikase* Number One abolished saluting and authorized soldiers and sailors to form committees to determine which, if any, of their officers were acceptable. A rumour that the land was to be divided out had not been confirmed so far, but a mere hint of the possibility spread like wildfire through the fighting forces and every train crawling back from the fronts was crammed with men who, voting themselves leave, were determined upon staking a claim. Tens of thousands of them, hungry and cold, added to the capital's problems; and as the wage-earners among the population had ceased altogether to work, the streets were congested.

Admiral Prince Kaivanov had protested most energetically in Sevastopol against a decision that officers, bowing to the men's wishes, should forthwith remove badges of rank. On reaching Petrograd he may possibly have had second thoughts on this question. Certainly he would never have reached Palace Quay if his servant had not cut from the shoulder-straps of his fur-lined blue pilot-cloth coat the eagles sewn on them.

His son and daughter escorted him round the great residence, in which countless servants were striving to deal with the savage disorder. The Master of the Stables had brought his grooms, ostlers and coachmen; dishwashers and lamplighters had been pressed into service; and the Steward harried chambermaids and footmen alike.

The tour of inspection began in the lower hall, but had barely started when Prince Kaivanov sat down. Deeply affected, he fumbled for a handkerchief and, more than a suspicion of moisture in his eyes, blew his nose.

"I still can't believe it," he muttered sadly. "My dear Vera Nikolaevna gone; it seems impossible. As sweet and charming a woman as ever lived. And I suppose our darling little Mimi is dead also."

"We've searched everywhere, Papa," said Anastasia, "and all Isvoltoff's clerks are out inquiring now. But so far we haven't come across a trace of her."

A picture of gloom, Sergei shook his head and lost colour when he spoke of the temporary mortuaries he had visited, in each of which hundreds of corpses were arranged in lines, many of them mutilated or charred beyond recognition.

"She must be dead. I . . . I . . ." he mumbled, "I only hope that her end was merciful, poor darling."

"My dearest Mimi." Her father was quietly crying. "She was delightful, wasn't she? It has always been a source of profound contentment to me that you both were so fond of her."

Tears filled Anastasia's eyes. "We loved her, Papa."

Vision blurred, Admiral Kaivanov stared about him, and sniffed. The lower hall stank of spirits and putrefaction. Pools of sticky liquid marred the floor, and the bodies of several domestics were still in the lift-well where they were killed, crushed by the lift which had deliberately been sent plunging down on them. The marble walls were chipped, and the heads of nymphs on either side of the broad staircase had been broken off; heavily nailed boots had ruined the shepherdesses on a tapestry wantonly used as a rug, and ancient jewelled ikons were no longer there, only the fastenings remaining.

"My God!" he said suddenly.

Anastasia checked him. "Wait, Ivan Mikhailovitch. Wait until you have seen more."

They went next to the state ballroom where gold trellis-work in the gallery had been hurled down to the floor, to join gleaming candelabra which, to judge by bullet marks in the moulded ceiling, had been shot down as the easiest way to ensure their fall. A broken chair had probably been the instrument used to shatter the fountain, where sparkling water formerly trickled from one shell to another.

For a few moments the head of the house of Kaivanov eyed the forlorn spectacle, and then turned to his children.

"Praise be that your dear mother cannot see this," he said simply. "Let us thank God she is safe in the Caucasus, away from these horrors. At least we have that for which to be grateful."

Really it was too funny—the idea of the old bird, fresh from his latest *bonne amie* at Sevastopol, turning on the soft pedal about their mother, whom he met hardly once a year. Son and daughter howled with mirth.

The joke sustained them past the litter-filled marble swimming-pool and through the dining-room, where medieval plates for offering salt and bread were missing and the only stamped leather left on chairs was that close up to the studs. So the trail of destruction continued—in the picture gallery some inventive creature had given the family portraits a macabre appearance by cutting out eyes, and in the Banqueting Hall vengeance had been taken on variegated wooden panelling and canvases of hunting scenes.

"Wild beasts," Admiral Prince Kaivanov commented. "But there shall be a reckoning for this."

The library was reached by a long corridor, along which doors had been torn from hinges, mirrors starred, and caviare and splinters of gold-rimmed glassware trodden into Persian runners.

"And worse than beasts." Prince Kaivanov continued his theme as he lowered himself cautiously into a damaged chair. "They at least are satisfied when hunger is appeased."

Anastasia looked vainly for a cigarette, until her brother gave her one. "They even killed the black swans and the deer at Tsarskoe Selo," she said witheringly.

Her father's glance roamed about the library. Books were strewn about, bronze figures of warriors leaned drunkenly, and busts of musicians and poets, swept from their pedestals, lay on the floor amid a sea of precious parchments.

"Even such innocent creatures, Stana," he said.

Sergei Ivanovitch, after giving his sister a light, applied the match to his own cigarette. A stream of fragrant smoke came from his nostrils.

"Of course you know about the massacre at Kronstadt, Papa?" he said. "A hundred and fifty officers put through a hole in the ice, including three of your term-mates at the Naval Academy, all admirals."

Prince Kaivanov shivered. "No, I hadn't heard about that."

"Yes," Sergei continued, "the sailors have been the worst element of—— God damn it, the lousy dirty swine," he shouted, dropping a folio of rare manuscript with excreta inside a fold, swearing again on discovering into what he had stepped. Blaspheming freely, he scraped his boots on the fire-dogs of the grate.

Shocked by the fate of many brother officers, Admiral Prince Kaivanov took no notice of his son's justifiable anger and disgust.

"A hundred and fifty," he muttered.

It was a blessing that, in twos and threes, a score of their friends called within the next quarter of an hour, on a round of ghoulish visits to ascertain the damage others had sustained, after creeping from hiding holes to inspect their own wrecked homes.

Princess Savoseva was among the arrivals. Dressed in odds and ends, it was characteristic of her that she was more worried about her wardrobe and the state of her auburn hair than about the disasters which had overtaken them.

"My dears, hasn't it been simply dreadful?" she shrieked as she ran in. "And do you know,"—her slightly protuberant blue eyes were tragic—"Those fiends *ravaged* my clothes cabinets and I haven't a stitch left fit to wear."

In the presence of many attractive women, Admiral Kaivanov was forgetting his anxieties.

"You need a drink, my dear," he said as he kissed her hand. "And a drink you shall have."

"We *hope*," Anastasia murmured.

Her father nodded. "Yes, there's that, of course."

But the assistant to the Master Cellarer had been faithful to his charge. The keys to the wine cellars were found on his body, beneath his shirt and against his skin, tied to a piece of string.

Gradually, under the influence of stimulating liquor, the future was more rosily viewed. The hum of conversation in the library grew and people who had not laughed for days began to do so. Indeed an impromptu luncheon party had been quite gaily bruited when the announcement of a newcomer, a young man by his demeanour so obviously the bearer of ill-tidings, sobered everyone.

"Cyrus Konstantinych, old man," Sergei said with concern.

In the silence, Count Petrov slowly walked towards them, his hair no longer shining and well-groomed, no longer the dapper staff officer.

"Cyrus Konstantinych!" Anastasia cried, hurrying to him. "Have you found Mimi?"

Ashen-faced, dark circles under his eyes and horror in those eyes, he looked vacantly at her.

"Yes, starving," he replied dully. "She was leaning against the stage door of the Mariinsky . . . waiting for her mother. Will you come with me at once, Stana?"

"Waiting at the stage door, my boy?" Admiral Prince Kaivanov inquired. "But——"

"What has happened to her?" Anastasia asked imperatively.

Count Petrov's lips were quivering. "She's been raped, Stana . . . raped many times . . . raped until . . ."—he nearly broke down completely—"raped until she went out of her mind."

They crowded round him, tried to comfort him, tried to persuade him that all would be well. And they mingled their tears with his.

Fully five minutes elapsed after he and Princess Anastasia had gone before they started to chatter again.

Petrograd chattered a great deal in those days.

The Provisional Government, far from being united, chattered away wildly. And the chattering Cadets on the Council quarrelled bitterly with the chattering Mensheviks of the Workers' Soviet, almost to the point of violence on occasion.

Another party, quite insignificant, was much more quiet. This minority party, the Bolsheviks, covertly watered the seeds of discord in other plots, and by equally subtle underground measures forwarded their own ambitious aims.

3

The days were lengthening, the Neva cracking and groaning, and soon immense blocks of ice would be floating down from Lake Ladoga. But this spring the Governor of the capital, in a freshly-painted barge, would not be ceremonially meeting the Governor of Peter and Paul in mid-river; this spring brightly-clad men in green rowing-boats would not be pulling out for the Opening of the Waters. It could be seen when the Neva was free for navigation—that would have to be all; no merry-making.

There were too many matters of grave import to consider; too much to be heard.

For instance, this mild-as-milk, soft-spoken fellow Vladimir Ilyich Uljanov, more often called Lenin, who had been one among a carriage-load allowed by the Kaiser to enter Russia through Germany. A bald-headed little runt worth listening to, and no error. Wasn't it strongly rumoured that he had given a street sweeper the Nikolai Bridge? And most assuredly the wife's cousin heard him present Saint Peter and Saint Paul, with all the Tsars' grand tombs, to a drunken *drosky* driver; and heard him advise the tipsy idiot that all he need do, if he *really* wanted it, was to go along with sufficient pals to grab it.

The catchphrases Lenin fired off made an ordinary chap ponder, too. *The Hour of Bolshevism has Struck*—it rang impressive; *Peace, Freedom and Bread*—right sensible, yes; and *Peace to the Huts, War to the Palaces*—well now, that sounded real promising, and it wasn't surprising that a lot of the Provisional Government's soldiers were thinking of changing to Lenin's side.

You couldn't leave out little Lenin's wife either. Comrade Krupska spouted some wonderful stuff for a woman.

And what about Comrade Trotsky, who all but fired the *Cercle Moderne* with his eloquence? He had quite a few brilliant notions.

Then that silver-tongued Kerensky. What an orator! He made salt tears run down your cheeks, made you feel as if you ought to snatch up the nearest rifle and gallop like hell to the front, to start up the new offensive against the Fritzes he was always crying for. A spellbinder, wasn't he?

But what was it Lenin said: *His Home and His Land For the Soldier*? Yes, there was a lot there. Perhaps little Lenin was only chaffing about giving away a fortress like Peter and Paul, but maybe the right idea was behind it.

It was a strange Easter. Slavonic litanies were chanted as of old, and gifts were made: of painted eggs, almond cakes of a kind, and chocolate birds of a sort of chocolate. *Christ is Risen* was heard, but there was nothing lighthearted about the response: *Verily He is Risen*. Officers of the Provisional Government's Army kissed their men, but the sour smell of food on moustaches had replaced the odour of wax and scent of old days. The Tsar was a prisoner, and whether or not he was kissed at Easter nobody knew. It was known, however, and tears streamed in every crowded church about it, that for the first time in three hundred years the name of the Autocrat was omitted from the *Te Deum*.

It was all extremely perplexing, and throngs moving between Lenin and Kerensky wore puzzled frowns.

Late spring, when Kerensky definitely began to win the day, brought a change for the better. Before very long the sea would be warm enough for the bathing beaches at Syestroryetsk to become pleasant meeting places, and society able to settle down to its own preoccupations.

Less than six months before—though to them it felt that number of years—two young gentlemen of the *Corps de Pages* had sampled crystallized dainties in Eliesieff's, shortly before Christmas.

Now, late one evening, both dressed very dingily, they were killing time on the outskirts of a crowd.

"I say, Feodor Antonych," Count Wiazovsky complained, "I don't see any sense in messing about here."

The growl of a dozen nearby listeners silenced him.

The moon, beyond the Kchechinskaia Palace, clearly showed the red flag floating over a residence once the property of a dancer favoured by a Grand Duke, and now used by the Bolsheviks for their headquarters. The same moon, as if it were a stage property, brought the front of the Palace to contrasting darkness, forming a broad black mount surrounding a balcony illuminated by red-tinted searchlights.

Solitary on this balcony, with a minimum of gesture, Lenin spoke to those who eagerly hung on to his words.

". . . the decision, comrades, rests with yourselves, my duty is but to give you the facts. You are men and women of intelligence, and it would be an insult for me to say more. Private property . . . is plunder . . ." His voice was low. "So plunder the plunderers."

That was how he ended; so quietly, so dryly.

After that, a red demon in those blood-red lights, he raised his arm, clenched his fist and waited three or four pregnant seconds, prelude to an exit, unseen in the darkness when every light went out, so much more striking than the never-ending histrionics of the sallow-faced, fussy little Napoleon, Kerensky, the head of the Government.

"A pretty pass when a man can speak like that and still live," young Eghbokoff said bitterly. "And——"

He broke off to keep a vigilant eye on an armoured car, a black Sheffield-Simplex belonging to no one knew whom. The vehicle was of alarming repute and would often, vomiting flames, turn its machine-guns on a crowded pavement for no other reason, it was believed, than to provide a laugh for a drink-exhilarated crew.

With several hundreds more he stood up again when the menace passed from sight.

"God, what have we come to?" he growled, pointing to a giant-sized poster referring to the Imperial House. "'The Whole Dynasty must be Drowned in Mud'," he read out. "God, when I think of it. . . ."

"It's pretty hellish stuff to look at," Count Wiazovsky said. "What do you say if we drive out to the Islands? To Sergei Ivanovitch's spot."

"Not damned well likely, not when that dear mother o' mine is indulging in baby-snatching. She's got her claws into a silly devil who's hardly out of his shell."

Count Wiazovsky nodded understandingly. "Bloody, I know, Feodor Antonych. But," he went on with overdone casualness, "would you mind if I went, old chap?"

Young Eghbokoff eyed him shrewdly. "It's that bitch Anastasia Ivanovna, isn't it?" he grunted. "Well, if you don't mind preposterous digs about being a little boy, good luck to you, Bolo, my lad."

Sensitive, Count Wiazovsky hastily averted his glance from a man who, suspected by the Bolsheviks as a traitor, had been branded with acid across his forehead. The lettering was indistinguishable, foul with yellowish pus which affected one of his eyes horribly.

"I am quite capable of dealing with any slight, Feodor Antonych," he said.

"Ah well, I'll give up," Eghbokoff sighed, but became more businesslike subsequently on producing from an inside pocket a fat wad of Kerensky notes whose value was slowly but steadily declining. "Fancy a wager, Bolo?" he demanded briskly. "I'll lay you five to one in hundreds that far from pulling it off with Anastasia Ivanovna you'll not even——"

He was scathingly interrupted. "A Polish gentleman," Count Wiazovsky remarked, "does not bet on ladies' favours."

"Ho! ho!" young Eghbokoff chuckled. "My God, Bolo, you've got it badly."

At that they parted, one ambling off philosophically, the other racing along as fast as his legs would carry him to a cab-rank.

In the past six months Count Wiazovsky had changed immeasurably, and his expression sometimes, in unguarded moments, was that of an orphan adrift in a nightmare world. The murder of a beloved father at Kronstadt had affected him cruelly, and he was ever haunted by the manner of his mother's death, alone and surrounded by jeering street crowds.

Shortly after midnight he arrived at a wooden house in a clearing in the woods, carrying an armful of long-stemmed pink roses obtained by waking a flower seller who was sleeping against the bole of a pine tree.

The gift to their hostess caused much amusement; Princess Eghbokova, speech slurred, commented shrilly, and her particular friend of the evening, a stripling Hussar Guard, laughed ungovernably; thirty more people childishly created a din, beating crockery with knives and forks.

Eyes blazing, Count Wiazovsky ate a cold supper and showed

such a tendency to toss off iced vodka that several level-headed guests signalled surreptitiously to the top of the table.

Princess Anastasia took appropriate action. "Boleslas dear," she called out, "I'm fearfully hot. How do you feel about a breath of fresh air? If you've finished, that is."

"I'd . . . I'd love to, Anastasia Ivanovna," he stammered.

"All right, let's go," she said, smiling.

It was very beautiful that still night as they climbed a high-arched bridge near a leafy screen of beeches. Through gaps in the trees many branches of the river could be seen, fingers rippled silver by the moon, flowing silently towards the sea.

"This is wonderful." Count Wiazovsky whispered, as if frightened of breaking an enchanting spell. "To be here, and to be with you, Anastasia Ivanovna."

Anastasia laughed. "I think the vodka is either giving you courage or illusions, Boleslas."

Dreamily he shook his head. "Not illusions, Anastasia Ivanovna."

When they strolled along again he tentatively took her arm. "May I?" he murmured wistfully.

"Of course, Boleslas." She smiled.

Standing close together they paused at the edge of a bluff, gazing at a fleet of small sailing craft. An amorous couple drifted in a rudderless yacht, a piano tinkled in a riverside house, and somewhere a man sang a gloomy song in a minor key.

"Anastasia Ivanovna," he faltered. "I . . . I. . . ."

Inquiringly she glanced at him, a pallid, hollow-cheeked youth who would nevertheless become, she decided, a disturbingly attractive young man. As to him, he was looking intently at her as if bent upon capturing forever this picture of her, an exquisite young woman bathed in moonlight.

"I'm head over heels about you, Anastasia Ivanovna," he blurted out.

"That's most gratifying," she commented lightly. "Do please go on, darling; women positively *adore* these revelations."

He made a passionate gesture. "Don't, Anastasia Ivanovna, for God's sake don't spoil it all with flippancy."

She was less patient: "All right, Boleslas. But don't be so silly."

The reaction was violent. "Silly!" he said with offensive curtness.

Anastasia's dark eyes flashed. "Yes, damned silly. And stop behaving like an infernal fool."

A flurry of emotions, fury predominating, changed the shadowed contours of his worn face as he stared at a boat slipping by on the shimmering waters. When in control of himself, he turned to her.

Bowing, he said, coldly courteous: "Perhaps you would prefer me to escort you back, Princess."

They walked in silence, neither speaking until the wide-open doorway of the villa was reached. Peals of laughter resounded inside, and a gramophone blared away, noises destined to be repeated night after night until the time came to leave for the season in Finland.

No one was in the hall, though each of the rooms leading off held its little party. There, in the soft light from oil lamps, Princess Anastasia noticed how very strained he looked.

"Thank you," she said, her voice warm. "And I'm terribly sorry, Boleslas, but I shall always remember the honour you have done me. *Always*, Boleslas dear."

This touch of kindliness played havoc with him and his face puckered. "There's no need for you to be sorry, Anastasia Ivanovna."

She squeezed his arm. "Don't you think it could be Stana?" she asked.

Blindly he nodded. Tears were streaming from his eyes, and his lips seemed to be framing words which were long in coming. Eventually he spoke:

"I'm so damned lonely now, Stana," he said.

It took her a couple of seconds to grasp his tragic meaning, but after that she acted speedily, as speedily as she again acted not many seconds later when, realizing how ashamed he would be if his weakness were seen, she heard the lively voices of late visitors approaching the villa.

Deeply moved, she kissed him. "Poor Bolo, you miss your people so terribly, don't you?"

"Oh, Stana, it's hell on earth. I try to force myself to forget, but——" Panic-stricken he glanced towards the door. "God!" he ejaculated. "And here am I, blubbering. I must get out of sight, but——"

Clutching his hand she drew him with her, up creaking stairs and along a passage.

Pearly light suffused the low-ceilinged room they entered, the moon softening the vivid colours of rugs on polished pinewood floorboards, and converting the slight unevenness of a peasant-craft patchwork bedspread into a stretch of shining hills and dark valleys.

Cheeks streaked with moisture, Count Wiazovsky gazed about wonderingly.

"This is your bedroom, Stana," he murmured, breath catching.

"My very own," she replied, smiling.

Wanly he attempted to joke. "If someone walks in you'll have to think afresh about me. Hopelessly compromised, what else could you do?"

Laughing, she pushed across the heavy door-bolt. "There, that covers that. And now," she continued gently, pressing on his shoulders, "I want you to sit down, Bolo, and talk your head off to me. About anything . . . about your mother and father, if you wish."

For a while there was silence and then, his face working, he haltingly began.

"You see, Stana, we've always been three. There couldn't have been more because . . . because Mama was paralysed when I was born. For father and me that made the invalid-couch in her *boudoir,* or her bed, the centre of our world—oh, I know we Poles are sentimental, but . . . but. . . ."

"No, no, Bolo darling. And please go on."

Young Count Wiazovsky made an effort. "Father and I were such pals, always . . . whenever possible I'd be shooting and hunting with him, and when I was a kid he'd take me to Kronstadt. I . . . I loved being with the sailors . . . they were jolly, then . . . and. . . ."

Anastasia's arm tightened round him. "Try not to think of Kronstadt, Bolo. Put aside everything else and just remember proudly that he would die as a gentleman, a Polish gentleman, with courage."

Eyes momentarily glowing, Count Wiazovsky nodded. "Oh, I know that, Stana. He wouldn't flinch whatever they did to him, not even in the last seconds as they pushed him down the hole in the ice."

"I'm sure of that, Bolo," she said.

He sighed. "And that's about all, Stana."

Princess Anastasia hid her surprise and, thinking it might be wise to leave him by himself, she spoke of Mimi.

"I'll slip along to see her for a minute or two, Bolo."

"She was very sweet, wasn't she?" he remarked heavily. "How is she?"

"Quite . . . out of her mind, and the doctors have had to keep her under more or less ever since. Somehow they managed to get the drugs, though now they're trying the effect of lessening the doses."

Lips uncertain, Anastasia went to her half-sister's room. Breathing deeply, Mimi was very still, far off in a morphia-induced sleep. She seemed wizened and strangely old.

"My poor darling Mimi," Anastasia murmured.

When she returned to her own room she was in nearly as bad a state as Count Wiazovsky, who had deteriorated rather than improved in her absence. Both made valiant attempts to take a better grip on themselves.

"Bolo," Anastasia said as she wiped her eyes, "you haven't really finished talking to me, have you? I'm certain there's something else. Why don't you tell me? It'll do you good."

He began abruptly, when apparently lost in a dream about the trees outside.

"Yes, it's Mama," he said rigidly facing the window. "She was never anything but full of fun . . . she teased us, and she laughed like a girl. And she was so pretty, Stana . . . I can see her now, looking exactly——" A heartrending groan shook him. "No, I can't," he corrected himself desperately. "All I can see is them picking up the bed and throwing it out of the window. I can see it dropping, but I can't see what happened to Mama . . whether the bed turned over on her, whether she was killed at once. Sometimes I imagine her dying in the street for hours, almost until I got there, waiting to smile at us and to tell us not to worry . . . and it's like being crucified."

Without warning, young Count Wiazovsky collapsed. Sinking forward he started to weep almost soundlessly, weeping, weeping, weeping—weeping until he could weep no more. When his shuddering body quietened, Anastasia spoke to him.

"Bolo, dear, the bed's in shadow. Lie on it and rest."

"Supposing I fall asleep, Stana?" he asked wearily.

"Then you'll have spent the night with a young woman who already has a rather tarnished reputation. But I shan't let you leave here until you're able to meet the world. So please don't argue."

Eyes closed, head sunk into a pillow, Count Wiazovsky felt her place an ice-cold cloth on his aching forehead. It was fragrant and refreshing, as soothing as the hand gently stroking his head. Emotion welled in him. She was wonderful, so very wonderful, so. . . .

When he awoke a shaft of moonlight fell upon the bed. In its pure, cold rays he saw she was beside him peacefully sleeping, lovely dark hair disarranged, her dress not hiding the rich, curving lines of breasts and body.

"Stana," he whispered, heart thumping.

His involuntary start disturbed her and sleepily she opened her eyes, dark shining pools.

"Hello, Bolo," she said, smiling. "I got so damned stiff in the chair, and I thought you wouldn't mind if I stretched myself alongside you."

"Mind!" he muttered, and repeated himself. "Mind! How could I mind when I've wanted you so. For months and months before . . . before Mama——"

"Steady, Bolo dear," she warned him.

"Yes . . . yes, I'll keep off them," he gasped. "But for months and months before I lost them I thought of you until I was nearly crazy, as Poles do when they love."

Distressed and moved, she glanced at him, and saw in the moonlight a romantic-looking creature with tortured eyes.

"Stana," he resumed throatily. "When we came in earlier . . . *you* kissed me. May *I* now be privileged to kiss you?"

"Yes, Bolo," she said at once.

His mouth pressed against hers and as he drew her to him, head swimming, he began to tremble.

"Poor Bolo," she murmured, sympathy for him welling over. "Poor old Bolo."

His grasp tightened as though it would hold forever.

CHAPTER III

PETROGRAD was excessively hot, fierce sun by day, airless at night. Hawkers of ice-cream, lemonade and pickled apples listlessly pushed top-heavy two-wheeled barrows along unswept streets stinking with kitchen waste and bedroom slops thrown from windows; naked urchins were able to go farther and farther down the flights dipping into the Neva; the tellers of the All-Russia Congress sweated when, for form's sake, they counted the unanimous vote by which the delegates declared themselves finally and completely antagonistic to the Provisional Government.

Troops at the front, Kerensky's mighty offensive just beginning, sweated for a few days, and then cooled off on deciding to refuse to obey their self-appointed officers.

Three thousand Kronstadt sailors, the loyal spear-heads of the Revolution, sweated under their heavy arms as they swooped down on the capital; Cossack horses sweated as they drummed wildly down the Nevsky to charge against the red-rosetted invaders from the naval base; the troops of the Provisional Government sweated when taking aim from behind the parapets of the Quay.

Kerensky sweated until his forces obtained the upper hand; the Bolshevik leaders, the Kchechinskaia Palace in danger of becoming a smoking ruin, sweated as they dived for pre-arranged burrows.

It was very hot in Petrograd when Kerensky, with magnificent magnanimity but less foresight, said: "We must shed no more blood"; and, in full proof of humanitarian goodwill, released Bolshevik prisoners into the oven-hot air, a stark change from chill underground cells.

It was very hot that summer as certain Ministers resigned in a pet when Social-Somethings fell out with Social-Something Elses, when the fate of Russia swayed this way or that, when division after division of German troops could safely be transferred from the Eastern to the Western front.

It was quite hot in Finland also, though there were tempering sea breezes, shady trees, and beautiful residences planned to keep cool.

For a full hour the sun had sunk beyond the Gulf of Finland; the westering glow was deepening. Lights were springing up in the windows of Princess Savoseva's villa, where a gigantic sturgeon had been placed on the dining-room table, and blue boxes of caviare surrounded by chips of ice.

There were about a dozen people in the hall. Under the coat-of-arms carved above the simple, massive fireplace a first cousin of the younger Kaivanovs adroitly performed a trick with a bottle of vodka sealed with the Imperial double eagle. He slapped the base, with slightly curved palm, that's all. It looked simple.

"Splendid, darling." Princess Savoseva clapped her hands as the cork hit the beechwood ceiling. "And now what?" she asked archly.

"Oh, chuck down another drink, Olga Ivanovna," Princess Anastasia told her rudely. "It helps to promote lust later on."

Her hostess gasped. "Really, Stana, I think that is quite unpardonable. *And* suggestive. *And* crude."

Restless, Anastasia rose as if she had little use for present company. "Dreadful of me," she remarked.

Each member of the small group glanced at her as she stalked off, and then at one another.

"I don't know what on earth has come over her," Princess Savoseva complained, still ruffled. "Really, she has never been in anything but a black mood lately."

The Kaivanovs' cousin chuckled. "Stana has always been renowned for her moods."

Princess Merzelena, convinced despite his protests that Prince Sergei had been steadily growing more uneasy throughout the day, satisfied herself about him and joined in the conversation.

"Personally," she said, lips thinning, "I have never found Anastasia Ivanovna other than detestable. Of course, I may have been unfortunate. . . ."

She shrugged and again turned towards two tall windows opening on to a broad balcony, against which Baron Matviei Tchalmin, scowling ferociously, was talking to her lover. Curtly rebuffed a few moments before when he endeavoured to intercept his companion's sister, Baron Tchalmin's swarthy complexion was deeper-hued than was normal with him.

"What the devil is the matter with Stana, Sergei Ivanovitch?" he demanded. "Dammit, she ticked me off just now as though I were something obscene."

That morning Prince Sergei had heard Princess Savoseva casually mention the names of a few people who might be calling in before the end of the day. To his consternation one of them was a lady, not of his sister's and her friends' circle, to whom lately he had been paying appreciable, though discreet, attention. On the one hand he felt excitement rising in him about even the bare prospect of her arriving; on the other, he had forebodings as to what embarrassing possibilities there were if she did. Yet again he glanced outside.

"And aren't you, a trifle, Matviei Jacobych?" he asked, boldly casting off unpleasant speculations. "My God, I'd say you were, you old lecher."

Unaware that Baron Tchalmin suffered him merely for strategical reasons, Sergei revelled in the terms-of-equality friendship he had struck up with the gayest and most degenerate spark in Town.

"You would," Baron Tchalmin muttered. Smoothly successful hitherto in his womanizing, he was completely baffled by Princess Anastasia, with whom he had not advanced an iota for weeks. But if his failure was a matter of chagrin to him it made him also more determined not to relax. "Possibly," he grunted.

"Women!" Sergei gesticulated freely with his hands. "Anyhow, old chap, what about a Turk?"

As he pulled out a cigarette case a small gilt box shot to the floor, the lid opening to disclose two compartments containing pink and white tablets respectively. Stooping, he picked it up and in one astonishingly swift motion removed from sight potent specifics prepared for him in Georgia from a centuries-old recipe.

"What the hell are those for?" Baron Tchalmin growled. "Heartburn, angina, or flat feet?"

Red-faced about the *contretemps*, Sergei was saved further awkward questions by the appearance of the lady who had been in his thoughts all day. Slipping a sly leer and a smutty aside to

Baron Tchalmin, he hastened to her and devotedly kissed her hand.

"So you have managed to come, my dearest Irma Adolfovna," he said warmly. "I've been on tenterhooks this past hour . . . with my eyes glued to the clock. . . ."

The Countess von Schmalandorf was the Russian-born widow of an Austrian gentleman who years before, when Prince Sergei was a small boy, in fact, had shot himself on the morning following his nuptial night. She was extremely attractive; a credit to dressmaker, hairdresser and maid, and illustrated to perfection that beauty treatment can be a fine art.

"Impetuous creature, aren't you," she replied, insolent glance flickering towards a lady who had risen abruptly at the far end of the room. "But perhaps you are not a strictly truthful boy."

Usually rather languid, Princess Merzelena quite rapidly skirted furniture and other obstacles as she headed for the new-comer. Meantime Prince Sergei, with the charm which had such a magic effect upon women of a generation older than his own, protested strenuously about the insinuation. But his voice speedily tailed off.

"My dear Irma Adolfovna." Princess Merzelena held both hands out in greeting when she joined the couple. "How very nice to see you again."

Countess von Schmalandorf's response was no less cordial. "My dear Varvara Mikhailovna," she gushed. "This is *quite* enchanting. It must be ages since we last met."

"Oh, *utter* ages," Princess Merzelena agreed.

The two ladies chatted away vivaciously, Princess Savoseva's highly-titillated guests watching the little drama whose first act ended when Princess Merzelena fondly squeezed Sergei's arm.

"Darling," she cooed. "Do fetch me a handkerchief from my room. You'll see a sachet about somewhere."

Prince Sergei's throat was dry. His first two words in reply were whispered, the second pair emerged explosively.

"Of course, my dear," he said.

Countess von Schmalandorf was too adroit to allow this. Amusingly and exaggeratedly she dwelt upon the heat of the afternoon and its disastrous effect on her.

"My dears," she said, "I'm so parched that I am certain I shall die here on this spot if I don't have a drink. And," she smiled bewitchingly at a luckless young gentleman who was in the unfortunate position of being neither quite off with the old nor on with the new, "Sergei Ivanovitch, *darling*, I just can't wait a second. So do hurry to save me."

Apprehension was visibly damping Prince Sergei's smooth

brow when a flash of inspiration enabled him to wriggle out of a nasty dilemma. Murmuring: "Bottle of just the precise medicine in my room," and muttering: "Kill two birds with one stone," he departed post-haste on his twin errands.

Princess Savoseva partially stifled a giggle, but as Princess Eghbokova was not concerned in the courtesies as between hostess and guest she had no need to discipline herself. Her hard laugh rang out.

"Stana seems as sullen as ever," she remarked when Princess Savoseva returned to her after welcoming the latest arrival. "Positively vixenish."

Princess Savoseva shrugged. "One becomes so inwardly weary of warding off a man if one really wants him. Personally my view is that Stana has put Matviei Jacobych long enough in his place."

As the other members of the house-party, with the exception of Princess Merzelena, had gathered round Countess von Schmalandorf, they wandered towards Princess Anastasia, who lately had visibly shed some of her bloom. As her closest friends had been sympathetically declaring for some time, that was not surprising when she worried so constantly about Mimi Ivanovna.

"Cheer up, darling," Princess Savoseva said to her. "If you don't, you'll slip into a decline or something equally dreadful."

"Then Matviei Jacobych *will* lose interest," Princess Eghbokova nodded warningly.

Irritably Princess Anastasia turned on them. "What the devil do I care about him?" she snapped. "And why the hell should I go into a decline?"

"*Dar-ling*, you are in a dreadful humour," Princess Savoseva wailed. "We're only troubled for your sake. Because you look so frightfully peaked."

"Peaked!" Anastasia's slumbrous eyes quickened.

At that moment she saw danger, and instantly took the bull by the horns.

"Yes, I am peaked," she agreed hollowly. "I suppose it's inevitable."

If this remark surprised them, as it did, they were far more astounded when she, who never cared what she said or where she said it, put a finger on her lips and nodded her head sideways towards a deep, flower-bowered recess.

Dumbstruck, her friends followed her into the privacy of a small extension jutting out from the main room.

"What is it, Stana?" Princess Savoseva gasped.

Making sure that no one was within short range Anastasia whispered into the super-attentive ears of both ladies.

"*Pregnant!*" Princess Eghbokova goggled.

Cutting short a high-pitched squeal of astonishment by clapping a hand over her mouth, Princess Savoseva resumed in a carefully lowered voice.

"So that's it," she said with an air of triumph. "I've wondered and wondered why you've been so unkind to Matviei Jacobych. It's because you blame him. And you shouldn't, Stana, not *entirely*."

Princess Anastasia ignored this and started to dwell in some detail upon an austere residence, smelling strongly of disinfectants, in the fifth line of Petrograd's Vasili Ostrov—where ladies of rank could have a certain imperative service performed for a commensurate fee. Accommodation had already been reserved for her.

"But I have now decided not to go," she told them with impressive gravity.

This unexpected *volte-face* had its effect upon her audience. Both spoke at once. Neither received an immediate reply.

Dreamily Anastasia looked about her. The servants had lighted tall candles whose soft glow shone upon bright blue silk monograms on table napkins, a red-and-blue hemstitched tablecloth, and the Savosef crests on gleaming china. There was a delicious smell of mushrooms frying in sour cream.

"I'll tell you why, my dears," she said, a tender light in her eyes. "Because I can't, because I know it would be wrong, and above all because . . ." she faltered and, under the stress of intense emotion, clasped her hands tightly on her breast, "because I don't wish to. Oh, my dears, can't you understand how glorious it will be for me when I have fulfilled woman's true purpose in life?"

Princess Eghbokova's perception was always quicker than that of her hostess, who was gazing, mouth open, at the Madonna-like pose. That was why Princess Savoseva nearly jumped out of her skin, startled by ear-piercing laughter at close quarters.

"You devil, Stana." Princess Eghbokova nearly choked. "If you hadn't overacted at the end I'm damned if I mightn't have believed your rigmarole. But that prudish miss stuff. . . ."

Anastasia laughed. "Could have been worse. I'll split my sides for weeks whenever I remember your moon-struck faces."

The commotion attracted attention, and when Prince Yura Nitchkoff, of the flat-nosed Nitchkoff family, learnt what it was about he at once suggested a toast to the "might have been." In his exuberance, as he swept his arm, four tea-glasses in silver holders were sent flying.

A better idea was provided by the Kaivanovs' cousin, who filled a wide-bowled glass and pushed it into the hand of the "mother-not-to-be."

"Do the toasting yourself, Stana," he said, grinning. "What about declaiming that old family thing of yours . . . to the glory of something or other."

This notion caught on and Anastasia was boisterously lifted by four gentlemen on to a table. With glass raised above her head and in quite her old form, she did her best.

"To that blood-thirsty old boy, the Ataman Guchkor Kaivanov, who with a handful of loyal men," she screamed, "conquered and . . . dammit, I've forgotten. . . ."

Baron Tchalmin's pale eyes had been filled with admiration as he looked at the sparkling young woman on the table, and it was he who, encouraged by a dazzling smile, stretched up his arms and swung her by the waist to the floor afterwards.

"Thank you, Matviei Jacobych," she said demurely.

Laughingly he bowed in acknowledgement. "My dear," he said a shade wryly, "that was quite the most intimate service you have permitted me so far."

"So far, Matviei Jacobych?" she inquired, dimpling.

The change in her attitude had tonic properties on him, and with precisely the right mixture of dashing assurance and the cavalier's deference to a lovely young woman, he explained:

"Let us tread warily, my dear. But may I presume so much as to say that had you been bringing a less phantom-like child into the world I should have considered myself the most favoured of men to be its other parent."

"You!" Anastasia's eyes widened innocently.

In *his* old form now, and too experienced to be deceived by her wiles, Baron Tchalmin chuckled. "Yes, my dear."

To all of them she seemed genuinely perplexed. "But . . . but Matviei Jacobych, the point is. . . ."

"Little minx, aren't you?" he remarked good-humouredly. "And what is the point, my dear?"

It is against all probability that her answer represented the truth. But, a wonderful lead given her, a situation had been brought about—cleverly though hellishly, she admitted to herself —in which she could most hurt a man of his special conceit.

"A certain doubt which persists in my mind, my dear Baron," she told him with cruel distinctness, "as to whether you are capable of becoming a father."

If she had slashed his cheek with a whip he could not have recoiled more suddenly. Face aflame, trembling from head to foot, he stared half-insanely at her before spinning on his heel. Without bidding farewell to his hostess he left the villa and was not seen again that night.

As Princess Merzelena murmured venomously to her left-hand

neighbour at the supper table, it was a remark "which no decent woman would have made."

But Princess Merzelena had been in a smouldering temper for hours, and she herself was soon involved in a quarrel with Countess von Schmalandorf, conducted harridan-style on the princess's part and with cool and devastating effrontery on her opponent's. This resulted in a carriage being brought to the door shortly after midnight, in which Princess Merzelena, Prince Sergei's discarded mistress, started out alone.

These were welcome and enlivening interludes. Another, of a much more minor nature, occurred when one of Princess Savoseva's servants arrived from Petrograd the next evening bearing a telegram despatched by Prince Savosef in the Crimea. The utter scorn on Olga Ivanovna's face convulsed everyone when she read out her husband's message, which demanded she join him forthwith.

In the blue, star-lit night Princess Savoseva's house-guests and visitors sat on the veranda: gossiping, flirting, arguing the evolution of man, drinking, differing and making friends again. The latest item of news from Petrograd was discussed—an optimistic speech by the semi-Jewish lawyer, Kerensky, who slept in the Emperor's bedroom in the Winter Palace.

Prince Yura Nitchkoff sighed. He was sharing a wickerwork *chaise-longue* with his hostess.

"God-awful, isn't it?" he muttered. "When you think what those devils did. . . ."

"How is Mimi Ivanovna, Stana?" someone called from a very dark nook. "You brought her here, didn't you? Incidentally I dropped in on Cyrus Konstantinych the other day, and he looked frightful."

Abruptly Princess Anastasia put down her glass. "He's wonderful with her, *wonderful*. You see she can't bear people near her; men, rather. . . ." Tears welled in her eyes and, in sympathetic silence, her friends waited until she was able to resume. "She speaks more often now, but only meaninglessly, and wherever she is, in whatever room, she stares nearly all the time either into a corner or at the ceiling above her head."

"But why?" several people murmured.

Anastasia had difficulty in continuing. "In Vera Nikolaevna's lower hall a piece of moulding fell down long ago—you know how difficult it was to have repair work done—well, Cyrus Konstantinych is nearly sure that the damaged spot is what Mimi was. . . ."

A young man in the next chair leaned over. "Take it easy, Stana darling," he said.

". . . what Mimi was looking at when she was raped and raped," Anastasia said in a desperate rush.

A murmur of horror rose about her. "It makes one feel physically sick," mumbled her cousin, who indeed sounded a little sick. "But why, Stana, does she stare into a corner?"

"We . . . we don't know," Anastasia replied through her tears.

Those were the days in Finland; periods of wild gaiety, times of heartbreaking sorrow and repining. Lively tea-parties under the shade of orange-coloured awnings, joyous dancing to the strains of gipsy orchestras at night—and then, as counter, more rumours about the collapse of the Army, and place-names proving the tremendous German advances.

"That dinner-party you've arranged for when we return to town," Princess Savoseva said mournfully one afternoon. "You'll never be able to give it, Stana."

Anastasia tipped back a broad-brimmed straw hat with which she had been shading her face.

"You talk as if the rabble will regain control, Olga Ivanovna," she retorted, rolling on to her knees to glance challengingly at friends sunning themselves on the warm sands of the beach. "But I shall expect you all there. At least *I* don't intend allowing a few revolutionaries to put me off."

The next day, though the summer had not quite waned, she left for Petrograd.

The daughter of the house of Kaivanov had an engagement which, for all her waywardness, she would never have thought of breaking. Her closest companions understood that a kind old gentleman named Collins would be starting out for his homeland shortly, and she intended to see him off. He was to receive certain gifts before he left: a jewelled dress watch, diamond studs, and a gold-fitted dressing-case, marks of Kaivanov esteem and gratitude. Prince Sergei, who had also sheltered beneath Mr. Collins's roof in critical days, did not accompany her—he was in the throes of a passionate affair with the cool and collected Countess von Schmalandorf, whose ardour seemed to exceed his own, to the amazement of all who knew her.

By immense labours the British Embassy had arranged for as many as possible of their nationals to be repatriated to England and, owing to the war, this meant for the travellers a journey of some uncertainty and risk.

As the train drew away, and it was no longer possible to see Mr. Collins, Princess Anastasia Kaivanova's bright smile vanished. She turned and, replacing her handkerchief, started to walk along the platform, which was almost ankle-deep in old paper, fruit skins, chewed seeds, and offal even less polite.

"The filthy swine," she said aloud.

The root cause of her fury, however, related to the condition she was in, not to the sorry state of the capital.

Nevertheless, a summer's brief span had brought tremendous change to Petrograd. Traffic had to take care of itself, and every hoarding and every house-end was filled with the propaganda posters of the contending parties:

TO HELL WITH THE DARDANELLES—WHO WANTS CONSTANTINOPLE?

This demand, in scarlet lettering, attracted the eye five stories high.

WE WANT OUR HUSBANDS AND SONS HOME!

—a cry from the heart on a banner, one end of which was secured by a rope around the bronze neck of an Imperial statue.

A third, belonging to a rival school of thought, presented an idea on a more noble scale. It read:

KEEP FAITH WITH OUR GALLANT ALLIES: YES, WE KNOW YOU WILL

Princess Anastasia's long automobile, dull grey paint now daubed over glossy daffodil, waited outside. Her chauffeur wore a cloth cap, soiled linen jacket, and tweed trousers. As he opened the rear door for her she snapped:

"You know where, next. Then put the car away again."

Valya Igorovna, sitting on an occasional seat facing her mistress, gaped at the many gambling dens which had sprung into being, and at swarms of people fighting their way into shops to buy anything on offer while their money had some modest value. But the maid's lively brown eyes almost started from her head when she glimpsed a regiment of women soldiers stepping out, rifles at the slope, bayonets fixed.

"Look, Highness," she gasped.

It was a city of unease, in which orators shouted each other down and dazed crowds wandered aimlessly.

Recently Kerensky had denounced General Kornilov as a traitor, though he had earlier appointed him Commander-in-Chief of the Army. General Kornilov, wearying of the Provisional Government's policy of no policy, retaliated by sending General Krimoff against the capital with his famous Savage Division.

These hell-for-leather troops advanced valiantly, and then reeled in confusion under a non-stop pamphlet attack.

A few minutes later, in Vasili Ostrov, a dark alert-faced gentleman bowed over the hand of his distinguished patient.

"Everything is in readiness, Highness," he said gravely. "If you will be kind enough to follow me."

Princess Anastasia loosened her white dust-coat. "Before then," she remarked ungraciously, "I think it might be advisable to give you this."

The fifty one hundred rouble Nikolai notes crackled. But they vanished from sight, apparently unseen by the recipient, in the deft manner associated with the leaders of his profession.

"My dear Princess," he said reproachfully. "Perhaps a little discomfort, but no more than that. There is no reason whatsoever," he brought his glance down from the lofty ceiling of his impressive room, "for you to feel alarmed."

Scowling, Anastasia turned on him. "Who the hell thinks I'm alarmed?" she demanded.

The doctor tut-tutted. "My dear lady——"

"Oh, let's get on with it," she interrupted him brusquely.

Deferentially he led them to a white-painted bedroom, commodious and spotlessly clean. It was well-appointed, as could be expected of a specialist with an immensely wealthy *clientèle*.

Valya Igorovna began to lay out diaphanous night-wear and lacy little bed jackets, and the surgeon had another brief conversation with his patient before bowing himself out.

2

There was wild activity in the kitchens of the Kaivanov mansion on Palace Quay. The Master Chef cuffed a dishwasher, screeched, held his plump hands to high Heaven, wept, and at last dipped a finger in steaming *schi* soup. There was a palpitating hush as the *artiste* tasted his creation.

A massive trolly stood ready for loading for the first long journey to the banqueting hall; the red soup would be placed on the top tier and meat-filled pastries, hot from the oven, on the shelf beneath, together with bowls of thick cream.

The babel broke out again. The Chef examined the sterlet, frowningly eyed crisp fowls and the pickled cherries which went with them, and prodded a roast of stuffed mutton. He also glanced searchingly at venison, slow-cooking tree partridges, and a fruit-and-nut pudding.

In the gloom of the wine cellars the Master Cellarer wrought amid champagnes, Crimean wines, Caucasian wines, wines from sunny France, wines from torrid Spain, long-stemmed bottles from old Germany, and green bottles of Shiraz. His voice echoed in the arched vaults as he bawled authoritatively at his four aproned assistants.

Prince Sergei Kaivanov and his sister were entertaining their friends.

Heavy sideboards in the Silver Chamber were loaded with choice dishes: cold smoked fish, tiny salted cucumbers, caviare, hot mushrooms, stuffed eggs with sauce, and other appetizing fare to which guests helped themselves before dinner in the banqueting hall beyond.

Prince Sergei wearily picked up a small gold-enamel plate veneered with a fine skin of glass and forked on to it a diminutive wine-flavoured sausage, a second sausage grilled in butter, both steaming; to these adding a heaped tablespoonful of finely-chopped vegetable salad.

Bearing this he set out, a young man looking very much the worse for wear, pouchy-eyed and sallow, to rejoin the Countess von Schmalandorf, who was standing well clear of the throng.

"Thank you, darling," she said, smiling warmly at him.

Liveried servants were serving glasses of vodka, and lively chatter and laughter resounded everywhere. Nothing but gay faces could be seen, though singularly enough Princess Eghbokova's expression completely changed, becoming a trifle resentful, when she glimpsed young Count Wiazovsky. But after all it *was* awkward, she told herself, mentally tossing her head, when a friend of one's son was present on an occasion promising so much fun.

Some reflection of her feeling revealed itself and her friend and hostess, who was passing, paused to speak to her.

"Don't be so downcast, Valya Androvna," Princess Anastasia whispered mischievously. "If you must take your hair down later there are plenty of rooms to disappear into."

"But why did you ever ask him?" Princess Eghbokova said, her voice plaintive. "It *will* cramp my style and its most inconsiderate, Stana."

"Because he still broods horribly about his mother and father," Anastasia retorted. "He needs shaking out of it."

Duties demanding attention, she continued her way, here and there exchanging a few words with guests while gradually moving towards the door.

Her passage was surreptitiously watched by Count Wiazovsky. Since that unbelievable night one thing was painfully clear to him. So be it then: a gentleman of pride does not remind a lady of what she has been to him if her manner subsequently indicates that the episode has been of scant importance to her.

When Anastasia entered the middle vestibule the remote smile of a hostess with much to do broadened into a genuine smile of welcome when she saw a very *petite* young girl in a magnificent gown tottering on abnormally high Cuban heels from the staircase gallery. Xenia Menshek-Pelikova was very resplendent, and glittered with diamonds from the *kokoshniki* perched on her flaxen hair to the decorations of her shoes; in between these points, around her throat and arms and on her dress, more diamonds winked amidst fat rubies, luscious pearls, and emeralds.

"Hello, Xenia Borisova," she cried out.

The girl's green eyes were shining and excited. "Oh, Stana, it's divine of you to have invited me to one of *your* parties," she exclaimed. "I've been thinking of nothing else for days and days."

"Mmm," Anastasia murmured.

"Prinked myself up rather decently for it," her guest admitted.

"Oh, wonderfully, and that rag you're bundled into is utterly exquisite," Anastasia commented. "But darling, don't you think you may be spoiling its effect a teeny bit by portering a load of family heirlooms?"

"My jewels," Xenia muttered. "Yes, I did wonder about them."

Anastasia sighed. "Wonder no more, my dear. An Oriental potentate would be consumed with jealousy if he saw you."

"My God!" Xenia said tragically.

Her hostess took a few reflective paces. "Xenia, darling," she began, pulling a wry face, "of late I seem to have acquired a tedious mother complex. But if I might venture to advise you——"

"Please do, *please*, Stana," the girl begged.

"Right!" Anastasia said briskly. "Stagger off to my boudoir as best you are able, and let my maid relieve you of a substantial part of your weight. Then glide back again and stagger all the men—you will, darling."

Xenia blushed. "You *are* nice, Stana," she said. "But . . ." she went on eagerly, "what shall I keep on?"

Crooking a finger, Anastasia spoke to a footman, instructing him where to take her *protégée*, and then stood off to inspect her.

"A ring for each hand, a bracelet for each arm, and the rope of pearls, of course," she announced firmly. "The *kokoshniki* is too old for a child, but it's very charming on you so leave it and don't disturb your hair."

"Is that *all*?"

Anastasia was staring with acute distaste at an oval brooch on the girl's low-cut corsage.

"All," she retorted. "And if ever I catch you with that meat-dish on again I'll liquidate you. Now off you go."

Giggling, Xenia obeyed the order, while Anastasia returned to the Silver Chamber, smiling.

Fully thirty more people were due to be announced, and it was over an hour before the guests wound in a procession of couples into the banqueting hall, where a line of flaming candles shed a pool of soft light on napery, silver and gold.

Dinner was eaten very leisurely, servants bringing round yellow-wrapped cigarettes after each course. As time passed the smoke grew denser, laughter shriller, many pairs of eyes more excited, and some eyes a little glazed.

Baron Tchalmin sat at the right of his hostess at one end of the massive carved table.

"You seem very pensive, Matviei Jacobych," she said to him.

"Just wondering, Stana," he replied. "Just wondering why the hell I can't keep away from you."

"An important point, Matviei Jacobych," Anastasia agreed lightly.

After that she spoke to her left-hand neighbour, her glance often straying to a point midway down the table, where Count Wiazovsky and Xenia Menshek-Pelikova were seated together. In the earlier stages of the meal she had been amused by the manner in which the young couple aped the behaviour of a man and woman of the world. Now, dark hair almost touching flaxen, they were relaxed, joking with one another.

Anastasia smiled at her own thoughts.

Baron Tchalmin broke into her reverie, dragging his glance from lovely neck and bosom.

"Pleased with yourself, aren't you, Stana?" he asked bitterly.

She laughed. "No, satisfied rather, Matviei Jacobych."

"Satisfied you're making a fool of me, that's it," he retorted, voice thickening. "If not, why that damned secretive smile?"

"My dear," she said, turning to him with immense concern, "I believe we are at cross purposes. My satisfaction is not in any way concerned with you."

"Now look here, Stana."

Anastasia, however, infuriated him still further by showing she was much more interested in the Major-domo who, after speaking to her brother at the other end, now marched majestically behind guests' chairs at the left-hand side of the table, lower domestics scurrying out of his path.

Reaching her, the household's senior servant bent his back low in obeisance, and repeated the message his master had ordered him to bring.

Anastasia nodded. "The lady's grandmother has died, is that it, Felix Pavlych?"

"Yes, Highness, she ascended but a few minutes ago. A painless departure, I understand, and at peace with God, Highness."

Dismissing him with a word of thanks, Anastasia murmured: "You will forgive me," to either side, and leaving her chair, walked down the room to the old lady's granddaughter. Leaning over the girl's shoulder she said gently:

"Will you please come with me, Xenia, my dear?"

Within five minutes she returned, alone. Her friends were discussing the news, decidedly affected at the thought of a youngster now without kith or kin. The Menshek-Pelikoffs had been neither a prolific nor a lucky family for several generations.

She sat in the vacated chair. "Bolo," she said, "will you be kind enough to take Xenia Borisova home?"

"If you wish," Count Wiazovsky replied a trifle stiltedly.

Little Xenia Menshek-Pelikova had not appeared when, in heavier outdoor clothing, he entered the lower hall, where Anastasia awaited him. They had a short conversation and, skilfully handled, he gradually thawed.

"I'm afraid this isn't the pleasantest of tasks for you, Bolo," she said gravely. "But I particularly wanted someone . . . someone sensitive and understanding to accompany her. You see I'm rather attached to her—she *is* such a pet."

After seeing off the couple from the carriage-porch, a romantic-looking youth and a pretty girl with red-rimmed eyes who seemed comforted by his gentle attentions, Princess Anastasia went back to the banqueting hall, where the party had resumed its old swing.

From that stage nothing else could be expected other than increasing uproar, and two hours later, at three o'clock in the morning, the Countess von Schmalandorf slid her hand over Prince Sergei's.

"Darling," she said, her grip tightening. "Don't you think we might withdraw to your suite now?"

Her lover groaned, almost audibly. "My dear," he replied feebly, glancing at her with ill-concealed distaste, "I fear we must forgo our enchanting pleasures for once. Surely you realize, Irma Adolfovna, that as host I must remain to support my sister?"

Countess von Schmalandorf's laugh rang out. "I can't say that I have noticed you taking an onerous view of your duties as host so far."

She was drawing him out of his chair when salvation appeared in the person of Count Wiazovsky. Pallid, forgetting to remove his fur cap, the youth swayed uncertainly.

Profoundly thankful for a sound excuse, Prince Sergei released himself from Countess von Schmalandorf's hotly-clinging hand and hastened down the room.

"My dear Boleslas," he said, "whatever is the matter, old chap? Nothing wrong with Xenia Borisova, is there?"

"Nothing yet, Sergei Ivanovitch," Count Wiazovsky replied sombrely. "But I shall go to her again in the morning—later this morning, that is."

No wiser, Sergei asked: "Yes . . . yes, if it pleases you. But why, my dear fellow?"

Tears in his eyes, Count Wiazovsky slowly and sorrowfully shook his head. "Because she has no one, and neither have I. Doesn't that make it fitting for me, Sergei Ivanovitch, to lend her what support I can?"

By then, smiles were general. Princess Anastasia expressed the opinion of the majority.

"You've been drinking since you left here, Bolo."

He smiled crookedly. "Yes, I've quaffed deeply, Stana, but the draughts I swallowed were of fear."

She scrutinized him more closely. "You Poles, everlastingly on a stage," she teased him. "All right then, if something *has* happened, tell us what it is."

"A Bolshevik *coup d'état*," he said quietly.

"A Bol——"

Princess Savoseva screamed. "My God, he means it, and what shall we do? If it's worse than it was at the beginning of the year, I——"

"Shut up, you featherbrained fool," Anastasia snapped. "And nonsense, Bolo. There hasn't been a sound all night, at least nothing more than the usual amount of firing."

Count Wiazovsky nodded agreement. "That's because it has been a comparatively bloodless change-over. Oh, it's true enough—I sent the carriage on so that I could nose about a bit."

His manner carried chilling conviction. Exquisite jewellery threw out a myriad glittering points of light as women shivered.

"That's it," he wound up, summarizing. "The Bolsheviks have taken over the railway station, the Arsenal, Peter-Paul, everything which matters. And Kerensky has flown and the Duma is abolished as from now."

Breaking a stricken silence someone murmured. "It's . . . it's hopeless."

Baron Tchalmin startled them all with a vindictive outburst. "This is the British Ambassador's fault as much as any man's. At the same time as he has encouraged the namby-pamby liberals he's taken good care to keep on terms with the Bolsheviks, damned *friendly* terms if you ask me."

"That's perfectly true," Princess Eghbokova screeched. "I heard at a 'five o'clock' that he had attended the Bolshevik leaders' meetings. And I know he went in disguise to the funerals of the traitorous devils who were killed in the February revolt."

Rocking a little, Princess Savoseva drained off a glass of wine, not her own. "I wonder what will become of us," she muttered, slurring her words. "And don't think I didn't hear you insult me, Stana."

Prince Sergei stared at pictures and variegated panelling, mutilated beyond renovation, silent reminders of the assault upon the house not so many months before.

"The servants," he bawled suddenly. "Every door must be bolted and barricaded, the bars on the windows must be checked, and——"

His sister sharply interrupted him. "My dear Sergei, nothing seems to be taking place now and I don't think anything will before morning. We must see what the position is then."

As a sensible measure of precaution electric lights were switched off elsewhere, and the banqueting hall's candles were masked by being placed under the table. In their subdued glow the situation was discussed endlessly, and without disturbance.

Count Wiazovsky was perfectly accurate—the revolution directed by Trotsky from the new Bolshevik headquarters in the Smolny Monastery had been bloodless, a neat strategic conception carried out with inadequate resources and a small inner core of party members.

Next day it became generally known, naturally.

And how should this glorious victory be celebrated? many asked.

By making sure of a final reckoning between the classes, so vast masses of enthusiastic soldiers, sailors and workmen instantly declared.

Within an hour they were out of hand.

The capital of Holy Russia was given over to outrage and to blind revenge. The air was filled with the sounds of rifle fire, machine-guns, and dull reverberations from the Red cruiser *Aurora* which, anchored in the Neva, bombarded the Winter Palace, where remnants of the Provisional Government had taken refuge. There were screams and cries of agony; the Kronstadt sailors bayoneted the fifteen-year-old Cadets guarding that once-Imperial residence, and a regiment of women soldiers dissolved under a hail of lead. Grey-clad troops poured into the stations and raced out to join in the slaughter; the denouncement *Burzhuis* spelt quick, or maybe slow, death, and for that reason black-coated undertakers dared not appear. Thousands died:

murdered, burnt alive with petrol, crucified, torn limb from limb, buried to their necks only.

The change in their circumstances was for many people unspeakably calamitous. Surviving owners of proud names once again scurried to dingy hide-outs; the little Napoleon Kerensky, no longer able to ride a milk-white horse and wear semi-military uniform, fled also, dressed in seaman's attire, the safest passport; in the more promising districts, ghastly excesses continued for days and weeks: orgies of wanton destruction, robbery and violence.

Account had been rendered. Now it was in course of being paid.

These disorders had to be stopped, the chaos ended; the revolutionary leaders knew that. It was not enough officially to rename the Dvoryanskoyé Sobraniyé, the magnificent premises of the Nobles' Club, and to smash up gaming tables and deface princely coats-of-arms carved into chair-backs; it was not sufficient to destroy the Koopeitcheskoyé Sobraniyé, the Merchants' Guild, on Vladimirsky Prospekt.

The Council of People's Commissars for Overthrowing Counter-Revolutionaries and Saboteurs came into being. The Extraordinary Commission took over a fine building, in Grochowa, belonging to a finance company. A new secret police force came into existence—the Tcheka replacing the old Imperialist Okhrana. At its head was a Pole of good family named Dzierjinski. The sight of blood was repugnant to him, but there are other means of inflicting pain, and he found them; his assistants, in his absence, employed less artistic methods.

Looting gradually ceased and a measure of orderliness became discernible. The Commissars of the Soviet took charge with extensive powers, including the right of forced entry anywhere at any hour. The cold Terror had begun.

Slowly news dribbled south. The sailors of Sevastopol held their eighteenth meeting.

3

The house in which Admiral Prince Kaivanov had set up an establishment at Sevastopol with a most charming lady, the wife of a colonel serving in the Far East, was excellently sited. It looked across Kiezt Square towards the Fleet Landing Place, a white-columned ceremonial gateway standing at the top of a magnificent four-terraced flight of shallow, marble steps. The sparkling waters of the harbour lay beyond, and long lines of grey ships of the Black Sea Fleet secured stern-on to the extensive quay running along South Bay. The dockyard was at the other side of the inlet, and behind that the flag over the handsome naval hospital swayed gently in the light breeze.

It was very pleasant this late October morning, with the sun shining on a balcony where a table for breakfast had been placed.

"More coffee, darling. *Dearest,* more coffee."

The speaker, who wore a lacy wrap, was a very attractive woman with a pink-and-white complexion and features faintly Asiatic. She leaned forward again.

At her touch Admiral Prince Kaivanov waved vaguely towards a seaplane-carrier moored in the outer harbour.

"A thousand pardons, my pigeon," he said. "I am afraid I was rather in a dream."

Perhaps he sounded depressed; or it may be that her glance, attracted by a destroyer's motor-boat noisily zug-zugging up South Bay from the railway station, fell upon a multi-castellated old ship squeezed among others against the quay. *Pantelamon,* once the *Kniaz Potemkin,* was a disquieting sight to many people dwelling in Sevastopol in those trying times.

"What happened to the agitators who came down from the north, Ivan Mikhailovitch?" she turned to ask.

Prince Kaivanov's handsome face was haggard. "The men listened to them for a while, and then ran 'em out of the town. But I understand further subversive attempts are being made. The whole trouble of the business, my dear, is that we don't really know what is happening in Petrograd."

Overhead the pilot of a pusher-type hydroplane executed a foolishly dangerous manoeuvre for such a sluggish craft. In the dockyard workmen were swarming over the battleship *Imperatritsa Marya;* her sister ship the *Imperator Alexander III,* pride of the Navy also, swung from a buoy close behind the booms of the outer harbour. Great and modern ships both, with four turrets each on the centre line, each turret with triple guns, a remarkable innovation in naval architecture.

Admiral Prince Kaivanov's eyes rested for a moment on a roofless building. "We shall soon be able to put an end to the *Goeben's* insolent raids," he observed without much conviction, nodding to the *Imperator Alexander III.* "When 'the Devil of the Black Sea' comes up against our big fellows . . . though the position would never have arisen had it not been for the crass stupidity of the English in allowing the *Goeben* to escape into the Dardanelles in the early days of the war."

On the table were sweet currant-and-almond loaf and crisp rolls, orange jelly and rose jam, pats of deep yellow butter and a pot of honey. He did not seem interested in this pleasant fare.

From the harbour rose the shrill pipe of bos'ns' whistles, and the Lord's Prayer in thousands of deep voices; and thousands of shaven heads were bared, neither uniformly nor very smartly, as the flag of Saint Andrew was hoisted in the ships of the Fleet.

Prince Kaivanov, who had been standing punctiliously at the salute, resumed his seat. As he arranged his sword more comfortably the bugle call *Carry On* rang across.

"My dearest," he remarked, "I am inspecting the submarine base at Balaclava this afternoon. If you would care to accompany me I thought we might drive over in a barouche instead of an automobile. A most delightful drive if taken leisurely."

A crowd of white-clad officers strolled by for a knock-up on the Midshipmen's Courts; the sun became hotter; the bar of the Kiezt Hotel was crammed to capacity at noon. With full ritual ensigns were lowered at sunset; at night there was the musical tinkle of ships' bells and the routine calls of sentries in the sterns crying the customary challenge of "Who is rowing?" as boats neared or passed by.

As yet only the outer ripples of revolution were slapping against the sunny south.

Eleven days afterwards, on another bright morning, colours were hoisted with the usual rites, and ships' companies, bellies earlier satisfied with the Imperial Russian Navy's simple yet extremely wholesome food—the standard of which had been maintained at a high level since the *Kniaz Potemkin* disaster of many years before—began their routine tasks.

A small gunnery detail on top of "C" turret of the *Imperator Alexander III* jested with an electricians' party working on the searchlight platform circling the after funnel; a dozen men dangling over the battleship's yacht-like bows left paint-brushes in tins while twisting to hurl good-humoured abuse at a whaler's crew from the three-funnelled destroyer *Derski*.

At the hydroplane station further up the main harbour machines were launched by men thigh-deep in water; returning aircraft were dragged back to the top of the launching ramp where, tails propped up and fragile nacelles resting on the paved ground, the sitka spruce of their delicate frameworks was rubbed with the best quality linseed oil.

An hour before noon a workman gilding the spike-shaped ornament which rounded off the pyramidal summit of the three-tiered tower of the Dockyard Church called across to a mate busy on the cupola:

"Looks like there's something up again, eh, Bow Legs?"

Bow Legs glanced along South Bay towards the Station, where

a number of shunters, casting away their long poles, had started to run.

"And take a squint down the harbour. That is, if you aren't scared of turning round."

The elder, Bow Legs, chuckled. "I notice you always work single-handed," he bawled back.

His colleague shouted in response: "I'm like the sailors, one hand for the job and the other for myself. And be careful with that gold leaf. I'm inclined to think the *Batyushka* suspects we nobble a bit."

"I shouldn't . . . be surprised . . . considering what that old rogue the *Diakon* . . . collars before we get hold," Bow Legs jerkily snorted as he shuffled to face about. From that distance he could not hear what those on "C" turret of the *Imperator Alexander III* were saying to the electrical party; but he subsequently saw both groups swarming down ladders, and the painting party swarming up ropes. Boats were being lowered in every ship; shipwrights poured out of the Dockyard gates; mechanics from the hydroplane station raced along—everywhere men were hurrying, taking the shortest cuts to reach the Kulikovo Field.

The smooth arc of the cupola made a magnificent slide, and Bow Legs almost shot over the gutter.

"I'm not missing this lot," he remarked.

"Nor me either," his mate bellowed. "So look sharp. I want to know what it's all about."

Others wondered, too, among them nursemaids wheeling their charges in the Malakoff Park, a fine promenade with extensive views laid out amidst the thousands of graves of the Crimean War.

In the Kiezt Hotel officers drank steadily in the bar, laughed forcedly, joked with delightful Rumanian prostitutes, simultaneously wondering why the sailors of the Baltic Fleet had sent this special deputation. And a bunch of young pilots from the seaplane-carrier *Imperator Nikolai Pervyi*, with mixed ideas concerning "unlawful assembly", unanimously supported their fearless flight-commander, whose simple desire was to "bomb those bloody sea-lawyers to bits".

By then, at the great mass meeting on the Kulikovo Field, an orator still wearing the badges of a leading stoker had worked himself into a fine frenzy.

"Comrade Lenin describes us Kronstadt lads as the Saviours of the Revolution," he thundered. "But, comrade-sailors of Sevastopol, what would he call *you*?"

Another comrade from Kronstadt, a thin-lipped firebrand, was quieter and more dangerous.

"Warm here, isn't it?" he remarked sarcastically. "Nice to sit on your backsides while other folk do the job for you. Of course I understand the reason, fear makes cowards—now let me finish, comrades. . . ."

They heard him to the end.

There was a meeting also at Admiralty House, attended by officers wearing the black-and-orange knot of Saint Georgei, the deep crimson of Saint Alexander, the pale-blue of Saint Andrew, the ribbons of Saint Vladimir and Saint Stanislaus.

"We've given up our arms without a struggle, and we have surrendered our emblems of rank." Admiral Prince Kaivanov's dark eyes flashed. "We have yielded to the demand that only defensive operations should be undertaken against the enemy, and we have permitted ignorant seamen to stand over us on our bridges. How much more, I ask?"

A firm-faced gentleman detached himself from a small group who were quietly talking.

"The Commander-in-Chief will be here at any moment, Ivan Mikhailovitch," he said. "It will be better if there is less heat in the air when he comes in."

"Indeed, my dear Tianov," Admiral Prince Kaivanov snapped. "Nevertheless I shall give my views as and when I please."

Admiral Tianov's eyes narrowed. "For too long you've given your views, and far too often you've not been on the spot to implement them when the occasion arose. I remember something of your views during the war with the little men, a war in which, through unfortunate circumstances, you were not able to take a very active part. And I recall also your views at the time when poor old dead-and-gone Zelouky took your place at the last minute on a body of which I had the honour to be a member, the Court-martial sent down here to settle up the *Kniaz Potemkin* affair."

Admiral Kaivanov was fighting for breath. "By God, Tianov, if you are imputing. . . ."

"Gentlemen!" The voice was sharp.

The buzz of interest died as the senior officer in the room opened the door for the Commander-in-Chief. Heels clicked in a befitting silence.

Admiral Kolchak's eyes were tired, his strong mouth closely set.

"Gentlemen," he said slowly, carefully picking his words, "the position is extremely grave. Our men are on a hair-balance, nor can we weigh the scales to our side by offering them the contents of the Crimean banks, as the emissaries of the Soviet have done. Our inclination may be to fight, but until hostilities are actually provoked it is our duty, for Russia's sake, to bend rather than to break. In the meantime it is our task to provide for any eventuality. I should be glad to receive your suggestions, gentlemen."

It was decided, among proposals accepted, that another strenuous effort should be made to ascertain the situation in other parts of the Empire.

The wires leading from Sevastopol began to hum, and there were many: every telegraph post carried eleven cross-brackets each mounting eight pairs of insulators.

Preoccupied in these vital matters, it was towards evening before a member of the Naval Staff, glancing out from a window of Admiralty House, perceived with a start that the Dockyard chimney had, for the first time in the war, ceased to smoke.

CHAPTER IV

THE slowly-passing, misery-laden days of another bitter winter. Shivering men and women wandered aimlessly, hungry and despairing. It was the same in every drab street except Grochowa, along which few cared to pass—those doing so hurried fearfully, averting their heads from marble-faced Number Two, where the large daily suicide rate equalled on average the daily execution rate. Of the remainder forcibly taken there by the Tcheka, many died from feebleness or lack of will to live—and a few were eventually released, fortunate to be punished no more harshly beforehand than by being compelled to walk barefooted across an outdoor grating which, with thirty degrees of frost, ripped the skin off their feet.

On an afternoon well advanced in the new year, in a district of the capital which had become a vast exchange-and-mart, Prince Sergei Kaivanov trudged along in broken boots, carrying two bundles. Sunken-faced, his glance darted to the medley of second-hand merchandise in every shop window, personal possessions sold for next to nothing by those striving to keep body and soul together . . . silver dishes, cigarette cases, uniforms, furs, jewellery, gold-banded meerschaum pipes, beautiful walking-sticks, even dental plates—anything which might be used to buy a little food.

Into doorway after doorway he peered furtively, sidling into a shop only when sure it was empty.

A middle-aged man with fleshy lips, jaws champing, came briskly from the rear, wafting along an appetizing odour.

"Sixty roubles, my dear comrade?" he said, tossing back the

heavy-handled tooth-pick. "Why——" He clapped palms together and gesticulated before calling over his shoulder: "Rachel, my love, show this comrade that gold paper-knife I bought for twenty-three roubles yesterday. Yes, comrade, twenty-three roubles—no, don't trouble, love, if you're busy. Yes, comrade, twenty-three roubles. Now I'll tell you what, comrade, I'll take a chance and give you ten roubles."

Sergei, foot for safety on the larger bundle he had dropped to the dirty floor, leaned against a pile of packing-cases which, in those days of fuel shortage, were certainly worth their weight in silver.

"Twenty-five roubles," he said faintly.

"*Twenty-five* roubles!" The proprietor snorted with contempt as he reached for the tooth-pick and weighed it in his hand. "My dear comrade, I am here to do business, not to rob my unborn children."

"Twenty roubles, then," his customer said desperately.

The shop-keeper's brilliant, heavy-lidded eyes narrowed. "Twelve roubles and not a copeck more," he snapped. "Take it or get out."

For that amount a charmingly-fashioned article, Kaivanov coat-of-arms on the haft, changed hands. Its new owner counted eleven notes from a thick roll, made up the balance with stamps, but palpably hesitated before parting with the money.

"This little *burzhuis* relic, comrade, is it your own property?" he murmured, washing his hands and smiling oilily. "You see, comrade, the Tcheka takes an interest in these matters."

Prince Sergei knew this trap. "I stole it," he replied defiantly.

"And let's suppose I suspect you didn't steal it, what then? As a loyal supporter of comrades Lenin and Trotsky. . . ."

When Sergei, sweating profusely, reached the street again he was better off by five roubles, three of them in crumpled stamps.

A big crowd milled between the stalls of the old clothes market, a few of which were presided over by men and women of the old régime, who had optimistically persuaded themselves that their names were not included in the black list of those due for liquidation when found.

Sergei carefully made his choice as to whom he should approach, avoiding a stall-keeper sounding insane, a woman looking too much like typhus, and a youth altogether too shrill. In this quest he was reasonably successful and, after a couple of minutes of hushed bartering, disposed of one of his bundles, containing eighteen embroidered towels and two horse blankets.

Next, closely hugging the more valuable burden, he pushed

225

through to the other side of the market where, after alert reconnoitring, he decided upon opening negotiations with a youngish man, perhaps seven or eight years older than himself, who in the past fortnight or so he had noticed doing a very brisk business, both buying and selling. Distinctively marked by a V-shaped shrapnel scar on one cheek, this individual was making no attempt to disguise a cultured accent as he chaffed with those fingering clothing piled up on an improvised counter.

Unfortunately Sergei's whispered attempt to attract the stall-keeper coincided with the start of a campaign to draw customers. After violently ringing a cracked bell the man, who was fairly tall, mounted a box.

"This is the moment you have all been waiting for, ladies and gentlemen," he shouted, flourishing the bell again. "So gather round and direct your attention to the many bargains I shall shortly offer you at figures so low as to be unheard of. You may, ladies and gentlemen, rightly wonder why I should sacrifice my valuable stock at absolutely give-away prices. Very well then, I will gladly tell you why . . . for one thing, ladies and gentlemen, I have begun to suspect that my tenure of this attractive corner site may not be as secure as I believed, a lamentable thought for any go-ahead businessman . . . second, very unbusinesslike admittedly, I confess to a desire for different surroundings, an urge to wander, shall we say. Where my fancy will next take me I am not sure. Our sunny Crimean Riviera certainly attracts me, but I am inclined to think I shall pay a visit first to our mother city of Kiev, where I shall pray on the holy relics for this benighted land of ours."

Dangerous sentiments, these, in public, and Sergei sweated anew, aware of the secret police's habit when swooping of gathering into their net everyone in the vicinity. But he nearly expired when their author, bending down to pick up a woman's jumper and a man's thick flannel shirt, addressed him in a most confiding manner.

"You were suggesting some commercial transaction, my dear sir?"

Hurriedly Sergei glanced round, saw a crowd closing in, and then encountered the mocking gaze of the dealer's steely-grey eyes.

"Hardly been worn," he said throatily, opening the mouth of a sack to show his sister's ermine coat. "Guarantee it perfect, but I'll come again when you're quieter. Two hundred roubles."

The stall-keeper laughed. "It would be dirt cheap at two thousand, but believe it or not I should be very fortunate to obtain seventy-five for it. Yes, working as I do on a basis of small

226

profits and quick returns I fear my limit is fifty . . . subject at that to a meticulous examination."

"A hundred and eighty," Sergei muttered.

The man with the scarred cheek seemed perturbed. "Really, my dear fellow," he expostulated. "Even if I succeeded in interesting one of the Tcheka's overdressed tarts in it I doubt if I could push her up to a hundred, with all my powers of salesmanship."

Hemmed in by the throng now pressing round the stall, all of whom were absorbed in the proprietor's quietly-explosive sallies, Sergei was becoming extremely nervous.

"How much will you give, comrade?" he asked hoarsely.

The steel-grey eyes were icy with disdain. "I have told you my figure," the stall-keeper said very distinctly. "And for Saint Stephen's sake don't call me comrade! It is an expression I frankly loathe, though I will agree that that can be due to my inability to keep pace with the glorious march of human progress as outlined by our benefactors Lenin and Trotsky."

"You're going to be in a bloody lot of trouble soon, comrade." The speaker, a swarthy-faced man, wore a lady's astrakhan coat beneath which appeared black evening trousers tucked into what had been gleaming cavalry boots. "The hell of a lot, any minute, comrade."

Resting his hands on one of the pieces of floorboarding forming a table top, the stall-owner leaned forward towards the interrupter.

"Most interesting, sir," he said, nodding his head appreciatively. "And I suggest we debate the question when I have finished with this other gentleman. Yes, as I was saying, I have a definite distaste for being addressed as comrade either by the cravenhearted or by. . . ."

Fearfully Sergei edged away, relief seeping through him with every yard gained. But on the outskirts of the still-growing crowd, when close to a few people enviously hovering near a stand displaying tempting portions of foal-meat, he had a paralysing shock as a hand clutched his shoulder from behind.

Spinning about, he gaped at a man whom he had last seen in his own home as a guest. The change in Baron Tchalmin was tragic; yellow-grey webs of matter extended between trembling lips, and his skin had that bloodless sheen associated with absence from sun and light.

"Good God, Matviei Jacobych!" he exclaimed. "Where have you been?"

"Underground since October . . . chased from cellar to cellar . . . I'm starving, Sergei Ivanovitch."

"We all are, Matviei Jacobych."

In a little while, as always when friends met, notes were compared and news exchanged. Sergei learnt that, among others, Princess Eghbokova and her son were dead—the boy killed while fighting with a scratch unit of youths, his mother slowly frozen in a solid lump with her bathwater, beneath which she had been pinned by an upright piano.

Baron Tchalmin shivered. "What are you doing now?"

"Trying to sell a fur coat of Stana's, but I'm damned well leaving it over until tomorrow."

"A fur coat." Baron Tchalmin's dulled eyes flickered.

A sudden clamour arose at the opposite side of the square, where scores of noisily shouting people were strenuously pushing towards the stall-keeper with the scarred cheek. Hands waved in acceptance of his offers. Obviously this haste to reach him had nothing to do with his strictures on the new order. It was very evident that a sensational clearance sale was in progress.

"Had a shot at a deal with that lunatic," Sergei said resentfully.

"You know who he is, don't you?" said Baron Tchalmin. "One of the Andreyoukovs; Nikolai, I think." As Sergei shook his head, he went on: "It would be before your time, of course. Crackpots, all of them."

"This one," Prince Sergei growled, "can thank his stars that he's not being interrogated in Grochowa just now, and anybody who was near him as well. Did you hear him?"

Baron Tchalmin's unpleasant-looking lips curled. "Enough."

Long after Sergei tired of the Andreyoukovs, Baron Tchalmin continued to talk venomously about them. It was as though, wretched and quaking himself, he found compensation in venting his spleen on stouter-hearted contemporaries.

"Well, old man!" Sergei mumbled eventually, "I think I'd better get on with my infernal shopping."

"Might as well trail round with you, Sergei Ivanovitch," Baron Tchalmin muttered. "You know, old boy," he resumed as they moved off, "I've been pondering about that coat of Stana's, the point being that I have some pretty juicy contacts. What kind of a price have you been offered so far?"

A tiny warning, echo of the cunning in Georgian blood, rang in Prince Sergei's brain.

"Oh, a hundred and fifty roubles, Matviei Jacobych," he said airily.

Whistle of derision cut off glutinously, Baron Tchalmin turned to him. "My dear chap, ridiculous. I'm quite sure I can get you two fifty or three hundred. Suppose I nip off with it, beat up an offer, and meet you again in half an hour?"

"The trouble, old man," Sergei said with apparent candour,

"is that Stana made me promise I wouldn't part without cash."

"Dammit, she wouldn't mind if I were handling the proposition," Baron Tchalmin protested.

"If all went well," Sergei said. "But it's her coat after all, and if you were collared when you were off with it . . . need I remind you, old chap, that Stana can be a devil." He smiled indulgently. "She'd give me hell, Matviei Jacobych."

In days which seemed a lifetime ago, Baron Tchalmin had known Princess Anastasia to his cost. "All right, Sergei Ivanovitch," he sighed, "I understand."

Prince Sergei made several purchases, bargaining for a rasher of horse-flesh, a twist of suspect flour, and three offensively-smelling black eggs.

The next transaction, a scrape of butter from a country speculator, had just been completed when every soul in the vicinity was petrified by the staccato sounds of shooting.

In the split second before a mass dive for shelter began, Baron Tchalmin acted. Lips curled back, eyes bestially eager, his arm flashed out like a wild-beast's paw to snatch the sack from his friend's grasp.

"Hey!" Sergei screamed after the fast-retreating figure. "Stop, you damned thief."

The vanguard of terrified people swept him off his feet, and after that it was self-preservation only. Scrambling up and struggling to a doorway, he flattened himself back against those deeper in the recess. From that uneasy position, although frantically-running creatures often obstructed the view, he gleaned something of what was occurring when he saw the old-clothes dealer with the scarred face, automatic pistol in each hand spitting wickedly, slowly withdrawing into a passage.

Within a few moments Sergei also noticed—as did fourteen hundred other eye witnesses huddled along the sides of the deserted square—that five men were lying on the ground, three probably dead and two spasmodically twitching.

Swiftly the whisper spread identifying these victims: "Tcheka agents."

That left two thoughts only in every panic-stricken mind: How long would it be before avenging squads from Grochowa cordoned off an area from which every person would be hauled off for brutal examination, and how large would that area be?

The ensuing rush started as if a soundless signal had been heard simultaneously by all. Old jostled with young, the frail with the strong.

Through street after street Sergei ran, ran until he was far enough distant. Weakened by privation, vision out of focus, he leaned against a tramways standard and painfully gulped in air.

When he was able to do so, which coincided with a shivering fit, he resumed his way towards Cherydskia.

When only two blocks separated him from the dismal home he shared with five other people, Count Wiazovsky, carrying a load of picture frames, crossed his path diagonally. Neither tatter-demalion acknowledged the other, but the younger casually fell into station about three paces ahead in the peasant manner. It was a convenient mode of endeavouring to convey the impression they were not together, and also gave a slender chance to one if the other were halted for questioning.

Walking along facing strictly to the front they talked in lowered tones, lips barely moving. Sergei reported on his narrow escape, and Count Wiazovsky on his day's foray.

"Those frames, Bolo," Sergei asked. "Are they solid wood?"

"You should have a squint at my thumb-nails, Sergei Ivanovitch," Count Wiazovsky said between his teeth. "Broken to bits digging into the mouldings to make sure before I brought 'em. There's a thinnish covering of plaster, but the wood is first-rate underneath and they'll burn well."

"And did you go to Palace Quay again?"

For the last few days the young Pole had spent his mornings ferreting among the ruins of the Kaivanov mansion, usually salvaging enough to bring in a few roubles on the market.

Further prospects were being discussed when, with terrifying unexpectedness, they sighted three well-fed, warmly-clad men stationed in the semi-gloom of an alley.

Prince Sergei and Count Wiazovsky were scrutinized keenly, though nothing happened beyond that. But as they continued, slipping and sliding on the icy litter strewn about the hummocky, snow-trodden pavements, each felt for a long time that unseen eyes were still glued to their backs.

The room was damp, cold and verminous, and from the blocked water-closet at the bottom of the stair-shaft an unpleasant stench arose. Torn lace curtains across the middle separated the sleeping places of the sexes; a small window in the outer part, looking across a range of roofs overlaid with smut-soiled snow, let in even less light than it should as two broken panes were stuffed with rags and paper.

A moth-eaten wrap dropped from Princess Anastasia Kaivanova's shoulders as she turned hysterically.

"If you say that again, you stupid little fool," she screamed, "I'll . . . I'll—why the hell I ever made myself responsible for you . . .

'oh, Mimi, don't say it again, I shall go mad if you do. Do you hear me?"

Mimi Kalutkina, seated in a broken-down rocking-chair with the remnants of a carriage rug round her, almost ceased her endless rocking. She turned a pitifully young-old face towards her half-sister.

"Do you understand, Mimi?" Anastasia cried desperately. "Do you, you fool?"

The curtain parted as Xenia Menshek-Pelikova came through. She was wearing a man's high-necked shirt beneath a man's tweed jacket reaching to her knees, and her flaxen hair was almost hidden by a shawl over her head, as was the other women's hair.

"Must you, Stana?" she begged, standing with arms folded and hands balled in her armpits to keep them warm. "It doesn't do any good."

Anastasia's lips quivered. "She'll have to be disciplined for her own sake, or what chance will any of us have of getting away? And you needn't preach, Xenia. I'm not the only one who flies off the handle."

Little Xenia Menshek-Pelikova's green eyes filmed. "I know, Stana dear," she said. "It's so hellish I suppose we can't help ourselves."

"I wouldn't care a damn if we were *doing* something about it," Anastasia said as she sank on to a pile of dirty bagging, the men's bed. "What gets me down is this infernal waiting about for day after day, month after month."

Xenia sighed. "Yes," she said.

The day was fading quickly and, carefully striking a match, Anastasia lighted two lamps made out of medicine bottles with stay-laces for wick. In the smoky, yellow glow from them the two girls examined a fringed blue tablecloth and decided that, with care in cutting, an underskirt could be made from it.

"The poor darling hardly ever moves," Anastasia murmured, "and if we can whip something together it will help. When I think of her sitting there hour after hour——" A tear trickled down her cheek, and impatiently she dashed it off with the back of her hand. "Hell, I am in a damned low state today, Xenia. About time I shook it off."

Xenia smiled affectionately. "You haven't been often, Stana. In fact it's absolutely true, as Bolo said, that you've kept us all up."

"He's not done so very badly himself," Anastasia remarked.

"I think he's been really wonderful, Stana."

Anastasia laughed in her old style. "Well, well," she said,

repeating these two words even more teasingly on noticing her companion's blush.

In better heart they were pursuing their plans for Mimi's comfort when, five stories below, the front door slammed with an onrush of through draught. Immediately both young women became rigid. Then Anastasia glanced fearfully towards the dark stair-head, and Xenia Menshek-Pelikova's right eye resumed its periodical, sickening tic.

"The first man——" Mimi began mechanically.

In a flash her half-sister muzzled her so effectively with her hand that only the faintest whimper could be heard.

But there was nothing challenging in the shuffling sounds made by the paper-thin footwear of those mounting the flights of steps, and the girls' taut limbs relaxed.

On entering, Prince Sergei crossed to the window, placing on the sill the sparse provender earmarked for the next day.

"You've sold my coat, Sergei Ivanovitch," his sister said eagerly. "How much did you get?"

"Is isn't sold as yet, Stana. As a matter of fact I came across your old would-be flame Matviei Jacobych, and . . ."

Xenia smiled at Count Wiazovsky who, after bowing to the ladies, went off with the purposeful air of one who, tasks of consequence awaiting him, cannot delay. The man of action, he broke up picture frames in a most workmanlike style.

"You've brought more than last night, Bolo," she said.

He shrugged. "Oh, not too bad."

"Jolly good, I'd say," she complimented him. "And they must be *much* scarcer."

He straightened. "They are, my dear; you wouldn't believe it."

And so, very much as boy and girl, they set about building a fire in the crude stove, she laying the smaller chips in the bottom, he preparing the thicker pieces which would give them all the greatest pleasure of the day, a spell of warmth.

Meanwhile the argument about the ermine coat was proceeding.

"But it is a risk, Sergei, so why the devil did you?" Anastasia snapped. "You know perfectly well we mustn't break into the Nikolai money Isvoltoff let us have, and a bird in the hand is worth two in the bush, as old Brownie used to tell us."

Sergei blustered his way out. "Now look here, my dear girl, Matviei Jacobych has first-rate connections and when I met him fifty roubles was the best offer I'd had. Believe me, I'm too wary a customer to be swindled to that extent. Of course, Stana, I'll admit that if his number is already on a bullet and I don't see him again I'll feel damned silly, but . . ."

Again the reverberating crash of the lower door, an agonizing wait, and the release of pent-up breath when the footsteps were recognized.

"It's only Cyrus Konstantinych," Anastasia whispered.

Count Petrov, with a week's dark stubble on his chin, resembled in only one aspect the dapper, rather short, military *aide* of other days—he still looked determined and alert. Waving his hand cheerily in general greeting he wandered across watchfully to Mimi Ivanovna.

"Hello, darling," he said smilingly. "Here's your old Cyrus Konstantinych once again."

Following his instructions neither Prince Sergei nor Count Wiazovsky ever went near her, and he was extremely guarded himself. The arm he slipped round her shoulders rested lightly, and he did not attempt to kiss her. Standing loosely linked with her, but otherwise ignoring her, he chatted with the others.

"Anything particularly interesting?" Count Wiazovsky inquired.

"Judge for yourself." Count Petrov grinned. "This morning I was enrolled as a Soviet worker of the second grade."

"No!" Xenia exclaimed.

"God, but you've a nerve, Cyrus Konstantinych," the young Pole said admiringly.

Triumphantly Count Petrov held up a package. "And as such, ladies and gentlemen, I am entitled to certain perquisites," he boasted. "*Voilà*, my daily ration, two herrings and a pound of bread. A trifle more of this and we shall be dining sumptuously, eh?"

Before any comment could be made on that, a tremor shook Mimi Ivanovna.

"His smelly hair fell on my face," she said listlessly.

Swiftly Count Petrov acted. "No, darling, all that was a bad dream. Don't you remember my telling you how easy it is to mistake. . . ."

Possibly, in his earnestness, he gripped her too tightly. For a second, when pressed against him, she was perfectly still, but after that it was tragically different. Like a frantic animal, eyes rolling insanely, she beat his chest with her small hands, and scored his cheek with her nails.

"Go away, you horrible beast," she screeched. "You horrid, nasty creature. If my Cyrus were here he'd *kill* you. Oh, please . . ."

"There, there, darling," Count Petrov soothed her. "I'm here now, Mimi dear, and I shan't let anyone hurt you."

Just as suddenly she subsided, her head drooping, and made no protest when her half-sister and Xenia led her to the rocking-chair, which Count Wiazovsky had placed squarely in front of the stove.

Blood dripping from his chin, Count Petrov looked at his friends and noticed their expressions, in which sympathy failed to mask desolation.

"No, you're all wrong," he whispered. "She *is* a fraction better. I had my arm round her quite a while, and it isn't long ago that she went crazy instantly I laid a finger on her. She *is* changing."

"Perhaps so," Anastasia muttered, blinking a little.

Flames were leaping in the stove and, with a larger supply of fuel than usual, for once food could be heated thoroughly. Sour, grey potatoes were put with cotton-seed oil in one tin can, and the chopped husks of sunflower seeds in another to prepare a bran. A lidless pan was used to boil water for the *ersatz* coffee, and a couple of pieces of wire from the picture frames were doubled and bent into hooks for grilling the herrings.

Soon they were eating, Count Petrov feeding Mimi with a spoon as soon as she showed signs of rejecting the obnoxious fare, coaxing her to swallow messes which were, for all their scant food value, her sole chance of survival.

A little later the finest hour in the twenty-four arrived when, avoiding thoughts of stabbing indigestion pains lurking to assail them, they talked nostalgically in the firelight about happier days.

"I wonder if they'll ever return," Anastasia murmured. "Why had all this to happen?"

Slowly Count Petrov shook his head. "It was bound to, Stana. If years and years ago families like ours had strenuously supported those few of noble birth who advocated less autocracy and greater liberality it might have been different. A strong middle class would also have counted enormously."

"Those were my father's and my grandfather's ideas," Xenia Menshek-Pelikova said. "But Daddy was murdered all the same."

"But wasn't that because he had the ill-luck to be in the company of those less enlightened?" Count Petrov asked. "I think so, my dear."

Count Wiazovsky cleared his throat. "Russians of all kinds have been guilty of many gross errors," he announced tartly, "and not the least of these has been to keep my countrymen in fetters. Had Poland been a sovereign state, a friendly nation on your borders——"

Xenia giggled. "Oh, Bolo," she said, "I feel sure you're on the threshold of describing to us the glories of the ancient kingdom of Poland."

Flushing deeply, Count Wiazovsky brushed from his eyes a

thick lock of dark hair. But by some miracle he kept his temper.

"My dear Xenia," he said in a surprisingly gentle voice as he stared intently at her, "perhaps some day you may really know the magic of my beloved Poland. It will be Poland's privilege also, for she will see you."

Moved by the couple, Princess Anastasia was smiling mistily at Count Petrov when, driving away all thoughts of an incipient love affair, the entrance door at street level crashed.

"I'll spy out the land," Count Wiazovsky said under his breath.

Count Petrov nodded. "Then come back, Bolo. And all of you remember to leave the talking to me if it's a police raid."

Behind him Anastasia was already busy, pinning up purloined Bolshevik posters and draping red material round cardboard-mounted newspaper photographs of Lenin and Trotsky.

Within less than a minute they were aware that these emergency arrangements were not necessary; a woman's long-drawn-out sobs and the sorrowful voices of the men who were virtually carrying her between them up the flights, conveyed that clearly.

When Count Wiazovsky returned it was to tell them the latest disaster befalling the tenants of an end room on the floor below, two brothers and their sister, kindly and decent people whose offence consisted in being small factory-owning *burzhuis*.

"The girl went to Grochowa yesterday and they were kind enough to inform her that her husband was due for release this evening," he said, a mixture of sickness and hatred in his expression. "Tonight she's learnt he's been released all right, though not so quickly—by a bullet in the stomach. Rare jesters, the Tcheka, aren't they?"

"God!" Anastasia muttered. "I must go down to the poor devil."

It was very dark in the stairway and, as the balustrade had been used for fuel long ago, she had to feel her way, hand on flapping, loose wallpaper and freezingly cold wall. For a quarter of an hour she stayed with the distraught young woman, the comfort she tried to bring her as ineffectual as it would have been had she remained all night. Sadly she went up the stairs again, quickening her step on the slippery landing on hearing her brother shouting:

"It's all damned well, Cyrus Konstantinych, but——"

"Not so much row, Sergei Ivanovitch," Count Wiazovsky interrupted warningly.

Prince Sergei slumped on a stool, and began to bang his fists on a shaky spindle-legged table.

"We've got to get out, we've damned well got to get out," he screamed. "If we don't get out soon I'll kill myself, I'll——"

Count Petrov gripped him by the throat. "I'll kill you myself if you don't pull yourself together."

"You infernal fool, Sergei Ivanovitch," Anastasia hissed. "If a street patrol hear they'll fly up here like a shot."

The atmosphere was charged with emotion, but Count Petrov startlingly changed it with a crisp inquiry as to how much money could be mustered.

"We're making a mighty commotion, aren't we, darling?" he said smilingly to Mimi Ivanovna as he stroked her hand. "Yes," he continued, seeing puzzled faces turned towards him, "dig out every copeck you have."

From hiding-places in clothes, footwear, under floor-boards, behind bulges of wallpaper, and in holes drilled up candles which were never lighted, their hoarded funds appeared—a few precious five and ten rouble gold pieces, some fifty rouble Nikolai bank-notes, a pile of crumpled Kerensky, a handful of low-denomination coins, and a cigar-box full of many-coloured postage stamps.

"H'mm, seems sufficient," Count Petrov murmured. "Well, ladies and gentlemen, there are prospects for us—don't estimate them higher—that I've been sitting on tightly for the past few days, but in the circumstances . . . the fact that we're all near the end of our tether . . . I think I ought not to keep them to myself any longer."

Intent already, their eyes opened wider when he produced a bag of lump sugar. None of them had seen sugar since before the October revolt, and *lump* sugar was a pre-war memory.

Never a movement missed, he picked up the coffee pan, nodded with satisfaction on perceiving a small quantity in the bottom, and began to dip the rough squares.

"I was just as astonished by the sugar as you are, but enterprising enough nevertheless to transfer its ownership immediately from the proletariat to the dispossessed," he remarked grimly. "And now, if you'll mend the fire, Bolo, we'll gather round it."

Recklessly Count Wiazovsky used up the remaining pieces of wood. In the light of leaping flames they packed together, a small semicircle as close to the stove as a fender.

"Here, Mimi darling, try one of these sweets," Count Petrov said, holding a piece near her mouth. "Ah, that's it, my pet."

They all sucked away gingerly, even Mimi Ivanovna—none daring to crunch, each bent on prolonging the delight.

"Listen," Count Petrov resumed very quietly. "I'm in touch with a fellow who is a marvel at forging rubber stamps and documents, and unless he's nabbed beforehand I am reasonably sure I shall have identity papers and travelling passes, for all of us, within a matter of days."

Anastasia clasped her hands together. "Oh, Cyrus Konstant-inych."

"Is it true, old man?" Sergei said hoarsely.

Quizzically Count Petrov was eyeing his fiancée. "Finished, darling?" he asked. "And what do you want now from your Cyrus?"

Another round of home-made sweetmeats, each eagerly taking a lump with a dubious coffee flavour.

"Our surest plan is to aim for the Ukraine, where some kind of separatist movement is afoot," Count Petrov went on. "I also understand that it is a rallying ground for forces that are being raised to drive northwards against the Bolsheviki."

Immense excitement has its aftermath and gradually, one by one, they began to gaze steadfastly into the red embers of the dying fire, each too full for words. It was not yet seven o'clock and within minutes they would be compelled to seek their make-shift beds, three squeezing for warmth in each.

Mimi Ivanovna stirred and leaned forward towards the coffee pan, her lined forehead puckering more deeply.

"Cyrus Konstantinych," she said plaintively.

Speechlessly her half-sister and her half-brother looked at her, their incredulity shared by Count Wiazovsky and Xenia.

"Yes, Mimi darling," Count Petrov said, a betraying catch in his voice. "Another of those sweeties?"

It was the first time since being stricken that his name, or any of their names, had passed her lips.

Count Petrov took two fresh lumps from the bag and, his fearless eyes swimming, dropped them in the pan.

2

For months in Sevastopol the pot had simmered but never boiled, and this was the condition early in the morning of the day following that on which Count Petrov, in faraway Petrograd, talked to his friends about the possibility of escape.

In those months Sevastopol had deteriorated still more, and nowhere was that better demonstrated than in the flagship, where her dress-as-you-please crew relieved themselves against turrets and superstructure, and spat chewed sunflower-seeds on the once-sacrosanct quarter-deck without fear of rebuke. Boats were hoisted awry, ropes which used to be cheesed-down meticulously were now tangled heaps, and at the stern a red velvet curtain replaced the blue diagonal cross of Saint Andrew.

By the middle of the forenoon there was nothing to indicate that the day would be any different from the one preceding, but the orgy of bloodshed began at half-past ten—when ships' bells would have sounded melodiously over the water if watches had been kept. Attacks then started upon places where officers could be found in number: Admiralty House, the Kiezt Hotel, Army Liaison Headquarters, the Naval Club, the Dockyard, and in every warship in nominal commission. South Bay and the outer harbour crackled with pistol and rifle fire; machine-guns rattled and pom-poms barked.

Retaliation was spirited for a time, the majority of the defenders conducting themselves heroically, but, outnumbered and blasted by an immense weight of fire, there could be one outcome only. By three o'clock in the afternoon all effective resistance ended.

In this fighting the lower deck personnel of the Black Sea Fleet had been mauled to some extent and, shocked by the sad sight of dead and wounded comrades, thirsted for more officer-blood. This was the prelude to a period of indiscriminate slaughter, during which houses were broken into and many luckless gentlemen, from post-captains to young midshipmen, were butchered on the spot, often in the presence of their families.

At the end of this phase it was estimated that over three-quarters of the officers in the port had been dealt with.

Two unanimous decisions were then reached by show of hands. First, that a rigorous combing-out should be instituted, to be prosecuted until as many as possible of the officers remaining had been brought to light; second, that it would be more appropriate to the lofty aims of the new order if search and subsequent despatch were carried out less haphazardly. A touch of orderly dignity would add to, rather than detract from, everyone's legitimate pleasure.

For this purpose two parties amicably formed, one cynically asserting it would be the height of cruelty if a pampered officer's last sight on earth were not comfortingly that of luxurious surroundings. This party operated from the Naval Club.

The other party was more sentimental—self-styled the Fleet Landing Place Liquidation Authority, it averred that any salt horse was entitled to die in his chosen element, the sea.

The F.L.P.L.A. set to work with a will. Scores more victims were flushed out and, ringed in ten deep, were prodded along and driven down to a touchingly suitable spot for execution, the Fleet Landing Place.

On the wooden pontoon at the bottom of the flights of steps these officers were arranged in batches of about ten at a time along the outer edge, facing inboard, firebars fastened to their feet.

An immense crowd watched with interest, breath bated at

crucial moments, vociferous when it was commonly considered progress was too slow. Never before in its history had the Fleet Landing Place and terraces been so crammed with people; excited observers also clung to the beautifully-designed lamp-standards flanking the steps, and were jammed on the top of the column-supported ceremonial gateway at the head of the broad marble staircase.

Testifying to their numbers were the power and the volume of the yell which rent the air when those grey-faced officers, thrust hard in the chest, tumbled backwards into the sea.

Satiation breeds boredom, and after a hundred and three men had perished in this simple fashion a more ingenious procedure was adopted. The innovation was due to an engine-room artificer who suggested that it would be extremely funny if the next contingent returned to the fleshpots of the flagship's wardroom by the underground route. Officers, he explained waggishly, seldom used their legs, and he was willing to wager each one would be breathing very labouredly indeed as he tried to take a step in the desired direction.

When understood, the idea of a sea-bed promenade was wildly acclaimed, and someone knocked off the neck of a bottle—*ex* the Admiral-Superintendent's cellar—for its instigator. Thereafter, until supplies ran out, officers were bound in pairs arm-in-arm as if walking together, and then put into a pinnace brought alongside the pontoon by a crew who had fought for the privilege. As the boat moved away these couples, feet weighted as before, were dropped overboard at regular intervals, sightseers' glances being riveted in succession on points where a steady stream of bubbles could be expected from below.

When human stocks had been exhausted the stalwarts of the F.L.P.L.A., replenishments their objective, climbed the flights of steps. But, after passing through the archways, they pulled up short to gaze with critical interest at the scene in Kiezt Square, across which a few hundred howling members of the rival organization, the Naval Club Liquidation Authority, were racing towards a tree-bordered avenue, cap ribbons flying.

Their objective, Ekaterinskia, where many senior officers and officials of the great southern base resided, was neither particularly long nor its slope steep. Nevertheless, though only fifty-one, Admiral Prince Kaivanov was not quite in the condition he might have been. Despite his start the mob in filthy white trousers and dirty jumpers caught him as he was stumbling past the wrought-iron gate of Number Eighteen.

"Have I ever harmed one of you in my life?" he gasped.

"He talks," the cry went up.

A pock-marked stoker chuckled. "Let him, comrades. Tomorrow he will only stink."

"Men . . . gentlemen, I beg you to listen to me," Prince Kaivanov pleaded, his face distorted. "If you do, I promise you will have no cause to regret granting me . . ." He screamed with pain then.

A cutlass, swung playfully, ended his wordiness by cleanly chopping off three of the fingers with which he was clinging to a railing.

Elated with this outstanding achievement, the N.C.L.A. bundled him with their other captives and returned down Ekaterinskia. At the entrance to Kiezt Square, however, progress was barred by the F.L.P.L.A., who were most disgruntled at being robbed of prey on their own doorstep.

For several very noisy minutes it appeared certain that a bitter fight must ensue. But before the ultimate calamity could occur, that of bloody fraternal strife between devoted comrades, proletarian commonsense came into its own. Curiosity also played its part with the F.L.P.L.A.—for some time a persistent rumour had been passing round, to the effect that the boys of the N.C.L.A. had developed a unique technique.

Immediately a solution was reached tension evaporated, and the utmost good fellowship was revealed on a thousand faces as five hundred and seventy-eight good-humoured, back-slapping members of the F.L.P.L.A. joined forces with their good-humoured, back-slapping comrades of the N.C.L.A. The united force, with thirty-four wretched officers shuttled about in their midst, crossed Kiezt Square and streamed up the main shopping street as far as the magnificent entrance of the Naval Club. They surged boisterously inside, heading for the white ballroom where another quota of officers had been penned along one side.

Proceedings then began.

No novices themselves in their own sphere, the F.L.P.L.A. watched their colleagues with rising approval as a heap of bloody-headed, broken-skulled bodies by the concert grand piano grew bigger.

"Cracking nuts", these grand lads called it.

The exercise was not complicated, each execution beginning with the raising of the piano's heavy walnut lid, which was propped up with its stay. Meantime the victim, usually ashen-cheeked but resigned, was placed and held firmly on a waist-high side table by an enthusiastic squad, head projecting sufficiently over the end for his forehead to rest on the upper edge of the piano's curving side. The lid-stay was then removed and, additional momentum provided by brawny arms, down the lid came: "Crash-smash!" it was over, and "Next please".

The head of the house of Kaivanov was reserved until the end when, eyes rolling and blood dripping from the stumps of his fingers on to trousers and shoes, he was roughly dragged into position.

As soon as the roar of execration provoked by the sight of a flag officer tailed off, a yeoman of signals was responsible for a hot argument springing up.

"Now I ask you, isn't it only proper to single out an admiral specially?" he inquired with assumed solemnity. "Comrades, wouldn't we be doing wrong if we liquidated this gentleman just as we've done kids of midshipmen and young lieutenants who used to have nothing more than a couple of silver stars on their gold epaulets?"

At least ten minutes elapsed before it was decided that Admiral Prince Kaivanov should have the unique honour of dying to the sound of music furnished by himself. He was at once shoved to the other side of the piano where, moaning and gibbering, he was so placed that his face rested on the ivory keys.

Although harsh discords certainly were heard in consequence, the new method was not very efficacious in a killing sense, the small lid at the front of the piano too light and its arc of travel too short for cruelly telling blows; indeed after the lid had been lustily banged down by six pairs of hands for the eleventh time a wit remarked that if things continued as they were it would be only Christian to fetch the admiral a headache powder.

Tears of laughter were still streaming down hundreds of weather-beaten cheeks when a ship's carpenter provided the solution. It was most simple—he just turned an ornate little key.

Eventually Admiral Prince Kaivanov died, with the sharp latch of a lock buried in his cranium and his shapely nose resting brokenly on middle C.

3

A raw white fog swirled up the Neva from the sea. Beds were cold, few slept more than fitfully, and many of the enfeebled slipped into their last sleep.

In a room high up in Cherydskia a carefully screened candle had been burning since an hour before dawn. In its dim flickering light, while the sweat of weakness and excitement fought with the penetrating chill from damp walls, Count Wiazovsky and Xenia Menshek-Pelikova prepared a stew of sour cabbage and mouldy pork, lukewarm fare not likely to sit easily in gastric stomachs. After that, final preparations for departure were made; pitiful possessions were gathered together and every stitch of ragged clothing put on.

Count Petrov glanced keenly about, checking everything. "Ready?" he whispered then.

"Ready, Cyrus Konstantinych." Princess Anastasia nodded.

As if she were a jointed doll Count Petrov stuffed Mimi Kalutkina into an additional light-padded winter coat. She ignored him both then and when he tied a woollen shawl around her head, but looked down wonderingly as he knelt to make sure of the fastenings of her peasant felt overshoes.

"There, my darling," he said softly, pulling down the ear-flaps on his worn fur cap before taking her hand. He jerked his head to the others.

Anastasia and Xenia Menshek-Pelikova picked up their bundles, Count Wiazovsky threw a sack over his shoulder, and Prince Sergei dropped the cooking utensils—tin cans and a dinted pan—into a valise made from the curtain.

Treading carefully they descended the dark clammy stair-shaft to the front door. When outside, avoiding pavements littered deeply with offal thrown from windows above, they walked in the middle of the road, frozen snow crunching beneath their feet, dagger edges of ice occasionally and painfully penetrating thin footwear.

The streets were empty but now and then various objects seemed to rush on them out of the fog: derelict tramcars, upright or on their sides, and a *drosky* horse, which must virtually have been a skeleton before it died, whose stiff vitals were being gnawed by snarling dogs. Festooned everywhere, difficult to perceive until near, were frosted tangles of tram, telephone and telegraph wires.

When under the station's lofty barrel vault, in which few panes of glass remained, Count Petrov entrusted Mimi Ivanovna to the two women and pointed towards a crowd near the booking-office who were bargaining noisily. Prices of tickets were no longer fixed, and a small syndicate of railway officials were doing quite nicely for themselves.

"I'll get the tickets," he said. "There shouldn't be any difficulty about that part."

The station was packed; many had been there all night, some longer than that. Peasant speculators, clutching nets in which live fowl had been brought, were returning to the country; and pallid townsmen in patched, striped trousers, were adventuring into the country, would-be speculators in unfamiliar commodi-

242

ties. The air was rank with the smell of sheepskin coats and unwashed bodies.

When Count Petrov came back he spoke under his breath: "I've got 'em. There's a train to Zhlobin in two hours. When we reach there, well . . ." he shrugged.

Innumerable were the false alarms, innumerable the times when passengers, huddled during the intervals in groups on the paving stones, jumped to their feet as the asthmatic clank of an engine was heard. Actually the locomotive of the Zapolye-Zhlobin train was three hours late in leaving the sheds.

Count Petrov sheltered Mimi Ivanovna as best he could, the others pressing behind. Progress was very slow.

As the close-knit little party approached the barrier the searching nature of the inquiry to which travellers were submitted became apparent. Papers were frequently impounded, their owners' faces often betraying deadly despair. These people, the rejected, were hustled off to a luggage bay, where they swelled the numbers of those already in the custody of an armed section of down-at-heel soldiers.

At this crucial phase Princess Anastasia suddenly spoke to her friends, her whispered words few and urgent. Within seconds, an initial blankness vanishing, their faces lighted up with comprehension.

"Improvise like hell," she went on as each of them nodded. "Anything that occurs to any of us."

At last the moment came. Count Petrov held out their papers.

They were taken by a Red Guard, with buttons off his greatcoat and cigarette stuck to bottom lip. He handed them to an individual responsible for checking the authenticity of rubber stamps and signatures. This hurdle cleared after anxious moments, the documents were passed with a suspicion of deference to an extremely tall civilian, fleshless almost, who coughed constantly.

The lean man's burning glance bored into Count Petrov. "And you, comrade," he began silkily in a very precise voice, "are Egor Mikhailovitch Snadinzots, delegate of the Soviet of Gorodnya, returning with . . ." He pressed a stained rag to his mouth, ". . . returning with your wife and four others, as named, to the . . . er . . . pleasures of Gorodnya?"

Count Petrov's eyes narrowed. "Anything wrong with Gorodnya?"

The sharpness of his tone disturbed the senior investigator, who looked up from the papers he was now leafing over.

"No need to take offence, comrade," he murmured. "I am sure Gorodnya is all a loyal Communist would wish it to be."

Xenia Menshek-Pelikova's high-pitched squeal of contempt

243

attracted widespread attention. Red Guards, Soviet officials, railway staff and the public gaped at her.

"What do you know about Gorodnya, comrade telegraphpole?" she demanded. "Yes, it's you I mean, who's robbing a plasterer's lath of a job."

Three of her companions, their annoyance clear, spoke to her at once. The person insulted also addressed her. Neck sticking out, flushing angrily, he wagged an irate finger.

"I don't want any sauce from a chit no bigger than a tower of copecks could be built up to," he snapped.

"Think something of yourself, don't you?" Xenia retorted spiritedly. "We're all equal nowadays, aren't we. Anyway I'll say one good thing for Gorodnya—we don't have swankpots who talk like you. H'are you h'Egor Mikhail——"

A roar of laughter greeted this imitation. "That'll do," the man with the cough snarled.

Count Petrov rolled a globule of phlegm with his tongue and spat dexterously. "No more from you, my girl," he said sternly.

"If," Princess Anastasia remarked loudly, "somebody doesn't watch me carefully I shall set about her, the empty-headed little fool. She's got a very nice lad for a sweetheart, and when the Government shares out the land——"

The altercation had aroused so much interest that scores of people, passengers hanging on in the hope of other trains and those with even less to do, pushed into the back of a crowd straining to miss nothing. Count Wiazovsky's howl of renunciation caused more feet to scamper.

"I wouldn't wed her now, not if I was given the whole of . . . of . . . of Poland," he bellowed.

Vixenishly little Xenia Menshek-Pelikova disposed of him. "You're that ignorant you don't even know where Poland is. And as for wedding anyone, I can tell you I've better fish to fry than——"

"If you as much as mention that chap you've gone out of your mind about," Anastasia shouted, "I'll see you have more than you bargain for."

The lean-faced man tried to take a hand, shaking the papers at the culprit. "Now then," he bawled.

Xenia's ear-piercing scream defeated him. "I'll mention who I like," she said, quivering with rage. "And I'm *not* going back to Gorodnya, so there."

Anastasia's answer to that was to smack her face ringingly. Xenia recoiled a step, her green eyes devilish, and then, with a screech of fury, hurled herself upon her larger opponent.

An enthralled ring watched the fight between the two young

women, neither of whom spared herself. They slapped and clawed and spat at each other, and, clinging together and whirling madly, hair tumbled down their faces, bumped so violently into the senior Party member as to prostrate him so long with a bout of coughing that the struggle had ended before he was fully recovered. By then the antagonists were standing apart, Princess Anastasia's breathing distressed and Xenia Menshek-Pelikova weeping noisily.

"What's it about?" he asked feebly.

"She's picked up with a sailor here, and she wants to stop," Anastasia gasped. "The fool thinks he'll wed her."

"He will," blubbered Xenia.

"Listening to such blarney," Anastasia scoffed. "Don't you know, fathead, that a sailor has a wife in every port?" At least two hundred people laughed at this remark, and shrewishly she turned on them. "What's it got to do with any of you nosy folk?" she demanded. "Go on, answer me, one of you."

Too intimidated, none did, but the brief interval enabled the tall man to make an effort to restore order into proceedings sadly out of control.

"Is she going, or isn't she?" he growled.

The reply came as a determined, vengeful chorus.

"She's going," Count Petrov roared. "And when I meet her father. . . ."

"We'll tell him something," Prince Sergei seconded.

"She's going all right," Count Wiazovsky chimed in nastily. "Ignorant I may be, but I'm not 'lowing. . . ."

Deafened by the babel at close quarters, the ill-looking official lost his temper.

"She's going all right because . . ." he started yelling, but broke off when shaken by a severe spasm. Again the rag appeared from his pocket, and when he resumed it was in a whisper: "Because I'm sending her."

Busily tucking in strands of hair beneath her shawl, Anastasia bent towards him sympathetically.

"Are you taking anything for that cough of yours?" she inquired. "There's a syrup you can brew from a special sort of berry—we pick 'em in a meadow outside Gorodnya, at the end of summer that is, and its better to get up early so that the dew's still on them. . . ."

Half-despairingly, the tall man glanced at her as he pushed the papers into Count Petrov's hand. Grey-complexioned, clutching a post for support, he pointed to the wicket.

"Nothing will help me," he said in a tired voice. "Now through here the lot of you . . . and get back to Gorodnya."

Still quarrelsome, they obeyed him, Xenia Menshek-Pelikova bleating away and the others berating her, a pretence which on a diminishing scale they were compelled to pursue until their train creaked in.

The train was made up of covered cattle trucks, open timber-conveyors, ordinary coaches, a postal van, and two first-class coaches stripped entirely of the plush on the seats.

When it stopped Count Petrov was well placed, opposite the door of a fourth-class compartment. With his shoulder to the fore and his arm about Mimi Ivanovna, he held back a swarm of people until his friends had scrambled in to occupy a bone-hard bench at one side.

Another train, well-appointed, stood on the adjoining line, the rabble kept clear of it by the winking bayonets of Red Guards. It was reserved exclusively for the all-powerful Commissars of the Soviet.

It was a journey of frequent stoppages during the remainder of the day and throughout the cold night, with frequent searches and repeated examinations of papers.

The next morning, when running through the famine lands, still more could be seen of what war and revolution had done to Holy Russia. At wayside halts young children, glaucous-lipped and swollen-bellied as the result of eating grass, whinnied sub-humanly and dived away from strangers as would wild beasts; and occasionally, dragged along country roads at a snail's pace by feeble horses, muck-encrusted farm-carts could be observed filled with emaciated bodies, stripped of clothing, on the way to burial.

The first major stop was at Luga, where a thirteen-year-old boy in a light-blue frock coat was pulled out and harshly interrogated, though he had torn off silver-braid frogging and red velvet collar. Suspected rightly as belonging to the Imperial Lytzey School, an academy catering for the lesser nobility, he was left behind on the platform, a bundle in a viscous puddle.

On and on the train jolted, sometimes covering many versts during which nothing but ungathered crops were visible, fields of black stooks stretching into the distance; often halting until a sufficient head of steam was raised. So passed the day.

Shortly after midnight the disturbance staged in Petrograd was discussed in carefully-hushed tones. It was less risky then: the last of their fellow-passengers setting out with them from Petrograd had left the train, their places taken by strangers, who were asleep.

"Damned good notion of Stana's," Count Petrov said.

Sergei shook his head wisely. "Mightn't have managed it otherwise, Cyrus Konstantinych."

Count Wiazovsky smiled affectionately at the author of the scheme, and Xenia Menshek-Pelikova, drowsily resting her flaxen-haired head on his shoulder, smiled too.

"I hope, Bolo," Anastasia inquired, a hint of mischief in her voice, "that you weren't too adamant about your matrimonial intentions, or the lack of them?"

As grimy as any of them, Count Wiazovsky's teeth showed very distinctly as he grinned. "I hadn't much of a part, Stana. But I threw into it all I'd got."

Xenia glanced up at him. "You were perfectly offensive about me, Bolo," she said, dimpling.

Count Wiazovsky stifled a chuckle as he squeezed her hand. "If I hadn't been scared stiff I should have burst myself when you referred so nastily to my haziness about . . . about where I was born."

"But, Bolo dear," Xenia said softly, "you led me up to it *marvellously*."

After giving the couple an amused glance, Anastasia leaned cautiously across her half-sister. Mimi Ivanovna's eyes were closed and she was sleeping peacefully, the lines in her face less apparent.

"We've been very fortunate with Mimi, Cyrus Konstantinych," she murmured. "One can't be sure about her, and she might have said something disastrous. You know she does talk a little more now, though what she says is quite ga-ga, of course."

"Mimi is improving," Count Petrov told her decidedly. "For instance, it has been quite impossible to prevent her being pushed by men—and it hasn't disturbed her greatly."

For a few seconds Anastasia stared both at him and at the girl cradled by his arm.

"She may be looking a little less . . . less ravaged," she agreed, as if surprised. "Yes, perhaps she has improved slightly, Cyrus Konstantinych."

"There's no doubt," Count Petrov said stoutly.

The compartment was lighted by an oil lamp in whose dim rays its occupants could be seen: squeezed on the seats, spread in strange attitudes on the floor, stretched out haphazardly in pairs on narrow wooden sleeping shelves; some very still and others twitching; snoring, groaning and muttering.

"God, what would I give for a bath," Anastasia whispered. "But perhaps it won't be long now. When *do* you think we shall be reasonably safe, Cyrus Konstantinych?"

Count Petrov shook his head. "I don't know, my dear, but I

shall begin to feel happier when we've left Zhlobin behind." He sighed faintly. "We've Vitebsk, Orsha and Mogilev before then."

At none of these towns and cities did difficulties arise, though there were the usual alarms at each.

Vitebsk . . . scene of a particularly intensive search, where an old man was killed in his compartment to save his tired old legs the walk to the tribunal.

Orsha . . . centre of a grain country which had never been without the staple of life, where white bread was sold in the station and spittle ran like water as men and women fought for crusts.

Mogilev . . . where Nikolai II signed the Instrument of Abdication; the place at which Colonel Nikolai Romanov, in a workman's blouse, saluted his staff for the last time as the blue Imperial train started on its journey to the capital—a journey which, by order of the Duma, was never completed. Mogilev, where an over-eager man, breaking an ankle when jumping from a carriage roof, was trampled to death under a mass stampede for Troika cigarettes and a good place in the hot water queue.

Zhlobin . . . where the station-master three days before, on telegraphed orders, innocently lined up his staff on the platform and with them was mown down by machine-guns when an armoured Tchekist train thundered through.

Three days and nights of it altogether, in a stoveless, icy compartment reeking with dirty humanity.

For Count Petrov's party the journey ended at Homel, where the train was completely ringed by armed guards as it jarred to a standstill. Checking of papers was swift, scrutineers searching for a single item, a slightly indistinct letter on a violet-coloured rubber stamp.

"Out, the six of you," the Red soldier snarled.

"I strongly protest," Count Petrov retorted. "These documents were issued by the Petrograd authorities and have been perfectly acceptable to local Soviets along the route——"

The Red soldier reversed his pistol, poising it in readiness. "Get out or else," he growled.

They were herded into a parcels office, together with sixteen other shaken people, among whom Count Petrov recognized an artillery officer he had last seen during bogged-down battles against the Germans in the Pripet Marshes. This gentleman had gleaned catastrophic information, subsequently imparted to Princess Anastasia.

"They've found out in Petrograd about the forger chap," Count Petrov whispered, "and their telegram has caught us up."

Another ordeal followed quickly, the march through the town, during which the men were prodded with bayonets and the women's ears were assailed by the obscenities of a vindictive throng hurrying along with them.

As the gates of the prison opened the captives glimpsed a pile of corpses, and a working-party of enfeebled persons of both sexes digging graves.

The dank underground cell into which Count Petrov and his companions were thrust was illuminated by the light from the stone-paved passage outside; it filtered wanly through a small, partially-broken fanlight above the heavy door. Neither table, bench nor chair was there, and its sole amenity was an evil-smelling circular hole in the floor, over which prisoners could crouch to relieve themselves.

In the early evening footsteps were heard, the jingle of keys, and an impatient oath. As the door swung back a group of men gaped in with frank curiosity.

"'Ere you are, comrades," the leader jeered. "We've a reputation in this spot for fattening up folk before we start on 'em properly."

Salted herring, cold potatoes, black bread with not too much stalk and string in it, and a pitcher of brackish water were provided, wonderful food compared with recent fare. Famished, they ate little. It stuck in their throats—this was the end.

No one visited the cell again that night, but they heard screaming. The next day also passed without incident, but in the middle of the night following, gaolers roused them for the preliminary interrogation, which took place in a large room on the same level.

Conducted by an intellectual Trotskyist, the preliminary investigation was lengthy but not brutal. Brutality came into its own as they were being taken back to the cell.

"The awful beasts," Xenia Menshek-Pelikova shouted, half-sobbing with rage. "The utterly awful——"

"Shut up, Xenia Borisova," Count Petrov snapped.

But the penalty had already been paid, an iron-heeled rifle-butt crashing into her left breast. As she cried out Count Wiazovsky whipped round to crack his thin fist between the piggy eyes of a gross-looking soldier.

"You dirty swine, you," he yelled. "If you dare to touch any of these ladies again——"

Grunting with annoyance the five guards smashed him to the floor. The sickening thud of blows began, and he would have been killed then had not Xenia, leaden-cheeked with her own hurt, hurled herself between him and his viciously-striking assailants.

"Oh, please don't," she begged. *"Please."*

After that it was all over with tragic speed, both Princess Anastasia and Count Petrov failing in their desperate appeals to prevent anything worse. Kicked in the groin, Anastasia remained upright only by clinging to her brother. Slashed across the forehead, a thin flap of which hung down, Count Petrov reeled in agony and would have fallen had not his arm been round Mimi's shoulders.

A guard laughed slyly. "So it seems, comrades," he remarked, "that we have ladies here, real ladies."

His voice echoed in the clammy passage whose single light shone eerily upon the hollow-cheeked, poorly-clad prisoners: Prince Sergei looking sick with fright and his sister sick with pain; Count Petrov, features obliterated by a moving curtain of blood, and Mimi Ivanovna, unharmed, staring as if fascinated by the cob-webbed ceiling.

"And if that's correct," another guard chortled, "then we've also three gentlemen on our hands."

"One assuredly, and that's the young cockerel," grinned his neighbour, a squatly-built man who was tightly gripping Xenia Menshek-Pelikova. "Doesn't seem to have much spunk left in him now, does he?"

Xenia had had her lesson and, pride and intense pain both forgotten, she started to plead, blaming herself and entreating them to punish her alone for what had happened. For so long as it pleased her gaolers to listen they did so, but when they wearied she was silenced with a cruelly-cutting backhander to the cheek, delivered by a hand on which many diamond rings sparkled, some of them women's.

"No, I don't reckon this gallant defender of the ladies is all that cock-a-hoop," the guard with the sly laugh commented. "That's my opinion."

It proved to be his colleagues' opinion also. Semi-conscious, Count Wiazovsky had been dragged to his feet and propped against the damp wall, a slender fellow, chin sagging on chest, whose dark hair tumbled poetishly over a fine brow.

A guard with a squint brought matters to a conclusion.

"A talker, is His Honour," he growled. "Let's freshen him up so that he can talk a bit more. Should be interesting, comrades."

Eyes lighting up, a young guard with a receding chin asked quickly: "In the Bath House, eh?"

The proposer's lips thinned. "Aye, we've everything convenient there."

The squat man squeezed Xenia Menshek-Pelikova's waist. "We'll take this little piece along with us as well. What we do to her might persuade him to chat more easily, and she's some recanting to do herself if you come to think of it . . . awful beasts, eh, my little lady?"

A treat in store, the guards hustled the other prisoners into their cell. Prince Sergei, kicked hard, slithered on the floor and skinned his elbow against the soiled edge of the circular hole. But Mimi Ivanovna was hardly molested, possibly because of a strangeness in the eyes which has caused men down the ages to cross themselves in superstitious terror.

When Anastasia's nausea subsided she spoke shakily to Count Petrov, who had succeeded in tying a scarf turban-like over his wound.

"What will they do to them, Cyrus Konstantinych?"

He replied without moving, his head resting in a corner against cold stone. "I don't know, Stana, though I fear it is God help us all, my dear. But I won't allow them to ill-use Mimi, *never*."

Mimi Ivanovna was sitting close to him and, gently detaching himself from her, he rose painfully and tottered across the cell. Reaching on tip-toe to the fanlight he gradually shook loose a longish shard of glass, means by which so many revolutionary captives had released themselves from miseries beyond endurance.

Mimi Ivanovna watched him without curiosity, her half-brother and half-sister with a deathly chill in their hearts.

"My God!" Sergei groaned.

"Oh, Cyrus Konstantinych," Anastasia whimpered.

Unutterable grief in his tone, Count Petrov muttered: "I don't know how I'll ever nerve myself to . . ." Unaware of what he was doing, he touched his throat, felt the windpipe. ". . . to do it to her. But I shall."

Then, forcing himself to cheerfulness, he limped back to her. "Hello, Mimi darling," he said. "Come along, snuggle up again."

None of them could even have estimated how long it was before anyone returned to the cell. It might have been thirty minutes, or thrice that. Their earliest intimation was of the tread of feet, followed by a sharp click as the wards of the lock disengaged.

As the door opened they fleetingly saw their companions silhouetted against the yellow rectangle of light, each supported between two men. The victims were tossed inside as if bales of goods, one to lie still where he dropped; the other, despite fresh hurts, scrambled to her feet as the cell door slammed.

"They've done terrible things to Bolo," she cried broken-heartedly. "Cyrus Konstantinych, *please*. . . ."

But Count Petrov was already on his knees, peering at a froth of red bubbles on the young Pole's lips and at an ominous wet stain about his middle. Quickly he loosened clothing, closing his eyes momentarily in horror on perceiving deep and quivering gashes in a white belly.

Prince Sergei quailed. "Oh, my God," he mumbled, retching violently.

Count Petrov's voice rang with command. "Sergei Ivanovitch, it's probably a vain hope, but we must try to persuade them to fetch a doctor. Hammer like hell on that door, and keep hammering until someone comes. And one way or another we must improvise dressings and a bandage. . . ."

Anticipating this, Anastasia had pulled up her dress and was frantically tearing strips from her threadbare underclothing.

When an absorbent pad had been made, Count Petrov bound it in position with whatever they could divest themselves of for the purpose, and carefully drew together the ragged garments previously unfastened.

There was nothing else to be done, and he got up stiffly. Meantime Xenia, who had folded her jacket into a pillow, remained on the mildewed floor, sobbing almost soundlessly as she stroked the young Pole's hot forehead.

"They won't hear, so don't knock any more, Sergei Ivanovitch," Count Petrov said wearily. "Besides. . . ."

He was drawing a deep breath when, as she straightened from spreading her coat over a comrade staunch in many trials, he encountered Anastasia's anxious glance. She raised her eyebrows inquiringly. Sadly he shook his head.

Mercifully Count Wiazovsky did not take very long to die. For a while he whistled and wheezed through the blood-bubbles on his mouth and once, in delirium, made an effort to sit up, mumbling disconnected sentences.

But at the end he had a lucid moment, and perhaps in that moment the Almighty spared him from agonizing pain.

Flutteringly his eyes opened, his glance resting on the girl so near to him.

"Xenia . . . my very dear," he murmured weakly.

He was smiling at her when he died.

When his head fell back, and Count Petrov told her it was over, she wept unrestrainedly on the dead boy, cheek pressed against his breast, her arm across him.

Thinking it best, they let her be for a while, and then Anastasia, tears falling, drew her up.

Green eyes distraught, the girl turned to her. "It was my fault, Stana. If I hadn't——"

"Xenia, dear, you mustn't say that," Anastasia interrupted her, sympathetically but very decidedly. "You mustn't, because

Bolo would hate you to do so. If you think of what he really was in his heart you'll know I'm right, darling."

Behind them Count Petrov grasped Sergei's arm. "Give me a hand," he said. "We'll lift him to that side . . . well away from where we sit and from that stinking hole we all have to use."

This task had been completed when visitors arrived, unseen and silent adversaries who blinded them with dazzling beams from electric torches.

All that the victims saw occasionally was a rod or a stick flashing through a shaft of light; all they heard, if they heard at all, was the dull sound of metal or wood thudding on thinly-covered bones.

The flogging lasted for four minutes.

Nearly twenty-four hours later, at the midnight hour made fashionable by the Tcheka for summary sessions and executions, the surviving members of Count Petrov's party were brought to trial.

In Communism's high hierarchy a rift was revealing itself, slight but growing. Far away from Homel a struggle between two schools of thought had been resolved. Comrade Trotsky—no less than Comrade Lenin—advocated the signing of peace with Germany, but not at the price of yielding immense areas of Russia's fairest lands. On the other hand Comrade Lenin was prepared to accept peace even on the enemy's inordinately severe terms. He ventured to say quite plainly:

"Without a respite all our work may be undone, comrades. Without the *peredishka* the Communist millenium may never be."

The meek, quietly-persuasive little man had his way. It was all very simple . . . retreat when nothing else profitably offers, promise anything to obtain a settlement when opposing forces are too strong, stealthily infiltrate again when matters settle down— this must be Communist Russia's policy for many decades to come.

In Homel the differences between Trotsky and Lenin were reflected more harshly, comrade-soldiers to a man showing a lessening willingness to co-operate with their former comrade-workmen allies. This was established at the trial of Count Petrov and his friends, which took place in the once spick-and-span room of the murdered Police Chief. A red cloth covered a large table behind which three chairs were placed; Red sentries, with rifles at the "easy" and cigarettes in their mouths, lolled at the entrance. Doors constantly banged as sightseers drifted in and drifted out.

Irritated by the conditions, the President of the Tribunal of three beckoned impatiently. He was an elderly schoolmaster with snow-white hair, well-meaning and largely self-educated.

"What is it now, comrade?" he testily asked a middle-aged man in a green eye-shade who was bustling forward officiously. "And how many more times are the deliberations of this Court to be interrupted?"

The telegraph operator bent to whisper to him, and the two other members of the tribunal, in besmirched Army grey, leaned sideways to listen also.

The President stared incredulously. "Nonsense!" he snorted. "Ridiculous! As if . . . nonsense!"

The prisoners waited apathetically, a sorry lot: Prince Sergei Kaivanov, hareskin cap ludicrously to one side, livid bruises on his face, his sister with pulped lips moving but no sound emerging; Count Petrov, viciously battered about the head, unconscious and faintly moaning; Xenia Menshek-Pelikova, grinning queerly, scarlet weals standing out against the deadly pallor of her cheeks.

The President cleared his throat, coughed importantly, and glanced over his eyeglasses which, for reading, were low on his thin nose.

"Now let me see," he began. "Where were we?"

The Red soldier on his right poked him roughly. "How much more messing about is there going to be, comrade?" he growled.

"Aye, how much more?" a beady-eyed onlooker shouted ironically from the public benches.

The President rapped smartly with an inch-long stump of chewed pencil. "In the capacity and office in which I sit here, as elected by comrade-workmen and comrade-soldiers," he started off sharply, "it is my duty——"

"Get on with it or I'll get on with it myself," the Red soldier roared.

A flush crept up the President's scraggy neck. He fingered the nipper of his steel-rimmed pince-nez and fumbled with the papers before him.

"As duly appointed President of this Court of Summary Jurisdiction," he resumed not too certainly, "I must——"

His military associate on the left jumped up to make a general appeal: "You know me, comrades," he said, grinning mirthlessly. "What do you all say if I take over the job?"

It was evident, from the storm of applause, that this move was popular.

"I protest," quavered the President.

The protest was overruled. Its maker left hurriedly, his departure accelerated by a few kicks and a more severe bashing near the door.

The new President faced his very indifferent victims with remorseless eyes. "Well now, you ladies and gentlemen, as you've confessed yourselves to be, the question is——" His venomous glance darted towards a young Red Guard who was bullocking along the side of the wall. "What the hell is it now?" he bellowed.

The young man was in such a hurry that his shoulder caught a picture. A poster also fell, one depicting a workman riding on the back of a predatory-beaked factory proprietor who was on all-fours—the man of wealth's talon-like fingers glittered with gems, and gold streamed from his pockets as he crawled along.

The brief colloquy between the messenger and the new President ended abruptly, the latter abandoning his seat so precipitately and hastening out of the room so speedily that he remembered the prisoners only at the last minute.

"Take 'em back to the cells," he shouted from near the door. "We'll deal with 'em afterwards."

The gaol was very quiet that night, never the suspicion of a scream, not a hint of a brutal blow.

At dawn the flagged corridors resounded to the tramp of disciplined feet and harsh commands in alien voices. The cell door was burst open and a German sergeant looked in.

"Medical orderlies here," he shouted over his shoulder.

Later in the morning, in a fine house commandeered by the occupying forces, the released prisoners sat down to a meal: a watery bean soup, tolerable bread and sausage, some German rations, and wine not too bad.

A German major, singling out Anastasia, clicked his heels and bowed.

"Sorry the food is so poor, not even campaign stuff, but supplies haven't caught up with us yet, Princess," he said, adding in a low tone: "Our surgeon tells me you will all have to spend a couple of weeks or so in hospital, and that Count Petrov in particular needs considerable medical attention. We are arranging horse transport, the idea being to get you to Kiev, where there is every facility, as soon as possible."

Anastasia's dark eyes filmed with the tears of weakness. "You have all been wonderful to us, Major."

Nearer the top of the table, sick and dazed, Count Petrov yawned.

"Damned . . . damned good job your people arrived when they did, sir," he muttered to his neighbour, a Bavarian colonel with a close-cropped poll. "Damned good . . . Mimi darling, are you . . . where . . ." His head sank until the field-dressings swathed thickly round it rested on the table.

For generations Xenia Menshek-Pelikova's family had owned properties in the Ukraine.

"Kiev, did you say, Major?" she asked with an effort.

The infantry officer nodded. "We have already taken over the city and our forces are still proceeding eastwards."

This was how they learnt of the Treaty of Brest-Litovsk, which gave away so much of Holy Russia.

"Infamous!" Prince Sergei cried shrilly.

But he rose at once and, his face an expressionless mask of frigid courtesy, apologized to his hosts for a lamentable breach of manners.

One may be grateful for kindness and sympathy, but gratitude does not imply the acceptance of an iniquitous document to which blood-stained hands had affixed their tortured country's seal—to which other men who prided themselves on being gentlemen had, as the second party to it, signed their hands.

In doing that, German aristocracy had betrayed their own order, in the opinion of Prince Sergei Kaivanov, and were now themselves beyond the pale.

CHAPTER V

KIEV, "the mother of Russian cities", the cradle of Russian Christianity, with venerable churches, monasteries, and relics of Saints, and now the capital city of a new-born country, the "Free State of the Ukraine".

In this picturesque city of green-tiled and gold-gilded cupolas and towers, the banks were open, money was plentiful with a sufficiency of wealthy refugees from Petrograd to show how to spend it at the smart shops over which temporary signboards, displaying the names of the most famous establishments from the Nevsky Prospekt, had been placed.

The arms of Austro-Germany, which bolstered up the state, were not too apparent; the wide streets, filled with luxurious but dated Mercedes and Benz cars, blood horses, trotters, and handsome carriages, were guarded by Ukrainian Police bristling with lethal weapons—nothing about them to offend Russian suscepti-bilities. There were good food, fine wines, charming women, and delightful entertainment: soporifics which aided men and women to forget gruesome tales about the horrors of the distant Lubianka.

In the relaxing environment of Kiev, so helpful when planning great military operations, the representatives of two quite separate Russian forces enthusiastically toasted the day when the

Bolsheviks should bite the dust. Both agreed that the "Free State of the Ukraine" was a farcical creation of the Central Powers for their own convenience—that was the sole point upon which they were in accord.

The Don Cossacks, prepared to accept German aid in their fight against the Red Armies, had no hesitation in describing the Volunteers as drawing-room lap-dogs; the Volunteers had no illusions either—to them the Don Cossacks were uncouth peasants as well as traitors.

Under veiled Austro-German rule the two parties fought wordy battles. Members of one looked through members of the other at theatrical entertainments in the Kupeitchesky Gardens, and sneers were exchanged when they met while sauntering along the broad Krestchatik before morning chocolate.

The lounge of the Bristol Hotel was crowded with attractive *cocottes*, sparkling Russian girls, fair-haired Odessa Jewesses, and military dandies in dashingly-cut leg-o'-mutton breeches. There were strikingly-attired Polish officers, Don Cossack officers, Volunteer officers, and officers in the conspicuous new Ukrainian uniform, who caused amusement among the more polished by the breadth of their dialect. German and high-capped Austrian officers were also present, and they did not fraternize with each other at all.

A small group of well-groomed young men and women stood near the Palm Court. The speaker to whom they were smilingly listening, a radiant creature in a captivating hat, *svelte* short linen coat, and clinging wine-coloured slit skirt, looked very different from the bedraggled young woman who had bolted Army rations in a German mess not much more than a month before.

"But damn it all, Anastasia Ivanovna, how did you manage it?" asked a slim Volunteer officer. "There isn't a square inch of accommodation in the place, every hotel has been requisitioned by . . ." he glared at a Don Cossack who had chanced to glance that way, ". . . by some measly authority or other."

Princess Anastasia Kaivanova laughed, nodded to three friends passing in through the revolving doors, and then switched her dark eyes back to the inquirer.

"My dear," she said, "I suggested to the Chief of Staff that he could hardly expect me to sleep in the street——"

"And, of course, he offered you his bed, provided——"

"For God's sake be quiet," a tall blonde shouted at him. "I want to know how Anastasia Ivanovna grabbed that perfectly gorgeous *wagon-lit*."

"Just the way I say, darling," laughed Anastasia. "You know it makes quite a perfect little residence. A little noisy at times, of course, though much better since I had the coach removed to one of the outer sidings."

Always restless nowadays, Xenia Menshek-Pelikova wanted something different. "What about a drink?" she asked Prince Sergei; meantime her green eyes insolently held those of a Caucasian officer in another group. "*Now*," she concluded irritably.

In so short a period she had altered extraordinarily. The change in her face was profound—it was hard, very hard.

A move was made to the thronged bar where, at the far end, making a good deal more noise than was their usual custom, a dozen close-cropped Silesian officers were celebrating the thrust on the Western front which had sent a British Army, Gough's Fifth, reeling in its death agonies.

"And Mimi Ivanovna, Stana, what will she have?" another Volunteer officer asked.

Anastasia turned from him to her half-sister. "I don't know," she said dubiously.

"How is she getting on, Anastasia Ivanovna?" a young woman with a penetrating voice asked. "You know, sometimes she gives me the creeps."

"A Vienna-trained doctor has been trying to treat her." Anastasia shrugged. "But candidly if headway is ever made, I think only Cyrus Konstantinych will make it."

It seemed fairly safe to speak in front of Mimi Ivanovna, and they were heatedly arguing about reactions, complexes and repressions when Count Petrov arrived. The last of his bandages had been removed the previous day; the scars on his forehead were still very livid, and he looked extremely ill.

He smiled at Mimi, his eyes only for her.

"Hello, darling," he said lightly. "What do you say if we leave this noisy mob and have a drink together in a quiet corner?"

Some faint flicker of animation crossed her face as she stared at an arm crooked invitingly.

"Hang on, old thing," he said casually. "Ah, that's better, darling," he continued, gently drawing her away. "And now for that peaceful little spot."

The refuge he found was beyond the Silesian officers. Peremptorily waving away a white-coated waiter until he had seated her in a comfortable wickerwork chair, he then smiled at her over the narrow table.

"Sherry, sweetness, eh? I believe they have some rather decent stuff, and frankly, darling, my beastly old head isn't up to cocktails. So I think my Mimi must martyr herself and join me in a perfectly innocuous sherry." He laughingly stretched across and lightly touched her hand. "Do you remember how we sometimes used to call at that little place before going on to Kontant's? The sherry there was rather good. Now what . . ."—he frowned heavily—"what the deuce was that place called? Dash it——"

"Dalusbin's," Mimi Ivanovna said unexpectedly.

So often had Count Petrov made a cast without result. "My God, Mimi," he said excitedly.

But her flash of intelligence was short-lived.

Anastasia, who had seen something of his agitation, turned to her companions: "Mimi *is* improving. I really believe it now," she said.

"A ghastly business," said the slim Volunteer officer, his eyes darkening. "God, but won't we serve those Bolsheviki dogs with their own medicine when we begin to move. And I'll wager Cyrus Konstantinych is with me in that."

Xenia Menshek-Pelikova, as pretty as ever save for dark stains under her eyes, swung round to him.

"We're all with you, fool," she said shrilly. "Why should Cyrus Konstantinych or anyone else be picked out?"

A quiet-looking young man turned to her. "Ease down, Xenia Borisova," he said.

"Oh hell, what does it matter," she retorted, lips trembling. "And I want another damned drink."

It happened a few minutes later, a piercing scream rising above the buzz of conversation and clatter. In the strange hush ensuing everyone heard a young woman's agonized cries.

"Chuffka!" she screeched. "They slit his throat and . . ."

Anastasia dropped her glass. "That's Mimi," she gasped before she ran off. "And now I can guess why the poor dear used to stare at the floor so often."

Quivering from head to foot. Mimi Ivanovna was in a deplorable state, beyond restraint and oblivious to the curious gaze of scores of people.

"He was always so friendly with everybody, darling Chuffka." The torrent poured from her. "And one of them was petting him. . . ."

Holding her hands, Count Petrov was doing what he could to soothe her when, out of his eye's corner, he glimpsed the innocent cause of the terrible mischief, a white Borzoi held by a very full-bosomed woman. "For God's sake, madam," he shouted, "get that dog out of sight."

Reddening angrily, the lady he spoke to drew herself up haughtily. "Do you know whom you are addressing?"

Mimi Ivanovna was panting for breath. "Then darling Chuffka tried to crawl to me as he was dying. And blood was pouring from him and they wouldn't . . . wouldn't . . ."

The plump self-important personage, wife of a Volunteer Army Corps commander, found herself briefly confronted by a pale but blazing-eyed termagant who snatched a plaited leather-lead from her.

Anastasia took the animal, a surprised but friendly fellow, to the hall porter and gave him instructions. The Borzoi had just been ushered into a small cloak-room when his irate owner arrived.

"I think, *barishnia*," she said puffing with annoyance, "that both you and the man with the mad girl owe me an apology. What my husband would say to that ill-bred lout who positively bawled at me I can't even conjecture."

"The lout is Count Petrov, my mad sister's fiancé," Anastasia remarked icily. "And I am Princess Anastasia Kaivanova."

These were names to reflect upon, and embarrassment and discomfort revealed themselves in the expression of a silly and flustered woman.

"Why you hadn't the wit to shift your dog is beyond me," Anastasia continued. "Didn't you realize the effect he was having?"

The older lady floundered. "Perhaps I was a little slow in realizing——"

With a startling change of front Anastasia smiled graciously. "Oh, I do owe you an apology, naturally. But I am afraid that as I must hurry back the explanation will really have to wait. You *do* understand, don't you?"

The General's good lady showed her relief. "Of *course*, Princess. I am only too sorry that our acquaintance . . ."

She went on far too long and, furious with the delay, Anastasia stamped her foot.

"Oh, jump into the Dnieper, comrade," she snapped.

Leaving behind a lady crimson to the point of apoplexy she hastened to the bar.

Mimi Ivanovna had quietened down, and though she was still trembling both her half-sister and fiancé agreed that a stroll along the conservatory-walk, away from inquisitive eyes, might do her good. Each taking an arm they led her out.

A few minutes later Count Petrov risked a step he had been contemplating with trepidation for some days.

"Mimi dear, it was terribly sad about Chuffka, but it was quick and it may have been better for him," he said in an even, commonsense tone. "We've had a wretched time since then as you know, darling, and the old boy would have suffered terribly, wouldn't he?"

Beads of perspiration spotted his forehead as he watched her.

Anastasia, surprised and frightened also by this abandonment of pretence, accepted the cue when nothing disastrous happened.

"Yes, he's been saved ghastly hardship, Cyrus Konstantinych," she agreed. "And he loved his morning jaunts with Mimi and he wouldn't have understood why we had to keep him penned up in Cherydskia, in that poky, dreadful room. As to the terrible food he'd have had. . . ."

"Poor Chuffka," Mimi Ivanovna murmured.

Count Petrov nerved himself again. "Yes, the food question would have been fearful for him. He was particular, and I'm sure he would have slowly starved rather than eat awful muck."

His fiancée drew a deep breath. "And he was rather a greedy darling when there was something he really liked. And he could be a naughty thief, too, between meals, though he knew I would be cross with him."

She gurgled joyously and, not daring to speak, Count Petrov and Princess Anastasia glanced at each other.

"Yes," Mimi Ivanovna giggled, "it was because he had such a sweet tooth. He could recognize a box with a ribbon on it, and . . ."

She continued to chatter away—as a little girl, of perhaps seven or eight years old, might have done.

Every now and then people appeared in the conservatory but faded away as soon as they saw the occupants. The truth about the episode was now known throughout the hotel and many pairs of eyes were dim with tears.

But a fresh diversion shortly enabled them to forget a lovely girl's tragedy. Tempers in the bar, smouldering for some time, burst into a fierce flame. But there was no real fight—a German brigadier spoke too sternly. As game-cocks who are confident bear themselves, Volunteers and Don Cossacks strutted back to their respective parts of the bar.

2

The Golvaschuk Restaurant was particularly animated that July night. Marvellously-gowned women abounded and—excepting a sprinkling of Germans and Austrians in sombre uniforms—the men were colourfully clad, many scintillating with orders. Glassware tinkled and corks popped; laughter vied with the exciting rhythm of a Rumanian orchestra, and waiters in loose linen trousers and long white blouses girdled at the waist served the best of wine and food.

261

Between the ivory-and-silver screen hiding the service door and the flower-surrounded bower of the orchestra, a large party of Volunteer officers was seated round an oval table. One of them, wagging an unsteady hand to attract the wine waiter's attention, disclosed on his wrist a thick gold cable-bracelet to which a diamond-studded identity disc was attached, a tasteful touch which his friends also affected.

"Another bottle, two-three more bottles," he said thickly. "Damn it, are we to sit dry all night?"

"At once, Excellency."

The Volunteer subsided grumblingly into his chair, and listened again to a conversation whose every second sentence revealed the urge to take the field.

"To the happy day," a gangling young man shouted.

The orderer of wine chimed in: "Yes, and when we start we'll soon disembowel those bloody Reds. And,"—he focused uncertainly on a trio of Don Cossacks at an adjoining table—"we'll do it without the aid of a pack of traitors. Blasted country louts."

It was fortunate that the three Don Cossack officers were engrossed by a private difference. The point at issue was the death of Rasputin.

"I tell you he was shot," one shouted angrily.

His comrade to the right was so incensed that he rose, and, hands resting on the table, glared at him.

"Did I contend otherwise?" he bellowed. "But I did say he was given cyanide first. And I say the cyanide was as likely to have killed him as the bullets."

"Then why shoot him at all?" the other rumbled with scornful laughter. "Of all the crazy notions. Did you hear that?"

The third gentleman, to whom he appealed, had already given them scruplous chapter and verse, apparently now ignored.

"Haven't I told you Grigori Efimich was killed neither by the cyanide nor the wounds," he yelled. "Water was found in his lungs and therefore, you stupid dolts, he was drowned."

The situation was saved by the arrival of a smiling Cossack general, with an attractive woman on his braided arm. The time it was the Cossacks' turn and every Cossack in the restaurant stood and swayed to attention—and every Volunteer, supercilious smile on his lips, blandly ignored the distinguished newcomer.

Trouble was soon brewing elsewhere, however, and the orchestra leader, keenly watching a group of Volunteers in the middle, rapped hurriedly with his bow, signal if needs be for a musical counter-barrage.

A wasp-waisted stripling was at the root of the impending disturbance.

"Personally I should not permit it, Sergei Ivanovitch," he sneered glancing towards an alcove in which a young woman was dining with a Don Cossack. "Of course," he shrugged delicately, "opinions vary and I merely state my own. But if *my* sister—though it is quite fantastic to suppose she would demean herself or her family by consorting in a public——"

Goaded beyond endurance, Prince Sergei Kaivanov jumped up with a muffled oath, almost over-balanced as he turned, and lurched across the room.

Dazzling in a low-cut gown, Princess Anastasia Kaivanova leaned over the table in the alcove, eyes dancing, perfect teeth framed by scarlet lips as she smiled. She was finding this Don Cossack distinctly amusing.

"I gather you don't think highly of them, Count Andreyoukov," she said lightly. "Too many drawing-room soldiers, musical comedy warriors, eh?"

The Don Cossack looked up from his sucking pig. "We haven't any time to spare, Princess. This may be our only real chance, before the Bolsheviks build up an army."

"But aren't we building an army . . . two armies, in fact?"

A pair of steely-grey eyes surveyed her. "My dear Princess Anastasia," he said. "Just try to judge for yourself. Think of the immense number of officers happily skylarking here in Kiev, enough of them to whack the Bolsheviks by themselves . . . *if* nine out of ten would submit to serving in the ranks. Meantime out in the country, where our regiments are being formed, we just haven't sufficient officers." He ended dryly: "But perhaps there's wisdom in keeping most of these fellows away."

His voice carried and, hearing expostulations in two different quarters, he calmly eyed a fuming Volunteer staff colonel and a furious-faced young man wearing the silver aiglets of a Don Cossack A.D.C.

"My remarks really apply to the gilded staffs . . . of both forces, by the way," he went on with some grimness. "Too many popinjays in too many soft jobs."

Thoroughly enjoying herself, his companion laughed delightly. "I'm sure, Count Andreyoukov, you are pining to return to be the revered leader and brother of your men."

He carefully considered that. "Not noticeably so at the moment, Princess," he said after a while.

This fell very short of the fulsome, complimentary answer she was used to receiving. "No?" Her voice had a slight edge.

"Exactly!" he said crisply, perceiving about then a dashingly-attired young Volunteer officer who was standing beside the table

263

rocking a trifle on his heels. "And what do you want, my good fellow?"

Prince Sergei, gleaming from scented hair oil to brilliantly-boned cavalry boots, addressed himself solely to his sister.

"Stana," he began cuttingly, "may I escort you to the table of my friends. I find . . . I find——" He belched and paused in perplexity. "—I find I do not care for the company in which I . . . I find you, my dear."

Anastasia's sigh was long-suffering. "My one and only brother, Count," she murmured. "Sergei Ivanovitch, this is Count Andreyoukov."

Bowing stiffly, Sergei retorted coldly: "Indeed!"

Frowning appreciably, the Don Cossack had been eyeing him with vague wonder. Then his scrutiny grew more intent and, placing him, he cracked his fist into the palm of his hand.

"Unless I am mistaken, we have met before . . . er . . . comrade," he said, twinkling.

"Sir!" Prince Sergei drew himself up. "The term you have used——"

Checking him with upraised hand, Count Andreyoukov, apologized handsomely. "Perhaps that was a little unnecessary, my dear fellow. But may I remind you of the old clothes market in Petrograd?" He broke off to explain to his dinner partner.

From gaping, Sergei steadily bent lower, until his face and Count Andreyoukov's were not very far apart. Once he screwed up his eyes tightly, opening them to peer from extremely close quarters at a V-shaped shrapnel scar.

While this unusual inspection proceeded, Anastasia was being tutored in the basic principles of successful commercial practice.

"Turnover, achieved through small profits," Count Andreyoukov emphasized by tapping vigorously with a spoon. "Never forget that all-important maxim, my dear lady."

Princess Anastasia was biting her lip. "I shall make a note about it as soon as possible."

By then Prince Sergei had recollected, if hazily in parts, the day of Count Andreyoukov's grand clearance sale. On one matter connected with it, however, he was perfectly clear: Count Tchalmin's vindictiveness about the Andreyoukovs—which plainly evaluated that damned thief Matviei Jacobych as small beer compared with them.

"Do," Count Andreyoukov advised Anastasia warmly.

Triumphantly interrupting, Sergei pointed. "Remember you," he said.

Showing the utmost gratification, Count Andreyoukov signalled a waiter for another chair and insisted upon Princess Anastasia's brother taking a glass of wine with them before rejoining his party.

A changed man, Sergei accepted with alacrity. "I say, it was you who let loose at those Tcheka swine, wasn't it?" he asked.

Rather formally, Count Andreyoukov turned to his dinner partner. "You will forgive us if we talk shop for a moment, won't you? You see, your brother and I chanced to share a somewhat stirring day." Taking her consent for granted, which was as well, he nodded to Prince Sergei. "It's this way, my dear fellow . . . I happen to be a stickler about the sanctity of business hours and, as perhaps you will recollect, eager shoppers were storming every entrance. Yes, I considered it most disobliging when that troupe of Civil Servants gambolled in."

Convulsed, Sergei rolled in his chair. "Not all of 'em left, old man. You made dead meat of three or four, and winged another two or three."

"Really!" Count Andreyoukov murmured. "Circumstances prevented me from counting the bag."

Howling with laughter, Sergei thumped his thigh and slapped his new-found friend's back.

"Damned good, old boy," he bellowed. "By God, that's ripe . . couldn't count the bag, what?"

In this happy vein he remained so long as he was there. Then, highly elated, he bade them a ripsnorting farewell. Gaily waving, he stumbled off.

Count Andreyoukov coughed. "I have always thought it an excellent thing to make sure of being on good terms with the family as well," he mused.

Ill with long-repressed laughter, Anastasia hastily averted her glance, ostensibly to watch her brother, who was not being too well received by his brother officers. In point of fact the epithet "renegade" was used about him, and his previous taunter was outstandingly severe.

"Don't care if he's a Don Cossack or a Bashi-Bazouk," Sergei replied with the utmost good humour. "Grand fella, great pal o' mine."

"If it were my sister——"

"Tell you what, old chap . . ." an exquisite jest occurred to Prince Sergei. "You run over there and act as Stana's protector. And don't stand any nonsense from that softie Andreyoukov."

"Who?"

Sergei's face became stern, his expression reminiscent. "I saw this bird blot out six or seven of the Tcheka—yes, the hell of a tight spot that was. But surely you've heard of the Andreyoukovs? Good God, still wet behind the ears, little man?"

Furious about Prince Sergei's insult, the juvenile-looking

Volunteer began to shout at him, and this compelled several of their companions, who were trying to exchange tales about those wild customers, the Andreyoukov brothers, to shout also.

The orchestra leader was preparing for action when a Jewish millionaire with a window seat attracted attention by rushing out, napkin still tucked in collar, on seeing newsboys scampering along the broad street.

The special editions sold like wildfire, private quarrels were forgotten in universal grief; the Golvaschuk, unquestionably the brightest restaurant in Kiev, became an assembly of sobbing men and women.

In Petrograd the boys called "Death of Nikolai Romanov!" In Kiev placards proclaimed in blood-red type:

MURDER OF THE TSAR

The despatch ran:

On the night of July 17th, in accordance with the decision of the Ekaterinburg Soviet, the ex-Tsar Nikolai Romanov was shot. His family have been transferred to a place of safety.

Officers wearing black armlets and with sword-hilts swathed in black muslin, and young women and old women in heavy black veils and the sombre stuffs of mourning, began slowly to move along the streets of Kiev. Hundreds of bells filled the night air with their dismal dirge, and every church was packed.

In the Pestchersk quarter, a self-contained town in itself surrounded by high walls, the monks of the Pestcherskaya Lavre, the "city of caves", lamented for hour after hour. Old Saint Sophia was full, the new Cathedral of Saint Vladimir without an inch of spare space, the churches of The Three Saints and of Saint Andrew crowded with stricken souls. Poignantly priests delivered the solemn words, hundreds of vessels burnt incense, thousands of candles cast yellow shadows upon the faces of those who prostrated before the pictures of the Saints.

Two broken-hearted men jumped from the iron bridge over the Dnieper.

Hearts were filled with sorrow. They were filled with resolution too.

3

Kiev continued gay, though by late summer barricades stood at street corners and rumour after rumour flew from ear to ear. A machine-gun behind a sandbag barrier guarded every intersection; Austro-German troops patrolled day and night; the Ukrainian police shot at sight any civilian carrying a weapon.

The murder of Field-Marshal Eichhorn by the hole-and-corner

266

Bolshevik element in the city had caused the Central Powers, so their spokesman announced, to adopt a strong attitude. Many people declared, however, that rising Communist activity was not the real reason for the nervousness exhibited by the Austro-German High Command, and a few openly insisted that the Central Powers were in danger of being beaten by the Allies.

Meanwhile jazz bands blared, and places of entertainment did good business in that mellow October.

Night after night the five tiers in the immense auditorium of the cream-and-gold theatre were packed, night after night the possessors of some of the proudest names in Russia streamed past the statuary on the broad, marble staircase, or gossiped in the many-mirrored foyer. Night after night they laughed, night after night they cried when the orchestra struck up *God Save the Tsar*. And one night the audience were still weeping when leaving.

So sad it had been, that performance of *Uncle Vanya*—the blank shot in the wings during the second act, the young girl in the stalls who raved when she heard the sharp report.

"Her lover was shot by the Bolsheviks before her eyes——" The whisper ran round the house.

After the last curtain a disconsolate group, not quite recovered from this emotional upheaval, lingered outside the theatre.

"I've got a damned good idea," said Prince Yura Nitchkoff, who also had managed to escape from the north. "That cabaret on Zuratskia," he went on with a certain wariness. "How about it, Stana?"

Princess Anastasia made several blisteringly disparaging comments. She had been in a foul temper for days, often openly contemptuous towards the men of her set. In her awkwardness she was backed to the hilt by Xenia Menshek-Pelikova, who was now drinking too much in an effort to forget the past and seemed all too frequently to enjoy being contrary.

Prince Nitchkoff wriggled his flattened nose. "Oh, I say, you two," he expostulated.

When another establishment for supper had practically been decided upon the two women switched round with exasperating inconsequence in favour of the place in Zuratskia. But as soon as she reached there Xenia Borisova found fault with the gipsy band and the impromptu versifiers who specialized in sly allusions to patrons; and Anastasia Ivanovna in turn, disliked the negro ragtime, the service, the champagne, the food, and the girls dancing in the middle of the floor.

Prince Yura, who thought the dancers quite passable for the provinces, lost his temper.

267

"Damn it, could either of you do half as well?" he demanded.

"Of course, my dear," Anastasia drawled. "And even improve on it."

"Rather," said Xenia Menshek-Pelikova. "God, yes."

"Bunkum!" Prince Yura shouted.

Anastasia's eyes darkened. Within ten minutes she and Xenia began a strip act which brought the room into an ecstatic uproar.

When enthusiasm was at its height a Don Cossack officer, whose uniform earmarked him as from the training front, pushed aside the curtains at the back. Smiling with anticipation, he glanced about searchingly for a moment. Then, jaw determined, he plunged through a dense ring of spectators, occasionally to the misfortune of enraptured gentlemen who, to obtain a better view, were precariously balanced two or three on a chair.

On bursting into the cleared space in which the semi-naked performance was taking place he seized the dark girl's wrist, spinning her round in an inelegant scamper.

"What the devil do you think you're doing?" he growled.

Princess Anastasia's reply hardly sounded as though she had been counting the days to seeing him again, though that was the truth.

"And what the devil has it to do with you?" she asked, eyes blazing.

The inquiry was echoed by many among the male section of the audience.

Count Andreyoukov smiled sardonically as he picked out the more indignant. But humour died out of his grey eyes when he saw that they soon became unsure of themselves, and his tone was sharp as he spoke to a young woman who defied him with every gesture and inflection.

"Put your clothes on, Stana. I'm taking you out of here."

"You're not," she said, quivering with fury.

Still retaining his grip, he stared levelly at her. "If you don't get dressed you'll go as you are."

Every eye was on them, but the Princess Anastasia Kaivanova had always been supremely indifferent to being the central figure of a public scene. Despite that, she terminated the episode with a few savagely restrained words.

"For this, my dear Count," she said before leaving him, "you will suffer."

He waited outside the *artistes'* dressing-room. When she came he armed her through a gaping throng and thrust her into a taxi.

"The goods depot," he snapped.

"And may I ask why you are taking me to the *wagon-lit*?"

"To talk to you," he answered shortly.

"What about, my dear?" she said mockingly.

"I'll tell you when we get there," Count Andreyoukov grunted. "But in the meantime you might let me know whether you have made arrangements to leave for your villa in Livadia." He screwed in the seat and pointed in the direction of the artisan houses of the Padol quarter. "Stana, haven't you noticed that the local Bolsheviks have become much bolder, even to the extent of killing a German Field-Marshal? And hasn't it occurred to you what may happen if the Germans are compelled to withdraw?"

"But the glorious Don Cossacks, what will they be doing when their friends have gone?"

"Arguing with the Volunteers," he replied dryly. "By the time the armed forces of South Russia take action against Commissar Trotsky's vermin it may be too late . . . for some."

"You are extremely solicitous . . ." Anastasia shrugged disdainfully in her corner, ". . . for me."

Faintly smiling, he glanced at her. "Yes," he said as the car lurched through a gateway, "I think I am, Stana."

The great railway depot resounded to purposeful activity. Every night ten trainloads of fats, cheese, flour, fish, eggs, corn and sugar left for the empty-bellied lands of the Central Powers; and every day five hundred horses, soon to don the webbing-harness German ingenuity had fashioned to replace leather, went the same way too.

Under blue arc-lamps in the goods yard, parties of German and Austrian soldiers in forage caps were loading express goods trains. Steam drifted through the air; the sidings stank with sewage fallen from the lavatories on the rusty-wheeled coaches of the *Compagnie Internationale de Wagons-Lits*—for over a month the German sanitary officer responsible, usually so meticulous, had failed to ensure its removal.

The clock in the belfry over the Town Chambers boomed three times. Count Andreyoukov picked up his companion and, avoiding the filth as much as possible, carried her across the tracks towards a brilliantly-lighted coach, one connected temporarily to the city's electric mains.

"From the babel I think we must assume that your brother is entertaining on the grand scale," he murmured on setting her down. "But . . ." he nodded at the next *wagon-lit*, which was in darkness, "but perhaps we might borrow this for a few minutes."

She laughed scornfully. "A little apprehensive about meeting so many Volunteers, Nikolai Tikhonovitch?" she inquired.

His mouth tightened and, grasping her forearm, he forced her to turn-about. When they reached a narrow door he opened it with his free hand before assisting her up three brass-edged steps into the Kaivanovs' coach.

In the near half-portion of the long railway car there were nine or ten officers, neck-bands open, swords discarded, and as many women with hair tumbled to their waists. Signs of drunken carousal were everywhere: tumblers, fragments of glass, spilled ashtrays, bottles on their sides, and pools of liquid.

As far as Princess Anastasia was concerned the trollops might not have existed. Her brother was not in sight and so she appealed to her brother's friends.

"Gentlemen," she said icily, "Count Andreyoukov has been good enough to insult me. Perhaps you will be so kind as to ask him for an explanation?"

"By Saint Pavel of the Little Church," a Volunteer cavalry lieutenant yelled as he reached towards where his sword-hilt should have been, "by Saint Pavel, we'll teach this Don Cossack . . ."

Count Andreyoukov's steel-grey eyes sought those of the young woman by his elbow.

"So this is what you do to me, my dear?" he said.

Proudly she retorted: "I allow no one to treat me as you did, and this is merely a beginning." Her lip curled as she assessed her defenders. "For what it may be worth."

He nodded absentmindedly, more interested in the fuddled attackers, who were forming up in the aisle between the seats.

"Not too impressive from your punitive point of view, I agree," he murmured. "The mistake they're making," he leaned forfidingly towards her, "is to throw themselves into action without having made sure of sufficient space for manoeuvring. Why, my dear, only one of 'em can get at me at a time. This fellow in front."

Rear pressure urging him on, the spearhead of the noisy onslaught was within arm's length of Count Andreyoukov who, grabbing a handful of blouse, jerked him forward before hurling him against the second in the file. Cannoning violently into each other down their line, the Volunteer officers fell backwards in quick succession, a row of ninepins toppling, each pair of feet, from the second, pinned down by the weight of the man ahead.

It was evident that the tipsy, blaspheming heap, jammed in a tight passage-way, would not easily sort itself out.

"No, I fear I can't wait," Count Andreyoukov remarked.

Anastasia touched his chest. "Oh, Nikolai Tikhonovitch," she whispered, her voice breaking.

Count Andreyoukov bowed to her before leaving.

Nostrils quivering, Anastasia watched his broad shoulders

disappear. He did not look back, nor glance in as he passed outside.

For a while she leaned against a high-backed seat, her immobility ending only when she realized there was no possible hope of his returning. For the next two or three hectic minutes, while cursing officers and shrieking women crouched behind whatever shelter was available, she indulged in an orgy of destruction, sweeping glasses from trays, throwing bottles through the windows.

Just as suddenly she dropped limply into seat Number Five, her dark head sinking on to a baize-covered table.

"I'm leaving this damned place," she said shakily. "Now I *will* go to Livadia, but not because that fool wants me to."

Bleary eyes blinked, and widened further in amazement. Could it be that Anastasia Ivanovna had begun to cry?

When building a station at Kiev was projected, hundreds of designs from all parts of the Empire were submitted. In 1889 an eminent committee was appointed to make a final selection from the short list. It disagreed violently. Temporary wooden erections were the outcome until tempers cooled. This prospect was never realized, a succession of committees stubbornly dividing on the question throughout the years. In 1918 these temporary structures, apart from the effects of time and, more latterly, gross neglect, were precisely the same as nearly thirty years before.

The station was crowded with people, amongst them anxious-faced Germans who wondered about the disquieting news of the release from a Berlin prison of the Marxist, Carl Liebknecht; and Austrian officers, naturally good-natured, who crimsoned with fury whenever a German was encountered. A train would soon be leaving and outside the door of a first-class coach a lively group had begun to break up.

Count Petrov was now in the training area, and so it was her half-brother who handed Mimi Kalutkina into the compartment.

"You look, divine, my dear," Prince Sergei said as he kissed her hand. "And that will be my report to Cyrus Konstantinych the very first moment I see him."

Immediately behind, Prince Yura Nitchkoff was talking to a Volunteer staff-captain to whom, at the beginning of the week, Xenia Menshek-Pelikova had announced her betrothal.

"By God, if it is true that the Germans are finished," he said boisterously.

The staff-captain was an extremely dissipated-looking gentleman, his expression oddly melancholy.

"When we Volunteers begin to move, what?" he suggested.

Prince Sergei reproved him over his shoulder. "Obviously you mean the Armed Forces of South Russia," he said gravely.

This sally caused a bellow of laughter.

In a recess a short distance away, her shoulder touching the rusty side of the public hot-water boiler, Princess Anastasia listened with the utmost attention to a very smart, flaxen-haired young woman who, out of breath, had just arrived.

"Sorry I've been so long, Stana," Xenia Menshek-Pelikova was saying. "But I knew you wanted to be absolutely sure. Yes, Nikolai Tikhonovitch left four days ago. And if it interests you, he took fifteen women with him."

"What!"

Xenia giggled. "Dancers," she said. "From what I was told he is determined his regiment shall have some of the pleasure hitherto exclusively appropriated by 'the braves of the base'—his words."

Dark eyes soft and reminiscent, Anastasia smiled mistily. "Isn't that just like him?" she murmured. But after that, as if conscious of a tendency to weakness, she abruptly dismissed Count Andre-youkov from the conversation. "I wish you'd change your mind and come to the Crimea, Xenia darling. And even at the risk of being snubbed there's a question I intend asking before I go—aren't you simply chucking yourself away by marrying that . . . by marrying so soon?"

Defiantly Xenia Menshek-Pelikova stared at her. "I'm marrying him because he's had plenty of sorrows himself and drowns them in drink as I do, which makes us a very suitable pair," she replied. "And I'm marrying him because the drunken sot is fool enough to be just crazy to marry me, and I don't care a damn either way. What the devil does it matter now? Nothing matters, not a thing."

Sadness was depicted on both their faces as each of them thought with aching regret about a young Pole. But neither mentioned Count Wiazovsky's name.

"All right, darling," Anastasia sighed after a brief interval. "I suppose you must go to hell in your own dashing style."

Xenia's laugh was brittle. "Or perhaps, as you would say, Stana dear," she said, wrinkling her nose mockingly. " 'One lives but once'."

Time was passing but, before they sauntered along the platform towards their friends, Anastasia handed her companion a letter written the previous night to cover the eventuality which had arisen.

"Darling," she said with unusual earnestness, "will you hunt

272

out an *absolutely* reliable messenger to take this to Nikolai Tik-honovitch? For God's sake don't lose it, will you?"

Xenia Menshek-Pelikova's recklessness and hardness were on the surface only. Tears filled her green eyes as she nodded.

"No, I won't," she muttered, as if heartbroken. "And I hope you'll quickly settle your misunderstanding with him, or what-ever it is. And may the good Lord bless you both, Stana darling."

Sympathetically Anastasia squeezed her arm as they started to walk along.

Within ten minutes the party which had gathered on Kiev station to wish God-speed to Anastasia Ivanovna and her half-sister were driving out to the open-air theatre for the last per-formance of the season.

The train, pale wood-smoke fanning upwards from the loco-motive's funnel-shaped stack, was no more than ten minutes late as it swung round the curve of Sevastopol dockyard. Despite many material handicaps, German railway engineers had achieved marvels with the transport system of South Russia.

The glowing afternoon sun was cruel to the naval base, emphasizing the flaking gold on the cupola of Vladimir Cathedral and the grime on the windows of Peter-Paul, modelled after the Temple of Theseus at Athens; its rays picked out tattered strips of flag flying over the Naval Hospital, and illuminated a long line of grey ships of war, neglected and forlorn.

To these depths had sunk Catherine the Great's creation, "the second heart of Russia", the final humiliation being that in the gardens on the point across the waters of South Bay an Austrian military band was playing the *Wacht am Rhein*.

With sombre eyes Anastasia looked at the marble steps of the Fleet Landing Place and Government buildings and houses rising behind.

"This was where they killed Ivan Mikhailovitch," she said huskily.

"I know, Stana," said Mimi, nodding. "Frightful of them, to be so dreadful to Papa, don't you think so?"

Sobs shook Princess Anastasia as she gazed over the town in which their father had died so terribly.

"You do, don't you?" Mimi Kalutkina persisted brightly. "I am quite sure I do."

"Shut up," her half-sister screamed.

A few tears trickled down Mimi's cheeks, but as nothing ever went deep with her she was not hurt. Within four minutes she was clapping her hands excitedly when, sullenly watched by loungers who seemed to form the greater part of the population, she recognized the Renault limousine awaiting them at the station, and throughout the lovely drive to Livadia she constantly jumped with pleasure in her seat.

At the sea-shore villa there were more tears, but these were tears of joy.

"*Valya Igorovna!*" Anastasia cried shrilly; her maid, weeping too, fell into her mistress's outstretched arms. "How didst thou get here, Valya Igorovna?"

"Well, you see, Highness," the girl raised brimming eyes, "after you disappeared I . . ."

In the cool bedroom, scented by late roses clustering along the rails of a broad balcony, she described her trials since leaving Petrograd. She told of other things, too . . . the growing belief that the whole Imperial Family, not the Tsar alone, had been murdered.

"Mimi," Anastasia shouted, her hands clasped in despair. "Did you hear that?"

Shoulders drooping, she walked slowly along the balcony, glimpsing a red-shingle beach through the cedars and magnolias. Her glance passed from the Emperor's villa to Dulber, the estate of the Grand Duke Peter; she stared at the Imperial Road over which the slaughtered Nikolai had laughingly sauntered with his son and daughters to Ay-Todor, in whose gardens the Grand Duke Mikhail had erected a lighthouse to guide his children home when Black Sea mists stole insinuatingly over the land.

"It will be true," she murmured. "They are capable of anything."

"I shouldn't be at all surprised," Mimi said wisely. "You know, my dear, I always think——"

"And it may not be true," said Anastasia, emerging from her slough of despond. "Valya Igorovna, who is in residence here? Find out and . . . but unpack my things first."

"Her Highness the Princess Savoseva is here, Highness."

Princess Anastasia shouted with delight. How wonderful it would be to see Olga Ivanovna again.

Below, on a broad road by the gently-lapping sea, a patrol of German soldiers marched. Their officer's face was apprehensive, nor did it lighten when he acknowledged the salute of a sergeant of police. And the Russian police sergeant, deprived of his sword by one of the first ukases of the Provisional Government, grew even more apprehensive when he saw the officer's apprehension. Without the Germans what could a few police do, he reflected fearfully; and if the Germans had lost the war, or their troops were withdrawn to quell rebellion in their own homeland. . . .

It was peaceful in the Crimea now. But if the Germans left . . . a man of intelligence knew what that might mean.

Beyond the Bosphorus and the Dardanelles, at the other side of the Black Sea, a British Naval Commander-in-Chief was signing an armistice with the Ottoman Empire as the police sergeant gloomily pondered these matters.

Soon the trunk lines of Middle Europe began to hum: Spa-Berlin; Vienna-Berlin; Berlin-Hamburg; Berlin-Munich; Berlin-Dresden; Berlin-Leipzig.

Armament kings, bankers and businessmen spoke to colleagues far and near: "Geschlagen! *Geschlagen!* Unmöglich, *Unmöglich*"——"Beaten! *Defeated!* We can't be, we *can't* be" they mourned.

Through a vast spider's web of swaying lines their groans weighed down the wires: Mighty Germany—and now; "Das Spiel ist aus, *das Spiel ist aus*" . . . "We're finished, the game's up."

The High Command of the Central Powers hurriedly began to bring back to the Fatherland their still immense forces in lands overrun.

Willy-nilly, faced by the immediate prospect of stark change, Volunteers and Don Cossacks were compelled to consider seriously some working arrangement. Each of these armies submitted to the other a list of officers for liaison.

PART FOUR

1918 - 1920

*

CHAPTER I

THE World War had ended and everywhere the victors' forces were moving freely. In the Aegean an Allied fleet slipped cable in Mudros Harbour, to steam through the Dardanelles and the Sea of Marmora to Constantinople, where the warships anchored off Dolma Bagtché, the Sultan's white palace.

A few days later these multi-patterned vessels began to stem the fierce current of the Bosphorus. The sheer cliffs of Balaclava, north-eastward across the Black Sea, were their next landfall, reached shortly after a glorious daybreak. A pilot yacht awaited them there, prelude to the majestic investment of Sevastopol, where the Malakoff Park and waterside gardens were black with spectators.

Officers on the ship's bridges, sweeping the scene through binoculars, sometimes paused to admire the lovely marble lines of the Fleet Landing Place, or to wonder about a three-funnelled destroyer which, farther up the main harbour, had ploughed into the shore—she had struck at twenty-eight knots, wheel hard over under the hands of her young captain, who then died dreadfully through the verdict of a lower-deck committee with little use for high courage. Out in the fairway, of acute interest to professionally-minded observers, lay the battleship *Imperator Alexander III*; now renamed the *Volya*, she swung dirt-raddled at a buoy, green slime on her massive cable—a fate perhaps more ignoble than that of her sister ship, not far astern but wholly out of sight. The *Imperatritsa Marya* had been scuttled by revolutionists who, running amok in destructive transports, never considered that a change of name would more reasonably preserve a fine ship for their new Elysium.

Before the incoming warships picked up their allotted anchorages scores of small boats began to pull out, down to the gunwales with Russian officers enthusiastically bent on greeting these allies and friends.

In the days to follow senior officers visited the ships also, often with serious matters to deliberate, among them the re-establishment of disrupted communications. In consequence British destroyers, when on routine calls at Black Sea ports, frequently carried urgent Russian commands and accommodated in other fashions.

H.M.S. *Nighthawk*, giving passage to a British naval lieutenant, was of these. A fortnight before Christmas, after calling at Yalta with mail for surviving members of the Imperial Family and at Novorossisk with despatches for General Denikin, she was speeding southwards—to sub-tropical Batoum, a languorous place whose main drawback, in the eyes of a destroyer captain particular about the cleanliness of his command's decks, was the state of the mole upon which the pipe-line from the oilfields terminated: oleaginous, clinging slime reflecting every colour of the spectrum.

At Batoum, H.M.S. *Nighthawk's* passenger, official business transacted, ordered himself a sumptuous lunch at the *Hôtel de France*. Over this meal he pondered about his next mission, one far from being of an official character.

The first leg took him by train to the old Russian capital of Trans-Caucasia, where he sought assistance from the British Military Mission. On Tiflis station a khaki-clad political officer, white band on cap, gave him exact directions.

The Military Mission was quartered at the Hotel London in Golovinsky Prospekt, on the side facing the steep ascent to the Fortress of Kalah. Along this fine boulevard were extremely contrasting sights: wildly-driven Russian military automobiles and yellow-skinned Bucharans urging overburdened camels; the magnificent palace of the Governor-General and the grim execution ground near it.

The officer commanding the Mission was tremendously helpful, and tremendously curious about the reason for a naval officer's appearing.

"Amsibu, eh?" he muttered. "Why, of course, my dear chap, certainly I'll fix up a car and driver for you."

"Thanks, sir."

"Mmmm . . ." the Army murmured. "Rather an unusual errand you're on, Crowther, what?"

The Senior Service's representative, a sallow-faced, stockily-built young man of about twenty-six, nodded.

"On the face of it, yes," he agreed. "But I suppose there's such a thing as *noblesse oblige*, sir. Anyhow, that's all I know—that a member of the Imperial Family had a word with the C.-in-C., and that was that."

The Colonel-in-Command stroked a ginger moustache as he gazed out at pink-and-white colonnaded barracks, golden cupolas of green-and-white churches nestling in the crannies of the higher slopes, and at the cliff below a prison formerly reserved for political offenders.

277

"Tell you what, Crowther," he said eventually, "I think I'd better let one of my fellows go along with you. And an interpreter, of course. Deuced queer country if you get stuck. And while you're waiting what about a bath to freshen you after that filthy train journey? They're rather good here. Take a pew while I arrange things."

The senior officer of the Mission then excused himself. In the next room he consulted his subordinates, who to a man thought the whole business funny. Well, if the Navy imagined it could butt in on the Army's preserves. . . .

In due course, accompanied by a lieutenant of ingenuous mien and bland inquisitiveness, Edwin Crowther visited the public bath-house, where he endured sulphur-water smelling of bad eggs and a relentless massage by a bearded Persian. When returning, immensely revived, he passed through the factory quarter in the depths of a ravine, saw crude machinery turned by creaking water-wheels, and gaped at chain armour for which men down from the mountains bargained in ancient streets.

The car was waiting at the Mission together with an Intelligence captain who, during the drive, innocently drawled leading questions.

"Simply magnificent," the unwitting object of these suspicious speculations ejaculated. "Never seen country like it in my life."

When not immediately concerned with the antics of a Georgian chauffeur who took hairpin bends inches only from the outer edge of dizzy drops, Edwin Crowther stared in wonder from snow-clad peaks to the luxuriant growth of the valleys, from venerable watch-towers to creaking, primitive modes of transport.

The gleaming palace of Amsibu was another revelation.

A stout woman, sitting on a deeply-cushioned divan, received them.

Princess Kaivanova had changed grievously from the slim, exquisitely lovely Princess Zeneide whom Prince Ivan Kaivanov had passionately wooed as a young naval officer. As she apologized for the indifferent quality of her English she waved them to chairs.

"My dear Lieutenant Crowther," she said, snapping her fingers occasionally as she sought for an elusive word, "it is mos' charming of you to have journeyed so far with my daughter's letter. You will excuse me."

Watched warily by the Intelligence officer, she thrust a gold paper-knife under the flap of a crested envelope.

Meantime Edwin Crowther wandered to an open window from which he eyed lofty towers set with coloured faïence tiles, an artificial pool whose mirror-like surface reflected tapering poplars, pink marble terraces in sweeping flights, and mosaic pavements with all the delicacy of old Valenciennes lace.

It was a noble prospect, implicit of aristocrat prestige, sufficient to cause wishful thinking in the son of a manufacturing family which, after amassing wealth great by British provincial standards within a couple of generations, now strove to disassociate itself from the stigma of "trade".

He turned when he heard Princess Kaivanova clapping her plump hands. She spoke to the servant who bent before her.

"These gentlemen are staying the night and will be dining, of course. Make the necessary arrangements."

"Yes, Highness."

Princess Kaivanova was sadly affected when, holding a Navy and an Army arm, she took them on a gentle tour through the miniature landscape gardens. The folds of her pendulous chins began to quiver, her flabby, dead-white cheeks shook, her kohl-rimmed eyes soon were streaked with tears.

"My husband was murdered by the Bolsheviks," she said tremulously, "and for months I did not know whether either my son or my daughter lived. I suppose you have seen them, Lieutenant Crowther?"

"No, as a matter of fact I haven't, Princess."

Panting a little, she went on unheedingly: "My very dear son, gladly prepared to risk his life to avenge his beloved father. But I am too distrait, so perhaps you will escort me back. I must compose myself, I must write to my daughter. You understand, gentlemen?"

"Of course, Princess," said Edwin Crowther sympathetically.

Tragically courageous, she smiled as she dabbed her eyes. "Thank you," she said. "My servants will attend to your wishes. Would that, instead of the poor hospitality which is all that one can extend nowadays," she smiled again, almost vivaciously, "I could honour you as I would wish."

In the ornate room to which he and his companion were conducted the Army captain made a gesture embracing the confines of Amsibu.

"Nearest thing to the Arabian Nights I've ever come across, Crowther," he declared, glancing at a liveried servant who had silently entered bearing a small tray. Offered a thin-stemmed glass, he savoured the fine Echmiadzin. "Poor hospitality," he murmured, cocking a whimsical eye. "I suppose dinner will be for the three of us—on newspaper."

Twenty-two covers were laid for dinner, however, with a servant behind each chair. There was superb food, flowing wines, laughter and jesting among a company bearing renowned

Georgian names—Seshlyks, Akashidzes, Chikesskas, Gham-bashaidzes, the men handsome and the women, when youthful, unbelievably lovely. Putting personal griefs behind, Princess Kaivanova became exceedingly lively by the time of withdrawal to an immense apartment with malachite pillars, and she was arch indeed when, later, hanging on to the Intelligence officer, she waddled past narrow fluted columns towards *chaises-longues* and canopied hammocks placed discreetly apart on a star-lit terrace.

"Poor hospitality," the Intelligence officer groaned the next morning as the car swung into a tree-lined avenue. "I say, old top, I don't want to tell tales out of school, but I think our hostess's finishing establishment must have had a superb record in passing on favourites for royal harems."

"God, what people and what a place," Edwin Crowther remarked thickly. "And I've gathered this little retreat is merely *one* of the Kaivanovs' estates."

The Armenian interpreter in the front seat craned round.

"More than one, bloody well," he announced shrilly. "They have three-four-five palaces as big as that. And a Tsar he has slept in all of them. I tell you esteemed gentlemen that Kaivanovs is in list of four importantest families in accursed Russia. From the blood of the peoples. . . ."

Edwin Crowther was staring back at Amsibu, a Khan's palace in a Persian garden. In the distance Georgian patrols signalled to one another with bird-like calls, but in the fields there was not a sound from workers who for generations had so happily sung mournful songs when toiling through the day.

2

Within the past twelve months Sevastopol had passed through two distinct phases. Now, a third and quite new kind of phase opened with the departure of the German battalions. These forces had not been replaced by troops of Russia's friends, and as the Allies' warships lacked the means to police large seaports the Reds started cautiously to creep out of their hidey-holes.

But sporadic incidents could not affect those men and women in Sevastopol to whom life promised to begin anew. Large White armies were in being, and great events ahead. That was enough. In the meantime it would be folly not to enjoy themselves.

A magnificent ball was planned to take place in the Naval Club, to which their "dear friends and allies" were warmly invited.

On the afternoon of the ball a party of Russian officers visited a British battleship, and it so happened that these gentlemen—

why and how it came about their surprised hosts were never able to fathom—stayed on for dinner. These unexpected guests wore a strange motley: full ceremonials with gold braid and decorations, service uniforms new and old, mess kit, shabby ill-fitting civilian suits and other makeshifts.

After dinner the pattern of events followed faithfully upon that now anticipated by foreigners: quarrelsome arguments on metaphysical subjects, wild laughter, periods of abysmal despair, and a haughty though child-like withdrawal by a gentleman who, discovering in a remark some reflection on himself, tossed off his drink and bowed to the company before stalking out, only to return a few moments later, when he apologized and wept.

Shortly before ten o'clock a few flushed and harassed Englishmen were immeasurably relieved when the Fleet Paymaster and Gunnery Officer entered the wardroom.

"Reinforcements," the Executive Commander muttered, adding thankfully and a shade too loudly: "God Save the King."

An individual wearing field-grey trousers tucked into ammunition boots and a monkey-jacket bearing the shoulder straps of a Russian lieutenant-commander, took three impulsive paces forward.

"God Save the King," he cried fervently, prior to waving his glass aloft, one foot on a chair. "Gentlemen," he shouted, "the King of England."

This led to further toasts submitted by both sides in turn, the fifth being to the heir to the British throne.

At this stage attention became riveted on a cavalry subaltern who, in some agitation, was consulting a friend sitting on the piano stool. His Royal Highness the Prince of Wales had a sister —a disastrous breach of etiquette might have been committed in not honouring her first. Tongues wagged, tempers waxed hot, and the vital centre of dispute shifted farther down the wardroom. The officer on the stool, wearying of the niceties of protocol, swung round and struck a few wild chords, and then, not satisfied with the volume, threw open the piano top and immediately flung himself into the *Song of the Volga Boatmen*. As his countrymen's voices rose in deep, unerring rhythm half a dozen British naval officers dropped limply into chairs.

About then, fortunately, the officers' boat was called away.

"Well, I suppose we'd better push along," the Gunnery Officer remarked to one of the guests, a young man of almost feminine beauty, with sleek jet-black hair, dark eyes, and proud aspect. "Or this beach affair of yours will be over before we get there."

Wearing a perfectly-cut Volunteer uniform, Prince Sergei Kaivanov looked exceptionally elegant.

"My dear fellow," he said, smilingly taking a long cigarette holder out of his mouth, "I fear you English are far too much influenced by the hands of the clock ever to make the most of life."

"H'mmm," the Gunnery Officer murmured.

When heavy overcoats and boat cloaks had been put on, the wardroom quickly cleared as hosts and guests left for the picket boat. The night was crisp and beneath the frost-twinkling stars the run in was made speedily, although at the Fleet Landing Place it was necessary to lie off for a few minutes until boats ahead discharged their passengers.

This was the moment when Prince Sergei, voice throbbing with tragedy, chose to inform a close-packed company that on the sandy bottom beneath them, weighted with firebars shackled to their skeleton feet, were the water-swayed remains of over two hundred officers.

"God!" someone whispered.

"My father died too," Prince Sergei continued sombrely. "But it was at the Naval Club, and I shall show you how."

To many of his hearers this seemed hardly the most suitable note with which to begin a social affair, and they said little either then or when landing and climbing the shallow risers of the Fleet Landing Place to the stone-paved square beyond the ceremonial gateway at the top. The municipal electric power station, whose operations were erratic, was working that night; the Kiezt Hotel was brilliantly illuminated, and a single-decker tramcar groaned agonizingly, every foot of its noisy progress marked by constant fireworks from the overhead wire.

Wood smoke from household stoves added a pleasant tang to the air and, despite the late hour, the main street was crowded. Shop-windows along it had little to display, but the *cafés-chantants*, filled with the blue haze of tobacco fumes, were crowded with hilarious parties of men and women. It appeared as if every regiment possessed by Imperial Russia was represented; men fair-haired and dark-haired, aquiline or flat-nosed, melting-eyed or with slits of eyes, narrow-waisted and tall, squat and stout, but all identical in the profusion of lethal weapons they carried.

"It only wants José Collins," the Torpedo Lieutenant remarked dryly.

By now they were near the Naval Club, a massive, well-embellished building.

The ball, with its deathly-silent moments of immense sadness and uproarious moments of hectic gladness, took a form which, for all its oddness, entranced the stranger. There was dancing, of course, but this was interspersed with excitable speechmaking, and always there was endless drinking. A *prima ballerina* was present, and she, together with a few members of the Imperial Ballet who had escaped to the south, was delighted to entertain her friends—that was a spectacle never to be forgotten, great *artistes* in their own most fitting Russian environment.

During a brief interval, a small group of British naval officers gathered near the dais in the white-pillared ballroom. Occasionally some of them surreptitiously eyed a grand piano.

"Well, I don't know," one murmured dubiously. "This cracking of skulls business was a ghastly way of taking revenge, but on the other hand you just can't get away from the fact that the Whites do a lot of pretty grim things to Bolshy prisoners."

A Marine officer nodded. "Six of one and half a dozen of the other when it comes to sheer mercilessness."

An engineer commander frowned slightly, recalling a distasteful memory of a day in 1914 when the Germans raided the Straits of Penang. He could still see the bodies of dozens of very young Japanese girls which had floated out of a Russian cruiser caught unprepared.

"No," he began thoughtfully, "I wouldn't care to imagine either a White or a Bolshevik army let loose at home."

A watch-keeper from a battleship chimed in : "Of course these birds do exaggerate. For instance," he jerked his cigarette towards a scarred Steinway. "This quite fantastic piano business—'liquidating', I gather, is the correct term—do we really know it's true?"

A well-informed destroyer captain began to reply, but broke off to greet an officer to whom he had given passage to Batoum not very long before.

"Evening, Crowther," he said, and then continued : "Oh, there isn't a shadow of doubt about the piano incident. But what shook me tonight was the dolled-up bloke who favoured a practical illustration with the lid. Strange, isn't it, that a chap should dwell on the thing with such nauseating detail when his own father was a victim? An admiral, I rather believe."

"Young Kaivanov's father certainly was an admiral," the Engineer-Commander murmured.

Edwin Crowther turned sharply to him. "Kaivanov, sir? Shouldn't be surprised if I've met his mother."

The watch-keeper chuckled. "Have you met his sister, that's more to the point?" As with many other young men Princess Anastasia Kaivanova had made a strong impression on him and, quite unthinkingly, he glanced round the colourful press in the hope of seeing her. He noticed her almost at once, buffet-bound with another young woman. Both young ladies were laughingly clinging to an elderly general, much to his pleasure.

"There she is, Oofy," he said, indicating the trio. "The dark girl."

To his chagrin, Edwin Crowther had acquired this nick-name at Dartmouth, as the result of less fortunate term-mates discovering the lavish amount of pocket-money he received from home.

"Where?" he demanded.

"There," the watch-keeper said. "Trying out her undoubted art on an old boy for once."

The fleeting view was tantalizingly short for Edwin Crowther, but he saw enough—a young woman with raven-black hair, lovely dark eyes, and a perfect figure. She was wearing a ball-dress both ravishing and revealing.

"What-ho," he cried, prinking his tie humorously. "Yes, I must certainly be presented to her. As an old friend of her mother——"

He had inherited the single-mindedness of a grandfather who, from the humblest of beginnings, had founded a commercial dynasty. Determined to make the acquaintance of Princess Kaivanova's daughter, he succeeded in doing so shortly after the Foreign Minister of the self-appointed Government of the Crimea completed an emotional speech. When they were left by the gentleman who effected the introduction he began easily, bent on achieving a personal note from the start.

"I've something of a surprise for you, Princess," he said smiling.

Her eyes, slumbrous and almost black, opened a little wider. "A surprise?" she said. "Oh, but I simply adore surprises. What is it?"

"Well, you see, not very long ago in the course of my extremely arduous duties, I was——"

A young lady with a roguish expression, obviously pent-up with excitement, joined them. Briefly, in French, she apologized for the intrusion, and then began to whisper to Princess Anastasia, who was soon giggling. Finally the pair of them, clutching each other for support, reeled with amusement.

"No!" Anastasia gasped joyously.

The other nodded violently. "I swear, Anastasia Ivanovna."

"But how, darling?"

"I think . . ." the answer was given with an air of mock censure, "it would be better if we did not inquire into that. All I can say is that they've disappeared, ribbons, lace, everything, and she just daren't show herself."

"How delicious," Anastasia gurgled.

This interlude ended as swiftly as it had begun, when the

roguish-looking young lady rushed off with a swirl of silken skirts.

Edwin Crowther smiled again, indulgently. "Secrets, eh?" he said. "Anyhow, about this little surprise of mine. What do you say, Princess, if I collect a couple of drinks *en route* to a snug sitting-out spot where I can tell you what it's all about?"

Before she could answer, two young Guardsmen, Pavel and Volhynsky, seized her arms. They, too, apologized profoundly for the interruption, though their charm could hardly be expected to compensate the Englishman, who was left alone. Before disappearing through an arched doorway, however, Princess Anastasia sufficiently checked her escorts' impetuosity to turn and make what amends she could.

"Do forgive me," she called back. "These dreadful creatures are too, too impulsive and I did so want to hear that surprise. You'll tell it me later, won't you?"

"It's a bargain," Edwin Crowther said, smiling.

But as he headed towards the bar his smile, a little set, quickly disappeared, though the rush of colour in his sallow cheeks remained for a while.

The night's high-speed gaiety, interspersed with melancholy interludes from which there was always an amazingly quick recovery, continued unabated until the ball was officially ended by the playing of six or seven national anthems. Then, glad to escape from this final ordeal, which in following the rigid example of their hosts kept them standing interminably at strict attention, the officers of the Allied navies went outdoors, into the still-thronged streets of the great base. Occasionally a few desultory rifle shots would be heard, coming from where no one knew, the bullets almost spent.

CHAPTER II

DESPITE the pessimistic opinions of level-headed judges during the remainder of the winter, the summer following was one of extraordinary progress by the anti-Communist forces. Everywhere Red armies reeled back under hammer-blows. The end, it was widely felt, could not long be delayed.

Meantime the world outside settled down to the joys, and rather disconcerting trials, of Peace; to victory marches, to slogans—"Hang the Kaiser" and "Make Germany Pay", and to such sensational news as that of the scuttling of the German Fleet at Scapa Flow.

These various items became known to officers and men of

Allied warships in the Black Sea largely through intercepted Wireless Press messages.

During those hot months destroyers, cruisers and battleships, now mainly British, constantly traversed the waters of the Black Sea; at times through minefields, dubiously charted, of Turkish, Russian, German, Bulgarian and Rumanian origin; steaming frequently off shores on which lighthouses functioned haphazardly or not at all.

In the course of time ships' companies came to know many strange and delightful places: Odessa, with its lovely blue-eyed Jewesses and superb buildings of Italian and Maltese marble; Constantinople, from the Sweet Waters to Skutari, from Pera to Stamboul; Constanza, the place of Ovid's exile, the termination of Trajan's Wall, and the home of many of the most attractive women in the modern world.

Homer spoke of Balaclava, and a few classically-minded sailors, pointing to the narrow, winding entrance and steep, foliaged sides, paid tribute to the accuracy of the poet's description.

For those travellers so inclined it was a liberal education. To many it was as pleasant to meander among the Tartars, Karaite Jews and gleaming mosques of sleepy Eupatoria as it was to saunter in the Crimean Riviera with its princely palaces, sprawling sea-shore villas and sophisticated people.

Fashionable Yalta was crowded, in so far as a really fashionable resort is ever crowded. Along a curving road against which the sun-sparkling sea lapped gently, men and women strolled. In gardens close to the road wounded officers, nursemaids, with gay ribbons fluttering from caps, and healthily-brown babies enjoyed the shade beneath cedars and dark-green cypresses. Pretty V.A.D.s were there in plenty, their *chic* white tulle caps, hardly arranged to the correct Red Cross pattern, revealing tendrils of hair which, artistically curled, were also a breach of regulations.

Few residences were unoccupied. On the wooded heights climbing behind the gardens, on which pink-and-white houses perched in terraced vineyards, it was rare to see a villa without green awnings.

On the shore road quite a few people loitered to watch a barouche standing near the white posts at the top of the slope leading from the private jetty of the Yacht Club. Into this highly-varnished vehicle Prince Savosef was handing three very striking women.

"Why you wish to go out there, my dear," he grumbled to his auburn-haired young wife as he gingerly placed a gouty foot on the step, "whatever can possibly interest you in . . ."

Princess Savoseva's slightly protuberant eyes were hardening when she noticed a couple of English naval officers. One of them rather gave the impression that he was trying to slink past. Smiling delightfully, she beckoned to him.

"Ah!" she called out roguishly, shaking an admonitory finger. "Now I know why you have deserted me lately. And when," she pouted prettily, "does your marriage to Irene Sergeivna take place?"

Lieutenant-Commander Staitherton flushed furiously as he crossed to the carriage.

"Oh, not until towards the year end, Princess," he told her hurriedly. "And now may I present to you a shipmate friend of——"

Her lengthy sigh dried him up. "These dreadful men," she murmured. "The things he said to me, the undying devotion he protested . . . ah, well."

"Lieutenant-Commander Crowther," mumbled Staitherton, thoroughly confused. "Crowther . . . Prince and Princess Savosef, Princess Anastasia Kaivanova, and——"

Recently promoted also, Edwin Crowther smiled. "I've already had the pleasure of meeting Princess Anastasia," he said. "But it was quite a long time ago."

Anastasia's hand went to the bosom of a simple-looking but very expensive dress.

"That secret," she said, accusing him. "And you never told me what it was."

"You hardly gave me a chance, Princess," Edwin Crowther replied dryly.

Her eyes narrowed with amusement. "So, so," she said.

Staitherton had not finished. "And Crowther," he said, "this is . . . er . . . Miss. . . ."

Anastasia leaned forward. "Mimi Ivanovna has changed the name which eludes you, Commander Staitherton," she told him. "Count Petrov came from the front ten days ago and they were married before he returned."

"Congratulations, Countess," he said. Always a trifle uncomfortable in this, to him, strange girl's presence, he eyed her a little uncertainly. "Yes, deuced good," he added, groaning inwardly on hearing his companion's acceptance of Princess Savoseva's invitation to join them.

Prince Savosef, with infinite care, was shifting a foot in whose veins, unless rumour lied, ran Imperial blood.

"Rather a squash," Edwin Crowther remarked when climbing in. "I'm so sorry, sir."

"Not at all, dammit," Prince Savosef yapped.

When the barouche moved off, Countess Petrova at once began to be vivacious:

"Quite one of the nicest weddings I can remember," she tittered. "Not big, of course . . . my husband is fighting with the White forces. Too bad if he were killed, wouldn't it be?"

Nonplussed, Crowther did the best he could. He evidently satisfied her, for she turned her attention to his shipmate.

"You think that too, Commander Staitherton?" she asked, her lovely sapphire-blue eyes fixed earnestly upon him. "You think it would be rather dreadful if Cyrus Konstantinych lost his life?"

"Lord, yes," stammered the object of her inquiry.

Countess Petrova stared over the sunlit sea. "I should be a widow," she soliloquized vaguely. "But you know I have really been all sorts of things. In the February revolt . . . my experiences were utterly incredible. Positively not a girl in Petersburg can remotely compare with me."

The horses's hoofs sank into soft sand wind-blown on to the road. Livadia was ahead, while Yalta, where a destroyer lay alongside the dog's-leg breakwater, dropped steadily farther behind, as did a grey battleship anchored close to the land, with the advantage of a steep-to shore.

A lofty, white-painted flag-post gradually drew nearer, close to a creeper-covered pavilion with a veranda on three sides, which stood in the middle of a smooth and extensive lawn bordering the sea. When the carriage stopped Prince Savosef distastefully eyed the pebbly beach beyond the Club's carefully kept green boundary.

"I hardly think it wise for me to venture down there, Olga Ivanovna," he said fretfully.

His wife laughed lightly. "Of course not, my dear."

He fumbled for a cigarette-case. "Very pleasant here," he commented, glancing tentatively at her. "I think I might as well wait for you. Don't hurry yourselves, I shall be perfectly happy enjoying——"

"Don't be so ridiculous, George Filippovitch," Princess Savoseva said sharply. "Go for a drive or something . . . much more sensible."

Prince Savosef had been too often worsted by his dominating young wife ever to be able to put up any worthwhile resistance. He faded miserably away when, turning her back impatiently on him, she waved gaily to a group of male acquaintants.

With Princess Anastasia and Princess Savoseva in front, the two Englishmen and Countess Petrova following, the party crossed the beach, the leaders pausing every few yards for brief but lively talks with friends. On that short exclusive strip were some of the fairest women of Muscovy, and many men bearing the Empire's most noble names; flirting, playing like children, enjoying every second. It was natural that hearts should be light in Chursuv Bay —there was delight about the White Armies' gigantic forward sweeps, which promised the restoration of so much held dear.

Quite half an hour after Princess Savoseva and her friend decided upon the party they would join, Crowther made a second attempt to gain Princess Anastasia's attention. Rolling on his elbow towards her he said:

"You know, Princess, I met your mother——"

A sudden outburst of hectic argument, in which a dozen men and women took part, each endeavouring to be heard, again defeated him.

But Edwin Crowther had patience and was not ill-contented; it was pleasant to lounge and bask on the hot rocks, to sit beneath multi-coloured umbrellas while drinking ice-cooled Crimean wines and eating appetizing honey cakes. Bathing was an experience also, naked in the Russian custom, though the sexes segregated themselves each in its own custom-appointed portion of the beach.

The sun's fiery orb was descending towards the unseen lands of the far-off Kuban when Princess Anastasia, jumping to her feet, attracted attention by vigorously clapping her hands. The signal seemed to be understood, for everywhere people began to rise and stretch themselves, preparatory to sauntering towards the Club and the road beyond, abandoning wraps, parasols, and beach gear to the care of servants who would later gather them together. Before very long a line of more than a hundred and fifty people was climbing a twisting, greenery-overlaced path towards the rambling Kaivanov villa which, amid magnolias and olives, nestled under the shelter of a lovely bluff.

In the house the staff had everything in readiness; a notable array of immense plates piled with innumerable delicacies and a choice of drinks no less comprehensive.

The party was in full swing when Lieutenant-Commander Crowther, glimpsing his hostess, cornered her.

"Look here, Princess," he started breezily.

A shrill voice intervened: "Stana, my pet, I hope you haven't forgotten about the picnic at Oreanda tomorrow."

Anastasia's head turned. "I had, darling," she screamed.

Through the hum and chatter a few comments were audible:

"Anastasia Ivanovna has a memory like . . ."

"Except when it concerns . . ."

This caused a howl of glee and, presumably as the result of further observations, a series of roars of laughter.

Quite unmoved, Anastasia looked over the rim of her glass. "You must come with us tomorrow, Commander," she said. "We're driving to the ruins of a desperately old palace—marble columns, grottoes, waterfalls, and all that—one of the most beautiful places in the Crimea."

"I'd love to," said Edwin Crowther. "But . . ." he smiled. "But before we discuss that let me finish something I had a shot at starting ages ago."

Just then he was bumped violently by a couple of bronzed and barefooted young men, clad in linen trousers only, who between them were swinging Princess Savoseva off her feet. She was shrieking joyously. The taller of these high-spirited gentlemen apologized to the Englishman, the other addressed himself to his hostess.

"Listen, Anastasia Ivanovna . . ." he started off.

"Yes, do, Stana," Princess Savoseva giggled.

Familiar now with what might happen, Edwin Crowther acted promptly. Laughingly but none the less he firmly grasped Princess Anastasia's arm, drawing her through one of the arches pierced along the outer wall of the long room. Between fragant shrub-filled tubs on the broad veranda, leaning against a stone balustrade with his back to a magnificent scene of cloudless sky, lush vegetation and golden-hued sea, he endeavoured to explain:

"I've been trying to tell you all this afternoon that I met your mother in the Caucasus. I took a letter to her. . . ."

An expression of amusement, aroused by his impulsiveness, was replaced by a faint frown of perplexity, which in turn vanished when she remembered.

"Why yes, of course," she said, nodding. "That is why your name is a little familiar. It was very good of you, Commander."

Edwin Crowther grinned. "I'd humbly suggest that it had more to do with the C.-in-C."

She shrugged. "I did ask His Imperial Highness to speak to your Admiral."

"And I'm deuced glad he did, Princess," Crowther said warmly. "I had a marvellous trip. And, I say, what a wonderful place you have at Amsibu. Your mother was kind enough to allow me to wander wherever I wanted, and I took full advantage. Charming! Really charming."

"Candidly," she replied, "I haven't been there for years. It is so abominably out of the world, and one positively rusticates there. My mother likes it, though she used not to. Of course she's Georgian. But for me——"

Edwin Crowther laughed understandingly as he flipped open

his cigarette case. "Try one of our gaspers, Princess. . . . Yes, I know what you'd prefer, the jolly old bright lights in winter, a run over to Paris now and then for refitting——"

Her dark eyes mocked him. "So . . . you are very experienced, Commander."

He flushed at her bantering tone. "Well," he began again, "I do possess sisters, and the Mater——"

"Stana, Stana." The feminine voice was very peremptory.

Anastasia promptly excused herself, though before leaving she suggested with an innocence which would not have deceived anyone who knew her well, that if looking over houses appealed to him he might prowl round.

"You must let me know later on what you think of it," she wound up.

"You bet," Edwin Crowther promised.

What with the throng and friends who detained her every few yards, Anastasia was fully five minutes before joining Princess Savoseva, who at once insinuated that she had a crush on the sallow-complexioned, stocky naval officer.

"Really, dar-ling Stana," she went on. "I would hardly have thought he was your type."

As though utterly exhausted, Anastasia allowed her head to loll and her arms to hang limply at her side.

"Aren't these English wearying?" she sighed deeply. "Tell me, my dear, what does one do with them? And do they ever grow up?"

Princess Savoseva tittered. "It's rather fun if they can be made to imagine that a hot-blooded uninhibited Slav woman is developing a frantic passion for them. Truly, darling, you can actually watch fright and a hunted look appear on their clear-cut boyish faces. Delicious!"

Anastasia shrugged off the notion. "Surely very small game, my dear, as you have virtually admitted."

Two beautiful young women à deux was certainly not a sight to be borne with equanimity in that company, and a moment later these ladies were surrounded by an hilarious group of gentlemen, men of their own world.

The room was sufficiently distant for the noise of the party not to be heard. On the walls, between cases containing an astonishing range of fishing-tackle and handsome guns of differing bores, were autographed photographs of members of many reigning European houses, big game at their feet.

When interrupted, Edwin Crowther was devoting considerable attention to two pictured groups, one taken at a Royal shooting lodge in the Scottish Highlands, the other of a sporting King surrounded by friends at Newmarket.

Lieutenant-Commander Staitherton sounded ill-humoured. "Distinguished connections, eh?" he grunted. "It'd arouse the locals, wouldn't it, if you could shove up that sort of regal stuff in your father's gun-room at home."

Too ready to suspect a slur, Edwin Crowther's lips thinned slightly as he turned.

"What the devil is the matter with you?" he demanded.

Too preoccupied with his own troubles, Staitherton failed to notice his companion's sharpness.

"That bitch the Savoseva woman," he growled. "Damn it, Oofy, there's never been anything beyond the ordinary courtesies between us, but she's behaving as if I'd left her on the altar steps. If Irene ever hears a word of her infernal nonsense. . . ."

Quite recovered, Edwin Crowther chuckled. "My guess is that Princess Savoseva's reputation is pretty well known to all the Russkies, and you can bet that anything she says will be taken with a big pinch of salt."

Gloomily Staitherton eyed him. "You never know with women. What about our hooking off?"

That was hardly in his companion's plan. "Might as well stick it out to the end," he said.

Staitherton laughed hollowly. "End!" he scoffed. "These convivial gatherings never end. Gor' blimey, ain-'tcha been in Russia long enough to know that?"

On this occasion the irate speaker speedily found himself wrong. In slightly over an hour they were both in a Yalta café, a plateful of highly-sugared cakes on the table between them. While eating these and sipping fragrant lemon-flavoured tea Staitherton gave his views on a recent situation.

"Primeval, these people," he grunted. "A Cossack posse races in with a letter, the exotic Anastasia tears it open and then, before anybody can get a hint of what it's about, she turfs everybody out. Bedlam isn't in it."

"Oh, they're lively enough sparks," Crowther agreed easily. "And it adds a spice of life, doesn't it?"

His shipmate made no comment on that. "Anyway, thank Heaven she shooed everybody off the premises," he remarked with relief.

In this he was not absolutely correct, for Princess Savoseva had stayed on. Actually, at that moment she was agreeing with some of his strictures.

"You're a fool, Stana," she shouted. "He hasn't written you a line until now, and it is almost a year since you left Kiev. And has the crazy creature—and the Andreyoukovs have always been crazy—really *begged* you to meet him at Rostov? Of *course* not. He's merely told you that his division is being moved from the Kiev to the Rostov front."

Princess Anastasia's bedroom was strewn with intimate pieces of feminine wear; flustered, Valya Igorovna placed *crêpe de chine* wisps into a pigskin trunk, or with shaky hands took them out again when her young mistress, excitedly selecting from fitted wardrobes or from innumerable open drawers whose neatly-stacked contents had been hopelessly jumbled, changed decisions this way and that.

Completely ignored, Princess Savoseva continued shrilly: "Because the fool deigns to write, you immediately shed every atom of womanly dignity and fly off to your place at Yasni Dulba. Why? Because it is not so very far from Rostov, where you'll duly go in the utterly wild hope of——"

Her dear friend whipped round on her. "In the utterly wild hope of meeting a *man*, if you know what a man is," she stormed. "And he hasn't *begged* me to meet him, because if he were a man who went down on his knees I wouldn't have a damned bit of interest in him."

Princess Savoseva had difficulty in breathing. "What do you mean, I don't know what a man is?"

"Oh, get to hell out of here," Anastasia screeched. "Get out before I—not that pair, you stupid dolt," she flashed savagely, landing a resounding cuff on her maid's ear.

"Yes, I'll get out," Princess Savoseva gasped. "Yes, I'll get out and——"

"Go then, and not so damned much womanly chatter about it," Anastasia screamed.

Valya Igorovna was whimpering, Princess Savoseva panting, Princess Anastasia white with uncontrollable rage.

"Yes!" Princess Savoseva had taken grip of herself. "Yes, I'll go," she said, her voice dropping strangely low. "Yes, I'll go, Anastasia Ivanovna. I never want to meet you again, I never shall meet you again."

Anastasia's lips curled cruelly. "Some things in life may be missed," she retorted, laughing harshly, "but sometimes their absence may be the most blessed of blessings."

With unutterable hatred blazing from their eyes the two young women glared at each other. This was the end; no reconciliation could there ever be.

Nevertheless, despite this uncompromising parting, the stay lights on the grey battleship off Yalta were not yet burning when Princess Savoseva's purple Hispano-Suiza flew along the coast road to climb once again to the Kaivanov residence.

It is not easy to hear or to connect broken phrases when two proud ladies bitterly sob, all defences down, each in the fond embrace of the other. One outcome was clear—they all but fell to quarrelling once more when each furiously denied to the other any remote share in the original blame. This refusal of reasonable accommodation had the unfortunate result of leaving a tinge of coldness between them almost to the moment when Princess Savoseva was standing on the drive, tiny handkerchief in readiness to wave God-speed to the traveller. Then joint and simultaneous remorse wiped out the last blot on their friendship.

Two cars were needed for the journey, and as many spare tyres, the best virtually down to the canvas, as possible. Princess Anastasia and Countess Petrova were in the leading vehicle, together with Valya Igorovna and a chauffeur and footman; both men carried arms, as also did an assistant steward and three gardeners who made up the complement of the second car. It was true, praise be, that in South Russia such active Communists as remained hid in fear of their lives, but now and then a few would furtively emerge, to murder, rape and destroy before once more going to ground.

Leaving dense trails of dust behind, the small convoy rushed northwards to Simferopol in the heart of the Crimea over roads which, seldom good at any time, had now become never-ending sections of crater-like potholes.

Then out of the Crimea and westward, across the wild country to the north of the Sea of Azov, pressing ever steadily forward to the territory of the Cossacks. The broad waters of mighty Don were ahead, and Rostov, where General Denikin had established his army headquarters.

2

The immense gains of the summer continued without cessation and, given in advance a hint about an announcement of even more stupendous news, the distinguished assembly in the Opera House at Rostov-on-the-Don was agog one evening in the middle of October. A chatter of eager anticipation filled the lofty auditorium with the end of the first act, when not a seat was vacated by those usually seeking bars and foyer.

A minute or so elapsed before the expected development took place; the buzz of excited talk rose to a sharp peak and swiftly died. In the silence the rap of the conductor's baton rang out distinctly, the red velvet curtain swished open, and additional house-lights sprang into crystal-white brilliance.

A martial figure, chest radiant with decorations, boots gleaming in the footlights, and glittering spurs jingling, marched erectly from the wings to the middle of the immense stage, turned smartly left to front the sea of faces, saluted meticulously and, with the vast audience on its feet, remained at the salute while *God Save the Tsar* was movingly played by the augmented orchestra.

A fine setting for a fine announcement; the house resounded to a storm of applause.

The Area Commandant waved a beringed hand smilingly but deprecatingly. After all, he was but the bearer of news, only the humble instrument. He strove to make this clear, and received another resonant round of appreciation. He shrugged, gesticulated, and then almost beseeched silence.

At last it came. The General's expression became grave, stern, cold.

"Ladies and gentlemen," he began curtly. "Nearly a year before the end of the war which our gallant allies . . ."—he bowed to the representatives of the British and French missions, and waited until a thin clap faded of its own inertia—"which our gallant allies describe as the Great War, but which we . . ."

He allowed his features momentarily to relax, smiled ruefully, and, hand on hilt of sword, stood patiently until the ripple of amusement expired.

His arm raised, he next declaimed fervently: "It was then that General Korniloff left this loyal city with a meagre force of three thousand poorly-equipped men. Alas, my dear friends, that heroic soul no longer lives to see our triumph. Tonight, on the instructions of our beloved Commander-in-Chief, it is my privilege to disclose to you something of the full value of that triumph."

When the uproar subsided the central figure flung out his arms.

"At this moment, ladies and gentlemen, Admiral Kolchak moves forward relentlessly in Siberia . . ." (Cheers and indistinguishable cries)——

"Our Army of the Ukraine based on Odessa advances with unchallengeable verve . . ." (A deafening roar)——

"Our beloved General Denikin, aided by valiant Cossacks of the Don, Kuban and Terek, has captured Orel, within easy striking distance of Moscow and is pressing on at . . ." (Further cheering, shouting, a forest of uplifted arms—a thunderous commotion lasting four minutes.)

Slowly, watching intently, the Area Commandant unfolded a telegram containing the plum of all the news.

"And, ladies and gentlemen," he resumed, striving to ward off emotion, "I have lastly to inform you that General Yudenitch and his courageous cavalry are racing on Petrograd . . . and that at noon today . . . they were within sight of Saint Isaac's Cathedral——"

His further words were drowned in wave after wave of cheering. It was a scene of wild enthusiasm during which bitter enemies did not scorn to embrace, nor great soldiers and sailors feel shame for the tears streaming down their cheeks.

As soon as a reasonable semblance of order was restored, the General resumed:

"I am also, ladies and gentlemen, authentically advised that a train ordered by an individual named Lenin, the engine's boiler quivering because the safety-valve is screwed down, has been standing-by in Moscow station for several days and nights. . . ."

When the laughter caused by this sally faded, he added a tail-piece, his impassivity plainly in danger:

"Together with iron-bound boxes containing specie . . ."

That caused more laughter, much shouting, and booing both good-natured and blood-thirsty. When the audience recovered from these transports the Area Commandant, with statesmanlike ability, comprehensively reviewed the outer situation, bowing to Allied officers present when he dealt with their nations.

He spoke of French forces fanning out northwards of Bessarabia, and of the British acting as temporary guardians of the oil-fields of Azerbaijan.

These observations were greeted by half-hearted clapping or, more deadly, absolute silence, and soon there were really active signs of impatience about these tactful references to foreigners' contributions. The general feeling was that Russians, and Russians alone, had been the architects of Russia's re-birth and, immediately he mentioned warships of the United States and Japan in secure control of Vladivostok, a gentleman in the stalls was frantically applauded on rising tempestuously to express the common view.

The vibrant force of mass agreement pulsated in the air, and very wisely the Area Commandant reduced his contemplated peroration to a simple summary:

"Ladies and gentlemen," he said movingly, "all I need say is this, just this—that all that remains for us to do is to mop up the Green Guards, those pitiful bandits too insignificant hitherto to send major forces against. As to the larger fields, it is my duty and pleasure to tell you that the position of the Red hordes who have had the audacity to plunge Holy Russia into worse than anarchy . . . is untenable." Immeasurably stirred, he stepped nearer the footlights. "My very dear friends"—his voice faltered —"let us rejoice, for all is well. It is over."

Frenzied emotion filled the Opera House. Men clambered on to red plush seats, and showers of programmes floated down from the tiers; there was more shouting, more hysterical laughter, and more tears as the General, weeping himself, once again stood rigidly at the salute before bowing and withdrawing.

Surfeited with this heady banquet, the audience later on streamed into the brightly-illuminated streets of a city where costly French perfumes and soaps might freely be obtained but the necessities of life only with difficulty—apart from Cossack girls guaranteed hygienically sound.

The *cafés-chantants* were full; there were still excellent wines and choice foods for those with bulky enough wads of recklessly-printed money from which to strip off a sufficient weight of currency to pay the reckonings.

The reception and ball given by the Area Commandant's wife two nights afterwards to celebrate the brave tidings was nothing less than a glimpse of old Russia; a scene of scintillating beauty, with gallant men in striking uniforms, and fair women delightfully gowned, some wearing glittering *kokoshnikis* on their heads. Dancing would continue without intermission until dawn, when there would still be bright eyes and unflagging spirits.

A lively crowd swarmed round a buffet on which the choice was ample: lobster, caviare, chicken patties, fruit salads made from the sun-kissed fruits of the Crimea, pastry tarts, bowls of whipped cream, and chocolate ices. A glass of champagne, ladled from an ornate tub, seemed to be in every hand. Russia of old, and soon dear Russia would be as of old.

Princess Anastasia Kaivanova lightly, almost imperceptibly to any beholder, played a scale with her fingers on her escort's arm.

Count Nikolai Andreyoukov turned from a khaki-clad officer to smile at her. "Yes, darling?" he asked, lovingly quizzical.

Her eyes opened extremely wide. "Nothing, dearest," she replied as if very surprised. "I'm most interested."

A glint of disbelief in his own steel-grey eyes, Count Andreyoukov glanced again at her before continuing his conversation. This was about General Denikin's hard-fighting forces, an army composed nearly exclusively of officers.

"I take my hat off to those chaps," he said. "They haven't been too big for their boots or they wouldn't have served as rankers. That's my solution for the future—small forces to be trusted—and I am not enamoured of the latest idea, which is more or less the recruitment of all and sundry to fill gaps. Numbers mean nothing, guts everything, and there's still fighting to be done in my opinion, despite the good news. Of course there are units such as my own, with well-tested ordinary soldiers who are all right, none better, the salt of the earth. . . ."

Again he felt a tiny tattoo. "Yes, darling?" he asked, hiding a smile. "Still interested, my pet?"

She pouted. "Of course I am interested in your praise of your men. I think your devotion to them is superb, Nikolai Tikhonovitch, far transcending any other odd attachment you may have picked up carelessly here or there."

The colonel attached to the British Military Mission twinkled understandingly. Leave from the front was limited, and no girl can be expected to appreciate precious minutes being utilized for a lecture on strategy.

"Well, all the same," he wound up preparatory to moving away, "if your fiancée is determined to go to her place up the Don my advice is that she doesn't linger there overlong."

"But really, Colonel, isn't that frightfully absurd?" Anastasia's entrancing mouth curved scornfully. "Our armies here, at Odessa, in Siberia, all of them, have been advancing . . . twenty, thirty, fifty versts daily."

The two officers eyed each other. "Your point, eh, Count? The lines of communications, what?" the British officer said softly.

Count Andreyoukov nodded. "Exactly what I am afraid of, sir. Too much enthusiasm to push ahead and too little sound consolidation. And Yasni Dulba might be remarkably unhealthy if anything untoward happened."

Bidding farewell to the Englishman, Count Andreyoukov and his vivid companion went off to make their farewells to their hostess. On the way Anastasia waved to Princess Savoseva, who, in the joint throes of a further attack of remorse and a desire for a more stimulating round than the society of Livadia afforded, had followed her darling Stana to Rostov. That had been many weeks before but, despite Prince Savosef's relay of peremptory letters— with a pen he could produce an apt selection of autocratic phrases —his youthful wife was still enjoying herself with the many males attached to Headquarters.

Princess Savoseva, to her dear friend's parting salutation, retorted with a meaning smile before continuing to divide her attentions, wickedly and tantalizingly, between two hitherto boon companions who were now dangerously at loggerheads about her.

Soon Count Andreyoukov and his future Countess were being driven through brightly-lit streets which, even at that very late hour, were thronged.

"This is your last night, Nikolai Tikhonovitch," Anastasia murmured sombrely, snuggling closer to him while detachedly watching a mounted section jogging along on small, mud-plastered

Siberian transport animals, of which the cavalry horses of the White armies were now almost wholly composed.

"But I shall soon be back again, sweetheart. And then we can be married."

"Married!"

Count Andreyoukov's mouth quivered with amusement as he glanced at the dark head nestling on his shoulder.

"I believe you did say you wanted to be married, my darling," he chuckled.

She stirred sharply. "Of course I did. But why must we wait until——"

Braked with abandon, the car screeched to a standstill at a level-crossing. An armoured train, improvised from coal and cattle trucks, slowly shunted across.

Groups gossiped in the streets, their breath steaming in the keen air; others were reading red-lettered notices insisting upon the extreme necessity for taking every possible precaution against the spread of typhus—in particular, everyone was urged to wage relentless war against lice. It was pointed out that the best weapon consisted of frequently and thoroughly washing both body and clothing. Posted in a city where there was a dire scarcity of fuel, this bureaucratic direction was causing a great deal of acid comment.

Many people, huddled deep into the high collars of threadbare coats, shuffled from lamp-post to lamp-post, pausing at each to gape wearily at announcements they already knew off by heart; some halted to gaze with blood-shot, apathetic eyes at the flags on the war maps, or stared lackadaisically at a notification which set out in stark detail the official fate of Bolshevik deserters who might in the future fall into the hands of the Whites.

"A mistake, that," said Count Andreyoukov thoughtfully. "Hitherto we've received thousands of recruits from that source . . . Ah! It's off now."

The armoured train, *en route* to the area which the renegade cavalry general, Budenny, was impudently raiding with his tattered forces, rattled over the points.

Count Andreyoukov bent lower, pressed his lips against her responsive mouth; her arms tightened fiercely about his neck, her soft body melted into the angularities of his muscular frame.

"Why, Nikky?" she persisted, her lips parted, her dark eyes blacker than the night. "Why not, Nikky?"

"Why?" he repeated, teasing. "Now what *were* we discussing?" He began to laugh when she pounded his chest savagely with her small fists. "There, there, Stana darling," he said.

"Oh! Nikky, but why not?" she asked huskily, all fight gone

out of her. "Why shouldn't we? You leave in the morning and it may be months before you return. If . . . if you ever do," she ended, her proud voice small.

Their car screamed round the bend near the prison, where the hitherto daily volleys of the execution squads were now hardly ever heard. It had been a thrifty idea, saving precious ammunition, not to take away belts and braces from Bolshevik captives—the majority of whom had a fair notion of what the morrow had in store for them. A knife to cut down limp figures found at dawn dangling against the wall under window-bars was cheap enough, and lasted. It could be used again and again for this purpose; and was, in Rostov-on-the-Don.

"Because, Stana," Count Andreyoukov murmured tenderly, "I have a preference that you became my wife first."

His betrothed, bosom heaving, flung herself into the opposite corner. "You have the mentality of a petty *burzhuis*, Nikolai Tikhonovitch," she said with scorn.

The soldierly figure beside her shook with sudden laughter. "You're a little devil, my pet," he said, chuckling with appreciation. "Do you know, my little cabbage, that whatever else may happen to us I can't imagine any boredom in our married life."

"I hate boredom." She began to smile. "But all the same, Nikky the Very Proper——"

The one-sided argument, with Anastasia flaring furiously when his guffaws became too outrageous, started anew. And, when the chauffeur had been released from attendance until the next day, it continued in the furnished house she had rented in the (provincially) smart Katerinskia. On her part the dispute grew so heated as to make the awakening of Mimi Ivanovna and the domestics more than a possibility.

"That will do, my darling," Count Andreyoukov said eventually.

Her last flash of anger before dismissing him, his fiancée hurled down on to a Turcoman carpet a piece of caviare toast she had taken from the supper tray.

"I feel rather tired, Nikolai Tikhonovitch," she said icily. "Please go."

For a second or so only, which seemed much longer to both, he stared at her dark beauty, at the lovely lines of her figure outlined against the white enamel of the moulding-high stove; while she, fury vanished, looked back, seeing his firm mouth with its whimsical corners, and his breadth of shoulder as he stood near the door. Then, each speeding simultaneously, they met in the middle of the room, where she was hungrily enveloped in his strong arms.

300

"Nikky," she whispered.

"Stana, darling." His face was white with suppressed longing as he bent. Some ecstatic moments later he straightened again, smiling crookedly. "And now I'm shoving off before you twist me round your little finger, you little she-devil," he said jerkily.

The Princess Anastasia Kaivanova, with an expression of quite stupefied disbelief, watched the door close. For several seconds she was quite motionless, and then her lips began to tremble and her eyes to swim. But the tears of disappointment did not well for very long, and when, two or three minutes afterwards, she flew up the stairs there was scorching anger in her mascara-streaked eyes. Nikolai Tikhonovitch should be suitably punished.

On the following morning, beneath packs of snow-clouds distinctive against a blue-grey sky, the leave train creaked out of Rostov station, every window-frame jammed with the heads of men waving to wives, sweethearts and friends.

The sole exception perhaps, Count Andreyoukov had no share in these fond and sad partings—as the engine jolted the train into movement his fiancée nodded indifferently to him and, while he still leaned out and waited and hoped, half-turned to smile devastatingly at a very cocksure-looking gentleman, a distant kinsman on the Daleologin side, whose experiences with her in early days at Rostov had been as unfortunate as those of Baron Tchalmin in Petrograd. With this surprised officer, in whom the old desire rapidly kindled, she walked to the exit, without a backward glance.

A small group soon collected outside the station, irresolute as to what the next diversion should be.

"Can't any of you suggest something?" Anastasia snapped. "Do we have to stand here all the day?"

Countess Petrova nodded wisely at this display of overwrought nerves, and sympathetically squeezed her half-sister's arm.

"Poor Stana," she crooned. "And poor Nikolai Tikhonovitch. But why, my dear, have you been so unkind to him? How *could* you send him away as you did last night? Oh yes, I heard . . . poor darling Nikky, going back without——"

"Be quiet, damn you, Mimi," Anastasia said viciously.

Countess Petrova confided her thoughts to a twitching-faced young man who had arrived for leave the previous day.

"So silly of Anastasia Ivanovna to deny poor Nikky," she told him gravely. "Most unwise, you know, and . . ." she slid into a strange snigger, "and believe me, I *do* know. Of course darling Stana has not had my advantages, poor sweet. If she had had all *my* experiences with men . . . with men whose mouths dribbled, men with inflamed eyes and the most horridly cold-damp hands, men who were in such a positive hurry that . . ."

Sunken eyes haunted, ague aggravated, the officer with her stared numbly, refusing to credit his ears. He had a dull foreboding that his condition was rapidly worsening, that hallucinations akin to insanity now had an increasing hold on his sensitive, art-loving brain.

"Oh yes, rather." Countess Petrova chattered away vivaciously.

Behind them, the distant connection of the Kaivanovs slipped his hand under Princess Anastasia's elbow.

"Let me prescribe for your vapours, my dear," he said gaily. "A cocktail, then lunch with me at the Spelivi, a drive this afternoon, a tango tea, dinner——"

"A *partie carrée*?" A wonderful idea struck her, and she began to smile.

He eyed her speculatively. "I rather thought *à deux,* my dear Stana," he ventured.

He was quite passable, something new, and he would serve her purpose. And so Princess Anastasia, a flicker of anticipation in her eyes, challengingly met his arrogant glance. She laughed, she nodded, she took his arm.

This too, her sparkle showed, would reach the ears of Nikolai Tikhonovitch. It would be a fitting punishment for him.

CHAPTER III

ARRANGEMENTS for a passage in a British destroyer to Odessa, requested by the local naval authorities for Captain Prince Kaivanov of the Volunteers, had been completed, and the Russian liaison officer responsible for the details rose and shook hands across the desk. The room was in an upper story of Admiralty House in Sevastopol, with a view seawards of the concrete emplacements of the big guns of the base's land defences, now in a sorry condition.

"I think that covers everything, Prince," he said. "Better be aboard *Nightingale* in good time. And may I express the hope that you wangle a front-line posting for yourself before very long, so that you see more action than has been your lot in our struggle so far. I do, of course, understand and sympathize with your objections to the nature of this appointment on the Ukraine front."

Prince Sergei's mobile lips curved sarcastically. "An office stool, with all respect to you, sir, a job an older man could have done and freed me for active service. God, I protested enough, but it made no difference."

The naval captain, who was cleaning his monocle with a handkerchief, nodded down at the files before him.

"I've had the same trouble myself," he said, sighing, but thereafter put aside matters painful to both of them and launched quite cheerfully into a more congenial topic: the wedding for which guests were already assembling. "Afraid I can't get across to Peter-Paul. Duty Officer until midnight, which puts me out of range of any fun, *theoretically* speaking, that is. It may be, of course, that I shall conjure up some excuse for steering for the reception." He winked before becoming serious again. "Anyhow, my dear fellow, have a good time there yourself, and make it a pleasant memory to recall in the stickier times ahead to which I fear we must reconcile ourselves."

Sergei's laugh was quickly replaced by a scowl. "I'll do my best, sir. The only trouble is that one of the principals is an Englishman. God, how I loathe 'em. And the French."

During the last three weeks of November—which had opened under the happy impression that, apart from minor mopping-up operations, final victory over the Reds was already achieved—nothing but military disaster had dogged the White Armies, and after six months of unbroken successes this was a bitter pill to swallow. A powerful section chose England and France as the scapegoats upon whom to fix the blame.

This was Sergei's vehement theme for some moments.

"H'mmm, yes," the naval captain murmured. "I imagine we would have won long ago if our allies had provided a score of fighting divisions and sent us a steady stream of munitions. But both England and France are war-weary, which assists those anti-interventionist Parliamentarians and deputies who assert we let them down. You must remember, Prince, that our default enabled the Germans to switch entire armies from the Eastern to the Western Front, which might have lost our allies the war and most surely increased their casualties enormously."

Sergei eyed him coldly. "This 'default' you mention, sir," he demanded, "could we help it, be kind enough to answer that, if you can? And were we responsible for the demagogues who undermined our armed forces and deluded our people?"

The liaison officer reddened. "That raises another question, who and what were responsible for the agitators coming into being and enjoying such a receptive field for their activities," he said, barely controlling his temper. "And I would be obliged, Captain Kaivanov, if you would moderate your tone."

"And I, sir," Prince Sergei replied distantly, "would be obliged if you would confide your views elsewhere. I must add that they would not be tolerated in any mess of which I have been privileged to be a member."

He bowed from the waist, straightened, saluted, and, turning-about smartly, marched to the door and into the corridor beyond.

Outside, brilliantly-polished high boots shining in the winter sun, Prince Sergei walked towards the Fleet Landing Place, along an uncared-for pavement dangerous with glassy ridges of ice. At the far side of Kiezt Square he turned towards Peter-Paul, against which a line of automobiles and carriages was standing. His appointment at the Admiralty had made him late, and when he tiptoed into the Cathedral on that frosty late November day the first two portions of the marriage ceremony had been completed— the betrothing with its exchange of rings and, to the relief of the two bridesmen who held the heavy crowns above the heads of the couple, the matrimonial crowning with massive goldware belonging to the church.

The congregation pressed nearer the gold-and-silver holy table as the priest, wearing almost priceless robes, completed the Holy office.

"We thy servant, O, Lord," he intoned, "having ratified the contract and performed the office of marriage, as in Cana in Galilee, and laid the symbols of it, give glory to Thee the Father, and the Son, and the Holy Ghost, now and for ever, unto ages of ages."

Lieutenant-Commander Staitherton of his Britannic Majesty's Royal Navy and the Princess Irene Shulovskia were now, according to the rites of the Orthodox Church, man and wife, and a laughing throng surrounded them.

"My very good wishes, Irene Sergeivna," Prince Sergei said, kissing her hand before speaking coldly to the bridegroom. "And you, sir, must be greatly congratulated."

The bride, a sweet-faced girl glowing with happiness, thanked him on three counts: for his good wishes, for the magnificent present he and his sister had given them, and for the loan of the villa at Livadia for an all too brief honeymoon of three days only. Despite grave military setbacks recently, Russians present would either have scoffed or been furious had they been told the reason for the bridegroom's limited leave, but the fact was that British advices from both Odessa and Rostov-on-the-Don were far from reassuring.

Then followed a short journey to the bullet-marked Kiezt Hotel in an open landau drawn by grinning seamen and marines from the bridegroom's ship. On reaching the hotel the bride, clutching her husband for support and grimacing quite adorably with relief, kicked off her right shoe and took from it a ten-rouble gold piece worn for luck. That delighted porters and waiters and maids. Less amusing, however, was the conversation Princess Irene Staitherton had shortly afterwards with the commanding officer of the British squadron, who had known her father as the captain of a five-funnelled cruiser in Chinese waters. What made the conversation so much worse was that Admiral Prince Shulovsky had been murdered a few paces away, after insisting that the hotel's main entrance, barricaded against an inflamed horde of revolutionaries, should be opened for him to face them.

It was a poignant little interlude, but she was cheering up when the British Admiral left her, distress in his eyes and thoughts of a restorative drink in his mind. He was ambushed, however, by a bevy of elderly ladies each of whom expressed blunt dissatisfaction about the bridegroom's leave. Their leader, the bride's grand-aunt, had been a *maîtresse d'honneur* at the court of Alexander III and her manner was that of freezingly reproving a youthful delinquent.

Bombarded from all quarters, their victim capitulated to the extent of undertaking to bring his good offices to bear on Staitherton's captain, but the concession beyond which he could not be budged, an additional two days, was viewed with patent contempt by ladies who in more halcyon days had thought nothing of a six months' honeymoon.

A lively group nearby, composed of Britishers and Russians without scruples about being in company with them, were joking uproariously on the subject of the British Navy of another generation which, it was averred, would be largely under the direction of Anton Haroldovitches and Boris Frankovitches if the present tendency to Anglo-Russian marriages continued.

Misunderstanding their laughter the Admiral glared balefully at the party, which at least had its effect upon those officers under his command. They, however, soon had something less perplexing to cogitate about when a diplomat in morning coat and striped trousers, with a singular lack of diplomatic tact, delivered to each of them a copy of a small news-sheet which had appeared at irregular intervals since Russia's allies entered the Black Sea. A banner headline announced that this was to be the last issue of the bulletin "Published by the Foreign Office of the Crimea for the Allied Navy now in the port of Sevastopol." Its leading article did not hide the opinion that further efforts on behalf of so-called friends would be an out-and-out waste of paper.

But problems of high politics were not allowed to interfere with pleasure for long, and laughter and animated faces proved how much guests were enjoying themselves. Inevitably, despite its

Anglo-Russian significance, the reception soon developed into the purely Slavonic model.

Nevertheless, the gathering was of a nature with little appeal to Prince Sergei Kaivanov. Quite bored, he stood sourly watching four English naval officers bidding good-bye to three charming ladies whose exquisite dresses were in the fashion of 1915.

About then he had the amusing notion of suggesting to these sailor guests that a ride to the Sevastopol Upland might interest them. Even in winter the high terrain was lovely with fir and pine-clad gorges, frozen cascades and steep crags.

But the merit of his idea lay elsewhere—the alternative secondary routes to and from Balaclava traversed a series of climbing and viciously dipping bends, an extremely dangerous mountain rally course of thirty to forty versts, uneven-surfaced and suicidal unless taken with extreme care when icing conditions were prevalent. Then, too, his chauffeur had a reputation for complete insanity when behind the wheel of a car.

Sergei mentioned this proposal to a companion, a lieutenant of Lancers.

"With that madman of yours driving," this gentleman gloated. "My God! he'll shake 'em up."

"Quite amusing, isn't it?" Sergei said, smiling thinly.

The expedition was speedily arranged, and, loftily waving aside thanks, Sergei went outdoors while the party put on suitable clothing.

Automobiles were parked solidly on the cobblestones outside the Kiezt Hotel and, on hearing his master's peremptory voice, the chauffeur of a Mercedes jerked upright and threw aside a skin rug. For a fleeting instant his eyes were pools of naked hatred, but soon, only a few moments after the well-trained servant's expression of unfathomable neutrality was resumed, they became filled with a devilish sparkle.

"Assuredly, Highness, the accelerator pedal shall never leave the footboard," he stuttered with rising excitement, colour tinging his high cheekbones. "The *Angliskis* shall have wetted themselves before they return, Excellency. That is for certain . . . I do swear to it on the bones of my forefathers."

"Then thou wilt have done well," Sergei said, nodding approval. "And for every minute thou savest under forty-five thou shalt have ten roubles for thyself."

"It is mine already, Highness." The chauffeur boasted as though he were with a crony. "Verily I have the spending of it now."

"They are here," Prince Sergei warned him.

Nothing but courteous attention was revealed on the faces of both as the four sightseers climbed into the car, but Sergei's features relaxed when the powerful car spurted off to the boom of twin exhausts.

"Perhaps an odd drink or so now," he remarked to the Lancer in the best of humour, glancing at the vehicles around them, "and then we might borrow somebody's bus and drive gently up to the Malakoff to intercept 'em . . . *if* they return."

Fort Malakoff had witnessed much of the fiercest fighting of the Crimean War, and they reached it about half an hour afterwards. Overlooking town and harbour, this part of the old battlefield had been made into a very pleasant park. In it was the Panorama, a fine building whose circular interior wall was covered all round by a realistically-painted landscape depicting the besieged base and smoke from shells bursting over starkly gashed hills, the Allies' tented camps and an English blockading squadron on a choppy sea—as viewed from there one morning during that long-forgotten war.

Between the central observation platform and the canvas, each stage imperceptibly merging into the next, the battlefield was faithfully represented. In the far distance oxen-drawn ammunition trains and marching columns, minutely but skilfully modelled, could be seen on rough roads; in the middle distance long lines of cavalry and artillery-wheeled transport wagons, larger models, were disposed as they had been; while nearer to visitors' feet, just beyond the platform's guard-rail, was the debris of a bitterly-waged minor fight—powder cases, swords, rifles, an overturned field-gun, all genuine relics. The bodies of Russian, French and British infantry and gunners were heaped and dotted around a shallow pit, each figure clad in service-stained uniform of Crimean War days. These images were so true to nature as to make holiday-makers shiver—they lay bloodless-cheeked, infinitely pathetic, some as if asleep and others in contorted attitude, fearful wounds visible and agonized eyes looking up to the sky.

Prince Sergei had last been in the Panorama when his English governess took him, and he and his companion whiled away a few minutes there. But as they passed out of the war museum beneath he paused angrily to point at two warships in the harbour. They were Russian, spick-and-span, kept shipshape by care-and-maintenance parties supplied by a low-lying grey shadow secured to buoys fore and aft in the fairway, a battleship flying the White Ensign. These two ships looked unbelievably different from what they had been before the British refurbished them—that was all very well, to be applauded, but the hurt to Russian pride was that both the *Volya* and the delightfully-lined destroyer were also flying the White Ensign.

"War was a gentleman's affair in those days," Sergei snapped, nodding his head sideway towards the old forts. "Then you knew who your friends were—now these supposed friends unblushingly appropriate what is yours. Why the hell isn't Saint Andrew's Cross flown by those two ships? They're damned well ours, aren't they?"

The Lancer snorted. "They daren't say so outright, my dear Sergei Ivanovitch, but I gather the idea is that if we collapse they'll move 'em away so that the Bolsheviki can't get their filthy hands on them."

"If we collapse," Sergei scoffed. "True, we've had a few nasty knocks lately, but they won't cause a collapse. Good God, no."

The two gentlemen were so engrossed in this subject that some time elapsed before it was realized that all chance of a bonus had been lost by Prince Sergei's man. Speculation as to where the crash had taken place was spirited until both noticed a car moving sedately on the road alongside Inkerman Bay. As the Mercedes drew nearer its owner scowled savagely on perceiving the chauffeur, who, sitting sullenly on the back seat between two officers, carefully avoided his master's eye.

A Fleet Paymaster was driving. "I'm afraid we mutinied and took possession before reaching Balaclava, Prince," he called out smilingly as he opened the low door of the sports tourer. "Appeared the only thing to do if we were to see anything of the countryside."

"Really," said Sergei, his fury ill-suppressed.

In these circumstances the ensuing conversation was stilted, the Britishers contenting themselves with thanking him, civilly remarking also upon the exceptionally fine view from there of the Crimean War battlefields, of whose victims one hundred and twenty-seven thousand were buried in neat rows in a cemetery forming part of the Park.

None of the naval officers, when glancing down at the harbour, commented on two very spruce Russian-built warships which, if their ensigns offended certain Russians, were also a sore point in another connection to them. Every compartment having been used as a latrine, it had been a disgusting job cleaning those ships, worthwhile only on the authority of the Crimean Ministry of Marine that in the *Volya's* case sufficient Russian petty officers would be available to man her. This expectation had not been fulfilled. But even more disappointing was the experience with the destroyer which, after immense labour, had been re-converted into an efficient unit on the definite assurance that she would be crewed entirely by Russian naval officers, of whom there were easily enough. She still swung to a buoy, however, and nothing resembling even the nucleus of a crew had materialized.

"Well . . ." the Torpedo Lieutenant sighed, recalling hours spent in evil-smelling flats below the waterline, "I think I'll get aboard again."

A grimy collier homeward-bound for Cardiff had reached the harbour mouth and, Plimsoll line far above the water, was bobbing to the seas. The Engineer Commander, watching her, reflected about the considerable supply of fuel which had been built up in Sevastopol to provide for a small, newly-born Russian naval force. Nevertheless, eddies of vapour emerged from only one funnel in the long line of Russian ships in South Bay. The *Vladimir* was slow and lacked any offensive power whatsover, but was luxuriously appointed, and White generals and admirals used her at their whim, drawing on that stock of Welsh coal for the purpose.

"Yes," he grunted, "we might as well sheer off back to the Landing Place."

"It so happens I have to go there myself, sir," Prince Sergei announced more pleasantly, aware of a disconcerting gleam in a penetrating pair of eyes. "We shall, naturally, be glad to give you a lift."

Less than four minutes sufficed to bring the two cars to a dramatic stop against the marble archway of the Fleet Landing Place. On the lowest terrace Prince Sergei's valet awaited him, with a pile of personal luggage : three hide trunks and half a dozen gold-fitted Gladstone bags and pigskin suitcases.

"Savoy Hotel when the millionaires roll off the Southampton boat special," the Torpedo Lieutenant muttered.

He might have embroidered this, but just then there was a general stiffening to attention as the Admiral briskly crossed the pontoon towards his barge. This immaculate little vessel left immediately, after which a picket boat, which had been dutifully standing off until the S.N.O. embarked, came alongside.

A two-and-a-half striper of middle height stepped ashore and, sighting Prince Sergei, headed for him. Since those hot summer days in Livadia, Crowther had met Princess Anastasia Kaivanova's brother on several occasions.

"Hello, Prince," he greeted him warmly. "What are you doing here?"

Although Sergei answered disagreeably he gradually mellowed, perhaps owing to the trend of their talk.

"Odessa, eh?" Crowther said.

"Yes, a staff appointment, hell take it," Sergei growled. "A blasted pen-pusher, me. Of course I shan't be without grave responsibility—responsibility for a pre-luncheon *apéritif* reaching some rheumy-eyed generalissimo on the precise dot. God, what a prospect!"

Grinning appreciatively, but sympathetic all the same, Edwin Crowther shook his head. "Too bad, but what can you do about it? Damn-all is my guess, but if I were you I wouldn't worry. You know, in England we have a saying: 'You can't keep a good man down', and that applies anywhere if I'm any judge. You'll get your opportunity."

As Prince Sergei digested these not uncomplimentary remarks the furrowed lines on his forehead smoothed out, and from then on he was quite affable with the Englishman, who further pleased him by the steps he took on recognizing a motor-boat which was speeding in, bow-wave high.

The destroyer's craft was too small for a large amount of luggage and Lieutenant-Commander Crowther appropriated one of the broad-beamed pulling boats tethered to the ends of the pontoon. For reasons known to themselves, which might have related to their estimate of the changing war situation and their knowledge of the receptive memories of Red adherents, the local boatmen had vanished to a man and were no longer available for ferrying services on behalf of anti-Communist foreigners.

The baggage was stowed with the aid of three ratings who chanced to be standing by.

"You are too kind, my dear fellow," Prince Sergei said.

"Not at all, old man," Crowther demurred. "Only too glad to be of help."

Under his instructions towing arrangements were quickly completed, and soon the motor-boat, with the luggage astern in the other boat, was nosing in to pick up her passenger.

Prince Sergei held out his hand. "Many thanks indeed, my dear Crowther."

"Oh, it's nothing," the Englishman muttered a trifle absent-mindedly. "Nothing at all, old chap."

Heels clicking, Prince Sergei saluted smartly. "Chin-chin, old man," he said. "And may God be with you."

"Er . . . yes," said Edwin Crowther. "And by the way, your sister's still in Rostov-on-the-Don, isn't she? I just wondered."

"Do you blame her?" Sergei laughed. "Livadia in winter, ugh! Splendid for old fogies of ninety but no one younger. Of course Rostov hasn't a Rue de la Paix or your Bond Street, but..."

"But not too bad for a provincial spot." Lieutenant-Commander Crowther's nod was knowing. "Yes, I've got you exactly, old chap. Well, let's hope she's having a grand time there."

The two young men parted on more friendly terms than could

have been foreshadowed when they met a few minutes before.

Out in the main fairway, Prince Sergei and his valet were received aboard their destroyer by the officer of the watch, a sub-lieutenant, whose eyes nearly popped out of his head when he glimpsed a mountainous stack of baggage.

H.M.S. *Nightingale* sailed twenty minutes afterwards and later that evening paused off Eupatoria to send in a boat. By breakfast time next morning she was gliding up the estuary to Nikolaev, at the confluence of the rivers Bug and Ingul.

An almost-completed battleship, sister ship to the *Volya* and another scuttled at Sevastopol, stood in a building slip in Nikolaev's silent dockyard. Rust-streaked and lacking a single coat of protective lead paint, she lay unlovely on the stocks, with the jib of a powerful travelling crane, massive tapering gun dangling from it, hovering over her fore-turret as it had done one afternoon when a loftily-perched cranesman had heard the cry of liberty, equality and revenge.

Business completed, H.M.S. *Nightingale* was again speeding westwards before noon, the northern coastline of the Black Sea on her starboard hand. In the early afternoon the magnificent buildings of the Russian Empire's fourth greatest city became visible, and flights of monumental terraces leading down to the sea.

On landing in Odessa, Prince Sergei went along to Army Headquarters in Nikolaievsky Boulevard.

Too new in the command to have assimilated the fierce and unquestioning partisanship which is usually the hallmark of the trusted staff officer, he found the atmosphere in the commandeered hotel far from serene. He said as much to a close-cropped Courlander captain to whom he reported after some considerable initial delay.

"There's the hell of a flap on," this gentleman admitted. "Conflicting reports are coming in about the position both at Kiev and Kharkoff, and so far we haven't managed to sort it out. But I'll wager the Kharkoff part is nothing more than another local incident those numbskulls of the Don Army tend to get rattled about."

Prince Sergei tapped a gold-tipped cigarette on his thumb-nail while following his companion's glance towards a war-map which showed South Russia as containing two quite separate fronts, those of Odessa and Rostov-on-the-Don. In effect, however, these fronts were one only, a single though not continuously-held line of more than a thousand miles in which Kharkoff and Kiev were the key points.

"Appalling," Sergei remarked, already beginning to assimilate the requisite fierce and unquestioning partisanship. "To be perfectly frank I have a special reason for hoping those asses at Rostov don't make a trifling matter worse through one of the infernal blunders we know they're capable of. You see, my sister's there."

The other reassured him. "No need to worry, my dear chap."

Neither then nor during the next week or two, reckoned by such shallow indications as glittering social functions and passionate love affairs, did it seem that White supporters could have any cause for apprehension. The blow fell when preparations for Christmas celebrations were reaching their peak. Advices from the two commands, usually over-optimistic, became ruthlessly accurate inasmuch as it was possible. It was brutally clear that the armies on both fronts were in rapid retreat, though there were assertions that the withdrawal was orderly.

But two ghastly facts stood up clearly: Red forces had occupied Kiev, which constituted a long-term threat to Odessa; and, far more serious, Kharkoff's defences had crumbled, leaving virtually open country for Red cavalry to race south-eastwards in the confident hope of capturing a glittering prize: Rostov-on-the-Don.

2

In the industrial area stretching along the high, right bank of the Don, through gaps between silent paper mills, distilleries, flour mills, and desolate shipbuilding and timber yards, a steady stream of fugitives, despairing of escaping by more orthodox means, were crossing the partially-frozen Don by a winding route which took them past a dredger gripped by ice in the middle of the river, their sole faint hope the wastes of the Don Cossack country beyond.

In the centre of Rostov, two human currents surged in opposite directions along the curving, snow-mushy Borodinskia. Starving refugees, of the thousands pouring into the city, were doggedly forcing their way towards the station; riff-raff in uniform returning from the station, vigorously breasted that flow, a few of them halting occasionally to break into residences or Christmas-decorated shops with the one idea of finding a strip of red material which, in the hours to come, might purchase immunity. But nobody, so intent were all, gave more than a cursory glance at the bodies of men and women, spies and looters dealt with by the Whites as their last act of authority, which were strung from every lamp-standard. The weaker among the moving throng made what effort they could to avoid the hooligans who, when not knocking off the necks of wine bottles on any convenient wall, openly stripped clothing and possessions from those too far gone for resistance. The stronger cursed while endeavouring to avoid being crushed against a British Mark V tank which, abandoned by its White crew some hours before, divided the tight-pressed traffic in the treacherous-surfaced avenue.

Not very far from a building which on an oval, enamelled wall-plate displayed the emblazoned lion and unicorn of the British Vice-Consulate, two young women were standing on the top step of a large hotel. One of them, indifferent to the shocking spectacle just below, gazed with enchantment at flakes of slowly-falling snow; the other, brown eyes horrified, stared at a freshly blood-stained epaulette which progressed along the pavement as broken-booted feet, barely lifted, dribbled it on.

"So effective," Countess Petrova murmured. "I remember dear Mama dancing in a delightful scene at the Mariinsky in which tiny pieces of cottonwool . . . but really Her Highness is a long time. Really, it is most tedious. Hold this, Valya Igorovna, while I find out what on earth is detaining her."

Princess Anastasia's maid took the travelling-rug. "Countess, could I wait inside?" she faltered. "I . . . I don't like stopping out here by myself."

Mimi Ivanovna's dimple deepened, her sapphire-blue eyes filled with amusement.

"Of course, thou silly. For myself, I always think it so interesting to watch people, to see the expressions on some of their faces. One positively learns so much that way."

When the double glass doors separated her from those awful creatures outside, Valya Igorovna breathed easier.

Nodding graciously to the hall porter, a gigantic man whose complexion was pea-green with fright, Countess Petrova crossed the ornate gilt and red plush vestibule. Within a few moments she found her half-sister talking to the Area Commandant, who, less than three months before, had heartened Rostov-on-the-Don with his pronouncements.

"My dear Princess," he was saying, a slight snap in his voice, "I consider you have been distinctly fortunate to return safely from your estate up the river, as frankly we have been steadily withdrawing from the vicinity of Yasni Dulba. And as to your venturing overland to your villa in Livadia . . . absolutely out of the question, my dear young lady. Those damned Green Guards control every inch of the country to the west, and I'll vouch you wouldn't get ten versts before they stopped you."

Anastasia shrugged her shapely shoulders. "It seems to me that the Bolsheviks, and these new Green Guards who appear to be just as much against people like us, hold most of the country.

So in that case, General, would it be unpolitic to ask whether or not our forces are going to be driven into the sea?"

Moustache bristling, the Area Commandant glanced impatiently at his *aide-de-camp*, who was writing out the pass required by these infernal women.

"My dear lady," he resumed stiffly, "we—how much longer will you be with that confounded job, you?"

The A.D.C. shrugged also, at the blotched writing caused by blotting-paper which had seen better days.

"Just finished, sir," he replied coldly.

A bumping noise outside the door indicated to the General's super-keen ears that his trunks were being taken down to the servants' exit. The imminence of departure brought better humour.

"Not at all, Princess," he said. "We are merely executing a strategic retreat to Ekaterinodar."

"Which is three-quarters of the way to the coast . . . and to Novorossisk," Anastasia pointed out.

"Just so, but don't worry your pretty head about that, my dear young lady," the General said, smiling. "In confidence, I rather think that long before we have fallen back to Ekaterinodar our enemies will have been manoeuvred—ah, here's your railroad permit."

Countess Petrova intervened charmingly. "So good of you, General," she told him. "So much more pleasant to travel in comfort. When I was a child I simply revelled in the luxury of expresses, and I haven't changed a bit."

"Mmm . . . as for comfort," the General began dubiously.

Anastasia smiled provocatively at the *aide* while leisurely drawing on her gloves.

"It can't be as bad as when we escaped from the north after the October revolt," she confided in him. "First we waited on the station . . ."

Placing himself between the two young women, the Area Commandant took an arm of each, making no bones about urging them towards a door which his A.D.C., with intelligent anticipation, had already opened.

The Turcoman chauffeur, together with the limousine from Yasni Dulba and luggage hastily packed, had decamped more than an hour before, but up to now Anastasia had been under the impression that, if a staff car were not available through one of her friends, there would be no more than a slight delay in obtaining a cab. The nightmare struggle on foot she was eventually compelled to make came all the more hard.

The station was filled with a seething mob. Three small bodies, a boy and two girls, trampled to death in an earlier rush for a train, rested limply on an iron-wheeled trolley, and that of a young woman sprawled grotesquely between the rails of the track.

A railway official contemptuously waved aside Anastasia's military pass.

"I regret, *barishnia* . . . er, Highness, that travelling accommodation is now strictly under the control of the railway authorities. This piece of paper, *barishnia* . . . your pardon, Highness, is useless here."

The furious-tempered young woman he was addressing with thinly-veiled insolence bit back a scream of pain as a powerful elbow savagely jabbed into her back.

"But we must get to Ekaterinodar, fool," she said imperatively. "You must somehow arrange for us to have a compartment."

The stationmaster smiled slyly, twiddling thumb and finger suggestively. "It might be arranged, Highness," he conceded. "I say it might, *if* . . . you will please excuse me, Highness," he wound up abruptly but more politely, roughly brushing aside a poorly-dressed woman in his effort to beat a colleague in reaching a better prospect, an Armenian man of business holding a bundle of notes.

"My bag, Valya Igorovna," Anastasia demanded. "My bag, you stupid idiot."

"But, Highness——" The maid shrank back at the wild passion which the trifling delay had brought to her mistress's face. "You . . . you took it yourself, Highness. You told me to hold the small valise and . . ."

The one-sided argument was in full swing when Countess Petrova clicked her tongue in exasperation.

"How embarrassing," she said. "Surely when travelling it *is* essential to have ample funds." So far she sounded very sage, but towards the end of her remarks her tone became a little pettish. "Really, Stana dear, I don't want to reproach you——"

"Will you be quiet, Mimi?" her half-sister shouted. "Have you any money . . . you—*you*—*you*, dolt . . . Valya Igorovna?"

With trembling fingers the weeping girl opened a leather purse. "Only . . . only twenty roubles Nikolai," she snivelled, and went on to mumble miserably: "Eighty-nine Kerensky, and thirty-seven roubles Don."

"Then we're penniless, with no money to get away from here," her mistress yelled. "You crazy little fool. For this, I'll give you . . ."

Details of the threatened punishment were drowned in a howl compounded of rage and grief as a train crowded with wealthy speculators steamed out.

A young man standing near the barrier had had enough. He

was wearing a very fine fur coat of Russian origin, but his high-laced boots were American style and his uniform cap was of regulation U.S. Army pattern save for the ear flaps he had improvised. A cool-looking individual, he had decided the previous day that his assignment as observer attached to the disintegrating Army of the Don no longer had any validity, and since then had found his way down from the old front.

"Say, you," he growled.

Seized by the scruff of the neck, a revolver close to his head, a civil servant of the Third Category swiftly lost his self-satisfaction. Nothing but the most appalling fear was revealed in his expression.

"No more warnings," the American said grimly, his intent plain even if his fumbling Russian were less so. "From now on these folk are taking their fair turn, irrespective of whether you can rake in the shekels. Understand, fella?"

The traffic manager wriggled. "Your Honour," he wailed.

Near a broad shelf on which stood a big, tarnished hand-bell, used in happier days, when shining brightly, to warn passengers with a mellow, echoing clangour, Anastasia was explaining her difficulties to a Volunteer with whom she had a slight acquaintance.

"My dear," he waved gloved hands, "sorry, but orders are orders and truly I can't do anything. As a matter of fact I ought to be with our main bunch now, but my crowd defending the Sympagurlaf cross-roads hung on so long that we were damn near surrounded."

An engine, tender piled high with sawn railway sleepers, was backing into the station. The Volunteer hurriedly picked up a bulging suitcase.

"Well, cheers," he said with a touch of diffidence. "You'll be all right, Princess."

The relentless pressure of the mob, forcing towards a narrow opening, grew greater as the influx into the station continued. There were moans and strangled chokes; an elderly lady, unconscious remained jammed upright; a small woman disappeared entirely—there was an uplift of heads when the slowly-moving ranks reached her, as though there were a step in the paved floor.

A few men were working desperately to avoid crowd panic, among them the American officer. He was slowly edging across the human stream when, all arrogance gone, the daughter of the house of Kaivanov snatched his arm.

"I am . . ." she began quickly, her fingers tightening, "Princess——"

"I'll do what I can to get you aboard the next, ma'am," he said,

316

anticipating her. "We're trying to divide people out . . . safer . . . but if you'll hang on to my belt, and your friends hang on to you, we'll see what can be done."

Four minutes after that the barriers broke; it was then, almost before the sound of splintering timber died, that six thousand frantic creatures went completely mad in their efforts to reach the train. From the track Volunteer soldiers climbed into the coaches, while on the platform side doors were burst off in the *melée*, and limbs broken; within a very few seconds every inch of space inside the train was occupied—outside, every buffer mounting supported at least two persons, the roofs of the coaches were packed, and the footboards, where they were whole, were lined with clinging people.

The tall American, who had not escaped wholly unscathed, leaned into the glassless window.

"Well, that was that, Princess," he said.

Anastasia's shaky smile evaporated as she heard an angered growl from the square outside, where hundreds of fresh arrivals found their passage blocked by the living wall before them.

"You . . . you have been most charming," she said. "So helpful."

"Glad to have been of service, ma'am," he said.

She was reviving under his admiring glance and there was a touch of roguishness in her manner when she next spoke.

"How are you travelling? On the engine?"

"I guess not, Princess," he said, shaking his head. "You see, I've hooked up with a few of your tough guys, and as there are some more locos in the depot we're *persuading* . . ." he grinned boyishly, "we're persuading a bunch of drivers and firemen to bring 'em out and couple them on to anything that rolls, freight cars and cattle trucks included. The idea is to stay on until either Budenny's cavalry gallop in or until we've dispatched every poor devil we can, whichever is first."

"Of course," said Anastasia, shivering a little. "Yes, of course."

Her eyes were dim as she watched his retreating back. Wearily she closed them, only to re-open them with a nervous start as a howl went up to the steel-braces of the sloping, wooden roof.

"They're not coming in here," shrill voices hysterically screamed along the length of the oddly-assorted vehicles forming the train. "Hold that bloody door . . . full up . . . keep 'em out . . . by Saint Grigori, if they try to get in here . . . what the hell are the isolation camps for?"

The cause of the dread was a line of officers who, one by one, laboriously crept through a hole in the palisading between a square water-tower and a platelayers' hut. Tattered hospital dressing-gowns trailing in icy filth, they slowly advanced on hands and knees across the rusty metals of a siding, leaden-faced, gasping, slavering, the ravages of typhus written in their transparent cheeks. When nearer they stretched upwards towards the footboards with sticklike arms, clawing, mouthing, weeping—stricken beasts using the last remnants of strength in an attempt to escape from the coming slaughterers.

Countess Petrova's neighbour on the hard seat, a fine-looking woman, began to vomit.

To more than a thousand terrified persons it seemed a lifetime before the train made a jerky, wheel-slipping start, though actually not more than fifteen minutes elapsed. But at last they were steadily but slowly moving past tobacco factories, soap works and bell foundries: gradually Town Hall and fine Cathedral were lost to sight, and the many golden cupolas raised to God by wealthy inhabitants of the city.

Within twenty-five minutes the vista to either side was lonely, white and featureless. This was the northerly part of the Kuban; southward lay the hills and mountain passes.

The distance between Rostov-on-the-Don and the port of Novorossisk is over three hundred miles, and when the Area Commandant airily mentioned Ekaterinodar, the town *en route* to which withdrawal was planned, he was in effect admitting a retreat of more than two hundred miles.

Hitherto, throughout the Great War and the civil conflict succeeding it, Princess Anastasia Kaivanova had never given a thought to strategic concepts, but as the train jolted along, and during its many nerve-wracking halts, she began to view the General's design with the utmost suspicion. After all, Ekaterinodar was comparatively close to the sea—at Novorossisk there were ships and by now she was under no illusion as to who would be evacuated in them if final disaster overtook the White forces. It would be a military necessity.

"Valya Igorovna," she whispered to her maid. "We shall leave this train at Tikhoryetsk. From there we shall catch another, and leave these foolish people, who like sheep will run in front of the Volunteer army. But we . . . we will travel down to Amsibu."

From Tikhoryetsk a line ran down to Vladikavkhaz at the foot of the central Caucasian range, from where Anastasia believed there should be no difficulty in reaching her family's southern estate.

At this prospect, although her teeth still chattered, Valya Igorovna looked much brighter.

"Oh, Highness," she said, eyes filling with tears, "how wonderful it will be. There'll be the laundry and I shall be able to properly wash your Highness's silks—wash-women at hotels *never* do things as they should be done and . . ."

Despite bundles stuffed into broken windows and the presence of thirty-three people in a compartment intended for less than half that number, it was icy. Men and women shivered with cold . . . and with fear. The fear of being left had gone, but a fear just as strong remained, that the Green Guards might derail the train.

"I'll kill myself before they shall have me." This declaration came from a young man in field-grey slacks and a Tommy's jacket from one shoulder of which hung, lopsided, a gold-and-silver epaulette. "They'll never get me again, those Red swine," he added, jaw muscles uncertain with cold.

A troop-sergeant, long curl of hair looped Cossack-fashion over his left ear, swore viciously. "I'll take some of the murdering bastards along with me, choose how," he wound up.

Rather by gesture than in accomplishment the Countess Petrova moved away from him. She glanced frigidly at her half-sister.

"Frightful people here," she complained. "Really, Stana, it's too bad of you not to have seen we had better accommodation."

Princess Anastasia was staring out of the window, and for hours she continued in the same hunched position, incuriously eyeing a landscape which varied, although the signs of human disaster remained constant. Every few versts the corpses of typhus patients thrown from previous trains lay in queer postures at the side of the track; in the distance, along a road which was never far from the railway, an unbroken trail of bowed figures, darkly silhouetted against the white expanse, plodded in the direction of Ekaterinodar so far away, many carrying a potato sack or a knapsack improvised from a horse blanket; while some, in once modishly-styled fur coats, stumbled along with hat boxes and reticules. There were even those who tried to push perambulators, a hopeless effort.

At last she averted her glance from these poignant spectacles.

It was a terrible journey, its worst feature the conditions which prevented the observance of ordinary decencies.

In pre-war days, a slow, "hard" train took less than five hours from Rostov to Tikhoryetsk. On the present occasion passengers did not reach there until seven o'clock the next morning. Limbs paralysed after a Russian winter's night in an unheated compartment, sick with exhaustion and lack of warm food, they tottered along the uneven platform.

"Your money, Valya Igorovna," Princess Anastasia demanded hoarsely. "We must first eat and then I will see about a train for Vladikavkhaz."

Some forty minutes later, in the stuffy office of the White Army railway transport officer, she received two cruel blows. All communication with the Caucasus had ceased, she was told, as whole areas were in the hands either of Red sympathizers or tribes turned bandit; and that, owing to "the emergency", traffic by rail to Ekaterinodar and the coast excluded all civilians. The military had also requisitioned such few horses and vehicles as were available.

"But we cannot wait here to be butchered," she cried shrilly. "What can we do?"

"Only one thing I'm afraid, Princess," the R.T.O. replied regretfully. "It's hard, but I'd set out as soon as possible."

For several seconds Anastasia was quite nonplussed. "You . . . you mean *walk*?" she gasped eventually.

He nodded. "Thousands already are doing so, amongst them, I'm sorry to say, elderly ladies and delicate children. Yes, that's what we've come to. But harsh as the Command order is, it is the sole step possible if we are to have the time to build up another defensive position further south."

"*Walk!*" Anastasia murmured, still unbelieving. "But even if we tried we haven't money for food and accommodation."

The past few days had taught the R.T.O. the sorry local price for furs and jewels, but this was the only suggestion he could offer his caller. At least her sables were the most magnificent he had ever seen, and at her throat and wrists he had glimpsed the soft sheen and brilliant sparkle of superb pearls and diamonds.

This piece of advice immediately aroused Princess Anastasia, though her fury had nothing to do with parting with possessions whose intrinsic value meant little to her. She left him in no doubt as to the representations to his detriment she would make to the highest authority in the Empire at the first possible moment.

"Do as you will, Princess," he said wearily. "But even if at this moment you brought in every surviving Grand Duke, I should still not be able to arrange for you to travel in one of the troop trains. All I can do is to repeat my advice . . ."

"Keep your damned advice," she broke in.

Nevertheless it was the only course. Not easy, however, in a small town whose speculators—now considering moving on themselves—could pick and choose and set their own figure upon the variety of precious goods offered them so desperately. In the end she was relieved enough when two connoisseurs, a Greek-Armenian partnership, agreed to take her jewels and furs, and Mimi's, against peasant women's heavy outer clothing and a sum sufficient to cover bare requirements.

At last, in the early afternoon, carrying a supply of indifferent

320

food, she and her half-sister and the maid started out for Ekaterinodar, a hundred miles or so on.

At the outset, where their route wound along a snow-clad, treeless plain, the going was not too difficult, but later, after a dismal night in the hayloft of an extortionate innkeeper, conditions grew more severe. By then hills were rising about them and, in the brief intervals when sleet ceased to fall, the white-capped peaks of the Caucasian mountains could be seen. Gradually each step forward on slippery, hard-trodden snow or treacherous ice became more of an effort.

Bodies always chilly despite the exercise, they struggled through the lonely Kuban countryside, whose vast fields were in summer so gloriously golden with rippling wheat. All of them, before the next full day darkened, were too dazed to notice rafts crowded with White troops making a tricky passage down a fast-flowing ribbon of water in the middle of the river. Their sole thought that of escape, they were spurred on relentlessly by the news that the triumphant Reds, after taking Rostov, were speeding behind in pursuit. The many pitiful scenes along the roadside failed to move them; dead and dying refugees, and those who refused to leave their beloved, made no impression.

Nights were now spent by the three women in whatever shelter would serve: bee-keepers' huts, abandoned guard-posts on the higher passes, in empty granaries where their uneasy breath, mingling with the steamy cloud created by scores of other unfortunate people, slowly rose to freeze on the heavy rafters.

With mileages lessening every day and far below estimates, calculations went disastrously awry. At the end of a week their stock of provender was down to a mouldy slab of rye-loaf. By then the price of food, from being enormous, had become astronomical, and six days later Princess Anastasia's remaining money, save a handful of silver, passed to a village store-keeper. As was just as inevitable, those coins in due course were handed to a rapacious charcoal burner's wife in exchange for basins of watery vegetable stew.

On the fourteenth morning after leaving Tikhoryetsk they reached a district six miles from Ekaterinodar where a couple of thousand Volunteers, Cossacks and strays from dozens of White units, who had formed themselves into a determined, whole-hearted body, were building strongpoints to defend the exits from the frozen swamps to the north.

The following noon Princess Anastasia Kaivanova, Countess Petrova and the maid Valya Igorovna entered the town, whose population of seventy thousand had doubled in a fortnight. On frostbitten feet they dragged themselves feebly past magnificent municipal buildings and closely-shuttered, stoutly-barred wood-and-plaster houses.

With not a single copeck in any of three purses, with nothing left to sell either for food or to sustain them on a further journey to the coast, they joined the stream of starved and hopeless people circulating through the streets.

3

In January of the new year, after the fall of Rostov-on-the-Don, the war of mobility switched hundreds of miles westward, where it became the same story: of overrun and outnumbered White pockets of resistance continuing to fight and die to the last man against Soviet infantry coming more slowly along; and Red cavalry racing relentlessly forward, living on the country as they twisted southwards towards the Black Sea with the unpredict-ability of quicksilver spilled upon an ore-mining shaker-table.

The defending army's telephone and telegraph systems were functioning fitfully, and such information as trickled through by supplementary means was untrustworthy. It was definite enough, however, that in the early days of February patrols of mounted Bolsheviks had been sighted within eight miles of the outer suburbs of Odessa, though these ragamuffin raiders melted into obscurity when challenged.

Nevertheless the situation was nightmarish, and Base Head-quarters at Odessa was compelled to give serious consideration to the selection of a fresh venue for the direction of operations should evacuation of the city be decided upon.

It was also felt that the presence of a battleship might have a stiffening effect, and consequently a telegram was despatched to the Admiral-Commandant, Sevastopol. This important message did not reach its destination for over thirty-six hours.

Deluged with imperatively-worded demands from many quarters, the senior naval officer at Sevastopol fitted them in as equitably and advantageously as was possible, making the utmost of slender resources.

In the failing light of a grey wintry afternoon a member of his staff hastened from Admiralty House to the Fleet Landing Place, where a boat awaited him.

At midnight an old but handsomely-appointed White battle-ship sailed on the several missions assigned to her. In the darkness, every shore-sound minimized by fine but densely-falling snow, the *Vladimir* lumbered out to sea, leaving behind the unseen, white-mantled Crimean hills.

The toll taken by bullet and sabre was not the only enemy. Two days later Odessa Headquarters had another frightening burden to bear when the hospital service reported that figures for decimating diseases were leaping catastrophically.

This news particularly disturbed the Base Commander's second *aide*, whose preoccupations about health had often caused amusement in less strenuous days.

This hypochondriac gentleman shared with colleagues a very ornate room overlooking the magnificent Nikolaievsky Boulevard, and as he read the delayed telegram from the Admiral-Commandant, Sevastopol, he revealed something of his fears.

"We can fight the Bolshevik scum with our bare hands if necessary," he shouted. "But without suitable drugs and a sufficiency of medical supplies we can't fight the ravaging onslaughts of typhus and . . ." He paused to scrutinize the telegram again. "Hell damn it," he groaned.

"What the devil's the matter?" a third-grade G.S.O. asked.

"The *Vladimir*," the second aide retorted. "She's on a blasted Cook's tour instead of coming straight here."

The corridor door was opened by a young captain from Records who, after quietly showing a slip of paper to several officers, headed across the room to Prince Sergei Kaivanov, over whom he bent with concern.

"I say, Sergei Ivanovitch," he said hesitantly, "I hope to God I'm wrong, but I've a ghastly hunch that this is the name of the chap you told me your sister is married to."

"My sister!" Sergei said with surprise, but immediately muttered: "Of course," as he accepted the flimsy extended to him.

As he read his eyes filled with tears. "Records" were running weeks behind, but that did not soften the blow of Cyrus Konstantinych's death. Colonel (Temp.) Count C.B.A.K. Petrov, so the cold official intimation stated, had died on the last day of the old year, from wounds received in action.

"Yes, that's he, old man," he muttered, lips quivering. "One of the finest fellows I've ever known in my life."

"The bird who helped you to bring your sisters out of Petrograd?" the records officer inquired.

Nodding blindly, Prince Sergei rose from his chair and felt his way towards a window. Sympathetically watched, they let him be.

His thoughts a welter of despair and regret, Sergei stared out at the leafless trees surrounding the statue of the *emigré* Duc de Richelieu who, leaving France in the days of another revolution, had become Governor of Odessa through the goodwill of a Romanov Tsar. Below him, in the street, a skeleton battalion of cadets from the high schools and semi-military colleges marched with squared shoulders and resolute eyes through icy, brown slush towards the new, secondary front partially ringing the city, from which a thin stream of deserters had already started to sneak away.

"Poor Cyrus Konstantinych," he mumbled. "May he be at rest, may we all soon be at rest."

Despatch riders continued to hurry in; and two exasperated officers, failing to obtain a response, broke the coil-handles of telephones when furiously winding.

Quite unexpectedly, a quarrel flared up which did not end until the company had divided into two bitterly hostile camps. Differences arose when a major in Remounts referred sneeringly to "that English humbug Lloyd George", who not long before had spoken movingly about "England's debt to the Volunteers", but now was responsible for England's declining to afford the Volunteers further assistance.

An artillery officer lost his temper. "God, aren't I fed up with hearing addlepates blaming anybody but ourselves for our troubles," he roared. "Here we all are in cushy jobs, lolling on our backsides—"

Furiously the remounts major intervened: "You're sitting pretty, aren't you?"

"That's what I said," the artilleryman retorted. "And for so long that I'm sick and ashamed of myself for it. But tomorrow I'm clearing out of here to go up to the line, and as long as I'm doing my bit there I'm not choosy whether it's with a rifle or the guns. To hell with the gilded staff, and let any of the great men try to stop me."

"I'm with you, old chap," a lieutenant-colonel wearing the emblems of one of the most famous Foot regiments said with an air of relief. "What we need is men in the field, men who will resist to the last ditch. . . ."

The battle raged on, and it seemed that, if the expression on many faces was a sound criterion, Headquarters Staff would be strikingly attenuated the next day.

The commotion was subsiding when the Senior Intelligence Officer bustled in with news of the 3rd Dniepers, whose fighting colonel had been in dire disgrace three days before, through augmenting his command up to brigade strength with the remnants of other battalions without reference to higher authority, if you please. A commission of three was at once dispatched to investigate, but these luckless officers, on reaching their destination, were at once shoved in the front line. In due course Headquarters bellowed with indignation, but subsequently the mood changed —it was damned funny to think of the three outraged captives in

324

a trench or something, not one of them with any stomach for close and untidy warfare.

Since then, perhaps clutching at any straw, Headquarters had made a pet of the 3rd Dniepers' commanding officer, and there was spontaneous acclamation when it was announced that the miniature army was still holding its own.

The Senior Intelligence Officer wound up cheerfully. "Yes, we're perfectly sound on that sector. And now what about a peck of lunch?"

There was an immediate stirring. This was increased when a pretty young woman, hips swaying, her *décolletage* extremely low for a place of stern purpose, arrived with a green folder.

The head of Intelligence tugged his iron-grey moustache as he gallantly relieved her of a tape-fastened bundle.

"I'd better check these at once," he murmured. "Yes . . . er . . . I'll join you fellows afterwards, if I can manage it."

Tension declined miraculously. The laughter was a full-blooded roar.

This happier note continued well into the afternoon, until a new tone was heard in the voice of the Fourth Intelligence Officer, who for once failed to curse the vagaries of the telephone system as he hung up the receiver. Wearily he leaned against the wall-box.

Forgetting problems of forage, Prince Sergei asked: "What is it?"

"The 3rd Dniepers can't hold on," the Intelligence Officer replied huskily. "They're falling back in what order they can."

"God!" a machine-gun expert muttered.

The situation was debated at the highest level. Among those present at the conference was the Governor, the Base Commander, the Chief of Staff, a Liaison general from the Don White Army, two ministers of the Ukrainian State, a White admiral, and representatives of General Denikin and the Siberian Command.

Their decision, filtering downwards, ultimately reached Prince Sergei Kaivanov, who was instructed to proceed in search of the colonel of the 3rd Dniepers.

"You are to inform him in the strongest terms that he must reform a line and hold it at all costs, under threat of a court-martial if he fails," the G.S.O.I. said emphatically. "You will advise him also that sufficient reinforcements are on their way to him, or will be shortly."

Sergei fingered his chin. "Reinforcements, sir?" he said, raising his eyebrows. "But, sir, with all respect, are we in a position to promise any?"

Ears pricked up. But for several seconds, the G.S.O.I. did

nothing more than stare appraisingly at the proposed messenger, and when at last he spoke it was with astonishing suavity.

"I quite appreciate your sentiments," he said. "But junior officers can't expect to be fully in the picture, so do get on with the job, there's a good chap."

"Certainly, sir," Sergei replied with some austerity. "But perhaps I might be permitted to point out the impossibility of starting off tonight when every roadworthy car in the pool is away."

The G.S.O.I. slapped his shoulder encouragingly. "There are vehicles under repair in the Command workshop. I shall make it my personal business to ensure the mechanics have one ready by the time you reach there."

"Is that all, sir?" Sergei drew himself up.

The G.S.O.I. smiled thinly. "That is all, my dear Sergei Ivanovitch," he said.

Prince Sergei bowed and turned away, the G.S.O.I.'s face growing more expressive as he watched him.

When the second *aide* flicked open and held a cigarette case invitingly he shook his head slowly, but nevertheless absentmindedly stretched out his hand.

It was assumed that the 3rd Dniepers would fall back as compactly as possible towards Nikolaev with their right flank resting on the Bug.

With nothing more substantial than this supposition to guide him Prince Sergei Kaivanov travelled uncomfortably through the freezingly-cold night, past the extensive lagoons along the shore of the Government of Kherson and then cross-country over treeless steppes. Happily the moonlight was brilliant, illuminating the snow-covered landscape into the far distance and so affording every assistance to the open tourer's military driver, guard and passenger, all of whom, aware of the dangers of wide enveloping movements, were keenly on the watch for Red raiders.

Two hours after dawn, over a coarse breakfast in a tumbledown posting-house, a morsel of information was obtained about the locality of the nearest fighting, and some fifty minutes later and sixteen versts further along this was supplemented by the leader of a caravan of Rumanian gipsies. Not very long after that, a business-like outpost of the 3rd Dniepers brought the car to a halt.

From there the route was on foot, over reedy, frozen marshland to battalion headquarters on a sunken road.

The Dniepers' redoubtable colonel, blood-clotted flannel bandage wound round his forehead, was in an unaccommodating humour and, remembering how his predecessors had fared, Prince Sergei's responses were circumspect.

"That's the situation," the colonel growled. "And I would be obliged if you would tell the G.O.C., with my compliments, that if he believes he can do better he is welcome to come and take over himself."

"My dear sir, he will think no such thing," Sergei said warmly. "He and all of us are overflowing with admiration for——"

"Then why the hell don't you people follow our example, if it is worth following?" was the savage demand.

"We do our utmost, sir," Sergei said. "But, alas, we have many handicaps."

"And plenty of time to forget them in the amusements of Odessa," the colonel retorted. "By Saint Nikolai, I often think we poor mugs in the line are the only ones who know what is at stake and why we're risking life and limb. Do you know?"

"For Holy Russia, sir," said Sergei, very gravely.

A pair of tired, red-rimmed eyes looked searchingly at him. "Yes, and even more than that," the colonel said. "You see, men like myself and those I have the honour to command are on the whole very simple chaps, and to us the issue is whether we and our families can live our lives in freedom and decency in the future. Do you imagine"—he shook his head—"that we shall ever have freedom and decency in our beloved Russia if the Bolsheviks master us? Never! Or not for another half-century or more."

Fighting had flared up again, much closer, and added now to the chatter of machine-guns and the sharp crack of rifle fire there was the bark of heavier pieces and the whine from lobbing mortar shells. Ducking as he sped along, a runner reached them breathlessly. The 3rd Dniepers' colonel made one more remark as he dismissed the young officer from Base Headquarters.

"You are merely the courier, and I ought not to have belted into you," he said sadly, without passion. "I'm sorry for that, but I suppose it's because we here have got down to bedrock, to the ultimate truth, and we are impatient towards others with less vision. We know that, if we are to have even the faintest prospect of winning, every man on our side capable of bearing arms must come out to fight with us without counting the cost until we either turn the tide or are wiped out. Now be off."

In other circumstances Prince Sergei would have been seething with hurt pride, but he was too anxious for that. Thankfully leaving, he cautiously retraced his steps. The ground was too hard for entrenching, but a low bank afforded him shelter from bullets viciously buzzing overhead. Crawling or bent double, he gradually left the danger area.

327

After an alarming ordeal lasting thirty-five minutes he sank gladly on to the back seat of the staff car, but had barely recovered from a frightening experience when, twenty versts down the road, more serious trouble loomed ahead: bitter hand-to-hand fighting in the main street of a neat little village which had been peaceful enough earlier on. As the Lutheran Church erected by a German colony came into view round a curve, the military driver, sizing up the situation with praiseworthy rapidity, swung the car into the loading alley of a sugar factory.

From the upper storey of this building, joining villagers mainly of German stock, with Little Russians and a few Jews, Bulgarians and Bohemians, Sergei watched the swaying fortunes of a struggle for possession of a yard belonging to an agricultural implements works. Hordes of tatterdemalion Bolsheviks, who seemed apprehensive most of all about comrades behind them, charged again and again before finally overcoming nests of resistance sited in the shelter of tarpaulin-shrouded ploughs and reapers. Methodically the Reds disposed of wounded Whites with an easy bayonet thrust into soft bellies or a skull-smashing blow with the steel-tipped heel of a rifle butt.

A White battery, seeking to restore the position, started to do as much damage to the sugar factory as to the machinery depot. But gradually their shooting improved and the Bolshevik infantry withdrew. The Whites, very thin on the ground, followed up, and in a very short time the struggle had moved some distance away.

Prince Sergei, passing villagers attending to their own injured and wounded, picking his way through debris and down a flight of steps to the car, which had suffered nothing worse than dints from roofing tiles and a thick powdering of loose mortar.

That was the beginning of a frantic drive. Avoiding the more direct cross-country roads probably now in enemy control to the west, only tracks leading southwards were taken.

As dusk fell Sergei and the men with him were lost in a maze of hard bog; just before midnight, chilled and miserable, they glimpsed a silvery-shimmer in front, the moon shining on lagoons bordering the sea; and in the cold, grey light of daybreak, when trying to climb a steep bank beyond an icy, boulder-strewn ford eighteen miles from their destination, a half-shaft broke. Abandoning the Stutz, they began wearily and stiffly to walk.

Little by little the character of the white landscape changed: farmlands and fruit gardens began to be displaced by fine houses in park-like grounds, and as the versts were covered more and more dwellings appeared.

It was noon before they entered the outer districts of Odessa, unaware of having passed through a gap between defence segments irregularly posted round the city. Hereabouts the road was congested. To reinforce the newly-fortified zones a constant procession of ill-armed men, outward-bound, trudged on foot or rode sorry-looking animals; almost as many were returning, some openly defiant, others with a hangdog look about them.

Odessa's traditionally strong police force had disappeared and, in a well laid-out district with broad avenues and better-class shops, a large crowd watched from a respectable distance the battle between a scratch company of Volunteers and deserter-looters. This ended suddenly, after a passionate harangue delivered by an outstandingly seedy Volunteer. Accepting his words as good sense, a considerable proportion of his fellow Volunteers decided to join forces with their opponents in profitable raids on business premises and private houses.

Prince Sergei's driver and guard had slipped away, scenting trouble if they remained with him. He was indeed alarmingly conscious himself of the colourful staff emblems he was sporting, and felt as conspicuous as if he were naked. So, all the more thankfully, giving praise to the Almighty with a prayer last used by him in childhood, he saw a horse-drawn vehicle trundling down the street towards the sea. Aware of dark comments in his vicinity already, he began to run.

Reining in, the heavily-swaddled *drosky* driver stared down impassively from his high perch.

"Base Headquarters, eh?" he said, frowning. "On Nikolaievsky Boulevard, your Honour was saying."

Prince Sergei's voice was hoarse. "How the hell did you manage to obtain a licence to ply for hire?" he growled. "Surely to God you know where Base Headquarters is?"

The driver combed a long, thick beard with mittened fingers. "Ah," he murmured as though enlightened. "I believe it's coming to me, Excellency."

"As quickly as you can," Sergei said. "And . . ." in view of what he had seen it seemed prudent to avoid any possible incident, "you'd better set me down at the side entrance."

"Certainly, Excellency," the driver agreed handsomely.

Sitting far back in the fusty interior to escape observation, Sergei rode down to Base Headquarters, outside which he had another manifestation of the temper of the lower orders. Remarked adversely upon by tattered soldiers and their women, none of whom three days before would have been permitted to hang about anywhere near Headquarters, he searched in the compartments of his gold-mounted wallet for acceptable currency. The notes he had originally offered, fresh and crisp from the Bank,

were strewn on the pavement, where they had been contemptuously thrown.

There was nothing of the customary whining and cringing,
almost a sign of his calling, in the *drosky*-driver's manner.

"Ah, them's much better, your Honour," he nodded approv-
ingly, spitting within inches of his passenger's sadly-torn boots.
"No, no Denikin, Don or Ukraine roubles for me. They're nigh
valueless now."

Leaving those jeering groups behind, Sergei attained the
sanctuary of the big building.

Within a matter of seconds he had a devastating surprise—the
Staff's working quarters were completely deserted; not a soul
was in any of the many suites.

On the main landing, dire fear in him, he peered down at the
vestibule, from which the laughter and chatter of officers and their
friends always arose. The small tables and palms in tubs were
there as usual, but nothing which moved. Out of habit he
thumbed the lift's bell-push, though shakily-sure the loop of
steel rope in the shaft would not move.

Then, following the shining banister rail curving above him, he
raced up a flight of stairs to the next floor.

Beginning with the Base Commander's, he flung open bedroom
doors one after another. Signs of hurried packing were almost
everywhere—wardrobe doors open and soiled linen tossed about,
stuff much too good to discard in days of shortage, but left nevertheless; here an unopened bottle of pomade had been forgotten,
and there an extra pair of corsets overlooked.

Later, pacing restlessly across the corner of his own room, he
paused occasionally to gaze desperately out of windows to either
hand—through one he could perceive the Opera House and a
gigantic poster: "This Theatre Will Be Heated Tonight"; the
other window gave an uninterrupted view of a leaden sea, on
which an old, brownish-grey battleship was slowly steaming.

When, shock-dazed glance wandering farther afield, beyond
the city's snow-laden roofs, Prince Sergei saw the *Vladimir*, he
screamed with impotent rage. She was approaching the tip of a
long, stone mole, and until her stern swung past the seaward end
he never ceased to bawl blasphemous insults at his colleagues.

After that a single all-powerful instinct excluded anything else:
self-preservation. He was not the only one with a similar thought.
Humble white-collar workers and the numerically-small middle
classes had it, and their social superiors still more so, all knowing
the gruesome fate of their counterparts similarly caught in towns
and cities of the interior.

That lawless night dock labourers toasted in pillaged vodka

the retribution shortly to fall upon those who did not earn a living by toil and sweat; local Bolsheviks sallied out with machine-guns; and a party of sailors, breaking into a chemist's shop, roved the streets, frenzied with cocaine. Few householders slept.

At dawn it became common knowledge that a core of stout-hearted Whites alone prevented an overwhelming Communist flood from bursting through the north-eastern suburbs.

With only the most remote prospect of escaping by ship from the Red terror, horror-stricken people started to walk to the water-front. This movement began as a feeble trickle when to the north gun-flashes were reflected in the dark sky, and rapidly increased as the drumming of artillery fire grew more defined. By daylight men, women and children were trekking *en masse* towards the quays.

The narrow alleyway was in a section of the city in which detachments of Red infantry, infiltrating in darkness, had given to those living there a bloody foretaste in rape, murder and every bestiality, of what would happen through the length and breadth of Odessa before very long.

Filthy and shadowed beneath his eyes, Prince Sergei Kaivanov crept past privies and household middens. In the harsh light of day he looked a pitiful sight, clad as he was in patched woollen trousers so short that they failed to meet the ragged-edged tops of cracked half-boots he had acquired at one stage of his harrow-ing search for a suitable disguise. His gaping, three-quarter length sheepskin coat was black with lubricating oil, his gloveless hands were blue, and his round fur cap moth-eaten.

Nearby a church clock with a cracked bell struck ten. A few minutes later he passed beyond a street block, escaping by crawl-ing through slowly-trickling sewage in a tunnel well below frost level.

From a broken manhole at the exit it was not far to the Kiev road, where he fell in with a company of Whites. Every man among them was more or less incapacitated, but still able and willing to fight Red sympathizers who, hourly growing bolder, attempted from houses and other shelter to interfere with their passage to the docks. Seriously wounded young cadets were in their midst, tottering or on stretchers made from sticks and greatcoats.

In this manner Prince Sergei reached and passed the deserted inner basins, ice-bound and useless until spring came again. But further out there was activity, and the harbour's sea quays were dense with shivering humanity. Spread along them were thousands of people, some fully clothed, others with fur coats over night attire. There was also a sprinkling of super-optimists with heavy luggage at their feet.

Many ships lay against the wharves, carrying wounded or civilians signally favoured, so packed that not another soul could be permitted into them, though occasionally groups ashore attempted to take matters into their own hands. This happened as Sergei pushed into the crowd, when a machine-gun barked noisily on the boat-deck of a merchantman converted into a unit of the Volunteer Fleet. The swath of bullets cut down seventy or eighty innocent persons standing patiently on the quay, leaving a tragic gap in which dead and dying far outnumbered the small party of hysterical creatures who had tried to rush the gangway.

Four or five ranks ahead of Sergei, in the front line pressing against a rope barrier, a man in a sumptuous but overlarge fur coat thrust a greasy bundle of notes into the calloused hand of a gaitered petty officer who, supported by four armed seamen, guarded the approach to a British destroyer. Although at once rebuffed, the speculator shrugged, grinned broadly and, fumbling in the depths of his many garments, replaced Greek currency with French francs. When these were angrily rejected he showed himself utterly confounded, until a highly probable explanation occurred to him.

"Ah," he said, grinning. "*Angliski*, eh?" Get ver' goot paper *Angliski*. Vatch! Zen you will sell me steamer-passage."

Gleaming steel at close range is a most potent weapon and, with a cry of dismay, he frantically reared back. But he did not waste time in repining and at once glanced along the docks, his moist, dark eyes darting from ship to ship as he sought the merchant flags of Italy or Greece, both of which had prospered greatly in the past hours: either at the expense of his own kind, who were compelled to pay for transport in gold, or to the loss of others, who were granted standing room in return for jewellery the valuation for which was made by the maritime party.

Within seconds, as he perceived spaces where ships had been berthed not long before, his confident expression disappeared. A worried man now, he elbowed into the throng and, when able, began clumsily to run.

When next Prince Sergei saw him he was standing forlornly near the Grain Harbour, around whose southern jetty the bow of an outward-bound Italian vessel was appearing, swinging to starboard to steady on a course which kept on the seaward side of the massive Volnolum breakwater. Mouth working, the man gazed tearfully at passengers crowded six deep behind the rails. Wailing audibly, he clasped his brow.

"Serve the devil right," Sergei thought jubilantly.

Far beyond the Mole the 13.5 guns of a British battleship thundered, shelling Bolshevik roads of approach; near the Petroleum Harbour five screaming women and their chattels were being thrust off an Italian coaster to make room for an inlaid walnut bedroom suite; and a two-seater Bugatti was being hauled up planks into a Greek destroyer amidst the non-stop abuse of a crowd of Greek citizens who were not being permitted to sail away safely in their own country's warship.

Despite these disagreeable sights and sounds Sergei was in better heart. Possessing imposing credentials covering both his staff appointment and the importance of his family, he was so sure of asylum being warmly granted him in any allied warship that he had deliberately rejected the stress of a passage in a destroyer. His objective was a larger and more comfortable craft: a British light cruiser.

It chanced that her captain was just returning from a hazardous venture in the city, where he had personally made sure that all members of the British Military Mission had left their quarters in accordance with orders which might or might not have reached them. Near the gangway of his ship he was intercepted by a colonel of the Imperial Army, who bluntly asked to be transferred elsewhere in the Black Sea. In the circumstances it was a peculiar request but, burly, purposeful, and fearless in bearing, there was an aura about the soldier of the true fighting breed.

Prince Sergei heard the conversation and realized, as the naval officer obviously did also, that the colonel genuinely believed he could best serve the White cause where Cossack and decidedly heterogeneous infantry-*cum*-artillery combinations were reported to be still mounting stiff delaying actions south of the old Don front.

Regretfully the cruiser's captain shook his head, horribly aware of hundreds of dumbly-beseeching faces turned towards him.

"I'm sorry," he said with feeling, "but all I am permitted to do is to take aboard your service wounded. No fit Russian can be embarked."

A constant stream of stretcher bearers was passing and the cruiser's officer-of-the-watch, foreseeing disaster from heel-scrapings of ice accumulating on the steeply-sloping gangway, ordered fresh sand to be sprinkled.

Meantime his captain, weatherbeaten cheeks queerly white, was staring at a charming family of four—a youngish one-armed man of military bearing, the type which officers so well the non-fashionable regiments; his wife, tired but attractive despite shabby clothing, still with a glint of fun in her hazel eyes which the tumbling of her world had not been able to destroy completely; their sturdy little boy, who was talking solemnly to a frisky puppy tethered by a piece of much knotted string; and his pretty sister, a miniature of her delightful mother who, when she was not smiling engagingly at those about her, chattered gaily to her parents, a very composed Persian cat in her well-swaddled arms.

"No, it is quite definite," the light cruiser's captain said with an odd curtness. "I wish I could, but I can't. In fact," he ended on a savage note, "I wish to God I could take not only you, but thousands more . . . many of whom aren't as capable as you are of fending for themselves."

Red with resentment, the colonel bowed. "I shall not trouble you further, sir," he said huffily. "I daresay I shall myself accustom to street and cellar fighting, in which for once the 'liquidation' will be the other side about."

As he listened, confidence oozed out of Prince Sergei, for he dully recognized the scant possibility of the light cruiser's captain being any more accommodating in his own case. Shaken by cruel disappointment he turned about, pushed through the crowd and, dejectedly walking along a quiet wharf, racked his brain for a loophole.

Some time afterwards he wandered unsteadily into a small building in the empty Pratique Harbour. On the point of collapsing, he sank on to one of a row of eight side-by-side wooden topped sitdowns with which this lavatory of the Fourth Class civil employees was fitted.

"Had I been wounded," he muttered. "Father in Heaven, how I wish I had. Then there would have been no difficulty in——"

He had been gazing blankly at a line of straw-coloured wash-basins opposite, but as his words tailed off a semblance of animation replaced the deadness of his expression. For a few seconds, considering possibilities, he remained in the same hunched position, and then, as if a decision had been reached which must be implemented instantaneously, he delved with nervous haste beneath his sheepskin coat.

"Yes . . ." he whispered through clenched teeth.

On that icy afternoon sweat stood out on his forehead and blood ran from a bitten lip as his finger tightened on the Colt's curved trigger. But no sooner were his eyes closed tightly, in anticipation of grievous hurt, then they were opened again widely.

"No," he groaned, "I'd never be allowed to put a foot on the deck if they suspected it were self-inflicted. Yes, by Saint Hilarion of Kiev, those cold English fish would order me aside. . . ."

It seemed the end but, as it had done in crises before, the

cunning passed down to him by Georgian ancestry came to his aid, and, as if inspired, he set about creating the means to save himself. The greatest problem arose fom the strong trigger-pull of his revolver, and how to secure the weapon firmly enough took much contriving. Next, with another length of blind cord ripped from a window, and utilizing an iron clothes-hook in the passage as a pulley, he arranged a remote-control method of firing. At last, trembling, he faced the self-chosen instrument of his own pain and salvation, whose barrel was carefully directed.

At this stage he hesitated perceptibly, his face drawn with terror and pitiful irresolution. Twice his hand and arm moved a little, and twice he faltered. But the rising crackle of firearms and a shell bursting in the harbour nerved him to the final act, although he jumped frantically sideways as he jerked the cord.

The report reverberated loudly in the narrow confines of the tiled compartment. Scored across the fleshy part of the thigh, Prince Sergei staggered. Moaning, he stared down, conscious of a warm flow beneath his trousers. Immediately he spewed, sick with pain and affected by acrid fumes.

Twenty-five minutes later, after hobbling along in the penetrating chill of a northerly wind, he reached the light cruiser. She was on the point of sailing: captain on the bridge, a working party on the forecastle, while fore and aft of her along the wharf seamen were preparing to relinquish her last links with the shore, the hawsers.

Forcing himself out of a deathly-silent crowd, Prince Sergei limped towards a miserable-looking British naval officer who was standing at the edge of the quay abaft the ship's bridge; the unenviable duty of this young man, and that of a line of ratings who appeared to feel the occasion just as acutely, was to prevent any last-minute suicidal jumps. That done, they would rejoin their ship by motor-boat.

The next few moments, Sergei realized, would be as crucial as any in his life, and once more the Georgian strain in him asserted itself. As he and his friends had so often scornfully remarked, the English had the habit of quite ridiculous understatement, in which they most surely prided themselves. Very good! If casualness and playing down appealed to them, that should be his own approach.

" 'Fraid I am rather a scarecrow," he said to the English lieutenant, attempting a whimsical smile. "But for my sins I happen to be a member of the Base Commander's staff . . . left behind to do a trifling job o'work of a spying . . . shall we call it, of an Intelligence nature . . . hence the fancy rig-out. Not much, is it, but I flatter myself it could be worse."

Over the light cruiser's canvas bridge screens heads were peering. These observers, warmly-clad in hooded duffle coats, saw a pale young fellow who, despite the inadequacy of comic-looking clothing, seemed to be joking about his plight. With growing respect and commiseration they noticed a flow of crimson in the gap between trousers' cuff and the torn top of a boot.

"I say, you're wounded!" the lieutenant ejaculated.

Sergei shrugged that off. "Ran into a spot of bother near the Opera House," he drawled. "But I hared out as soon as I could, of course. But enough of that . . . perhaps you will permit me to introduce myself and show you my papers."

To beholders it was evident he was striving manfully to ward off ignominious surrender to bodily weakness, but growing faintness seized him and he was compelled to clutch a petty officer for support. Meantime a brief conversation was taking place between the lieutenant and the cruiser's captain, the upshot of which was that, in a chair formed by the arms of two seamen, Prince Sergei was carefully carried aboard.

Within three minutes the screws of the light cruiser began to churn and, as the space between ship and quayside slowly widened, a low-pitched sound, destined to linger for a very long time in many sensitive foreigners' ears, arose from the vast throng.

The cruiser began to throb with increased speed, the musical tinkle of ice cut by her sharp stem ceasing as she left inshore waters. Odessa, with its terraced granite front and magnificent marble buildings, was falling behind; the crowds on the quays, hope gone, were melting away with unbelievable speed, although to starboard a few score desperate creatures were running along the Reidovi Mole, their leaders imploringly clasping hands, kneeling in an attitude of prayer, as the ship swept past the lighthouse at the end.

Face strained, the light cruiser's captain focused his binoculars on the doomed city, where fires now raged in many quarters. Hordes of Red infantry were pouring through every approach, and down the Kiev Road exultant Bolshevik cavalrymen were madly spurring starved beasts. As the line of his glasses lowered he traversed the Nikolaievsky Boulevard, pausing to watch a solitary figure which momentarily disappeared behind the statue of the Duc de Richelieu, again picking up the same figure sprinting wildly along a side street.

That was Odessa, a city in which, according to the inevitable pattern, thousands of decent people would await massacre, looting and outrage. But these frightened folk would have a little respite, for the conquerors would raid the hospitals first—the wards were the easiest places in which to find, and to destroy, their enemy's officers and men.

"God!" whispered the light cruiser's captain.

After dinner, escorted by the Fleet Surgeon, he inspected the sick bay, now spilled over into many adjoining flats and cabins. Among those he visited was Prince Sergei Kaivanov who, if in some minor physical discomfort, was most peaceful in mind while recalling what he knew of Pera, the fashionable part of Constantinople, which he erroneously believed to be the light cruiser's destination. On this he was disabused—Novorossisk, in the north-eastern corner of the Black Sea, was to be the first port of call, and on arrival there all casualties were to be discharged to a White military hospital.

Quick-witted cunning had served Sergei well that day and, though taken aback, he was so much recovered already that he was able to draw smoothly on his resources.

"In that case, sir," he said deferentially, "I suppose you will pass quite close to Sevastopol, where perhaps you will have the extreme kindness to land me, so that I can report with the minimum of delay to the General. As you will be aware, sir, he left Odessa for the Crimea only a short time ago."

Sympathetically but firmly this request was turned down.

Sergei's new sombreness of mood was not improved when a well-meaning sick-berth attendant allowed him to glance through signal forms which set out the world's news as gleaned from that night's Wireless Press messages. Languidly he read them, paying little heed until he came across an item near the end.

This quoted a report (unconfirmed) to the effect that strenuous attempts were being made in the Crimea, still entirely in White Army hands, to reinforce and sustain Don Cossack forces fighting spiritedly in the Southern Kuban. It was anticipated that munitions and men, Kuban-bound, would be shipped to Novorossisk, the sole port capable of handling the traffic.

Novorossisk and its military hospitals were, of course, within the Don Army's area of command and, not troubling to suppress a groan, Prince Sergei shifted a little on his sound rump. For the next hour he stared at a light bulb, his fine eyes filled with fore-boding—the conclusion he dismally reached was that the exchange of Odessa for Novorossisk might be akin to jumping out of the frying-pan into the fire.

CHAPTER IV

AFTER the *débâcle* at Odessa, important meetings were held in Sevastopol, attended by a galaxy of senior officers who had succeeded in reaching there.

These gentlemen came to a virtually unanimous conclusion: that a comparatively small but super-efficient army should be built up in the Crimea for the conquest of Soviet-controlled Russia, its nucleus the disorganized White elements who, within the past two months, had entered Russia's Riviera through the Perekop Isthmus.

It was agreed that the ample breathing space required for the creation of a well-trained and well-balanced force would not be difficult to obtain. The Crimea's long coastline could not be assaulted by the Reds because command of the sea was securely in the hands of the Whites, thanks to possession of the Black Sea Fleet lying in the port of Sevastopol. Nor would Communist hordes be able to storm into the peninsula from the north—the narrow neck of the Perekop Isthmus, which a brisk walker could cross in an hour, was too easily defensible for that; and would, incidentally, serve as an admirable sally-port when the moment arrived for a rejuvenated and dedicated White Army to burst out.

Staffs were ordered to submit plans.

Among matters subsequently referred to Supreme Command (Crimea), with a request for guidance, was that of munitions, of which stocks were modest. This inquiry arose as the direct result of a frantic plea for supplies, received from Novorossisk. The reply to this was a refusal, sent back by the same means as that in which the original document had been brought, in a French battleship by courtesy of her captain.

The truth was that campaigns already lost did not appeal to Supreme Command (Crimea), although the question of man-power, under its own eye and immediate control, did. Consequently Novorossisk was simultaneously advised that, should White forces at present fighting in the Southern Kuban be driven back to the coast, every attempt would be made to despatch merchantmen to evacuate them, though it was also stressed that shipping facilities were very limited.

The decision of Supreme Command (Crimea) was completely at variance with the Wireless Press message (unconfirmed) read by Captain Prince Sergei Kaivanov, who would have felt even more disconsolate had he been in a position to know that henceforth the residue of Whites engaged to the north of Novorossisk would have to struggle on without assistance from outside. And that meant, above all, as he would have grasped still more forlornly, the combing-out of men from wherever they could be found.

The schemes and arrangements of Supreme Command (Crimea) never became known to White forces on active service in the Southern Kuban. In any event this mixed band, to which only those with warrior blood and strong convictions gravitated, was too busy for idle speculation. Gaily making-do, grimly taking deadly toll of the enemy, they had pride in themselves, a brotherhood in arms.

On the other hand, refugees in the combat areas had neither the stimulus of comradeship nor high purpose to sustain them. Without exception they were too wretched to think of anything except the most meagre necessities of existence.

2

Ekaterinodar, where terror increased hour by hour in those March days, where livestock trucks filled with the victims of typhus fouled the railway sidings, where the tiny hospital, drugless and without bandages, had three patients in each narrow bed, head to foot, some wounded and others with the dread pestilence.

Ekaterinodar, where Princess Anastasia Kaivanova was on duty for sixteen hours out of the twenty-four in return for musty groats and black bread and an attic shared with ten other girls, all of good family.

The *café-chantant* in which she earned these bare essentials was dirty, smoky, and stinking of skin coats and unwashed bodies. The tables were rickety, the lighting inadequate, the mirrors cracked; suggestive drawings and vulgarities were scrawled on the dingy walls.

Here were flashy small-time profiteers, blowzy prostitutes, and unshaven professional men beyond caring. There were second-rate White officers on base duty, who were often disputatious while sharing a few bottles of watered-down Crimean wine.

"I tell you Orlov is doing the right thing at Sevastopol," shouted a member of an exclusively military group occupying a large corner table. "He hasn't mutinied because he's suddenly developed Bolshevik leanings, but because he's got fed up to the teeth with our brass-hats. And, by God, I'm with him. These incompetent bastards have dragged us by the nose long enough."

A companion rocked derisively. "What the hell are you talking about?" he jeered. "The fellow's a bloody traitor."

At an adjoining table a gangling young man rose with manly determination, an angry flush mantling his youthful face. In an attitude of swaggering gallantry oddly at variance with the flapping of a boot heel, he sauntered across.

"Excuse me, Major Whatever-your-name-is," he said coldly. "Captain Orlov is a friend of mine and in his absence I do not propose to allow a temporary gentleman of doubtful parentage to malign him. You will be good enough to withdraw your lying assertion, sir."

The bellow of glee from supporters, opponents and neutrals alike which greeted this stinging sally had not died before the offending party, eyes flaming, jumped up.

"By God!" he said, almost choking.

If publicly insulted, a man is justified even in taking life—that was the unwritten law. So no one intervened, though vocal encouragement grew frenzied.

While the dispute was at its height Princess Anastasia, questing hands reaching to fondle her legs or pinch, picked her way across a floor littered with chewed sunflower seeds and fruit stones. Slipping through the outer door she climbed a flight of stone steps, to the street and to daylight, for the brief spell of fresh air she and the other girls were permitted once daily.

Scrutinizing every passer-by, she hurried towards the town centre, her objective a short street connecting two tree-lined squares, one an assembly point for troops marching up to the front, the other in which there was a shabby hotel where officers often called before returning to the fighting line. As always, hundreds of anxious women on the same quest were there before her, each hoping for a miracle, a glimpse of a friend or a beloved one.

Too frightened of her employer to remain outdoors longer than allowed, her vigil was nearly ending when she sighted an individual shambling past the Town Hall. High above the dejected walker's moth-eaten cap the hands of the tower clock stood, as they had done for weeks, at a minute after twelve, a time regarded by many as an omen of the most dread significance.

His name rattling in her throat, she flew across the ice-covered road, skirting three dying horses.

"Sergei Ivanovitch," she gasped.

Fright leapt into the dark eyes of the sorrily-dressed private soldier, whose whole demeanour was that of a man so reduced by fear as to be nervous of his own shadow.

"Stana!" he ejaculated, stopping abruptly.

Brother and sister had never been very fond of each other, but as they embraced, clinging together desperately, tears of joy streamed down their cheeks.

340

"Oh, Sergei Ivanovitch," she cried. "How good this is. For ages and ages I've been looking for someone who was one of us, but I never dreamed I might see you. I thought you were on the other front."

"I was," Prince Sergei said shakily.

Anastasia stared at him through water-filmed eyes. "But I haven't heard of anyone from the Odessa Command being transferred to this side lately, so what are you doing here?"

His mobile lips quivered as he pointed with a knobbly stick to the north. "I'm in the line, with a fanatical gang who vow that before retreating a step they always put ten of the Red vermin under the sod to their own one, and that when they do have to fall back they kill to the same tune as they go along. Lunatics, *lunatics*, Stana."

She had noticed his humble uniform. "You're . . . you're not an officer, Sergei Ivanovitch!" she exclaimed. "How is that?"

Before the explanation ended, his woefulness changed into indignation. Graphically he described how, wounded in the last desperate phase of the defence of Odessa, "which my gallant colleagues missed", he had been carried by the English into one of their warships, which was sailing for Novorossisk.

"Where I was taken to hospital and thrown out again before I could hardly walk," he continued with rising bitterness. "And if that weren't enough I was stripped of my rank on the spot and rushed off as an ordinary soldier to the front. It was entirely due to a commission sent down by the blood-thirsty crew I'm now with, and although the Hospital Commandant—a decent old boy who used to have some sort of Court appointment—protested in the strongest terms about such treatment of a gentleman in his care——"

In the Square a bugle sounded. Men began to double in response to stentorian orders bawled by an immensely moustached sergeant-major of pre-war vintage.

Sergei started to tremble. "I'll have to buzz off, or some of those brutes will be after me," he muttered. "This is farewell, Stana, my dear, for my days, my hours, are numbered. We're all destined before long to die . . . perhaps you also."

She was crying again. "Oh, Sergei."

Pent-up feeling about a man who, for old time's sake, could have treated him differently, suddenly boiled over in him.

"But if I die that damned Andreyoukov you made a fool of yourself about will die also—even if I have to put a meat skewer into his back myself," he said viciously.

Anastasia was swaying, nearly fainting with relief, hardly hearing him as he ranted about her lover's tyrannies.

"You mean Nikolai Tikhonovitch is with you?" she whispered. "Nikky . . . Nikky is there?"

"Yes," Sergei stormed, "and he's detailed me into a fatigue party. Cookhouse, latrines, any disgusting job, *me*."

She interposed imperatively, to tell him, in a torrent as swift as his own had been previously, that as soon as he was back he must seek out Count Andreyoukov.

"Common sweats like myself don't seek out colonels to give them personal messages," Sergei retorted nastily. "Besides, Andreyoukov is much too busy running the war in our sector to be bothered with trifles."

"He won't be too busy to take care of me," Anastasia declared proudly. "As soon as he learns of what I am suffering. . . ."

Time was passing, a column of men had formed and, as she vividly described her present existence, with its humiliations and indecencies, Sergei's eyes were darting about as though he were contemplating bolting. Several people were watching them, however, including the officer-in-charge, a fair-haired Balt who looked as though he were thoroughly enjoying life with a raggamuffinly but nevertheless highly-efficient outfit.

"Well, this is it," Sergei said hollowly.

A succession of staccato commands was heard; feet stamped raggedly to attention, the sound muffled by wrappings of felt on worn-out boots. Another sharply-barked order rang out and, stared at in apathetic silence by onlookers, the latest batch rooted out in Novorossisk for the labour brigade started off on their march up to the support lines. On each flank were guards, of whom Prince Sergei was one, detailed from the non-combatant branch, who had come down that morning—they were allowed truncheon-like staffs only. With the contingent also were seven N.C.O.s of the *élite* fighting corps, each with trigger-finger in readiness, lynx-eyed for any attempt at a breakaway.

Fully aware that her brother's thoughts would be wholly devoted to saving his own skin, Anastasia ran alongside the column as it wound through the gloomy streets of Ekaterinodar, exhorting with every step she took. But not until the leading files turned along a road beside the frozen Kuban River was she able to elicit any reasonably convincing response from him.

"You will tell Nikky about me as soon as you can?" she urged, clutching his arm more tightly. "And about the filthy *café-chantant* I have to work in? And the address: Maxim's— it's behind the Grain Exchange . . . down in a horrible cellar. You'll tell him that, at once? You promise, Sergei Ivanovitch?"

"Yes," Sergei muttered.

"You will swear to it," she demanded. "By all the Saints of Novgorod, Kiev and Moscow, and on their dear relics."

Dully Sergei nodded. "I will tell him, faithfully I will."

"Then . . . then he will save me, I know he will," she cried, weariness overcoming her. "God be with you, Sergei Ivanovitch, now and for evermore."

"And with you, Stana," he mumbled. "Yes, may His blessing be with you always, say I, your brother, my last words on this earth to you, for we shall not meet again."

Leaning for support against a rusty, street-sanding bin, Anastasia remained until the tattered company passed from sight. By then, revived by gladness and relief, a spurious strength had flowed into her body, and she ran back to the business area without the effort taking too much toll.

But the old fear returned when, a quarter of an hour overdue, she paused against a wall-sign, crudely-lettered: Maxim's. Fortunately her employer was occupied as she crept down the stairs, so that she was able, almost immediately, to tell her maid the joyous, unbelievable news. Their conversation took place as she changed beggarly outdoor clothing for bedraggled finery, in the dubious seclusion afforded by an old velvet curtain hanging across a recess in a passageway. The inadequacy of this dressing-room had been responsible for tragic happenings, two girls destroying themselves because of it; gently-nurtured, they could no longer suffer the men who often watched them through holes in the fabric.

Valya Igorovna's eyes were wide with wonder when she heard of the meeting with her mistress's brother, but they glowed with delight and hope immediately she knew Count Andreyoukov would shortly learn about their plight.

"Oh, Highness!" she exclaimed, sitting down abruptly on a box. "And *he'll* do something for us quickly. His Excellency never hesitated about anything."

For the first time for weeks Anastasia smiled, a tiny smile full of reminiscence.

"No, he never hesitated, Valya Igorovna," she said, her eyes moist with emotion. "Nor will he now."

This thought sustained her for the remainder of the afternoon, throughout the evening and for the greater part of the next day, stiffening her to suffer the many indignities which she had to suffer if she were to eat. But the next morning, from the moment of throwing aside soiled blankets and rising from a bedding of fusty rugs, she began to falter.

Almost to the exact hour and minute, it was four days since

Princess Anastasia had so unexpectedly encountered her brother, and there had been no word from Count Nikolai Andreyoukov.

In the middle of the afternoon, when musicians and performers in the main room of the *café-chantant* were allowed five minutes rest, Countess Petrova hurried from the kitchen. She had been cogitating a great deal about her half-sister and, although she proposed to comfort her as much as possible, she intended to make dear Stana realize that, as the lover of a fighting man, she had obligations also on her side.

Firmly resolved, she hastened to the candle-lit dressing-room, where three or four young women lay about as if too exhausted ever to move again.

Anastasia sat huddled in a corner, gazing into space.

"You know, Stana dear, this simply won't do," Mimi began firmly. "Of course you're troubled, that's only natural, but you can't expect Nikolai Tikhonovitch to abandon his regiment just because he has heard you are only a few versts away. It may be hard, and it is, but as the beloved of a soldier that is a lesson you will have to learn."

This said, she nodded to herself a little self-complacently.

"I don't want to be too cross with you, Stana," she went on, "but there is still another thing. You see I chance to know a great deal about men, and I can positively assure you they simply *loathe* women who mope. In fact, because he might think I was whining, I've never *dreamed* of telling dear Cyrus Konstantinych about our rather disagreeable situation."

Roused despite herself, Anastasia stared. "But he doesn't even know what has happened to us," she said.

Tears dimmed Mimi's sapphire-blue eyes as she caressed her half-sister's hand. "Poor, poor Stana," she crooned. "Really, things are becoming too much for you, aren't they? But of course Cyrus Konstantinych knows. I've written him every day since we reached here, and every day when I go out I post the letter. And I'll tell you an awful secret," she giggled. "When I go out I often steal writing material, from all kinds of funny places. Oh, I've become a ravishingly clever thief, truly so." Sobering, she rounded off on a much more serious, and definitely chiding, note: "Unhappily, Cyrus Konstantinych has not been able so far to reply to me, but *I* understand, and you must do so also. Men on active service often just haven't the time for letters."

"Oh, God!" murmured Anastasia, mainly to herself.

Her trifling respite was over and, sick with despair, she walked slowly along the passage and into the public part of the *café-chantant*, wearily mounting the tottery steps of the dais for her twenty minutes' turn. With the keen eyes of the proprietor upon her she forced a smile for the benefit of patrons, signed to the drooping fiddler, and began to dance.

The Greek was not at all pleased with her performance.

"Throw 'em up, my lady," he growled to her during the interlude. "My customers want to see something for their money. Either they get an eyeful, or outside you go . . . lively."

His dancer compelled her aching limbs, kicking a little higher still on resuming.

From a table near the dais a prominent local speculator rose unsteadily to clap loudly, an inane grin upon his pouchy face.

"Brav—bravo, my girl," he cried, hiccuping. "Now you come down and have a nice drink and a little pow-wow with me."

A concertina-stockinged drab with dishevelled hair, wearing a superfine wool costume trimmed with ermine, grabbed his arm.

"You sit down," she snapped. "What do you reckon you're doing?"

"Doing?" Her companion's thick lower lip jutting pugnaciously. "Anyway," he added, snarling, "what business is it of yours?"

She jumped up and, hands on hips and head sideways, shouted at him, shrill with rage:

"What are you after? That thin-faced piece up there that's showing all she's got?"

His yellow, unhealthy cheeks became a trifle red, but he showed black stumps of teeth in a broad grin.

"And very nice too," he announced. "A hell of a sight better than you can offer. And you can clear off now, my good woman, because I'm after a bit of fresh meat—if you haven't guessed."

"So you think," she sneered, "that I'll let you——"

There was a dull impact, solid flesh and bone striking softer flesh. She groaned on the floor, blood trickling from her mouth.

Scowlingly, the man examined his fist, cut by sharp teeth. His eyes narrowed as he looked down.

"I warned you, didn't I? Now get out of here and be damned quick about it. Do you hear?" he grunted, savagely booting her before returning to a more inviting quest.

Just one of those incidents; and few of those present in that place of uneasy laughter, where pots clattered and white-faced patrician girls scurried to fulfill orders, took any notice.

The man of action pulled Princess Anastasia off the dais, dragged her to his table and, sitting down, endeavoured to force her on to his knees.

"No?" he said, in quite good temper. "Well, I prefer women with spirit. Nothing like a woman of spirit once you've mastered her—and what the hell are *you* pushing your ugly snout in for?"

The proprietor inclined obsequiously. "Perhaps a little more refreshment?" he suggested. "A bottle of——"

"The best you've got." His customer gestured sweepingly. "Me and this shapely piece are going to celebrate." With eyes slightly out of focus his glance roved over the lines of the young woman whose wrist he was firmly grasping. Despite the privations she had undergone they were still alluring—and very evident, thanks to the insufficiency of the flimsy material from which her dress was made. Gloating with anticipation, he sniggered. "She'll be glad enough to sit on my lap before I've finished with her."

Under the menace of the Greek's eye, although love of life, strong in her yet, was the more compelling factor, Princess Anastasia Kaivanova took that human seat, her fury, hatred and resentment evident.

Ignoring this, the man laughed slyly and, without any preliminary address, began to explore her leg.

That was when they began to run in Nikolai Prospekt; that was when the throng in the *café-chantant* panicked on hearing the thudding of many feet on the pavement grating; that was when Valya Igorovna, in Nikolai Prospekt, spun round and hastened back to her mistress as quickly as her tired limbs would propel her.

The more humble members of the staff of the down-at-heels establishment known as Maxim's, kitchen maids and so on, were also allowed a daily spell of liberty, and on that afternoon Valya Igorovna had been out on what had become her routine round. Twice, there and back, she listlessly walked the full length of the main street, where every shop was a money exchange accepting nothing but jewellery or foreign currency against the indifferent commodities remaining on thinly-stocked shelves; and twice, as did everyone else without sad business in connection with it, she crossed the road before venturing hurriedly past an undertaker's typhus-infested premises from which open-topped coffins, hired out for burial, continually were being borne out fully-laden, their temporary tenants' leaden-coloured faces rolling from side to side with every jolt.

Every day except the Sabbath Valya Igorovna went to the fine Natural History Museum, where much of what she saw was beyond her understanding. Nevertheless, coming out once again lost in wonder, she was not too preoccupied to miss noticing that the bank was closing, always the most reliable sign of impending trouble. Nor had others—within minutes the news was flashing round that the front had broken up.

Thousands at once started to run, a mad hurly-burly of people whose sole instinct was to escape as quickly as possible with such possessions as they had.

On the corner of the Bourse, flying along, Valya Igorovna collided violently with a young man. Both lost their feet on the ice.

As they scrambled up they looked at each other, looked harder and harder. Of the two, the girl was the quicker-witted.

"Highness!" she gasped.

Prince Sergei had come out worst from the impact. "Where is this damned Maxim's?" he asked, voice high-pitched. "You . . . you, Valya Igorovna, that's it, isn't it? I must see your mistress as soon as possible. There is little time and . . ."

Brown eyes wide with wonder, Valya Igorovna gaped at him. "Her Highness is not far from here, Highness," she stuttered. "And if your Highness will condescend to accompany me, it won't be——"

"Lead the way then, fool," Prince Sergei interrupted her. "We haven't a minute."

And so, nobleman and servant, they raced off together.

At Maxim's the main room was completely deserted, though in the passage beyond they were thrust back by an onrush of terrified young women who, clutching bundles and bass game-bags, surged towards the steps and the street.

In the kitchen, Princess Anastasia was devouring horse-flesh from a dirty stew-pot, and Countess Petrova, festering sores on her hands from neglected chaps, hummed to herself while swilling crockery in a small tub.

"Highness," Valya Igorovna gasped. "They're coming."

For weeks now the hearts of White sympathizers had leapt into their mouths whenever it was rumoured that "they" were approaching, and despite many false alarms the old fears were still as potent as ever, which perhaps explains why Anastasia, prepared though she was by the events of the past few minutes, dropped an earthenware cooking pot. Head tilted backwards, she had been drinking the last few drops of a wonderful broth, one of Maxim's "specials", top of the bill-of-fare. Immediately then, however, her eyes were for her brother only.

"Sergei Ivanovitch!" she exclaimed, bosom heaving. "What are you doing here? And where is Nikolai Tikhonovitch? You told him about us . . . about me?"

Sergei shook his head. "I hadn't a chance."

Almost bereft of speech, she stammered. "You . . . you didn't speak to Nikky *at all*? Even though you knew about your sisters' terrible position?"

Nerves disastrously frayed, Sergei shouted: "There was the hell of a fight on when we got back, and it never stopped. Even if I had been allowed to try to reach him he wouldn't have been able to do anything for you—the most ardent lover couldn't have given himself a minute's leave in the circumstances. Yes, I'll grant even that. God! what we've been through. They attacked again and again, and the more we mowed down the more others seemed to rise out of the ground to take their places. Their casualties were colossal, but in the end," his lips quivered, "they finished us, *absolutely*. That's why I am here, because it is the only spot I knew where there might be food. We've got to make for the coast at once. Every second is vital . . . *vital*, do you understand, dammit?"

Anastasia screamed. "But what has happened to Nikky?"

"He'll have stiffened long since," her brother replied brutally. "There isn't a hope of anything else. Battalion headquarters was completely surrounded, and every one of those do-or-die heroes will have been wiped out hours ago."

Eyes filled with tears, Anastasia stared blankly before her. "So Nikky is dead," she whispered.

Beside himself with anxiety, Sergei shook her arm. "Yes, and if you want to share his fate you need only to wait here."

Four days before, his sister's hopes for the future had been high, resting as they did upon a man whose courage, daring and ingenuity she knew so well. But that was four days ago, and now, with him gone forever, she cracked.

"My darling Nikky," she whimpered. "Oh, God, I can't go on now."

Tenderly Mimi comforted her. "Poor dear Stana," she murmured. "But do try to pull yourself together, darling. Oh, I know it is dreadful, but a soldier's wife has to realize these awful possibilities."

Valya Igorovna became noisy. "And His Excellency would have expected you to do everything you could to save yourself, Highness," she blubbered.

Slowly Anastasia turned towards her maid. "You think that, Valya Igorovna? You think that because His Excellency never yielded to anything, himself, he would be furious if he could know that I was doing so?"

"Verily, Highness," Valya Igorovna wailed. "His Excellency would be angry enough to rise from the grave."

Accepting this estimate, Anastasia nodded. "So you would start out on another terrible journey?"

The maid swallowed. "Unless Highness stays, I should. I am very tired, Highness. But even if I walk until I fall and die in the snow it would be better than awaiting *them*."

Incuriously Anastasia watched her brother who, teeth gritting, paced rapidly between sink and the ice-room door: backwards and forwards, backwards and forwards.

"Yes, perhaps it is preferable, Valya Igorovna," she admitted. "I am soiled enough, but if I stayed I should be infinitely worse soiled. Yes, truly, His Excellency would rise from the grave at the thought of me, his beloved——"

Furiously Sergei halted. "You'll have your own opportunity of rising from the dead very soon," he bawled. "Chatter, chatter, chatter——"

"Please, Highness," Valya Igorovna begged. "Highness must hurry."

Sergei laughed harshly. "Or else," he said, running his finger round his throat.

Stooping, Anastasia wiped off the tears with the gossamer-like fabric of her dress.

"Yes, I will hurry," she said mournfully.

Within seven or eight minutes the party of four, clad in as many extra layers of outdoor clothing as they had been able to purloin, assembled again. The owner of Maxim's had disappeared and they seized what they could for the long and arduous journey before them—tea, black bread, preserved cucumber, pans, kettle, anything eatable, anything which would serve for barter.

Each loaded, they went outside, and found the town filling up with troops, the vanguard of the retreating forces.

In a small square near the Corn Exchange, Princess Anastasia and her companions joined the tail end of an exodus many thousands strong which was progressing slowly through the main street towards the Syeversk road.

When once again in a crowd they were in the familiar world of rumour. The Green Guards were near . . . Budenny's remorseless cavalry were only five versts away . . . were as much as eleven versts off . . . had been badly cut up. A paltry Volunteer force had capitulated . . . a large body of Whites, traitors every man, had attempted to go over to the Reds—and Don Cossacks, catching them, had put every misbegotten man to the sword. Rumour upon rumour.

Already the short walk had had its effect, eighteen debilitated men, women and children dying before the last of the refugees left Ekaterinodar. Few of the passers-by heeded their bodies. And, near the grain clerks' wooden office in the station yard, a kneeling woman, husband supporting her back, was giving messy birth to a child. Few noticed that, either.

The majority were thinking of Novorossisk; wondering if they would ever sight the sea; wondering what would happen if they did.

The distance between Ekaterinodar and Novorossisk was almost as far as that from Tikhoryetsk to Ekaterinodar, but the going was even more cruel as soon as the state highway, leaving the marshlands behind, entered the hilly region leading to the mountains.

There was little shelter throughout the whole route and only three small towns along it: Syeversk, Kholmsk, and Krymsk, backwaters sniffed at by the most modest-pursed traveller in less troubled days.

"A march of death", that was what many of those undertaking the journey named it, and a large proportion of them proved this assertion. On leaving Ekaterinodar the plodding column occupied a stretch of road perhaps two miles long, a body compactly moving forward. But as the hours passed, with the physically-stronger forging ahead and the paces of the weaker shortening, this distance was soon doubled—all under conditions which, for deep winter in the stern Kuban, could fairly be described as surprisingly good. It was moonlight that first night, and although perishingly cold there was no wind, even a breath of which would have penetrated bone and marrow so much as to destroy willpower and purpose save in the most determined. Despite this, eight hundred men, women and children had become still and silent for all time before the greyish-blue light of the moon had been replaced by the pale gold of dawn.

As if repenting of this initial kindness, the elements then did their worst for day after day—snow blizzards, fierce gales and buffeting squalls which raged over the road where it curled round the mountain peaks. From these desolate heights, looking back during one of the brief intervals when there was a clear view, it was possible to discern the remnants of the column, tragically sparse now, widely spread out as far as the eye could reach—bent figures, dark against the snow, moving painfully onwards.

Those who fell between Ekaterinodar and Syeversk were usually given a semblance of seemly burial: a few prayers and a light covering of snow. Thereafter even the most devout could not summon up the energy to attempt this simple office for the departed.

Nights were spent beneath the sagging roofs of Nogai Tatar hovels, where the ill and weary huddled round fires fed sparsely with scraps of kindling and dry dung.

Beyond Kholmsk snow ceased to fall and, visibility considerable, signs of activity were seen. Four times within the next hour, refugees were compelled to flounder into deep drifts at the roadside to allow passage to horse-drawn military sledge convoys.

About then also, well down the mountainside, two trains crowded with Army personnel steamed along the winding railway, the leading locomotive's plough raising a feather-white cloud. Elsewhere there was additional evidence that considerable forces were in motion—along the road behind, steadily gaining, soldiers were marching, while here and there on the high trails leading westwards detachments of White cavalry, strung out in long lines, moved doggedly forward.

To many these sights brought some comfort, though none to Prince Sergei Kaivanov, who shrank into the shelter of the towelling swathing his head and neck whenever fighting units were within recognizable distance.

The next day he and his party reached Krymsk, which was crowded with troops of tough appearance and civilians in the last stage of exhaustion. It was evident at a glance that the little town was being hastily converted into a strong point; machine-guns and a few field pieces were being sited, and buildings were tumbling down to the thunderous roar of explosives, to ensure a clear field of fire.

That morning the Kaivanovs had broken into a small wooden spoon factory presumably abandoned by its proprietor, which by some freak had escaped the attention of fugitives. There was a round-bellied iron stove, plenty of logs, and in a warmth none of them had for a long time known they took stock.

Prince Sergei, despite his fatigue, got up and began to pace restlessly. "We must push on to the sea," he said hoarsely. "In Novorossisk the High Command will have taken grip of the situation——"

His sister interposed impatiently. "Rubbish!"

"They'll have a better grip than the idiots who are trying to hold this spot," he retorted violently. "Who they are I don't know, but I'll wager they're jumped-up nobodies who haven't a notion as to what a staff course means."

"At least they are behaving as if they mean to fight," Anastasia snapped back. "And while we're speaking of fighting, Sergei Ivanovitch," she continued, her eyes narrowing, "how is it, that though my darling Nikky has had to give his life, you have managed——"

In a noisy outburst he checked her, and although much of what he said was wild in the extreme his remarks were based on a deadly core of cold fact. Certainly it seemed impossible that the White forces in Krymsk could achieve more than a brief delaying action, and this being so it was only commonsense to leave quickly. To do this meant acquiring food, enough to keep them alive on the arduous walk to Novorossisk, thirty-five miles away.

Wearily Anastasia shook her head. "Yes, but how?" she said. "There are so many who will be thinking the same thing. And we have neither money nor anything left to exchange."

Countess Petrova laughed joyously, for this was when she came into her own. From a modest start with writing material she had progressed a great deal, and by now was openly boastful about her dexterity in thieving, which in truth was quite remarkable.

Smiling with delight, she jumped up eagerly.

"How?" she said with gleeful scorn. "Really, Stana, you do forget, don't you? But I shall show you once again, and when you see what I bring you won't need to ask 'how', you silly thou."

Despondently they watched her preparing for the foray, and even when she had gone out gaily, waving to them from the doorway with a commodious string-bag acquired mysteriously in Ekaterinodar, none of them spoke for several minutes.

The silence was broken by Valya Igorovna's whimper. It was strange how this strong-limbed girl, from sound peasant stock, had latterly failed so much more than her softer-bred fellow travellers.

"I can't manage any further, Highness," she said, tears coursing down her cheeks. "Highness must leave me here."

"Don't be so damned silly," her mistress replied irritably. "Haven't we enough to worry about without you putting on a performance?"

"I'm not, Highness," her maid wailed. "And if Highness will excuse, I will stay here."

"And what when those Red fiends lay their hands on you?" Anastasia inquired. "Stupid idiot, haven't we had an example of what they did to her Highness, the Countess? How if in nine months time—*if* you have sufficient reason left to wonder—you wonder why your brat has a yellow Mongol skin ... or Kalmuck slit eyes ... or——"

"Please! Oh, please, dear Highness."

Anastasia nodded. "Now maybe you realize why you must force yourself into walking to the sea."

Terrified but resigned, Valya Igorovna replied submissively: "Yes, Highness, verily I do."

Still irritable, Anastasia looked her brother up and down.

"So you ran away, that was it, wasn't it?" she inquired. "A deserter, aren't you?"

"Like hell I am," Prince Sergei flared up. "It merely happens, as often in confused fighting, that I have lost my unit."

"A deserter," his sister mused. "So that is why you hide in your boots whenever your former comrades-in-arms are about. Yes, *I've* noticed, Sergei Ivanovitch."

"It's . . . it's a damned lie," Sergei stuttered. "You . . . you nasty bitch."

"Bitch, am I?" she screamed, snatching up a chisel.

The sharp-edged tool missed by a hairsbreadth when she hurled it at him. That was the beginning of a row which raged to heights of fury, each rousing the other to greater excesses. But the pace was too hot to last and when, about three-quarters of an hour later, Countess Petrova skipped in triumphantly, both were subdued. In that interval, belatedly, Sergei had told his sister about Count Petrov's death.

"Well!" Mimi crowed from the threshold. "What did I tell you?"

Drifts outside had partially snowed-up the windows, and the upper panes were thickly frosted. In the grey half-light of the workroom it was not easy to discern the results of the expedition. Valya Igorovna, nearest the door, was the first to do so, and her eyes widened with astonishment at the sight of a bag bulging with provender.

"Excellency!" she gasped, also glimpsing the clumsy packages her mistress's half-sister carried in the other arm. "However did you get all that?"

With quite an air Mimi displayed her burdens. These she arranged on a packing-case, choosing a small saddle of mutton with crisp crackling for the centre-piece.

"My God!" Anastasia cried. "Meat balls, smoked fish and maize cakes. How the devil did you do it, Mimi?"

Countess Petrova's method was new, and she started to giggle as she related her conquest of an amorous cook-sergeant.

"And, by the way, he said the situation was well in hand," she interrupted her account to remark gravely. "Most confident, he was." Her smile returned as she waved a rye bannock. "I had, of course, to agree to an assignment of a certain nature tonight, if his duties permitted, and I had to allow a few crude liberties as a first instalment. But," she shrugged, "I am much too old a hand to be worried about anything like that."

She seemed to be in the mood for arch reminiscence and, while they ate, chattered away inconsequentially. Elated by her success it was not until long afterwards, when they were ready for starting out, that she recalled a tit-bit of news which obviously was not of prime significance in her view.

"Guess who I've seen?" she asked casually. "You, Stana, you should be the one to try first."

Accustomed to her half-sister's disordered outpourings, Anastasia took scant heed.

"Should I?" she said.

Mimi tittered, more interested now. "I think so, yes, indeed I do."

When she mentioned an officer's name, the Kaivanovs spoke simultaneously. Sergei Ivanovitch's response was a terrified, hysterical "Andreyoukov!" while his sister screamed two words: "Nikolai Tikhonovitch!"

"You've seen Nikky?" Anastasia went on without pause. "Why didn't he come back with you? You told him where I was, didn't you? When is he coming?"

Mimi remarked very calmly that she had not considered it fitting to bring herself to his notice.

Despite its wording, there was no sting in Anastasia's next question. She was too aghast.

"But why not, you infernal little lunatic?"

Slightly put out, Mimi retorted: "Would I rush out on to the Field of Mars if Cyrus Konstantinych were riding past, even if I hadn't set eyes on him for ages and ages?"

"But this isn't a smart military parade, you idiot," Anastasia stormed.

Quietly dignified, Mimi drew herself up. "Precisely," she replied, rebuke in every accent. "This is war, stern war, Stana, and women have a duty, too. And that is not to hamper their men. So I avoided Nikolai Tikhonovitch, who is on active service, please remember."

Wisely, Anastasia left it at that. "Where is he?" she inquired feverishly, fingers a-tremble with the buckle of a leather belt she had already fastened. "I'm going to find him now."

Sergei went off like a rocket. "You're not," he yelled. "We're shoving off without another second's delay, so let's have no more crazy nonsense. Dammit, haven't you heard the firing?"

Eyes dark with determination and threat, Anastasia nodded in the direction of a passageway leading to the street.

"Sergei Ivanovitch," she said with deadly deliberation. "You'll promise to wait here with Mimi and Valya Igorovna until I return, or I shall fetch in some of your former comrades and turn you over to them for what you are—a deserter. You know what shrift they'll give you."

His legs gave beneath him and he dropped on to a stool.

"You . . . you inhuman devil," he groaned.

Assured now that he would remain there, Anastasia opened the door and hurried out into the freezing cold.

The high street of Krymsk ran in a slow curve, rising gradually. At the north end, where the newly-made defences were being concentrated, considerable changes had taken place in the past three hours. Sentries guarded the entrances to a network of temporary blockhouses, while strung out on a line from north-west to south-east hurriedly-built pill-boxes reared up.

At the start of her search Anastasia's hopes were high, but gradually her limbs flagged after many disappointments. One sullen party of men to whom she spoke, who were thawing out machine-gun parts on a fire, had never heard of Count Andreyoukov. Later though, when struggling along the fringe of a wood, she obtained definite information from a section of Cossacks, who pulled their horses to their haunches at her signal. Faces lighting up, they told her that "The Colonel" had returned to the town after inspecting forward defences. Whimpering feebly, she at once began to run back, slipping and stumbling on the icy, uneven ground.

The high street had emptied appreciably even in a short time. Refugees too ill for further effort had crawled or been carried into any building available, and others more capable were moving out on the final trek to the coast. The earliest to depart could be seen in the distance climbing towards the northerly spurs of the Caucasus, on a road winding over the heights to Novorossisk and the sea.

Outside the door of a dingy eating-house a crowd had gathered, largely composed of ne'er-do-wells and the semi-educated, none of whom felt that the Reds would harm them. On tip-toe they strained, striving to see what was taking place indoors.

Anastasia's heart leapt when, through a side window, she glimpsed her lover's broad shoulders. Pistol in hand he was facing a line of resentful men. Frantically she elbowed towards the door, hearing his stern voice as she did so.

"Enough," he said. "I need labourers, and by the Almighty you miserable scum just fit the bill. Out of here and up the street the lot of you."

A gigantic ex-N.C.O., swaying in a shadowy corner, began to move forward menacingly, a shambling beast growling in its throat.

"None of us is going, for we'd die like bears in a pit, that's what." His red-eyed glance roved over his comrades. "Arkasha," he snapped. "When thou drew the shortest straw thou bragged that if this happened thou would be the leader in throwing thyself upon . . ."

The men were whispering, bracing themselves for a mass rush, when Count Andreyoukov's Webley-Scott barked once. The N.C.O. clawed at the wall, rolling against it until he reached a doorway on that side, when his heavy body tumbled through the aperture and fell with a thud on the flagged floor of a kitchen.

"Any more objectors among you?" Count Andreyoukov demanded.

There were not. Death would soon come and now they knew it. Like automatons, they obeyed His Honour and marched out. A Don Cossack, cartridge belt diagonally across his chest and hand on hip, was riding swaggeringly up the street. Count Andreyoukov, bawling cheerfully to him, handed the captives into his charge.

"Nikky!" Anastasia gasped.

Swiftly, Count Andreyoukov turned, ineffable horror in his steely-grey eyes as he recognized her. For a few moments, as he drew her into the eating-house, closing the door with a kick, he seemed unable to speak.

"Stana, my darling," he said at last huskily. "What the devil are you doing here? I hoped you would be out of Russia by now, or at least in the Crimea, which I believe we still hold."

Tears of joy and relief were streaming down her cheeks. "I was at Yasni Dulba, and so didn't get away from Rostov soon enough," she cried. "Oh, Nikky, I've had the hell of a time since then."

She was gathered tightly in his arms and, after once again kissing him passionately, she murmured blissfully:

"But I don't want to talk about that, darling. Everything is all right now, so wonderfully right."

Compassionately he glanced at her. "Not quite, I'm afraid, dearest."

"Oh, it is, Nikky, there's nothing to worry about now," she persisted, laughing tremulously while lovingly touching the V-shaped mark on his cheek. "See what an utterly trusting wife you will have. Oh yes, I know how dreadful things are, but I have the most sublime faith in you. And Valya Igorovna has, too. As for poor darling Mimi—I am sure she will think the Imperial Army has taken her under its wing."

"They're both with you? How is Mimi?"

She sighed. "Eerily strange, darling. But she's happy somehow in her make-believe world, and doesn't know about poor Cyrus Konstantinych's death just before Christmas. I shan't tell her, either."

"I'm sorry about that, Stana. I only met him once or twice, but he struck me as a very sound customer. And wonderful with Mimi."

"Yes, he was, *utterly*," Anastasia murmured, weeping anew.

"Steady, my little cabbage," Count Andreyoukov said tenderly.

"It's . . . it's just because I am so, *so* happy, Nikky, darling," she whispered, eyes closed and cheek pressed against his breast.

He was petting her, gently stroking the nape of her neck, when an odd notion occurred to him.

"Petrov was on the other front. How did you hear he had died?"

"Sergei Ivanovitch told me, only today."

"Sergei Ivanovitch! Is he with you?"

Startled by the change in his tone, she looked up at him.

"Yes," she replied, at once perceiving the implication. "But, Nikky darling, you won't do anything about him, will you? Oh, I know he's awful, but he is my brother, after all, and I wouldn't want him shot."

Count Andreyoukov's lips curved ironically. "Don't worry, Stana, this outfit of mine is unique in many respects. For instance, though we render ordinary prisoners harmless for all time, we don't shoot 'em as is now the accepted convention in this war of ours. And as for deserters—we never have them, because we're far too choice a bunch for that."

"But if Sergei Ivanovitch left without leave?"

Dryly he retorted: "Sergei Ivanovitch was pressed into the sanitary squad or something just as ignoble, and we don't consider individuals like him as 'belonging'. The worst that can befall him is the whale of a thrashing if he bumps into any of my chaps."

Anastasia pouted. "You think the world of your wonderful men, don't you?" she whispered, absorbed in playing with one of his buttonholes. "Far more than of anything else."

"Do I?" Count Andreyoukov muttered, his arms tightening. But his lazy smile faded when, after losing himself in her dark eyes, he took deep toll of soft red lips held up invitingly. "My very dear," he said later.

"Oh . . . Nikky . . . darling," she said breathlessly.

It was not to be expected that a man with the commanding officer's responsibilities could disappear for long without being missed, and shortly afterwards a runner raced down the street with information about movements in the Communist lines. There were indications of the enemy launching the attack into which they were being neatly lured.

Count Andreyoukov went to the door, heard the news, and then returned.

"A little spot of bother may be starting, darling," he said, eyes sparkling. "We're letting them through as far as the sharper bend at the top of the street."

"But . . ."

Count Andreyoukov chuckled. "Ambush!" he said. "We've a remarkable flair for 'em. But come along, darling, and I'll stow you out of harm's way."

The command-post to which he took her was at the west of the town, a windmill in a timber yard, close to a frozen stream which at less inclement seasons drove a water-wheel. His personal sub-sotnia of Don Cossacks awaited him, grinning expectantly and already mounted, and he was also greeted with a whinny from his own beast.

Count Andreyoukov introduced his fiancée to his two most senior officers, a precise-speaking, middle-aged professor from the University of Moscow, and a broadly-spoken, alert-looking former ranker. There were other indications that, in this particular White force, promotion went by merit alone.

Indifferent to the presence of many bystanders, Anastasia grasped his arm with both hands.

"You're not leaving me, are you, Nikolai Tikhonovitch?" she asked.

"Just for a little while, but you'll be quite safe here, my pet."

"I wasn't thinking about that," she replied haughtily.

He smiled. "Of course not, my dear."

Her fingers tightened. "Couldn't I go with you, Nikky?" she asked in a small, imploring voice. "Honestly, I ride rather well. I was often out with our Cossacks at Yasni Dulba, and I'm not one of those fluttering females who can't fire a pistol without closing their eyes as it goes off. And . . ." she ended revengefully, "I'd enjoy killing some of those devils."

"I'll bet you would," Count Andreyoukov commented, shaking his head.

"Really, I wouldn't be a nuisance," she pleaded.

Grey eyes twinkling, Count Andreyoukov glanced round the circle of officers and men, all of whom were looking at the lady with open admiration.

Solemnly he addressed them: "I hope you gentlemen do not contemplate supporting this romantic application. It is embar-rassingly obvious that my betrothed has a burning ambition to perish with me if need be in an heroic exploit, so that our names may be legendary. I regret to say the idea does not in the least appeal to me."

"Nor to me," Anastasia said, laughing. "I wouldn't be in a position to hear about it, which I regard as an immense draw-back."

"One lives but once, eh?" he teased her.

"Naturally," she retorted. "And don't be such a damned fool, Nikky."

Count Andreyoukov smiled, the Cossacks bellowed with glee, and others present added their full-bellied quota of laughter.

"But can I?" she wheedled. "*Please.*"

"No, darling," he replied cheerily.

Scowling, she demanded: "Why the hell not?"

"Because not, my dear," he told her with quiet finality.

She was distinctly aloof when he kissed her the first time. But their second kiss, before he swung himself on to his horse, was different. Watched with sympathy and understanding by hard-bitten but sentimental men, who realized all too well what the ensuing minutes might bring, the couple embraced passionately.

Anastasia saw the engagement from a narrow window high in the windmill, her view intercepted at intervals by slowly-revolving vanes. The action began when small contingents of Reds cautiously advanced, their numbers rapidly increasing when it was found that opposition was extremely light.

Count Andreyoukov's second-in-command was more interested in an enemy team of six who, carrying a machine-gun with tripod and ammunition, followed up the Red infantry. They established themselves in a position which, although of little danger to the Whites, certainly covered the area on which their own men were operating.

The second-in-command grunted with satisfaction. "I reckon that spot will just about suit the Colonel's book," he said.

"What does he intend to do?" Anastasia asked him.

He laughed. "It's a speciality of the Colonel's, Princess," he remarked appreciatively. "We'd rather he didn't, but——" As if conscious of the possibility of alarming her, he dried up abruptly.

The conflict was becoming brisker, with White retaliation so severe at one point that a company of Reds halted in confusion, apparently prepared to turn tail. The machine-gun behind them chattered briefly, and seven or eight waverers dropped to the snow. A salutary lesson learned, their comrades gingerly advanced.

An observer in the windmill, a merry-faced old soldier whose blasphemous but delighted comment was lost in the rising din of battle, hurriedly left his window to cross the circular room.

"If *barishnia* would care to watch the Colonel," he shouted in Anastasia's ear.

Nodding eagerly, she hastened with him to the other side, from which she at once saw, clearly delineated against the white landscape, a line of fur-capped Don Cossacks in single file. Taking advantage of every scrap of shelter, working along convenient hollows, men and horses gradually drew nearer the central assault point through which the Communists had been allowed to penetrate. Her lover was at their head—she could see him quite plainly through the surviving lens of a battered pair of Zeiss binoculars which had been lent to her.

Breath catching, she asked: "What are they going to do?"

"Wait, *barishnia*," the old fellow replied.

The crackle from small-arms had risen to a fresh peak. From either flank concealed marksmen poured in withering fire and, encountering the stream of lead, the Reds recoiled. Immediately their own machine-gun opened up on them.

But Anastasia, more intent than ever she had been in her life, knew nothing of that. She saw only a group of horsemen gathered in a depression which in summer would be a pleasant, tree-screened pool. They did not remain there long. Count Andre-youkov pulled his stallion round to face the slope, kicked his heels and was off. He sped up the incline and over the top, segments of snow flying from the hoofs of his horse and those of his followers as they raced across a level stretch.

The machine-gunners realized their peril too late. The gun, which had been spurting a deadly hail to the front, swivelled violently, but by then wild-riding Don Cossacks, an intimidating spectacle at close range, reached them. Rising in his stirrups, Count Andreyoukov's sword flashed down.

The whole minor engagement petered out after this. Red infantry, suffering scorching fire from three sides, discovered it was safe to retreat. Panic-stricken they faced about and ran, leaving two hundred or more behind. White infantry emerged just as quickly and, secure for the moment, rapidly examined enemy victims, bending over them and carrying out a small maiming operation wherever necessary, a double cut with a knife. Soon scores of hamstrung Communists were heading jerkily towards their own lines, crawling on hands and one knee, each dragging along a leg which would make campaigning impossible for a long time, if ever.

Fresh firing swelled up. "What's that?" Anastasia asked anxiously.

"Support for the Colonel, *barishnia*," the ancient soldier told her, less ebulliently.

Sick with apprehension, Anastasia descended to the ground floor of the windmill and went outside. It seemed an eternity to her before Count Andreyoukov rode in, bringing with him the survivors of the machine-gun crew.

"Take them away and question them," he said curtly to a sedate-looking sergeant from whose belt an arsenal of weapons hung. "And report to me as soon as possible."

As the prisoners were led off, he dismounted. "Well, darling, enjoying yourself?" he asked.

She clasped her hands. "Oh Nikky, I've been petrified."

Slipping his hand under her arm, he walked with her through

the timber yard, as far as a small hut in which there was an astonishing array of wines and victuals.

"We've been doing ourselves proud lately," he said.

"I know, darling, because we acquired some of your stores," she told him laughingly, and was explaining Mimi Ivanovna's artfulness when stayed by a piercing scream.

"One of the machine-gunners," Count Andreyoukov said laconically.

"You torture them?"

"If necessary," he replied. "But bullies soon squeal, and that's what the political Communist is."

"And what do you do with them afterwards?"

"Send 'em by the shortest cut to the longest rest," he grunted.

Anastasia's eyebrows went up. "But I always understood you had strong views on the treatment of prisoners, and you certainly spare the lives of those captured in the field, as I've seen for myself. Damn silly it is, too."

Grinning broadly, Count Andreyoukov eyed her with great pleasure.

"My my, but you're recovering quickly, aren't you? Soon you'll be the hellish little minx I fell in love with. Yes, darling," —he was serious, now—" we shoot these machine-gun specimens because they're different, because of what they do and what they are—political soldiers under a commissar, who squat in the rear and destroy their own men. God, it makes one vomit."

As he opened a bottle of wine and poured a glass, he went on: "Drink this while I am away, Stana. I've various arrangements to make, and I've to see about food for your party."

She stared at him. "Food for my party, Nikky?"

He hesitated perceptibly. "You'll need food, won't you? It's a fair stretch to Novorossisk, you know."

"But——"

"Stana dear," he interrupted her, his cheeks paler. "Please believe that I shall do the utmost possible for you. The trouble is that I haven't a bean's worth in money or anything negotiable, none of us has, so it isn't all that easy."

When she was alone, prey to many strange and confusing thoughts, Anastasia drank a second glass of wine and ate a slice of bread generously spread with caviare. Restless and disturbed, however, hoping to catch sight of him returning, she spent more time in the window than on the chair near the stove. But she ceased to look out when three Reds were lined up for execution.

Shortly after the firing party's volley rang out, Count Andreyoukov came back.

"And now for this spoon-factory of yours," he said very firmly.

"And while I am escorting you there I'll tell you what I've fixed up."

She was seething with mortification and rage before they reached the top of Krymsk's high street but, as if completely unaware of how he was infuriating her, he continued with perfect calmness to detail the plans he had made. These, she decided venomously, wholly concerned the well-being of others: gallant old horses, a crippled driver with one leg, and two seriously-wounded men.

"These two chaps are in a bad way, Stana," he went on. "They haven't an earthly if they remain with us and it will be a weight off my mind if I know you are there to do what you can for them on the way to Novorossisk."

"I shall do everything possible," she said frigidly.

He glanced at her. "What's wrong, Stana?"

"Nothing," she replied, tight-lipped.

"There is, my dear, and I suspect it is because you think I should be doing more for you than I am."

"On the contrary," she said, "I think you are organizing everything quite, *quite* wonderfully."

A section of infantry passed, and he responded to their salute before quietly resuming: "I can't do more, Stana . . . I only wish I could. But at least you will be able to ride in turns, which will reduce the strain."

Anastasia laughed mirthlessly. "I'm looking forward enormously to the outing, Nikolai Tikhonovitch. Perhaps it won't be as amusing as a picnic of other days, but really wonderful after what we have endured."

Count Andreyoukov's voice thickened. "Don't be an infernal little fool," he snapped. "Can't I judge for myself what you've been through—you're lovely still, even a half-blind man would recognize that, but your face shows the privations and hardship you've undergone. And for God's sake don't make it worse for me than it is."

"Worse for *you*?" she inquired scornfully.

They had arrived at the passage leading to the spoon factory and, as she was turning into the entry, he spun her about, holding her so that she was squarely towards him.

"Yes, worse for me," he growled. "How the hell do you imagine I feel about sending you off on this ghastly trip? But what else can I do? Chuck up my job and go off with you?"

"There are men who would."

Steel-grey eyes hard, he looked at her. "Would you wish me to be of that kind?"

Although out of her senses with anger, she nevertheless shifted

362

ground. "You could have let us have decent animals, so that we could get through more quickly," she said bitingly. "Sergei Ivanovitch has told us how very difficult it is to obtain a passage in a ship at the last minute."

The lines of his face sterner than she had ever seen them, he dealt with that.

"We haven't spare horses, and to take a horse belonging to any of my Cossacks would be more grievous to him than the loss of his left arm. I wouldn't do it anyway, because it would be a gross betrayal of my duty and of my obligations to men who have been my loyal comrades through thick and thin."

"Because you don't love me," she flashed back. "I once told you, over a year ago, that you cared more for your men than for me, I was joking, but now I know it's true, Nikolai Tikhonovitch."

Count Andreyoukov glanced up the street as a large sledge appeared on the bend.

"No, it isn't, Stana," he said wearily. "But must we part so horribly? God knows what will happen to either of us, and I would prefer a very different memory of you."

"I prefer this memory," she told him cruelly, "of the man as he really is. If I live it will be a reminder of what a fool a woman can be."

"All right, my dear," he said, sighing.

She flounced off and, grey of face, he waited for the sledge. When it drew up he looked into the straw-filled bottom, on which two unconscious men rested, their wounds dressed with boiled strips of commandeered linen to the best of the surgeon-probationer's ability. Then, murmuring endearments and with tears springing into his eyes, he fondled the horses before speaking to the bloodless-cheeked driver, one of whose legs was a massively-swathed stump only.

"Don't dally at all," he said with quiet emphasis. "For your ear alone I've learnt that a large force is bearing down on us, and we may not be able to hang on. You have your revolver?"

"Yes, Colonel."

Count Andreyoukov nodded to the rope-yoked horses. "Put these two old faithfuls down as soon as you arrive. They deserve a quick and merciful end."

The driver blinked. "Yes, your Excellency," he mumbled.

From the rear of the passage, where she had been leaning, all strength out of her, Princess Anastasia called once again much louder.

Count Andreyoukov swiftly reached her. She was crying, almost child-like in her grief.

"Nikky, I'm sorry," she said brokenly. "I shall never forgive myself for my bitchy behaviour."

A smile smoothed out the lines of strain and authority in Count Andreyoukov's face.

"Don't fret any more, darling," he said gently as he took her in his arms. "The only thing which matters is right again, that all is now well with us."

She kissed him passionately, before frantically pushing him away.

"Nikky darling, please go now," she said. "Because I can't bear the thought of leaving you, and . . . and I want to get it over."

Count Andreyoukov's voice deepened. "I understand, my very dear."

But she rushed to him and, arms clinging tightly round his neck, kissed him again. Dark eyes overbrimming, she looked at him piteously.

"Nikky, we shall meet again, shan't we?" she said, begging for assurance. "Tell me that somewhere in the world we shall still find happiness together."

Count Andreyoukov's firm lips quivered. "We must trust in the Lord's goodness, my darling."

"Yes," she whispered strickenly. "And now please go, Nikky dearest."

Their last sight of each other was from the ends of the passage, she unreservedly giving way to her sorrow before turning away; and he, of a family renowned for generations throughout Russia for its courage, in hardly better case as he walked up the main street of the doomed little town of Krymsk.

CHAPTER V

THE weather was arctic and, around the shores of the Bay of Novorossisk, a grey-black sea rolled against the frost-bound, white-mantled land.

Outside the mole not a single vessel was in sight as far as the horizon, but within the harbour there were many, their rigging picturesque with sparkling icicles. Among them were several Levantine tramp-steamers whose owners and skippers had already made fortunes in the last moments before the Communist tide submerged many other Black Sea ports. In ones and twos, people with the means in gold or its equivalent kept joining these ill-found craft, which were more than crammed to capacity already.

364

As daylight started to fade Princess Anastasia Kaivanova was thrust none too gently down the sloping gangway of a small Greek liner bound for Constantinople and Trieste, whose captain had noisily and contemptuously refused to make a detour to Sevastopol.

"You may own a handsome villa in Livadia and you might have jewels sufficient there to buy this 'tub' of mine as you say," he yelled. "But you will never reach the Crimea in my ship, A.1. at Lloyds."

Although her resources were diminishing, Anastasia still had spunk in her, as she had shown in recent minutes when humiliated unnecessarily.

Slowly she turned, to gaze at him unwinkingly with dark eyes, a favourite trick of childhood.

"Nor will you ever again pass Rumeli Hissar in the Bosphorus, Captain," she called to him, her voice pregnant with fate. "Because before then, so it is written in the tablets, you will perish . . . *horribly*."

His jaw dropped. "What?"

Sadly Anastasia shook her head. "The women of my family have the gift, Captain. We can foretell these things."

The quayside was a mass of ice and she tumbled heavily when thrown ashore by two swarthy seamen. But the captain's scared expression compensated her for the pain and indignity.

The wharf along which she tiredly dragged her swollen feet was dense with people. Crazily over-optimistic merchants stood against heaps of indifferent goods with which they proposed making a fresh start in life elsewhere; there were perambulators and handcarts loaded with treasured household possessions, and sledges of all sizes, from children's to country carriers', piled with extraordinarily pathetic collections.

But the majority had little more than the clothes in which, shivering, they stood, All were alike, however, in that every now and then they turned their heads to listen to the rumble of the guns.

Further along the jetty a merchantman, crowded with people of all ages, from elderly men and women down to tiny tots and infants, was leaving for Constantinople and the immense reception camps set up there. Furnished by the British, she was being seen off by an army captain in a fur-collared British Warm, a member of the Refugee Control staff. This service of mercy had saved thousands: Constantinople was full of refugees and Prinkipo almost a Russian colony.

Since arriving in Novorossisk six days before, Anastasia had called upon this Scottish gentleman several times, and he knew what she wanted—the same as everyone else who haunted the harbour.

"Sorry, Princess, but we've no signal yet," he told her regretfully. "Our people are trying to send more ships up, but when they'll arrive . . ."

She sighed. "Is another matter. And by then it may be too late for us. I think it will be."

Negotiating the treacherous-surfaced planks of a board-walk, she headed towards the shore. On the seaward side a group of emaciated boys were stoning a few semi-frozen, oil-bound ducks with such small energy as they had, waiting for the bodies to drift within arm's length whenever successful. The spectacle of slow maiming was not diverting.

On leaving the harbour area and entering the town she encountered an old couple to whom she had spoken the previous day. They were sharing a plate of offal at the side-door of a squalid eating-house, an old lady in a tent-like coat made by roughly cutting neck and arm holes out of a small square of floral-patterned carpet, and a grey-visaged gentleman in an English Tommy's greatcoat to which Russian shoulder-straps with the badges of a full general were attached. They acknowledged her bow with magnificent aplomb.

She plodded on through streets deep in snow until, faint with the effort, she paused against the offices of the cement works, occupied by the British Military Mission and guarded by a handful of aged White guards. The day was fading, and as the town's power station had ceased to work kerosene lamps shone cheerfully inside. Through a moisture-streaked window she enviously saw a smiling Russian cook take round cups of tea and, mouth watering, watched an officer feeding bully-beef to a miserably-thin, uncertain-legged mongrel. Remaining members of the staff seemed to be engaged exclusively in burning papers.

When her palpitation lessened she started off again, floundering along until a huge grain elevator loomed into view, her refuge and that of scores more who were destitute.

When inside the cold and cheerless cavern, where living creatures lay about so still and silent that it might have been an ill-managed mortuary, she picked her way in the gloom towards the niche in which she and her party lived. They were all there. Countess Petrova greeted her with a gay smile, but Prince Sergei took no notice. For the last two days her brother had not spoken. Lost in depression he sat with his hands squeezed beneath his armpits, head sunk on his chest.

"Highness?" Valya Igorovna said feebly, a question in her brown eyes.

366

"No," her mistress muttered.

An hour later the paltry remainder of the hoard of food acquired at Krymsk was divided.

So star-lit night came, and fitful sleep.

During the interminable hours of darkness the sound of firing rose in volume, and often the sky was lighted by shell flashes. Encouraged by these portents, local Communists emerged in greater force than ever; the prison was broken open—by Green Guard raiders, it was rumoured the next day—and mob law ruled the streets.

The next morning the weather changed, blanketing snow showers alternating with clear periods in which blue sky was visible. There were other changes, also: discharges from heavy guns were nearer and consequently louder, and frequently, when conditions were suitable, puffs of smoke from artillery positions could be discerned with the naked eye. Sirens blaring, the tramp steamers all left in very short order; and, from daybreak, White troops marched in without intermission.

In the early afternoon, after eating a piece of cold fish provided by Mimi Ivanovna from a source not inquired into, Princess Anastasia left her brother—who never went out during full daylight—and her half-sister and the maid, to return to the harbour.

Only a few scattered snowflakes were falling then, but the silent crowd on the quay were, for the most part, too far spent to brush off the thick capes of snow which had accumulated on their shoulders.

A considerable commotion was taking place in a rusty-sided Greek liner, whose starving passengers had learnt that their exorbitantly-priced tickets did not include meals. Frantic, these pitiable creatures crowded round an officer.

The engine telegraph was ringing, which made the predicament of a sad-faced young woman all the more terrible. Clinging to her were two little girls, wearing outer clothing which, although cut down by unaccustomed hands, was warm and serviceable; but she herself was clad only in a cotton frock. In the space between wharf and ship's side, now gradually widening, a chinchilla pelisse rested on a shelf of ice. Shocked to learn that the tickets were for passage only, the mother had thrown the coat into the clutching hands of a businessman on the quayside. When she demurred about an offer pitilessly inadequate, the mantle had been returned carelessly—it could be recovered, of course, when the ship had gone. Now, leaning over the rail, she looked down desperately at her sole valuable property.

"Vultures, battening on fear and misery." Anastasia hissed

367

before raising her voice to a compelling yell. "Can't any of you men do anything about it?"

But it was too late. The ship was drawing away.

Eyes pricking, Anastasia savagely turned to resume her daily tour, in which she never failed.

As she anticipated, the vestibule and stairs of the Refugee Control Office were thronged with down-and-out compatriots. The woman behind her, a Junoesque person in a threadbare velvet wrap-over and a mangy silver-fox tie, dispiritedly passed on the rumour that the control was closing down.

This anxious issue was cleared up during the course of the next interview, during which applicants outside the door, those who could understand, that is, listened with bated breath. The English sub-lieutenant was being exceedingly stubborn about a mother and daughter of his acquaintance.

The man with whom he argued was helpless, and surfeited with horrors. "I can't do a damned thing," he snapped. "The fact is we're packing up."

"Then there's only one thing to be done," the young naval officer said resolutely. "And, by God, I'll have a try at doing it."

After the sub-lieutenant stormed out, the Refugee Control Officer was heard to remark wryly to a subordinate:

"If all these romantic lads who want to save some girl were allowed to marry . . . why, the Orthodox parsons in these parts would be loaded down with Bradburys. But all that's quashed now, and he hasn't an earthly."

The depressing work of the Control went on. Vividly recalling a refusal which had caused a middle-aged ex-officer to shoot himself before his eyes, the duty officer was extremely careful with the old gentleman who succeeded the irate sub-lieutenant.

"Yes, another ship has been ordered up from Constantinople, and your family is booked for her, sir," he said. "But . . . well, difficulties aren't lessening, and I wouldn't depend too much on it."

The big room had been a bedroom, and an *oumovalnik* stood against the floridly-papered wall. It was a waist-high stand with plug-less basin and foot-pedal operating a jet which spurted water into the user's face.

"There is some doubt, I gather." The speaker supported himself on this piece of domestic furniture.

"Frankly, there is, sir. But we must hope for the best for everyone in every sense."

"Yes, yes, of course . . . hope for the best. And thank you for your extreme courtesy." The old man bowed, smiled grotesquely, and went out.

Clenching her fists, Anastasia trudged back to the harbour, so fiercely determined to find a way out that in her abstraction as she approached the wooden signal tower she collided slightly with a man in a duffle coat. Giddy through privation she swayed, but he prevented any worse mishap by grabbing her arm, apologizing in the most atrocious Russian as he did so.

To begin with his glance was merely rueful, but as recognition dawned he stared intently at this dark-eyed girl. She was filthy, blue with cold and virtually in rags, but the painful changes in her did not wholly conceal the riper beauty which had attracted him in the Crimea.

"My God!" he exclaimed. "You must forgive me, but this has rather bowled me over, Princess Anastasia—incidentally, my name is Crowther, and though perhaps I can't expect you to remember me too well we did meet a few times, the last time . . . well, it must be eight or nine months ago."

Her breath caught at this unbelievable contact with another world.

"Lieutenant-Commander Crowther, of course," she whispered. "You told me you had taken a letter to my mother in the Caucasus—was that at Sevastopol? And I did meet you occasionally after that."

"Whenever I could penetrate the screen of males hemming you in," Edwin Crowther said lightly. "And then invariably someone snatched you away."

Her expression changed, and she seemed to regard him in a different light. "Oh," she murmured. "Yes, perhaps I recall that also. But what are you doing here, Commander Crowther?"

He pointed seaward, towards a battleship, a light cruiser, and two destroyers, dimly seen grey shapes.

"We arrived in a blizzard this morning, and the snow has more or less steadily fallen off-shore ever since, which probably explains why you didn't notice us," he said. "But now may I ask the same question? What in the name of heaven are you doing here?"

"It is a very long story."

Officers and men of British forces serving in Russian waters were reluctant experts in the detection of malnutrition.

"Then tell me over a table," he said.

Even when willing to pay at the exchange rate of ten thousand roubles to the pound, which bought two slices of bread, it was a sheer impossibility to obtain a tasty meal in Novorossisk, but he got the best that the town could provide, refraining from watching her while she ate, another lesson the Navy had learnt.

When her appetite was appeased he mentioned a shipmate,

Lieutenant-Commander Staitherton, who had married Princess Irene Shulovskia in Sevastopol.

"Yes, of course," Anastasia said. "We lent them the villa at Livadia for their honeymoon. And how is Irene Sergeivna? I suppose you will know, Commander Crowther. And where is she? In England?"

Edwin Crowther laughed. "Yes, and the only conclusion I can draw is that the woman is involved in a whirl of gaiety."

"I'm damned glad," said Anastasia violently. "People like my own have made ghastly mistakes, and we're paying for them. But we never made a science of cruelty, which the Bolsheviks began in the Lubianka. They're evil, evil in a way I can only fumble towards understanding, and I'm glad Irene Sergeivna has got away and is having fun."

He had bought food to take back with them and was left with four pound notes and two fivers in his wallet. These he offered to her.

"Please," he said when she shook her head.

"It is delightful of you," she said, tears in her eyes. "But . . . but I think the money would be thrown away. Not very long ago I heard that your Refugee Control Office was putting up the shutters. Is that why you are here?"

She pinned him down in the end. "Yes, that's been my job on the beach here today," he admitted. "We're embarking them and the Military Mission fellows at ten in the morning. A destroyer is coming right in on the off-chance of any queer business."

"Yes," she muttered.

"Yes," he said. "And now I'm taking you back to this crazy shack of yours."

"Thank you," she said, her smile strained.

After that, in the unlighted streets of Novorossisk as darkness came, she had other worries. When a town was in its death throes, due shortly to be in Red hands, the reign of terror began at night and already there were shots, and anguished cries of pain, the accompaniment to brutality, robbery, murder and rape.

Meantime, throughout a hazardous twenty-five minutes' walk, Edwin Crowther had been concentrating as hard as his grandfather had ever done when founding a great business. At the end of those twenty-five minutes he had not reached a firm decision, but was balanced on a knife's edge.

In the grain elevator, where a few widely-dispersed, smoky yellow lights formed pinpoints in space, shadowy figures appeared and vanished. It was eerie in the gloom as he followed the Russian girl across the immense floor; less familiar with the place than she, he scraped his shins on low obstructions, kicked paliasses made from sacks, and jostled persons he barely saw.

That strange girl, Countess Petrova, was sitting between her half-brother, a sunken-faced spectre, and a young woman he was sure he had never known. All three, bagging over their legs, were leaning against a low wood barrier, close together for warmth. A lighted candle in the neck of a bottle emphasized their alarming fleshlessness.

"Commander Crowther has been good enough to escort me back," Anastasia told them. "We met quite accidentally; a delightful surprise."

A young-old face thrust itself forward. "How do you do, Commander Crowther," Countess Petrova said graciously. "Frightfully rude to ask, I know, but have we met before?"

"Er . . . yes, Countess," Edwin Crowther replied uncomfortably. "We drove together to Chursuv Bay, if you remember."

"Yes, of course; dear *dear* Chursuv Bay," she agreed sentimentally.

By then Prince Sergei had himself in hand, and was prepared for the picture he proposed presenting of himself, one which had served admirably with the English in Odessa.

"My dear Crowther," he said, rising and holding out his hand. "This is indeed a pleasure. Welcome, my dear fellow, to our amusing abode."

"Fearful!" Crowther said with palpable distaste. "It's frightful to think of you all here."

"Any chance you might get us out, old man?" Sergei inquired nonchalantly.

Edwin Crowther shook his head. "Not a hope, I'm afraid."

Visibly Sergei lost poise. "I just wondered with you arriving. Sorry to bother you and all that."

"The plain fact is that we have drastic orders nowadays."

"So we must die," Sergei muttered hollowly.

Between the harbour and there, Edwin Crowther's sallow cheeks had frequently flushed as he contemplated a most embarrassing action. But now, as he looked at Prince Sergei's sister, he realized he had made up his mind.

"Princess," he said, his voice betraying nervousness, "may I speak to you alone . . . on a little matter?"

Amazed, she glanced at him. "Of course."

Before awkward questions could be asked, he slipped off the duffle coat he was wearing over his greatcoat, put it round her and, grasping her elbow, returned with her through the lofty and largely windowless building.

It was much less dim outside. Stars were shining coldly, and towards the back of the town the glare from fires was reflected in the sky. The sounds of fighting had increased, adding a further sense of urgency to a situation critical enough.

Against this background, Crowther made an uneasy start: "I'm sure, Princess, that you are not likely to be under any illusion about the state of affairs, are you?"

She smiled mirthlessly. "No, if only because I have a very considerable experience in these matters. By this time tomorrow I am certain the Communists will be able to do as they will with us. As my brother implied, we are doomed."

Edwin Crowther shifted his feet. "There is a way out," he said, "but I'm hanged if I care about naming it."

"A way out?" She spoke flatly.

"Yes, Princess," he insisted. "I'm sure there is."

He had her full attention now. "Do tell me what it is, please," she begged.

He was silent for a few seconds, and then the words came with a rush: "If you would marry me it would be altogether different. I'm aware we haven't seen a lot of each other, but for me it would be a risk I'd gladly take."

"Marry you!" She spoke almost under her breath. "I . . . I am very honoured you should wish to do so, but I had not the least idea you cherished such serious thoughts about me."

"Why do you imagine I always tried to shove through that screen of males I reminded you about?" he demanded.

"So," she murmured.

Away to the left, fighting flared up in the vicinity of the Volunteer wireless station, upon which the Reds had opened an unexpected night attack, the harsh voices of the assault carrying with striking clarity through the crisp air. This was the beginning of the end—within five minutes every soul in Novorossisk assumed that.

"There's another aspect, too," Crowther went on. "It would mean the safety of your brother and sister, and I daresay your maid's. I've gathered she's your maid."

"If I married you?"

"Yes."

"But you can't love me, Commander Crowther."

Doggedly the Englishman answered that. "No, but one can't foresee the future. We could have a shot at making a go of it, couldn't we?"

She was trembling. "Making a go of it," she said painfully.

In the battleship off the mole a searchlight spluttered into life, its dazzling blue-white pencil sweeping along the black-and-white shore; sometimes the beam hovered, or swung with flashing speed; at others it lifted and probed different parts of the stricken town.

In the brilliant, stage-like glare Crowther fleetingly saw the Princess Anastasia Kaivanova, her face contorted. To him she seemed to be laughing helplessly, tears of amusement streaming; or it might have been that she was sniggering, giggling, or tittering, to which the stifled sounds she made equally applied. What he failed to understand was that her nerves had given way—that unmitigated relief and searing regret were warring within her.

"I'm sorry," he said thickly. "I realize my infernal presumption in dreaming that you would . . . would buy your life, as it were——"

"No, no," she implored him through her sobs. "It is only that I am horribly overwrought. You mustn't believe I am other than grateful for a gesture . . . of which I should have thought only a Russian capable."

"But will you marry me, Princess?"

Mistily she smiled. "If you knew my best friends, Commander Crowther," she said, mocking herself, "they would impress upon you that I am a firm devotee of making the best of this world."

"Then . . . ?" he asked eagerly.

Long seconds, and many of them, ticked by before she replied. "I will marry you," she said at last. "You have been most charming."

From their different points of view each was conscious of a cessation of strain.

"I'm . . . I'm damned pleased," Edwin Crowther muttered after a few moments. "And now we must do some really quick planning. My ship sails at noon tomorrow, which means that if our padre splices us it will be a close shave."

After a businesslike discussion it was decided, therefore, to seek out the nearest Orthodox priest, to arrange for him to marry them early the next morning.

"Suppose we'd better have a word with your brother before we pop off?"

"Sergei Ivanovitch!" Anastasia shrugged. "It is not in the least necessary."

Slightly taken aback, the Englishman nodded. "All right then, let's be off."

Fortunately the church was not far away, on the main road leading out to Ekaterinodar. It was just as fortunate that, though the streets were more menacing than earlier, Edwin Crowther had no reason to use the small automatic in his greatcoat pocket. It was less easy, however, to find the priest, whose house was shuttered and without sign of occupation.

373

The church was different, with many people in it, sensed rather than seen in the gloom, the sole illumination that from a tiny silver oil-lamp burning before a gaudy ikon.

Princess Anastasia spoke to a young woman and, on her directions, they went along a corridor, more or less feeling their way, as far as a door beneath which the faintest glimmer could be seen.

After some initial hesitation, and inquiries from inside, the lock clicked. Oddly enough, the priest's appearance was probably enhanced by the meagre light from a taper. Against the dark, shadowy background the yellow rays effectively brought out the gold ornamentation on the precious silks of his vestments and, a tall, commanding figure, he looked a presence sufficiently dominating to overawe anyone who might attempt to violate either the House of the Lord or those who sought sanctuary beneath its domed roof. But his eyes were terrified and, in striking contrast to a jet-black beard, his complexion was of the hue of lard.

With him Anastasia had a short but rapid conversation. At its conclusion she sank down and was blessed.

"That is all settled," she said, speaking in English again. "At nine o'clock in the morning."

"Fine," said Edwin Crowther. "I wish it were that now. I'll be happier when you're out of this place."

"Times passes," she remarked, her tone quite neutral.

When they were returning through the church a star-shell burst over the town. In its stark incandescent light Lieutenant-Commander Crowther saw many of the victims of the revolution who were sheltering in that holy place. It was a haunting sight, that of ordinary people awaiting death either in frightened suspense, out-and-out cowardice, or with calm humility. And there were wounded swathed in dirty rags, smelling hideously of gangrene, and others, tossing about, ravaged by typhus.

"That's an improvement," he muttered, breathing in fresh air when they left.

Down the Ekaterinodar road, inward-bound infantry and horsemen were slowly moving. Men staggered along, horses' necks dropped, riders' heads lolled.

"Cossacks, eh?" Edwin Crowther said.

"Yes, Cossacks," she mourned.

The rumble of the guns was more pronounced, the crackle of rifle fire more continuous, the glow of fires stronger, screams more frequent, bloody little affrays encountered more often.

"You'd better stay here tonight," Lieutenant-Commander Crowther said as they entered the grain elevator's lofty chamber. "I had thought you'd all be safer at the Military Mission, but conditions are becoming much riskier outside and it might be tempting providence to go along there."

As Anastasia passionlessly told her brother and half-sister the news, her future husband, glancing at his watch, discovered he was cutting things very fine. Hurriedly he went through his pockets, taking out anything which might be useful to them: cigarettes, matches, a handkerchief, a spare pair of gloves, small change in a variety of currencies and paper money just as varied.

"My *dear* Crowther, this is truly a surprise," Sergei said warmly as he shook hands. "A most welcome one, may I add. But for God's sake, old chap, take every care of yourself between here and the harbour. Wouldn't do to have you scuppered, would it?"

"No, and now I'll have to scoot," the Englishman said, more preoccupied about Prince Sergei's sister. "I don't think there is anything else, except to say I'll be at the church in good time in the morning."

Utterly drained for many reasons, Anastasia was sitting limply on a slatted box. But she smiled wanly and there was a hint of humour in her eyes when she spoke.

"I am afraid I can't seem a very attractive bride, either in appearance or mood. But that doesn't mean that I am failing to appreciate your wonderful kindness."

"Kindness be hanged," Edwin Crowther retorted.

"You know what I mean," she said.

"Yes, I think I do," he assured her sympathetically. "Anyhow I'll have to fly for that picket-boat or there'll be trouble all round. Good night . . . good night, everybody."

She was again staring into space. "Good night, Commander Crowther," she said absently.

Prince Sergei, who had become a new man, escorted their visitor as far as the main door. When outside, the Englishman briefly referred to the arrangements he expected to make about transportation to Constantinople, in the destroyer which would be lying at the quayside within a few hours.

Though much brighter, Sergei had one gnawing anxiety. "I say, old boy, isn't there just a slight snag?" he inquired breezily. "Don't your brass-hats frown on these last-minute marriages?"

"With junior officers, yes," Crowther agreed. "But I'm hardly in that category, and so I think I'll be able to wangle it with my skipper. Of course I shall swear that your sister and I have had an ardent understanding for ages, but lost sight of one another, as we have."

Immensely relieved, Sergei grinned. "Very fruity, old man, what! Nothing so juicy as pulling the wool over the blighters' eyes now and then. We birds at Odessa were dab hands at it. By the Great Catherine, what a bunch of lads we were . . . Oh, are you off?"

"Yes, and damned quickly," Crowther replied. "Good-bye, old man."

Sergei sped him with a wild salute. "Good-bye and good hunting, old chap," he cried out.

Then he walked back along the vast compartment, to find his sister, for the first time in his sight, crying her eyes out.

The long hours of a winter's night passed slowly for them. Countess Petrova, notwithstanding the cold, slept peacefully through the growing tumult of warfare bitterly waged not far away, but to the others it was a fearsome ordeal. Prince Sergei fretted constantly about his future brother-in-law, wondering if he had reached the boat in safety; Valya Igorovna, with scant faith in foreigners, snivelled frequently; and her mistress, alternating between abysmal despair and savage, impotent fury, thought of one person only, her very dear lover, Count Andreyoukov.

At breakfast-time the town was rocked by a tremendous explosion, when White infantry fired the port's petroleum tanks. These men, outnumbered by fifty to one, continued to make an heroic, fighting retreat house by house, street by street.

"They can't hold out much longer," Sergei muttered. "And as it must be climbing up to nine o'clock now I suggest——"

Simmering with rage, her humour then, Anastasia turned on him. "We've plenty of time yet. For God's sake stop fidgeting."

"I'm not fidgeting, and how do you know we've plenty of time?" her brother bawled. "We haven't a watch between us, and there isn't a damned clock in the town that is working."

Anastasia, her tone deadly, inquired: "You stupid fool, am I ready yet? Don't you realize," she added with a vicious coyness, "that this is the most important day in my life? As it is in any woman's life."

Sergei buried his head in his hands. "Oh *hell*," he wailed.

With taps frozen and every tank a solid block of ice, washing was an unconquerable problem, and the three women had to make the utmost of a small quantity of water in a tin basin. But they tidied themselves up by candle light as neatly as was possible, apathetically watched by a hundred or more people. Anastasia was, of course, outstandingly smart in a duffle coat.

"Dare I intrude with the remark that the minutes are passing?" Sergei asked sarcastically. "*Will . . . you . . . come . . . along?*"

This was the moment when Countess Petrova, who had seldom spoken since the previous evening, chose to air her views.

"Are you seriously proposing to marry this Englishman,

Stana?" she demanded, spots of vivid colour appearing on her cheekbones. "Because if you are I consider it abominable. Have you forgotten Nikolai Tikhonovitch?"

"No," her half-sister replied sombrely. "But Nikky is dead. And if he isn't he soon will be, so why should I care what I do?"

Mimi stamped her foot in vexation. "Really, Stana, it would serve you right if Nikolai Tikhonovitch were just behind a corner to hear you say such a silly thing."

It was as though she had touched off an immense charge.

"If Nikky were here I will tell you what he would do," Anastasia yelled, her voice echoing in the vast building. "He would throw me what food he could spare, and then hurry off to re-join his damned men. And I am marrying Commander Crowther as I promised."

"You are your own mistress, I suppose," Mimi said distantly. "But life has always been of more importance to you than anything else."

Exasperated, Anastasia snapped: "What *are* you drivelling about, you little idiot? One thing though, you'll lose your foolish ideas before very long, as soon as we are out of Russia and in civilization once again."

Mimi smiled secretively. "Those who live longest will see most, Stana dear, as your Brownie used to say."

Sergei sighed gustily. "If this small matter is now settled. . . ."

The always-feared Nord-Ost, blowing down from the mountains, was whipping up waves in the bay. Ashore, dense smoke poured from burning oil tanks, and the Union Jack flying over British Military Mission headquarters was being hauled down in a series of jerks. Farther away, on a snow-covered rise to the west of the town, a bedraggled Red horseman pulled up. He rapidly scanned the scene before him and then, twisting in a saddle held together by cord and leather thongs, swung his arm in an imperative sweep. At that signal hundreds of cavalry galloped forward on a wide front.

The bridegroom, who was waiting outside the church with Lieutenant-Commander Staitherton and the First Lieutenant of the destroyer in which the bride and her party would sail, hurried to meet Prince Sergei and the three young women as soon as he saw them.

"By Jove, I'm infernally glad you're here," he said, saluting. "Things are deteriorating at an appalling rate."

The destroyer's Number One, who had vividly-worded instructions from the captain, shooed them into the church without ceremony, permitting only trifling social niceties and the barest introductions. The wedding was conducted at the same speed, the waxen-faced priest gabbling the holy office through to its conclusion, when he snatched the notes for his fee and glided from sight.

Relieved from the bridesmen's duty of holding the heavy matrimonial crowns above the bridal pair's heads, not onerous in the circumstances, Staitherton and the destroyer officer exchanged a few quiet words.

"A race seems in prospect," the latter remarked wryly. "Who gets to that cockleshell of mine first? The Bolsheviki or us?"

Staitherton produced his conception of an Irish accent. "And if it's them your battered junk won't be there, begorrah," he said, grinning faintly.

The other nodded grimly. "Exactly!" he said. "The skipper will haul off if it becomes much stickier. Bound to do."

Edwin Crowther had no doubts about the growing perils of the situation, either. Briefly explaining to his bride the urgent need for haste, he seized her arm and, followed by his fellow naval officers, who had Countess Petrova between them, led the way outdoors.

It was a hair-raising trip. Bullets were spattering freely, and the rate of shell-fire had stepped up; men and women fell before their eyes. Some stretches were devoid of incident, but in other places they were compelled to dive into cover, waiting there until there was a lull in the hail of lead.

Inexorably the overwhelming pressure of masses of Reds was driving defenders back, and from the seaward end of many streets Communists could be seen at the upper ends, dodging forward. Every minute the noise of conflict grew more intense; every yard when out of shelter became more hazardous.

"Nearly there now," Crowther said to Anastasia when, after forcing through a stream of panic-stricken people stampeding across their path, they reached a small public garden. "One final dash will do it. Hope the others are safe."

The destroyer was visible to their right, along a broad quay; to the left survivors of an officers-only battalion climbed the steep gangway of a White auxiliary, an ancient craft with her port paddlebox shattered. Each was laden with equipment and carried a rifle, but everyone of them managed also to clutch a sword, the mark of his class from which he would not be parted.

"Phew!" Staitherton whistled when, hanging on to Countess Petrova, he joined the others against a wall.

"We must be on our marks to leg it," the destroyer's Number One muttered.

The occasion was far from propitious for a formal leavetaking, but to the astonishment of the naval officers this was what Countess Petrova embarked upon, shaking hands with each and thanking them sweetly. She kissed Valya Igorovna on both cheeks and Prince Sergei likewise before throwing her arms affectionately about Princess Anastasia's neck.

"Stana," she said, overcome with emotion, "I won't refer to anything I said earlier, because that would be stupid now. But please forget about it, and think only that I wish you all possible happiness, darling."

"What is it now, Mimi?" her half-sister asked a little despairingly.

Tears glistened in Mimi's eyes, but she smiled bravely through them.

"This gentleman's ship has to sail at once, he assures me, so there really isn't much advantage in my crossing that awfully-exposed quay twice, there and back, dearest."

Patiently Anastasia tried to deal with her. "But you won't be coming back, Mimi dear."

Countess Petrova laughed. "No, because I shan't be going, Stana, and that is why I must say good-bye to you here."

"Oh, Mimi dear, please don't," Anastasia begged. "Do be a good girl and don't be awkward."

As if she deserved reproof Mimi nodded. "I ought to have explained properly instead of being so mysterious, silly me," she confessed. "But the truth is, darling, I can't leave our dear Russia without Cyrus Konstantinych."

"Darling," Anastasia said more insistently, "Cyrus Konstantinych would be foremost in making you leave."

The din of battle was increasing. At that end of the harbour the crowd began to melt away.

Mimi dimpled. "Probably he would, Stana, but this once I am determined to be a wife who does as *she* thinks best."

"You must come with us." Anastasia's voice rose.

"I shan't," Countess Petrova retorted inelegantly.

"You must, Mimi darling."

"Shan't."

No other course possible, Anastasia told her half-sister that Count Petrov had been killed.

Mimi recoiled as if struck. "I . . . I think that is the most wicked thing you have ever said in your life, Stana," she gasped.

"But it is true, Mimi. I'm terribly sorry, darling, but it is."

Lips quivering, Mimi stared at the sea, dark and threatening against the white land.

"You have always been terribly wilful, Stana, but I would never have believed that you would make up such a dreadful lie to get your own way," she whimpered.

379

Desperately Anastasia tried again. "Mimi dearest, you know I love you, don't you?"

Seldom unresponsive to an appeal, Countess Petrova turned impulsively. "Of course I do, Stana darling," she replied fondly.

"I do, you know, Mimi dearest," said Anastasia.

Mimi's sapphire-blue eyes brimmed with affection. "We have always loved each other, Stana."

Along the waterfront, some distance behind the landward end of the curving mole, where a considerable throng had not as yet dispersed, a full-throated scream arose. Unarmed men endeavoured to protect their womenfolk and children, but their action merely spurred the Red horsemen to greater excesses. Swords hacking and swinging, the cavalry cut to ribbons every living soul before them.

Though familiar with many ferocious aspects of the civil war, the three naval officers had never previously witnessed anything so dreadful. Wordless and sick, they were gazing in horror at the scene of bloody carnage when Staitherton glimpsed a movement out of the corner of his eye.

He caught Countess Petrova as she fell against him. Shot through the temple, she was dead before he laid her gently on the cobble-stones.

"Oh, *Mimi* darling," Anastasia shrieked.

For a second, to avoid sight of the hideous wound, she covered her face with her hands, but then sank to her knees beside her half-sister's body.

"Mimi," she moaned. "Oh Mimi, my dearest."

Both Staitherton and his shipmate had satisfied themselves about Countess Petrova.

"It was absolutely instantaneous," Crowther muttered huskily to his wife. "She wouldn't know a thing."

The destroyer's Number One had seen danger, closing danger. Simultaneously, for the first time since reaching there, the prospect of a reasonably safe scurry presented itself.

"Sorry, but it's now or never," he said firmly.

Shoulders quivering, Anastasia sobbed. "But Mimi, we can't leave her here. Where everybody——"

"There's nothing else for it," her husband interposed gently. "'Fraid that's how it is, old thing."

"I'll stay and put her where she won't be trampled on," Lieutenant-Commander Staitherton said.

A signal passed between Edwin Crowther and the destroyer's First Lieutenant. Between them they raised Princess Anastasia to her feet and, when assured that Prince Sergei and the woebegone maid were ready also, dashed off at a rare pace along the quay, which was entirely deserted save for an imperious-looking, silver-haired old lady who had not lost her regal bearing despite a costume crudely fashioned from two French Army horizon-blue capes. Straight-backed, she was sitting serenely on a trunk.

When alone, Staitherton peered over the wall where it sloped lower, and decided to place the dead girl beneath the spreading branches of a yew. He had bent to pick up the body when hoofs and a pair of feet came within his restricted view. A youngish man, tall and erect, with the well-defined bluish-white scar of an old wound on his cheek, looked gravely down at him from a horse.

"May I assist you, sir?" the stranger asked.

"I'd be glad if you would," Staitherton replied.

Countess Petrova was featherweight light, easy to lift on to the coping stones of the wall. Scrambling up, they carried her to the resting place, where Staitherton straightened out her pathetic clothing and his companion crossed her hands on her breast.

A savage burst of firing made any further movement inadvisable for the present, though the English officer was on edge to be off as quickly as possible. On the other hand the Russian seemed strangely content and, as lead buzzed overhead, indulged himself in a contemplative survey.

"Another innocent victim," he mused. "Countries such as your own and the United States, each with a sufficiency of democratically-minded citizens powerful enough to hold a fair balance between reactionary and socialist extremism, are very fortunate, sir. Perhaps through that you may escape our dreadful fate."

"Nothing like this will happen to us, I'm damned sure," the Britisher said decidedly.

The Cossack turned to him. "I trust not, sir, but the Red doctrine is pernicious, and deep in some men is the desire to claw down the chap over the road who has done a little better in life than himself. Cloudy of intellect, these envious millions are the danger, ripe material for insidious-tongued men to play on. But I talk too much, sir."

Again he gazed at the dead girl. "Poor Mimi, so brutally used," he murmured. "God bless you, my dear."

This roused the naval officer, despite his anxieties. "You knew her?" he ejaculated.

"Yes," the other replied.

"And her sister? Or rather her half-sister?"

The Don Cossack smiled as though an immense weight had been lifted off his shoulders.

"Yes, I know her also," he said. "I thought I recognized her in the distance a few minutes ago, and when I was nearer I gave thanks to the Almighty when I saw how she left, with your fellow officers."

Lieutenant-Commander Staitherton jerked his gloved hand towards the destroyer at the extreme end of the quay, which Edwin Crowther and his party had just reached.

"We'll soon have her out of this," he grunted.

The Russian smiled again. "That is why I am glad, sir," he said.

Momentarily the British officer's lips tightened as he looked about him. "She'll be safe enough now," he said briefly. "Thank the Lord, we don't indulge in this kind of shindy in England . . . and we won't, believe me."

"England!" the Russian said sharply.

"She married a shipmate of mine this morning," Staitherton explained.

Ashen, the Russian officer said: "She has become the wife of a shipmate of yours?"

The Englishman nodded. "Not much more than an hour ago."

Count Andreyoukov stared along the edge of the shore where, close to a far extending white line of solidly-frozen sea-foam, hundreds of his broken-hearted men were slitting the throats of their beloved horses. Little by little his steel-grey eyes filled with tears.

The majority of those little horses were war-weary, enfeebled screws but, an animal lover himself, Staitherton was profoundly moved.

"Damnable, isn't it?" he muttered. "Will you have to put down this old boy, too?"

Either the sad-faced Russian did not comprehend or did not hear. But he made an effort to collect himself when the Englishman pointed towards the horse which was watching them inquisitively from the other side of the wall.

"Yes, I shall have to destroy him," he said strickenly. "Unhappily we cannot take our beasts to the Crimea, and we will not shame them by allowing them to fall into the enemy's hands."

"Don't wonder you're upset," Staitherton said gruffly.

The Russian, haggard from shortage of sleep, smiled strangely.

"Yes, I am upset, sir," he said. "But life must continue, as a very lovely lady of my acquaintance would entirely agree."

"Yes," Staitherton murmured, as he got up. "Well, I'd better push off. By the way, if you'd care to tell me your name I'd let Princess Anastasia know that I'd met you."

Slowly the Don Cossack shook his head. "In these days it is not the height of bliss to learn that a friend remains in our once holy and God-fearing Russia."

"I suppose not," the Englishman said. "And now I'll have to

risk it, or I'll be left. Many thanks and the best of luck."

Shrapnel scar standing out vividly against the extreme pallor of his cheek, Count Andreyoukov bowed. "And to you, sir," he said courteously.

Staitherton sprinted to the destroyer, against whose superstructure bullets occasionally pinged. As he jumped aboard he noticed thankfully that the battleship's picket-boat, which had been waiting at the jetty steps, was now lying alongside. That would save Oofy and himself going ashore again.

Below in the commanding officer's cabin, which had been allotted to Princess Anastasia, Edwin Crowther was hurriedly scribbling on a sheet of paper his father's name and address.

"Now when you get to Constant., buy sufficient clothing to see you all through to Paris or London, where you can outfit yourselves properly," he said to his bride. "And cable to the Pater for anything else you need, cash, advice, or whatever it is. And you'll tuck away safely the money I've just given you?"

"I shall take every care of it, Commander——" Anastasia smiled faintly at the slip. "Edwin, I should say."

Edwin Crowther laughed. "It would be more usual. You're my wife, after all."

She gazed unseeingly out of the scuttle. "Yes, I am your wife," she murmured.

"Yes, and as my wife don't you think I might kiss you before I leave?" he asked hopefully.

She allowed him to do so, but as a kiss it did not rate high, and his disappointment showed.

Whatever her inward fury about the sorry trick fate had played her, Anastasia was not without gratitude towards the man who had saved her, and she strove to replace deadly gloom with a semblance of liveliness and sparkle. Smilingly she held back her head, her lips parted, slumbrous eyes darkening; with consummate artistry she slipped into his arms.

It was given to few women, as many men knew, to kiss as could the daughter of the house of Kaivanov. Pulses leaping, utterly shattered by the experience, Edwin Crowther released her.

"Well," he said shakily, "that seems to have shifted us along the road of wedded bliss very nicely."

She was weeping again. "I say, Stana," he mumbled.

"Go, please go," she whispered.

Her husband hovered uncertainly. "Yes, I think I'd better. When I'll next see you I don't know, but we're long overdue to go home."

Coming from the deck overhead were sounds unmistakable to a seaman's ear, preparations for casting-off. As his wife did not reply he could do little about it and so, calling out "Good-bye, darling," he departed hurriedly, a slightly chagrined young man.

The thin plates of the destroyer were pulsating when Valya Igorovna slipped in to join her mistress a little later. For a while the two women, united in their grief for Countess Petrova, clung together, but after that they marvelled about cakes of soap, clean towels, and other wonderful amenities of decent existence.

It was well understood that in ships leaving Russia evacuees invariably congregated to watch the shores of their beloved country recede. The present voyage was no exception, and Prince Sergei, with his sister and her maid, stood so long in the stern that the watch-keeping sub-lieutenant expressed concern to his captain.

The commanding officer paused in his perambulations across the narrow bridge to glance aft at the melancholy-looking trio.

"They're frozen stiff already," he remarked. "But if you'd been out here longer you'd know they don't care a damn about it. Still, perhaps you'd better give Number One my compliments and ask him to invite them down for a drink."

In the wardroom Princess Anastasia disposed of six gins with a celerity amazing even to the Gunner, a hard-seasoned gentleman himself.

Then, smiling brilliantly, she excused herself.

An hour later Sergei picked his way cautiously past the depth-charge gear in the stern, where his sister, tears trickling down her cheeks, stared into the distance.

"I think you should come down now, Stana," he said. "This wind is devilishly keen, and you've seen all you can see. There isn't a spot of land in sight."

"No," she said.

"I wouldn't worry any more about Mimi," he went on. "It's crushing but, as the darling was, I think it is a happy release."

"I know that."

"Come along then," Sergei continued. "Not much sense in hanging about here."

Without moving her head she said angrily: "Will you leave me alone?"

"But. . . ."

"Clear off, damn you," she shouted.

A solitary figure at whose back officers and men gazed more and more uneasily, she stayed there, standing above the frothy mound bubbling at the stern. One watch went off and another came on but still she remained, anguish in her eyes as she steadfastly gazed in the direction of sad shores which long ago had sunk into the grey, wind-torn sea.